Praise for Katherine Sutcliffe...

NOTORIOUS

"Stunning . . . This is by far the best historical romance I've ever read. Sutcliffe has really outdone herself this time with this masterpiece novel, and I can't recommend it highly enough. If I had to use a scale of one to ten, *Notorious* would have to be at least a twenty. No, make that a fifty." —*Rendezvous*

"*Notorious* is dark and dangerous . . . and exactly what makes Katherine Sutcliffe's novels classics in the purest sense. This is absolutely one of the most compelling historical reads of the year." —Jill Barnett, *New York Times* bestselling author of *Wicked*

"An intense story of exquisite passion and deep emotions . . . *Notorious* is a luminous love story that shines brightly in your heart." —Kathe Robin, *Romantic Times*

"The incomparable Katherine Sutcliffe is in top form with her trademark blend of passion, pageantry, and thrilling romance." —Susan Wiggs

"*Notorious* has everything I expect from a Katherine Sutcliffe novel: breathtaking action, an exquisite hero, very vivid and evocative prose . . . Edgy and intense." —*The Romance Journal*

Book World
16 W. Water Street
Chillicothe, OH 45601
740-772-5732

continued on next page . . .

Devotion

"Exceptional . . . Katherine Sutcliffe leaves few emotions untapped in this exquisite romance . . . glows with compassion and the sheer power of love to overcome all boundaries."
—*Romantic Times*

"An exemplary romance—perfect in every way. Flawlessly plotted and written . . . this is one of the most exciting romantic stories of the year."
—*Publishers Weekly* (starred review)

Miracle

"Funny, endearing, heart-tugging . . . a must-read."
—*Indianapolis Star*

Titles by Katherine Sutcliffe

DARKLING I LISTEN
NOTORIOUS
RENEGADE LOVE
WHITEHORSE
HOPE AND GLORY
JEZEBEL
DESIRE AND SURRENDER
DEVOTION
MIRACLE
ONCE A HERO
MY ONLY LOVE

Darkling
I Listen

KATHERINE SUTCLIFFE

JOVE BOOKS, NEW YORK

This is a work of fiction. Names, characters, places, and incidents are either the product of the author's imagination or are used fictitiously, and any resemblance to actual persons, living or dead, business establishments, events, or locales is entirely coincidental.

DARKLING I LISTEN

A Jove Book / published by arrangement with
the author

PRINTING HISTORY
Jove edition / September 2001

All rights reserved.
Copyright © 2001 by Katherine Sutcliffe.
This book, or parts thereof, may not be reproduced in any form
without permission.
For information address: The Berkley Publishing Group,
a division of Penguin Putnam Inc.,
375 Hudson Street, New York, New York 10014.

Visit our website at
www.penguinputnam.com

ISBN: 0-515-13152-0

A JOVE BOOK®
Jove Books are published by The Berkley Publishing Group,
a division of Penguin Putnam Inc.,
375 Hudson Street, New York, New York 10014.
JOVE and the "J" design
are trademarks belonging to Penguin Putnam Inc.

PRINTED IN THE UNITED STATES OF AMERICA

10 9 8 7 6 5 4 3 2 1

I dedicate Darkling *to*

My incredible children
Bryan, Lauren, Rachel, Jennifer

I love you, my beautiful and brilliant darlings.
You make me proud every minute of my life.

My agent
Evan Fogelman
Evan, you believed I could do it when no one else did.

My editor
Christine Zika

For taking the risk.
I'll always be grateful.

GRATEFUL ACKNOWLEDGMENT

I would like to take this opportunity to thank a few individuals without whose help this book would have been much more difficult to write, and much less entertaining.

Anita Tinsley, R.N., for her medical expertise. Detective Al Morris, Killeen Police Department, Killeen, Texas; and Sr. Cpl. Rhonda Carrie Hollingsworth, Dallas Police, Northwest Patrol, Dallas, Texas.

A very special thank-you to Rachael Turney, my son Bryan's incredibly brilliant and beautiful fiancée. Punkin, few people have the tolerance to listen to authors wax on for hours about characters, plots, and plot twists. Your encouragement and belief in my capabilities helped me to set higher goals, and to reach for them.

Although Ticky Creek, Texas, is fictitious, the town and citizens were a compilation of many East Texas towns that I have known and loved in my life. I called on my own special childhood memories to flesh out my heroine's history. The Three Forks Café was actually Seven Pines Café. A rose by any other name would smell as sweet. To my grandmother Nora Jewel Allen, long gone, thanks for the memories. Nanny, you flipped a mean burger.

Darkling I listen; and, for many a time
I have been half in love with easeful Death,
Call'd him soft names in many a mused rhyme,
To take into the air my quiet breath;
Now more than ever seems it rich to die,
To cease upon the midnight with no pain,
While thou art pouring forth thy soul abroad
In such an ecstasy!

                    John Keats—"Ode to a Nightingale"

1

Fate was a bitch with a sick penchant for coldcocking men
at the zenith of their careers. Brandon Carlyle didn't think
too highly of Fate. Neither was he inclined to believe the old
adage that when God slammed one door, He opened another.
When God slam-dunked Brandon's life and career in the toilet, He had not opened another door. He'd simply flushed.
And kept flushing every chance He got.

Not that Brandon blamed Him completely. As his late pal
John Kennedy, Jr., had once described one of his rebellious
cousins, Brandon was, or had been, "a poster boy for bad
behavior."

But that was then, not now. Christ, he deserved a break.
Just a small one. Enough to make his climbing out of bed in
the morning worthwhile. Enough to keep him from expro-
priating his uncle Henry's Smith & Wesson .357 magnum
from the gun cabinet and blowing his own brains out.

He thought about that escape a lot these days. Just two
nights before, he'd stood for half an hour in front of the

glass-fronted weapon cabinet staring like a zombie at the impressive collection of rifles and handguns. His hands were sweating, his stomach roiling while he ticked off just how he could go about ending his life—or rather his existence. He had no life, after all.

He would take the .357 and drive down to Ticky Creek. His uncle kept a Sears bass boat there, decked out with a trolling motor and a sonar fish locator. He would motor up the creek a ways and put a bullet in his head. With any luck, his body and the gun would just disappear.

People would think he simply drowned while fishing. But then, his uncle would eventually miss his .357, and he would put two and two together. While the old man might survive Brandon's drowning, he wouldn't survive his only nephew snuffing himself. Brandon had enough on his conscience. He sure as hell didn't want to think that he would, in any way, cause the demise of the only person left on the face of the earth who gave a damn about him.

Obviously, he was feeling way too sorry for himself at the moment. Not good. Such self-pity led to black moods, and black moods agitated his temper, and his temper would ultimately get the better of him; he would start craving a fight . . . or a pint of Chivas Regal—both of which were tickets straight back to California's Corcoran State Prison to finish out his six-year manslaughter sentence. No thanks. Three years in that hellhole rubbing elbows with Charles Manson and Sirhan Sirhan had been enough to convince him that fighting and Chivas—as sweet as they were—were not sweet enough to tempt him back into his old ways.

Brandon briefly closed his eyes and took a deep, calming breath. For a moment, he forgot the letter in his hand, the one that had sent him into his mental tailspin. He focused instead on the television chatter in the background, the whir-ring and buzzing of a chain saw outside. His uncle Henry was readying firewood for the first cold snap, predicted for the end of the week—not that meteorologists in Texas had ever nailed a prediction during Brandon's lifetime, but best be prepared, nevertheless. He heard, too, the companionable conversation of Aunt Bernice's home health care nurse, Betty Wilson, as she went about the delicate caretaking of her stroke patient. Brandon was well familiar with the routine: at straight-up noon Betty would feed a tube down Bernie's throat and proceed to carefully syringe Ensure into her stomach. Bernice's pale blue eyes would continue to stare into space, and occasionally Betty would stop and wipe the thin stream of drool from Bernice's lips.

What lured Brandon into opening the long-closed door of The Shrine, he couldn't guess. Or maybe he could. It was the letter again, taunting and leering up at him in streams of flourishing black ink on stark white stationery. The door stuck, gave with a sudden scrape of warped wood against the linoleum floor, then sprang open with a creak and a rush of cool, stale air that felt and smelled like wind from a grave.

He left the door ajar just enough for the sounds of *All My Children* and Henry's saw to infiltrate the quiet of the room.

He felt as if he had been swept up in some macabre horror novel: a confused, brain-twisted protagonist being sucked down a vortex. Any moment he'd wake up to find himself knee-deep in excrement, because that's what hid beneath all the glittering, beautiful images lining the walls and shelves; images depicting a life of happiness and success.

Bullshit. It was all bullshit. An elephant graveyard, bones of his past jutting up out of dust and shadows. Musty, dark, and looming with treasures of his life, right down to the shimmering gold Oscar that resided by a life-size cardboard cutout of himself as Jesus Christ leaning against the wall like a mummy's sarcophagus. He stared at it, feeling his face go from hot to cold to hot again. The critics had crucified him for his role in *The Resurrection*—not because he'd done a shitty job of it—hell, he'd been nominated for a second Oscar for his portrayal—but because his own life had hardly reflected anything remotely resembling virtuous.

As a critic for *People* magazine had snubbed: "It is hard, if not impossible, to suspend reality long enough while watching *The Resurrection* to believe that the man on the screen playing Jesus Christ is anything more than the Hollywood Tomcat and Tinsel Town Terror who couldn't even attend the premier of the movie because he's locked away in Corcoran State Prison—for manslaughter, no less. And while *The Resurrection* may prove to be one of the most successful box office smashes of the year, we all know that the women lining up to see this movie again and again have less interest in the Divinity than in seeing the Hollywood hunk walk out of baptismal waters buck naked."

He gave a dry laugh. *The Resurrection* had not only proven to be the biggest grosser of the year, but of all time. Church attendance had risen twenty-five percent in the month following the movie's premier, as reported by *Newsweek*, which plastered his Jesus image peering out through cell bars on the cover. The article, "From Icon to Idol, Something Is Wrong with This Picture," included photographs of the District Attorney getting pelted by stones and protesters storming the prison gates demanding the "Lord's" release.

As if people's warped reasoning and skewed realities were his fault. Brandon shook his head free of the memory and reluctantly looked around the room.

More relics were showcased behind glass: an unopened General Mills cereal box with his grinning, snaggle-toothed image beaming up at the buyer. Sales had risen fifty percent within six months of his gracing the box, along with the commercial that debuted during the Super Bowl. That commercial had led to others: cola, candy, games, children's cold medicine, Jell-O pudding (which he couldn't eat, because every time he so much as smelled it, he puked).

By the time he turned eight, he'd landed his first television series, and his face was emblazoned across *TV Guide* four times over the next five years, each time after the show won an Emmy for Best Drama Series. The series had been about a family of delinquent foster care kids—Brandon billed over the adult star, who eventually became so pissed at being billed below a "brat whose mother slept with the producers to get the little shit his star billing" that he refused to renew his contract for a sixth season. Which was just as well. By the time Brandon reached his thirteenth birthday, the rumblings of trouble had begun to filter through Tinsel Town as ominously as earthquake aftershocks. The once cute as a bug, angelic-faced Brandon Carlyle had a King Kong–sized attitude and a streak of wildness that would eventually put Charlie Sheen and Robert Downey, Jr., in the shade.

Now Brandon peered down through the glass case at the preserved *TV Guides*. With each edition his image subtly shifted from the sparkling, wide-eyed enthusiasm of an eight-year-old, to the evolving sharp-edged adolescent with turbulent, cut-to-the-quick eyes that made most adults uncomfortable. He wasn't America's darling any longer; nevertheless, they came to see him on the big screen in masses because there was something hypnotic in the way he sucked them in and rattled their defenses. The critics likened him to James Dean and a young Marlon Brando. Cool. Tough. Wicked. Heartbreaking. Accomplished. Brilliant. Perhaps the finest young actor in the last three decades.

There were framed movie posters on the walls. And magazine covers. He'd made *People* eight times, once as Sexiest Man Alive. There was *Movieline, Entertainment Weekly, Vanity Fair*, and even *Cosmo*, as the man most women fantasized about while having sex.

Of course there were other photos. Brandon with women: models, actresses, a photo of him in Paris with Princess Diana snapped just weeks before her death. Another Rollerblading with John Kennedy, Jr., in Central Park. But the photograph most cherished by Bernice and Henry was the one that included them, taken backstage moments after Brandon had won his Oscar for Best Actor in a Dramatic Role, for *A Dark Night in Jericho*. He'd flown Henry and Bernice in on a Lear. Treated them to a shopping spree on Rodeo Drive, put them up at the Beverly Hilton. Before several billion people he'd dedicated his Oscar to Bernice and Henry for their love and support . . . and not a breath had been wasted on his mother, also in the audience. As the camera panned in tight, Cara Carlyle's expression had turned as stiff and white as a corpse's. The next morning the headlines had declared: "Mommy Dearest Snubbed at Oscars!" Cara's quoted response to Brandon's success had been. "The committee must have had their heads up their asses."

Darling Brandon. I don't know how much longer I can go on like this. Years of dreaming, hoping, watching. . . .

Brandon blinked the film of sweat from his eyes and reread the letter in his hand. Somehow, it seemed appropriate to read it here, surrounded by memories of who and what he used to be: a movie star, a heartthrob to millions. But that was then, when such success invited all sorts of perverted idolatry and fanaticism. Now he was a nobody living in Bum Fuck, Texas, a washed-up, has-been actor, a recovering alcoholic, an ex-con with about as much sex appeal as week-old roadkill.

I've been watching you. Always you. Morning, noon, and night. But you look right through me. Oh, how I despair. Cruel, cruel man. Because of you I have been half in love with easeful Death. Call'd him soft names in many a mused rhyme, To take into the air my quiet breath. When the time is right, my sweet Darkling, we'll be together. I didn't follow you from California to let you slip through my fingers now. Until then, I am simply . . .

Anticipating.

"Mr. Brandon?" A hand touched his back.

Brandon jumped and turned.

Betty Wilson, his aunt's nurse, took a startled step back, her eyes wide and her mouth slack in surprise. "My goodness, dear, I didn't mean to startle you. Gracious, you're white as a sheet. Is something wrong?" Her gaze dropped to the letter in his hand, and her thin, black eyebrows drew together.

Shaking his head, Brandon refolded the letter and slid it into the back pocket of his jeans. "No. Nothing wrong." He released a shaky breath. "The room. It's creepy. Like a boneyard. I don't know why I came in here. It's depressing as hell."

He stepped around her, back into the warmth of the sunny yellow kitchen with its frilly white curtains on the windows and the smell of a raisin pie wafting from the oven. The security of it nestled around him like a fuzzy blanket. His heart slowed; the rush of adrenaline subsided, leaving him a little woozy and feeling stupid for allowing the idiotic letter to unnerve him. He'd been getting letters from the same unknown correspondent for years.

"Anticipating" had adored him in one sentence; in the next, ranted that if she couldn't find satisfaction in their nonexistent relationship, she fully intended to take him out with an Uzi. The threats had been annoying and only a little intimidating during his flourishing career, hilarious when they were dumped in his prison cell. But when they began arriving at his uncles's farm four months ago, his annoyance had congealed into a cold knot of dread—especially since they were postmarked Ticky Creek.

The fact that she'd followed him all the way to Ticky Creek was bad news. Very bad. Her obsession with him was not some passing fantasy to be ignored any longer. Since walking away from Corcoran State Prison, he had managed to keep his whereabouts hidden from everyone except his agent and the minuscule populace of Ticky Creek, Texas. Ticky Creek residents protected his privacy. Brandon Carlyle was the hometown boy who made good, regardless of the fact that his career had ultimately crashed and burned. They didn't blame Brandon so much as they blamed his mother. Poor Brandon was a product of his upbringing, and there wasn't a soul residing in Ticky Creek who considered Cara Carlyle anything but a child-abandoning slut who went through husbands as often as she changed her Frederick's of Hollywood panties.

So how the hell did Anticipating find him?

Brandon searched his pockets for cigarettes.

Brisk and efficient, Betty reached into a drawer, plucked up a new pack of Winstons, and tossed them to him. His fingers ripping at the cellophane, Brandon walked to the window and looked down on his uncle, who had taken a break from his sawing to sit on a tree stump and catch his breath. His old basset hound Rufous lay at his feet, graying muzzle resting on the tip of Henry's Red Wing boot.

"Stubborn old coot," Brandon said affectionately as he slid the cigarette between his lips, then dug the lighter out of his pocket. His gaze searched the distant line of trees, looking for an Uzi-packing terror who called herself Anticipating. "We argued for an hour over which of us was going to cut that damn firewood. Says I'll cut my leg off, then no one in Hollywood will hire me. As if they will anyway." He sucked on the cigarette and enjoyed the bite of it in his lungs. He felt the tension in his shoulders start to relax.

"Now don't you be getting down on yourself again, Mr. Brandon. You'll be back on top before you know it. When the right part comes along." Betty lowered the oven door and, with oven-mitted hands, reached in for the bubbling, lattice-topped pie. She set it on the pie safe to cool, then opened the refrigerator to extract what was left of a ham and a bowl full of mustard potato salad. "Mr. Henry will want to eat before he goes to his doctor's appointment. Can I fix you a sandwich?"

Grinning, Brandon shook his head. "This isn't in your job description, you know. We pay you to see to my aunt's welfare. I think Henry and I can blow our own noses and slap a little mayo and ham on bread when we get hungry."

"I enjoy it." She beamed, showing slightly yellow teeth that were smudged with red lipstick. "You're like family to me, Mr. Brandon. It all gives me a sense of . . . purpose. I've got no family of my own, you know. Besides, if I wasn't looking after you and Mr. Henry, I'd be wasting my time on soap operas and Jerry Springer."

"There's always Oprah."

"Can't watch her now." Betty gave her shoulder-length, plum-red curls a shake. They bounced over her bulky shoulders that were clad in a crisp cotton long-sleeved blouse. "She's lost weight again. I hate it when she loses weight. She gets cocky. I can tolerate fat and cocky, but I can't handle thin and cocky. Oh, my, we're out of pickles. Remind me to add that to my grocery list. You know how Mr. Henry loves his bread and butters. Are you sure you don't want a sandwich?"

Her head swung around, and she stared at him with cow eyes the color of rich alfalfa. Brandon suspected she wore tinted contacts. No one's eyes were that green.

"I'll cut you a piece of pie once it cools," Betty offered. "It'll run if I cut it too hot."

"I'll grab something in town." He took another drag on his cigarette.

"I'll be cooking one of your favorites tonight," she announced as she reached for a loaf of Mrs. Baird's thin-sliced white bread. "Chicken-fried steak and fried fresh okra."

He watched his uncle bend over and scratch Rufous atop his head. The dog was sitting up now and staring toward the pine forest, head cocked and ears perked. His hackles were raised. "I won't be here for supper," he replied absently, and refocused on the distant trees. "I have a date."

"A date?"

Something in the way Betty coughed out "A date" made Brandon look around. Betty's square face, with its heavily colored cheeks, looked a little clownish as she stared at him in nothing less than astonishment.

"With whom?" she asked, pressing her hand against the tented gladioli on her chest. No doubt Betty was astonished, as was he. He'd rarely left the farm since moving back to Ticky Creek, and he never socialized.

"Charlotte Minger. She's a checker at Wal-Mart."

"Blond? 'Bout five-six? With an IQ of thirty if she's lucky?"

Brandon tapped his ashes into his cupped palm and grinned. "One and the same, except I think you exaggerated her IQ."

Betty's mouth flattened. "Why?"

"Why?" He raised his eyebrows and shifted his shoulders. "I guess she caught me at a vulnerable moment. It didn't help that she had on a skirt the size of a Band-Aid." Betty's eyes narrowed, causing Brandon's face to grow warm. He blew out a stream of smoke and shrugged. "Or maybe I'm just tired of living like a goddamn monk."

"She's half your age."

"Bullshit. I'm only thirty-five."

"If that gal is a day over seventeen, I'm Cindy Crawford. The last thing you need right now is to get yourself in trouble with a minor."

"She's twenty. I asked her."

"Check her driver's license. And besides, twenty is too young for a man your age."

Brandon laughed and crushed out his cigarette in the sink. "If you want to preach about old men and young babes, go yap at Jack Nicholson and Mike Douglas. Christ, we're only going for a burger, not to the Flea-bite Motel. I'll be home by eleven, I promise." He gave her a quick kiss on the cheek, and added softly, "But I thank you for giving a damn, Betty. It means a hell of a lot to me. You know that."

The phone rang. Brandon grabbed the receiver off the hook and walked to his aunt's bedroom door.

"Hello?"

"Darling, I was hoping you'd be in, and not out on that dreadful tractor. I have visions of your gorgeous body being chewed up and packed into little square things that are fed to pigs and such."

"Hello, Mildred." He glanced back at Betty and rolled his eyes. "I was expecting you to call last night."

"Darling, I was wining and dining Spielberg last night. I've almost got him convinced to use you in his next project."

"You're such a liar, Mildred." Brandon turned down the volume on the television and wondered who Mildred thought she was kidding. Then he reminded himself that such bullshit was the norm for agents. Part of their job was filling their insecure and paranoid clients with just enough fairy tales to keep them believing that their agents were actually earning their fifteen percent.

Receiver pressed between his ear and shoulder, he flipped a Kleenex from a box and carefully dabbed at his aunt's damp chin, then adjusted the lap blanket across her knees, gently tucking it under her bony thighs. "If you were the last agent in the business, Spielberg still wouldn't give you the time of day, much less eat at the same table with you."

"Oh, I forgot. I'm good enough only for egomaniac has-beens who actually believe anyone in Hollywood would want them after they've spent three years in prison for killing a sadomasochistic porno queen."

"Fuck you, Mildred." He slammed the receiver down so hard the phone bell pinged and the wall vibrated. It rang again immediately. He slammed it again, harder, causing Betty to hurriedly close the kitchen cupboard door before the glasses on the shelves tumbled to the floor. The third time it rang, he answered it, saying nothing, his fingers strangling the receiver so tightly his knuckles hurt.

"I'm coming to Texas," Mildred said. Clearly, she wasn't remotely intimidated by his heavy breathing or his borderline nuclear temper that, once exceeding its boiling point, became lethal, as too many producers and directors had discovered over the years . . . not to mention previous agents.

"I don't want you coming to Texas again." His voice shook with controlled emotion, making Mildred Feldman sink a little deeper in her chair and close her eyes, recalling just how throaty his voice could get, how tremulous it became in throes of passion. She'd had a lot of men, but never one so driven by raw emotion as Brandon Carlyle.

"By why not, Darling? It's been what, seven, eight months since they let you out of that horrible little cage? Surely by now you've pulled yourself together enough to get back to work. Surely by now you've grown tired of mucking horse shit and slopping pigs, not to mention rubbing elbows with a lot of Gomers. You must be going stark raving mad. Talk to me, Darling. Tell Mildred all about it."

Silence. Then, "I'm not ready. I may never be ready again. So why don't you just leave me the hell alone for a while? I have to think."

"You're not getting any younger, Brandon. There are a great many younger leading men stepping into your shoes. DiCaprio, Affleck, Damon. You're thirty-five, Sweetheart. Pretty soon you won't appeal to all those nubile females who made you the biggest box office draw since Tom Cruise strutted across the screen in *Top Gun*."

She picked up a copy of an old tabloid emblazoned with a bleary photograph of Brandon in handcuffs, sandwiched between two of LAPD's finest. "Let's face it, Sweetie, it may take you years to recover from this fiasco with Emèrald Marcella—if you recover at all. Remember, even before your Ferrari with Emerald in it took a deep dive through that guardrail, you were already up to your cute ass in problems."

"I thought an agent was supposed to boost her client's self-esteem."

"Only when the client dutifully kisses said agent's butt."

Silence again. He was brooding. Sulking. Simmering. Imagining nasty ways he could pay her back for rubbing the truth in his face. Obviously, he wasn't boozing, or by now he would have cut her to the bone with sarcasm and indignities.

Smiling, she slid her feet to the floor and sat forward, elbows on the desk, her long, red fingernails stroking the phone cord. "So, I'm coming to Texas. I'll check out the Dallas market, maybe see who's filming at Las Colinas. Maybe you could do a cameo. I'll make a few phone calls, run your portfolio by a few of the commercial agents in the area. We'll do dinner . . . or something."

Brandon hung up the phone without saying good-bye. Feeling that if he didn't hit something in the next few seconds, he was going to disintegrate before Betty's concerned eyes, he left the house. He stood on the porch with his hands jammed in his jeans pockets and his brain scrambling over all the reasons he should fire Mildred Feldman the instant she showed her nose in Ticky Creek. She was mean, spiteful, and one of the worst agents in the business. Only losers like himself even gave her the time of day. He'd considered firing her at least a hundred times. That idea had lasted long enough for a dozen agents to hang up in his ear.

What a bitch, insinuating that he was past his prime. Hell, his body had never been in better shape now that he'd sweated all the Chivas out of his system. His brain felt sharp and clear, most of the time, when it wasn't bogged up with self-pity and numb from tedium. There was still his anger to deal with, of course. He was cursed with a short fuse, which got all the shorter when he drank. He'd learned at an early age to give as good as he got, and most of the time what he got was a lot of abuse, physical, mental, and emotional. So he gave it back in spades. Why the hell not?

Rufous tore off down the long driveway, baying, ears flapping, ignoring Henry's shouts to heel. Henry rounded the house, shaking his head and laughing. A red bandanna flagged out of the hip pocket of his faded overalls. Something in Brandon softened and sank at the sight of his uncle, bald head shimmering with sweat and his face ruddy from exertion.

"Damn dog's got him a scent," Henry announced as he reached for the bandanna in his pocket. "I'm wondering when he's going to wake up to the fact that he's just too damn old to be chasing rabbits." He smiled at Brandon, his blue eyes twinkling with amusement. "Guess I've got a lot of room to talk, huh?"

"At least you're using good sense for a change, and not out there with him."

"Not 'cause I don't want to be, for sure. Nothing like a good rabbit chase first thing in the morning. Gets the old heart to racing."

Brandon looked away. "Speaking of racing hearts, you have your doctor's appointment. I'm driving."

Henry studied him. "Somebody's got you pissed off."

"Agents. They're all a lot of aggravation."

"Mildred again."

Brandon nodded and Henry chuckled, slapped him on the back. "I'm smelling raisin pie and mustard potato salad. By God, Betty is spoiling us rotten."

Henry ambled into the house, allowing the screen door to slam behind him. Brandon wondered how many times over the course of his thirty-five years of wandering back to Ticky Creek in search of emotional comfort and stability he had heard that old screen door slam. There were times when he lay in his bed in Malibu or some trailer on location and dreamed he was back at his aunt and uncle's farm, sunning himself on their porch, listening to Bernie hum as she cooked and cleaned and ironed. The memory always took the edge off his temper.

Somewhere near the front gate, beyond the boxwood hedge and the mini forest of crape myrtles that in summer became a frothy cloud of pink and purple blooms, Rufous's barking became frantic. No doubt the old hound had treed a raccoon or sniffed out an armadillo burrowed up in rotting pine needles. Frowning, Brandon stepped off the porch and started down the drive.

Mitsy Dillman slouched in the seat of her rusty, powder blue '68 Impala. She gazed through the windshield at Brandon Carlyle standing on the front porch of his uncle's house. It was a fair distance from where she had parked her car in the bushes just off the rutted tractor path that followed the perimeter of Henry Carlyle's five-hundred-acre farm, but she could tell he hadn't changed a whole hell of a lot since she'd last parked the old Impala here—seventeen years ago to the day. In fact, she still had the little calendar tucked away in the glove compartment with the date circled in red Magic Marker. Except, she didn't need no calendar to remind her of this anniversary. No sir. For the last seventeen years on October 20 she crawled out of bed and vowed that one day she would get even with Mr. Big Shot Brandon Carlyle.

Mitsy checked out her reflection in the rearview mirror. Damn, but she was lookin' crazier by the hour. Hormones, the doctors told her. Get used to it. She wasn't a spring chick any longer. Well, maybe it was hormones and maybe it wasn't. Maybe it was one of those chemical imbalance things that drove people to eat Prozac and Serzone like they were M&Ms. Except there were occasions when the medications had the opposite effect and drove the patient haywire—least that's what her brother said. They ran through post offices and school yards, blowing people away with semiautomatics, like the one resting on the car seat beside her, tucked under her denim skirt in case she was pulled over for a traffic violation. She sure as hell didn't want the la-di-da sheriff discovering she was packing heat, as the jerk liked to call it—thought he was freaking Dirty Harry just 'cause he carried a gun and wore a stupid badge.

Her brother, Jack Dillman, had always thought he was God's gift to women just because he could throw a stupid football. Oh, if the girls could only have seen him at home, whimpering every time their stepdaddy took a swing at him. It was only natural that after a linebacker seriously herniated Jack's spinal disk he became a cop. A badge and a gun made him feel powerful and restored the self-confidence that their mother's husband had taken from him. He was Big Dick Dillman, the Almighty and All-knowing . . . at least until Brandon Carlyle dropped into Ticky Creek on his infrequent sabbaticals from La La Land. Then Jack's self-esteem shriveled up to the size of a walnut. Christ, Jack hated Brandon Carlyle with a passion. But then, so did she.

Mitsy was a whore. She wasn't proud of it, but she accepted it. At least she was a pretty whore, not like some she knew who took pride in advertising the fact by wearing cheap, tacky clothes and layers of caked makeup. One thing for certain, she had never sat at home alone on Friday and Saturday nights during high school. Hell, it was nothing for her to have two or three dates a night. She had the horny sons of bitches taking numbers.

She had willingly spread her legs for the first time on her thirteenth birthday. Paul Gordon, seventeen, backup quarterback for the Ticky Creek Crusaders. She'd crawled out her bedroom window and met him where the railroad tracks intersected with Pike Road. He'd picked her up in his daddy's brand-new Ford truck and taken her for a spin out to the quarry. Once parked, it had taken him only ten minutes to talk her out of her cotton panties. He'd been clumsy. And scared. She'd had to remind him three times that if he didn't diddle a little with her first, to sort of get her juices flowing, it wasn't gonna be very pleasurable for either of them.

Paul had actually had the audacity to act shocked that a thirteen-year-old knew anything about diddling. He'd laughed and wanted to know just how long she'd been putting out; she'd thought about confessing it had been since the first time her drunk stepdaddy had slithered under her sheets in the middle of the night—she would have been about nine—but decided against saying anything. Even in the best of moods her stepdaddy was meaner than a timber rattler. If some bug-eyed social worker banged on their door, he wouldn't have stopped thrashing Mitsy for a week. Eventually, she had come to the conclusion that if she was gonna put out on a regular basis, it might as well be on her terms, and to someone who didn't smell like sour Schlitz and hot tamales.

She'd known Brandon Carlyle for most of her life; he was only one year older than her, the same age as her brother Jack. Their parents had attended Sam Houston High School together. Cara Stacy and John Carlyle had been those disgustingly beautiful and pop'lar people every other kid in school both idolized and hated. Most beautiful. Most handsome. Most pop'lar. Most likely. They'd started going steady their sophomore year, John hoping for a baseball scholarship and Cara thinking she would eventually win Miss America and find her way to Hollywood. But thanks to a leaky condom in their senior year, Cara wound up pregnant and John was forced to forgo baseball for a job at the local lumber mill to provide for his wife and son.

But Brandon had barely soiled his first diaper before Cara up and deserted husband and son for Tinsel Town. John and Brandon moved in with Henry and Bernice. (Cara's mother, her only living parent, had died six months before.) That situation rocked along until John got crushed to death four years later, under a pile of falling pine tree trunks. Cara, already somewhat successful in commercials and bit parts in soap operas, swooped into Ticky Creek and confiscated her son before Henry and Bernice could change out of their funeral clothes.

Cara Stacy Carlyle had proven that a woman with looks and a smidgeon of talent could escape Ticky Creek, Texas, and find success in Hollywood. Folks in Ticky Creek had often suggested that Mitsy was just as pretty as Cara Carlyle. At least they had during her high school days. And it was in this very spot, in the backseat of this very car, that Brandon himself had told her she had what it takes to make it in Hollywood—he would even introduce her to his agent. In the blink of an eye, she'd decided, with her legs wrapped around his thrusting hips and her eyes fixed on the overhead car lamp—their one and only fornication before he left the next day to make the movie that would ultimately win him an Oscar—that Brandon Carlyle was gonna be her ticket out of Podunkville.

At the time, of course, she didn't realize that she was already two months' pregnant. Father unknown; could have been any one of a half-dozen Ticky Creek bastards, including her stepfather. Didn't matter. She figured what Brandon Carlyle didn't know wouldn't hurt him; she'd pass the kid off as his. Except she hadn't counted on Cara. The Wicked Witch of the West Coast streaked in on her broom and bought her mother off with enough money to finance an abortion, a divorce, and, at least for her mother, a relocation to Tampa, Florida, where she married some mobile home salesman three months later. Both were killed in a car wreck on their way to Disney World during their honeymoon.

Good riddance, Mitsy thought as she watched old Henry Carlyle mount the porch steps and speak to his nephew. Her mother deserved it, allowing her husband to diddle around with her daughter. She deserved it for hauling her seventeen-year-old daughter to some filthy local quack to rip a fetus out with something that looked like ice tongs, leaving her insides so screwed up she was useless for having babies.

Dragging the gun into her lap, Mitsy watched Henry disappear into the house. She felt sick again, like all the times over all the years she thought about his screwing her in the Impala's backseat. Funny that she'd never been bothered by all the other men, breathing and drooling and rutting on her. She just lay back and let them have it. But she'd actually felt something for Brandon. He'd made her feel special. Took her on dates, bought her presents. Opened the car door for her like she was a real lady. Told her she was too pretty to be wasted on Ticky Creek. And she'd believed him. Every goddamn word. Every smile.

Then he'd dumped her.

Smashed her fantasies.

Made her feel for the first time like she was dog shit on the bottom of somebody's shoe, while he went on to win the Academy Award and dance until dawn with Princess Diana.

"Son of a bitch," she said through her teeth, and slammed the steering wheel with her fist.

2

Come on, sweet baby. My God, you're incredible. Turn those baby blues this direction, Sugar. Oh, mama, I can't believe it. *That's good. Give me that infamous Carlyle sneer now. Let's see some attitude.*

Alyson James shimmied a little farther out on the pine limb and refocused the lens of her Nikon on Brandon Carlyle's face as he stood on the porch, looking like a building storm cloud. Her heart hammered. Her breath lodged in her throat, making her face feel hot. She could visualize her editor's face when she slapped these up close and personals on his desk.

But that wasn't the best part. She would let him get all worked up, face sweating, horse teeth bared in a smile that made him look like a braying jackass, then she would inform him that he could kiss her patootie; she had already sold the photos to *People* and the story to *Entertainment Tonight*. Oh, sweet Mary, God must love her after all, to have dumped this slice of good luck in her lap, same as He had eight years before, when she had broken the first story of Brandon Carlyle's love affair with the bottle.

She had simply been at the right place at the right time, snooping around the LAPD at three in the morning, and witnessed for herself the laughing cops hauling Carlyle's skunked tush in—all making light of the fact that they'd picked him up for the third time in as many months. Something had soured a little in her stomach at the sight of him barely able to stand up, bending over and puking up on the cop's shiny shoes. Not that she was totally surprised. She was well acquainted with actors and how the realities of their lives were usually a far cry from what their adoring fans perceived. She'd been married to an actor herself at the time. Steve Farrington. Egomaniac.

She often wondered, and even worried, if, when snapping that photograph of Brandon Carlyle puking up his guts, his wrists handcuffed behind him, and the cops laughing their butts off, she had somehow been trying to get even with Farrington by humiliating Carlyle. After all, it was a way of showing the world that their godlike icons were no better than the sleaziest deadbeat drunks sleeping off their hangovers under bridges. The story had won her a job at the country's leading tabloid, the *Galaxy Gazette*.

And Carlyle's life had gone to hell.

Disintegrated.

And even though her peers had convinced her that Carlyle's life and career had already been on the skids, deep in the night the nagging thought plagued her that maybe they were wrong.

A well-known, high-dollar actress had been quoted soon after Carlyle's release from prison, as the press was buzzing about his demons and whether or not his time in the slammer had mellowed him: "The public doesn't see the ugly stuff that comes along with our business, and that's the kind of stuff that breaks us down. . . . No matter how much you pay some hospital or doctor, they can't fix you. You have to figure it out for yourself. Life is weird and messy, and you get through it. Brandon Carlyle is getting through it the best way he can. We're all pulling for him. We love you, Brandon, and miss you."

Brandon Carlyle had decided to get through the weird and messy stuff following his parole from prison by disappearing to Ticky Creek, Texas. Population five thousand.

At first, she'd refused to believe her cousin Sally. Brandon Carlyle living in Ticky Creek? Armpit of the deep East Texas pine woods? No way! The man Sally saw eating a cheeseburger and beer-batter onion rings at the Dime A Cup Café might have looked like Brandon Carlyle—as if anyone could look like the gorgeous god of Tinsel Town—but there was no possible way Carlyle would have buried himself in this logging mill town, no matter how badly he wanted to avoid press speculation. Carlyle was bright lights, big city. Party girls with gigantic breasts and sparkling smiles.

The Nikon whirred and clicked as Alyson zoomed in closer on Carlyle's face. He was pissed, all right. Big time. Positively smoldering, blue eyes slightly narrowed, mouth thinned, shoulders squared, and hands rammed into his faded jeans pockets like he was doing his best to refrain from choking someone.

"Always the bad boy, huh, Carlyle?" she said softly. "Always looking for a fight."

Closer . . . the lens sucked his image up into her face.

A niggling of discomfort fluttered in her stomach as she acknowledged the dark smudges below his eyes. And maybe he had grown a bit more gaunt and rawboned. No pretty boy, this. He was starting to look a little like a Joe Bob truck driver, hard and mean. Once, when hearing he had been hauled into jail on suspicion of murder, she'd refused to believe it. Carlyle might have been a brawler when he drank too much or got pissed off with the paparazzi, but he wasn't a cold-blooded killer. And when it came to women, he was a lover, not a killer . . . or a rapist, as the District Attorney had charged.

For weeks, a spellbound country had watched the shocking and horrifying story unfold. The funeral of the porn queen Emerald Marcella had held the television audience rapt. The entourage of instantly recognized attorneys marching in and out of the courts had refreshed memories of the O. J. Simpson case. The country had learned that America's heartthrob had been hauled in several times before the tragic accident that had taken Marcella's life, mostly for DUI and public intoxication. Twice he'd been ordered to undergo treatment at the Betty Ford Clinic. He'd spent thirty days in County Jail for assaulting a director who'd fired him. And the day after Princess Diana had been killed, he'd been arrested for attempting to run down the paparazzi outside his Malibu home, but since no one had been hurt, the charges had been dropped.

No doubt about it, the face filling her camera lens now belonged on a mug shot displayed on *America's Most Wanted*. Maybe he had finally gone over the edge. Maybe he had lost all control over his temper and turned on Emerald Marcella, raped her, and then, in an attempt to hide his crime, sent her nude body through a guardrail in his Ferrari. The coroner had declared that the crash had killed her. But he'd also testified that she had participated, or been subjected to, very rough sex a short time before her death. Brandon's skin had been found under her fingernails. Upon examination of his person, his face, chest, stomach, and thighs showed evidence of scratches.

A basset hound began to bay and run down the drive in Alyson's direction. She buried herself deeper in the pine needles, wincing as they dug into the back of her neck.

Carlyle stepped from the porch and started down the drive in pursuit of the barking hound.

Alyson did her best to shimmy her way back toward the tree trunk. The limb on which she balanced sagged and popped. She held her breath.

The dog ran to the high, pike-topped iron fence and proceeded to howl again. He'd spotted the car she'd parked just off the road, partially in a ditch, mostly hidden by a clump of cattails.

"Rufous, heel!" Carlyle shouted, stopping short when he saw the red rental car. He took a few steps backward, his expression turning from annoyance at the dog to sudden concern. His gaze swept the grounds as a woman bounced from the house, waving a cell phone in the air. Carlyle shouted for her to call nine-one-one and began backing up the driveway while the red-haired woman with highly painted cheeks and white shoes began babbling into the phone.

The tree branch creaked and groaned. This was *not* going to be her finest hour, Alyson thought, her panic mounting. Then again, it was probably no more than she deserved. It was just this kind of stunt that had turned Carlyle into a lunatic who would drive his car into a dozen photographers, scattering bodies across the lawn as if they were bowling pins. She wanted to crawl into her car and skulk back to her room at the Pine Tree Lodge.

But she was desperate.

And her only means of escaping future humiliation like this stood yonder in a tight white T-shirt and jeans that molded around his private parts like a lover's hand. Brandon was going to be her ticket to a legit job with a legit publication—one that didn't make her squirm in embarrassment when she was forced to confess who paid her a salary.

"Officer Cornwall is just down the road!" the woman called to Carlyle. "He's on his way."

Alyson rolled her eyes. *Great. Just great.*

A bald man in overalls walked out on the front porch, a sandwich in one hand and what looked like a glass of iced tea in the other. "What the hell is all the hoopla about?" he shouted.

"It's probably nothing," the woman replied, then shouted at Carlyle, "Get back in the house until Officer Cornwall gets here. Don't be taking any chances, Mr. Brandon."

Baying now like a hound from hell, the basset dived into the underbrush, plowing like a tractor toward her tree. After a moment's hesitation, Carlyle followed, wading into the waist-high brush, his face becoming redder and angrier by the second.

Sirens whooped. Lights flashed as a Caprice cruiser came wheeling off the highway and up to the opening gate.

The hound howled and ran in circles directly beneath her. The limb squeaked. Drooped.

Carlyle stumbled through the brush to where the dog was frantically digging at the base of the tree. He looked up. His eyes widened.

The limb snapped.

Carlyle ducked and rolled—too late. Her weight drove him to the ground, where he scrambled to knock aside the branch and grab a handful of her hair before she could recover from the impact. Suddenly he was over her, one knee digging into her stomach and pinning her to the ground, his teeth showing, eyes flashing, fist drawn back and prepared to smash her face to smithereens. She couldn't move or speak or breathe. She could only stare up into the man's furious expression and wonder desperately just how much plastic surgery was going to cost after he obliterated every bone in her face.

He didn't hit her, thank God, because he was a whole lot bigger and heavier and stronger than he'd looked from her precarious perch. And a whole lot better-looking, if that was possible.

"It's a goddamn woman," he snarled as the officer suddenly appeared over his shoulder, pointing a big gun at her and ordering Carlyle to back off and let him take over.

"Will somebody shut that dog up? It's giving me a headache!" the officer shouted.

The woman in white shoes and a flowered blouse whistled for the dog as Carlyle backed off, slowly, his eyes still locked on hers. She rubbed her head.

"Get the hell up," the officer ordered, wagging the gun at her. "Up. Up." He stepped back, lips pinched with nervousness.

Slowly, unsteadily, Alyson rolled to her hands and knees, managing to take a deep breath before climbing to her feet. Her camera. Oh, Christ. She glanced down at the Nikon, which lay partially ground into the dirt, and suddenly felt desperately sick. The lens had cost her four hundred and change.

Carlyle muttered something under his breath and reached

for the camera. Flashes of him smashing equipment in the past rolled in her mind. "Don't hurt it," she managed in a dry voice.

He removed the film cartridge and flung the camera back at her. She caught it and gripped it to her chest like a baby as she looked back and forth between Carlyle and the officer, who continued to point his cannon at her.

"You want me to take her in?" the officer asked, sliding a glance toward Brandon.

He looked her up and down, wondering to himself how he could have mistaken her, in that first flash of anger, for a man. The hair, he supposed. Cut so short. Shorter than his. And perhaps her height, five-nine, or maybe ten. But the body sure as hell didn't belong to anything except a female. Tall, willowy, poured into a pair of tight blue denims, her breasts nicely filling out a T-shirt emblazoned "Texas Aggies." Despite the fall the shirt was tucked neatly into the jeans; her very small waist was accentuated by a sparkling multicolored belt with a sterling silver buckle. She sure as hell hadn't bought it at Wal-Mart.

"Right," he finally replied, still looking into her hazel eyes fringed by thick, black lashes. There was a scratch across her right cheekbone that was beading, and a smear of golden pine sap across her chin. "Take her in."

Those gray-green eyes widened, and color rushed over her face. "You're not serious." She gave a short, disbelieving laugh. "Look, I apologize. You took the film. I was going to talk with you the first chance I got, anyway. But you're too damn hard to get to—"

"Obviously not hard enough." He gave her a derisive grin and turned away.

"I have a proposition—"

"So does every other woman in the universe, Baby. Not interested."

"Not *that* kind of proposition!"

Pausing, he looked back. Long legs braced apart and her arms clutching her camera, she glared at him through her tousled fringe of dark bangs, her face red with indignation, her eyes wide with worry. This is where she would beg, no doubt. Turn on the tears. But she didn't beg, didn't cry. Raising her chin a notch, she told him with equal derision, "Not interested, Carlyle."

He stared at her.

She stared back, the scratch on her face starting to puff and a solitary thread of blood trickling down her cheek. For an infinitesimal second something that felt annoyingly like respect flickered in his chest.

"Take her in," he repeated, as sweet and slow as molasses. "I'll be down later to press charges."

"You creep!" she cried. Cornwall holstered his gun and reached for her arm. She snatched it away, her gaze still fixed on Brandon as he joined Betty, and on Henry, who continued to munch on his sandwich and regard the interloper with an amused smile. "Arrogant bull. Fine. Be that way. You don't deserve me, anyway. Take your hands off me," she snapped at the officer, "or I'll see you brought up on charges of police brutality!"

Cornwall, who perpetually looked borderline skittish, took a quick step back and adjusted the gun on his hip.

"You're making a mistake," she declared, moving toward the cruiser, her gaze never faltering even as she tripped over a tree root and nearly dropped her camera. "I came here to help you. Don't stand there looking all full of yourself and tell me you don't need my help. If you weren't terrified of what the world thinks of you, you wouldn't be hiding away in this Twilight Zone of a town. At least give me a chance to explain!"

Cornwall opened the cruiser door for her, placed his hand on top of her head, and eased her down into the seat. She stared through the window at Brandon, her eyes big, her mouth petulant. He turned his back on her and walked off.

Charlotte Minger crammed three sticks of Big Red chewing gum into her mouth and tossed the silver wrappers onto Wal-Mart's glistening floor, grinning to herself. Cy Ricky

Wheeler was responsible for floor maintenance. Might as well give him something to occupy his time instead of hitting on her every chance he got. As if she'd go out with him! Just the thought of it gave her the willies. He looked like a cross between Ichabod Crane and Jiminy Cricket. And he smelled like Clearasil and B.O. As the recently crowned Miss Yamboree, she had her reputation to consider.

There was precious little left worth buying on the fifty-percent-off rack, she noted. Mostly summer stuff that the Goodwill would turn away. She didn't want to have to drive into town and poke around Patsy's Dress Shop. Patsy Crumm charged too much just because she had the only decent la-dies' apparel shop in Ticky Creek. Besides, Charlotte got a fifteen percent employee discount if she bought at Wal-Mart.

Then again, it wasn't every night that a girl had a date with Brandon Carlyle. In fact, as far as she knew, no one in Ticky Creek had managed to pin down the elusive hunk. He barely spoke to people, much less took them out for a burger at the Dairy Queen. She surmised that if she impressed him enough, on their next date he might take her to Tyler for Mexican food. Good plan. If the press caught wind of it and reporters just happened to be at the restaurant when they arrived, she'd get her photograph plastered in every maga-zine and tabloid in the country. She'd be famous overnight. The *National Enquirer* and the *Galaxy Gazette* would pay her a fortune to tell her story. Maybe Lifetime Network would make a movie about how she won and rehabilitated Brandon Carlyle's heart.

"Hey, Charlotte."

Charlotte looked around, into Cy Ricky's bumpy red face. "Hey," she replied, and turned back to the rack, removing a cropped western shirt with fringe on the hem.

"Thought maybe I could talk you into a movie tonight. We could drive into Tyler if you want. Go to the new Cinemark. I got paid today."

"I have a date, in case you ain't heard." She held the garment against her and assessed herself in the full-length mirror on the wall. The fringe was sorta sexy. And the rich purple of the material made her platinum hair look shimmery. The top might look good with her new Gap jeans, purchased last month at the Galleria in Houston.

"Oh, yeah?" Cy Ricky's mouth quirked to one side as he stared over her shoulder at her mirrored image. The Ping-Pong ball in his throat slid up and down as he swallowed. "Who you got a date with?"

"If I told you, you wouldn't believe me."

"Try me."

"Brandon Carlyle." She grinned and met his brown eyes in the mirror, anticipating his reaction.

He frowned and shuffled his feet. "Uh-uh. No way."

"The man himself. Like he came in the store to buy some malted milk balls for his uncle and some talcum powder for his aunt? He's been in before, of course, lots of times, and me and him sorta hit it off, I guess. I think he kept coming back just so he could see me. Anyway, he came through my checkout, and as I was ringing him up, he asked me out. Cool, huh?"

"I don't know." Cy Ricky shook his head, and his thin shoulders shifted uncomfortably. "He's old enough to be your daddy, Charlotte."

"Don't be stupid. And so what if he is? Movie stars always go for young women. Makes 'em feel studly or something, I guess."

"Your parents won't like it much, what with his reputation and all. Don't forget what he did to that porn star."

"She died in a car crash. It wasn't like he shot her or strangled her or something."

"He raped her." Cy Ricky's eyes bugged for emphasis.

"You've been reading too many tabloids, Cy Ricky. I watched Court TV. He testified that the sex with Emerald Marcella was consensual, and she was the one who got all hot and kinky and started doing weird stuff 'cause she was high on coke. She practically raped him."

"What are you gonna do after you eat?"

She turned the price tag over to check the cost of the shirt, decided that with her employee discount she could afford it, and tucked it under her arm. Maybe she should buy some new underwear, too. With any luck Carlyle would be in the mood for more than a DQ Beltbuster and a dip cone. And if he wasn't in the mood, well, maybe she'd just get him in the mood. From what she'd read about his sexual appetites, it wouldn't take much to get him buzzed.

She started for the lingerie department, Cy Ricky trailing at her heels. "Well?" he prodded. "Answer me."

"None of your beeswax, Cy Ricky. Why don't you go back to your mopping, and stop worrying about what I'm gonna do with Brandon Carlyle?"

"I don't like this one little bit, Charlotte."

"As if I care." Rounding a display of Halloween candies and ghoulish plastic masks, Charlotte stopped short. Sheriff Jack Dillman stood in her path, hands on his hips, his big gun fixed to his right thigh and his brown cowboy hat positioned low over his eyes. He glared down at her, unsmiling beneath his straw-colored mustache.

Without shifting his dark eyes from hers, he said to Cy Ricky, "Scram. I've got a bone to pick with Miss Yamboree here."

Cy Ricky scrammed.

Dillman's expression didn't change as he reached for the purple shirt with fringe and held it up between them. "Pretty. I assume you're gonna pay for this one?"

She frowned as her cheeks turned warm. "I don't know what you mean."

"I'm meanin' I got a call from Ben Roberts over at the Discount Drugs. He said you and he got into a little fray a couple days ago. Somethin' about you pocketin' some lipsticks and earrings and tryin' to slip out of the store without payin' for them."

Damn Ben Roberts, that piece of shit night manager. He'd promised to forget about the incident if she gave him a blow job in the back of the store after quitting time. Which she did. After all, she simply couldn't compromise her Miss Yamboree title. It was her first step out of Ticky Creek. Brandon Carlyle was going to be her second.

She chewed her Big Red and wondered what she was supposed to do now. In a quiet voice, she said, "If you're gonna arrest me, do it outside. I can't afford to lose this job."

"I ain't gonna arrest you. At least not yet. Ben Roberts is still thinkin' about whether or not he wants to press charges."

"Ben Roberts can take a flying leap—"

"Rumor is, you've got a date tonight with Brandon Carlyle."

She stopped chewing and looked around at Rita Weir at checkout five. Charlotte had confided to Rita about her date no more than half an hour ago, and already it was rushing through the store like a hay field fire. "Yeah. So what?"

"So we need to talk."

"You gonna tell me that he's too old for me? Or that I'm takin' my life in my hands by sharin' a freakin' burger and soda with him?"

"I'm tellin' you that if you want to priss your pretty little ass across stage durin' the Yamboree celebration, you'll listen to what I have to offer. Of course, if you'd rather have Ben Roberts press charges against you, that's fine, too. I'm sure First Runner-up Sally Davenport would appreciate havin' her picture circulated as Miss Yamboree."

With a sigh and a roll of her eyes, Charlotte set aside the shirt and accompanied Dillman out of the store.

*The county courthouse had been built in 1857 out of lime*stone blocks hauled all the way from a quarry near Georgetown, Texas. By the looks of the interior walls and floors, there hadn't been a great many renovations to the building in the last century and a half. The green paint on the walls was peeling off in large, curling flakes. The wood floor was dull, pocked, and rutted. Aside from a telephone sitting on Cornwall's desk and a soda machine humming against the far wall, one would be hard-pressed to believe they hadn't stepped into a time machine and been sucked back to the nineteenth century. She expected to see Marshal Dillon walk through the door at any minute.

For the last two hours, since Cornwall had hauled her away from the Carlyle farm, Alyson had waited in the small, stuffy room with only a view of the square to occupy her time. Normally, she might have found the goings-on up and down the bricked street relaxing if not amusing: two bald old men sat on a bench feeding peanuts to squirrels. A group of young people draped banners from streetlight to streetlight, the tall red and blue letters on the banners spelling out TICKY CREEK YAMBOREE. Across the courthouse lawn, vendors were setting up booths where they intended to sell cotton candy, taffy apples, and sweet potato pies to the hundreds of people who would pour into town to participate in the festivities celebrating the harvest of the revered yam. And across the street, between Martha's Old and New Antiquities and Crawford's Hardware, a group of men in grease-stained shirts were busily erecting carnival rides: a Ferris wheel, a carousel, an Octopus, and a Tilt-A-Whirl. There were game booths as well, tempting prospective players with heaps of brightly colored stuffed animals. Norman Rockwell would have felt right at home.

Alyson walked to the door and stared hard at Cornwall, who sat hunched over a tuna sandwich and a newspaper. He glanced her way, offered her an apologetic smile, obviously embarrassed over having to detain her.

"Aren't you supposed to be taking mug shots of me or something?"

"You ain't been formally charged with anything yet. That'll be up to the Carlyles. I don't expect Henry will do anything, but I ain't so sure about Brandon. He gets pretty sore when it comes to people intrudin' on his privacy." He chewed and swallowed. "Sure you don't want half my sandwich, Ms. James? It's good. Dime A Cup Café can't be beat when it comes to tuna salad sandwiches. They don't scrimp on the sweet relish and eggs, like a lot of places."

She shrugged. "Why not?" And while he was sharing a little tuna and sweet relish, maybe she could pick his brains about Carlyle's life in Ticky Creek.

Cornwall gathered up the paper plate heaped with sandwich, potato chips, and a dill pickle spear, and carried it into the holding room. He placed it on the table and backed away, rubbing his hands together. He looked a little like Barney Fife, only bigger and with more hair.

"Sorry 'bout this wait, Ms. James. I'm sure Brandon will be by shortly. I called the house. That nurse of Bernice's said he and Henry left for town a while back. Henry has a doctor's appointment. Got a bad heart, ya know. They gotta keep a real close eye on his blood pressure and such." He pointed out the window. "That's his doctor's office right there. Doc Simpson. Been doctor in these parts for forty years. I don't see Henry's truck yet. They may have stopped off somewhere. Feed store or something."

Alyson bit into the sandwich. Cornwall was right. Sure as heck beat the package of Twinkies and Dr Pepper she'd had for breakfast.

Cornwall slid his fingertips into his back pockets. "I'll try and talk to him if you want. Brandon, I mean. I think I can convince him not to press trespassing charges against you if you promise to leave him alone and go back where you came from. And promise not to tell anyone you saw him here, of course."

Alyson smiled and reached for a jalapeno-flavored potato chip. "I appreciate your thoughtfulness, but I'm perfectly capable of talking to Carlyle myself. Unlike a lot of people, I'm not intimidated by him or his tantrums."

"Naw, you don't look like the sort who'd be intimidated by much."

She smiled and made her voice a little sultry. "Am I supposed to take that as a compliment?"

He shrugged and grinned. "You got an air of confidence about you, is all." He leaned back against the wall. "You married?"

"Not anymore." She bit the end off the pickle spear and regarded the flushed officer. He was working up the courage to flirt, she could tell. "Are you married, Officer Cornwall?"

"Nope. Never met the right girl, I guess. Course there's not a lot to choose from in Ticky Creek. Most girls graduate high school and leave for Dallas or Houston. You know, they got aspirations of going to college or landing them a well-off husband. Can't say as I blame them. This town's idea of excitement is Friday nights at the high school football games and Saturday nights at the River Road Saloon—that's a honky-tonk 'bout ten miles out of town. Between here and White Sands. I suppose a woman like you wouldn't like a place like that."

"I grew up in a two-room apartment over a truck stop out by Seven Pines, near Longview. I've seen a honky-tonk or two in my time. My mother waitressed at the Pussy Cat Bar outside of Kilgore."

"Yeah?" His eyes brightened and his grin widened. "You don't sound like an East Texas gal. Don't look like one either."

"An East Texas gal gotta walk around wearing an old tow sack and have hay in her hair?"

"Naw." He shook his head and laughed. "That's not what I meant. . . . Anybody ever tell you you look like that actress . . . now don't tell me. Let me think a minute." He snapped his fingers. "Charlize Theron. Maybe it's the big eyes. And your mouth. You got a . . . nice mouth."

"Yeah?" She winked and slid her tongue along the pickle spear. "Your's isn't so bad either."

His jaw dropped, and he sank a little harder against the wall.

"I take it people 'round here don't give much thought to a movie star like Brandon Carlyle living among them."

He shook his head, attention still focused on the pickle.

"Does he behave himself?"

"Who?"

"Carlyle."

"Oh." Cornwall took a deep breath and slowly released it. "He stays to himself. Comes into town now and again and eats at Dime A Cup. Mostly when he brings his uncle in to the doctor. Henry and Bernice took care of Brandon and his daddy after Cara up and left Ticky Creek for Hollywood. When Brandon's daddy was killed down at the mill, Cara come back and took Brandon. Said no way in hell was she gonna let her little boy be brought up by a lot of backwoods hicks. Brandon was four, I think. 'Bout killed Bernice and Henry. Broke their hearts. They could never have kids, and looked at Brandon like he was their own."

"Obviously Brandon stayed close to Bernice and Henry."

"Real close. He come back to Ticky Creek ever' chance he got. At least Cara gave him that. Brandon was always a nice guy. Fit right in with the rest of us while he was here— or tried to. After a while it got pretty tough to treat him like he was just one of the fellas. Girls got all spoony over him, and that pissed the guys off. Then the guys didn't want him coming around, at least not while the girls were with them. Sometimes we'd all go off to the quarry and drink."

"Brandon could belt it back, huh?"

Cornwall rubbed the back of his neck, his expression bothered as he forced himself to shift his attention away from Alyson. No doubt he realized he was talking way too freely about Carlyle.

"It's not as if his drinking isn't public knowledge," she assured him.

"Right."

Time to steer him down another road until he relaxed again. "I suppose Bernice and Henry are glad to have him home again."

"Oh, yeah." Cornwall laughed. "Henry is beside himself. He sure needed the help after Bernice's stroke. Brandon's stepping in and taking over most of the farm chores lets Henry spend as much time as possible with Bernice. Not that Henry's able to do a lot to help her; he's got that home nurse to do all that. Betty, I think her name is. Betty Wilson."

The woman with red hair and white shoes. That one could be trouble.

"Was Henry aware of Brandon's drinking problem?" she asked nonchalantly as she took another bite of tuna sandwich.

Cornwall frowned and shoved his hands in his pockets. "Can't imagine he couldn't have seen it. We all did. Hell, once we all watched him kick back a pint of Jack Daniels in less than an hour. He couldn't have been more than fourteen, maybe fifteen at the time."

"What about drugs? Ever see him take any?"

"Nope." He shook his head, and his eyes narrowed in speculation as he focused on her again. "He don't drink anymore, either. Stays clean as a whistle. Part of his parole. He gets caught intoxicated, and he gets shipped back to Corcoran to serve out the rest of his sentence."

A door opened someplace, snapping Cornwall to attention. He moved to the door and looked out, made a noise in his throat, and muttered, "Ah, hell, I was hoping to get all this over with before Jack got back." He glanced over his shoulder at Alyson, his expression tense. "I'll be back. Just eat your sandwich and keep quiet."

"Something wrong?" She tossed down the pickle and pushed back the chair. Nothing like the scent of worry and anticipation to stimulate her need to poke her nose where it shouldn't be.

"Just that Sheriff Dillman and Brandon don't exactly see eye to eye, if you get my drift. Air gets a little thick when they're together." He cleared his throat. "Hey, Jack, you finished up in Nacogdoches already?"

Cornwall closed the door behind him, muffling the conversation between him and the sheriff. Alyson pressed her ear to the door, doing her best to catch any tidbits of information, then jumped back as the door swung open and the threshold filled with something that looked like he should be starring in the WWF. He glared at her with squinted eyes, his square jaw clenched and working. One hand rested on his gun. The other was hooked on his belt.

"This here is Ms Alyson James," Cornwall explained.

Looking her up and down, Dillman allowed a smirk to cross his lips, or what Alyson could see of them under his mustache. He reached around behind him; Cornwall slapped a paper in his hand. Dillman studied it a few seconds before raising his gaze to hers.

"Trespassin' on the Carlyle place, huh?" He didn't give her time to respond before saying, "Wondered how long it

would take before the lot of you busybodies and news vultures got wind of his livin' here. How many of you are
there?"

She shrugged and gave him an innocent smile. "Just lil'
ol' me, Sheriff."

"Just you." He snorted. "And don't patronize me, Mizz
James. I ain't in the mood to be patronized. Anythin' relatin'
to Carlyle puts me in a real foul disposition, so if you don't
want to spend the rest of the day and night downstairs with
a pair of drunks and a possible child molester, you better tell
me real quick what your business is and just when the hell
you plan on gettin' out of my town."

"She's a writer," Cornwall offered.

"Freelance," she added, putting a chair between her and
the sheriff. She was damn good at figuring out what buttons
to push on a person to tweak their more amenable attrib-
utes—a talent one developed quickly if one held any hope
of squeezing information out of reluctant interviewees. Take
Cornwall: five minutes in his company and she had assessed
that he was happiest kicking back at the River Road Honky
Tonk and schmoozing with lumber mill river rats over a
pitcher of cold Budweiser. He probably pinched the waitresses' butts every chance he got because it made him feel
like one of the guys. Her story of living over a truck stop
with a mother who waited tables at the Pussy Cat in Kilgore
had won him over in a heartbeat. It put them on a level
playing field.

But two minutes in Dillman's company told her that she
was going to be hard-pressed to find so much as a splinter
of amenability in him. Looking into his hard, whisky-colored
eyes was like attempting to stare down a cottonmouth.

"I'm alone, Sheriff. I hoped to discuss a possible book
deal with Carlyle. That is, if I can ever get close enough to
him without his having my butt hauled to jail."

"Alone, huh?" His mouth worked, causing his yellow mustache to move up and down and from side to side. His gaze
slid over her Texas Aggies T-shirt, hesitated, then back up
to her face. "Where you stayin'?"

"Pine Tree Lodge. Just out of town."

A door opened and closed. Cornwall looked around, his expression becoming more tense, if that were possible. "Hey, Brandon, how's it goin'?"

Dillman left the room, sucking the air out with him as he went. Alyson leaned against the chair and tried to breathe. First Dillman and now Carlyle. Drawing back her shoulders, she prepared for a second onslaught of insults, and thought she might be safer tossed to the drunks and molester in the basement. No doubt they would be friendlier company.

She moved cautiously to the door and peered out. Dillman stood aside, arms crossed over his big chest, glaring at Carlyle, who didn't so much as acknowledge his existence, though how anyone could ignore a man the size of a Mack truck Alyson couldn't guess. Cornwall stood behind his desk, presenting papers to Carlyle, who stood with his back to her. His blue chambray shirt was tucked into his blue jeans, and the blue jeans cupped his buttocks so perfectly that the sight made her mouth a little dry. The man had never needed a body double. He had the best tush in Hollywood; women packed the theaters by the thousands in anticipation of even the briefest glimpse of his naked buns. Sighing, she looked longingly at her camera on Cornwall's desk.

"Her story checks out," Cornwall said. "She told me she got into town two days ago. I checked with the car rental folks in Dallas, and she picked up the car Thursday morning at ten-thirty. She checked into the Pine Tree Lodge on Thursday around four in the afternoon. She's got an open-ended American Airlines ticket originating in San Francisco. I ran a check on her through the guys out there, and she's clean. Not even a traffic violation. Says she's a freelance writer and wants to talk to you about a book deal." Cornwall glanced her way and cleared his throat. "She don't act like a crazy, but I guess you've seen more of them than I have."

Thanks a lot, she mouthed at him, causing his face to flush.

Carlyle withdrew something from his back pocket and tossed it on the desk. "Got that in the mail today," he said. "Third one in as many months. A little coincidental that it showed up in my mailbox about the same time she shows up in Ticky Creek."

Both Dillman and Cornwall looked around at her. Carlyle turned, eyes as blue and cold as chips of ice spearing her where she stood in the doorway. There wasn't a smidgeon of sympathy in his expression.

Squaring her shoulders, she sauntered toward the three-some. "Sounds like I'm about to be accused of something other than falling out of a tree on the wrong side of a fence. Mind telling me exactly what other crime I'm supposed to have committed in the last forty-eight hours?"

Cornwall retrieved a paper from the desk and held it out to her. She sidled up next to Carlyle, her arm brushing his as she took the crumpled letter and casually perused it. Or tried to. Standing so close to the Sexiest Man Alive somehow diminished her ability to focus on anything other than the intensity of his stare, which made her skin feel as if she'd fallen in a bed of fire ants. She couldn't breathe the electrified air.

Clearing her throat, she finally managed to raise her eyes back to his and force a tight smile to her lips. "Sorry, Carlyle. If I've got sweet talk on my mind, I'll say it to a man's face. Or whisper it in his ear. I'm not shy about seduction. When I want a man, I'm about as subtle as a heart attack."

Cornwall coughed and reached for the can of warm Dr Pepper on his desk. Dillman snatched the letter from Alyson's hand and shoved it at Carlyle.

"There ain't nothin' in this letter that is remotely threatenin', Carlyle. Just some horny woman who ain't got the news yet that you're a pervert." With a smug grin, he lowered his voice. "Course, after spendin' three years in the pen, pretty boy that you are, maybe that letter ain't from a woman. Maybe after gettin' a taste of life on your knees, you've gone queer on us." Throwing back his head, Dillman laughed so loud that the sound echoed off the walls. Then, as quickly, his humor evaporated, leaving him glaring at Carlyle through a haze of contempt. "If you're gonna press charges against this woman, let's get to it. I got better things to do than waste my time on your stupid paranoia."

Carlyle carefully folded the letter, his face so red it looked almost purple. His jaw worked. His hands shook. Alyson took a step back, expecting him to explode, feeling a little sick to see him struggling so hard to combat the urge to rip Dillman's face off.

Yet, Carlyle did just that. He tucked the letter into his hip pocket, and without looking at any of them, left the building.

Cornwall's breath rushed from him like air out of a balloon. He sank into his chair and stared at the scattering of reports on his desk.

Dillman grunted, mustache cocked to one side as he looked at Alyson. "Guess that means you can go."

She reached for her camera, collected her purse. Turning to Dillman, she said, "I've met some real assholes in my day, but Bubba, you got them all beat to Sunday."

3

The weather felt too hot and sticky to be nearly Halloween.
Breathing in the humid East Texas air was like inhaling
through a wet bath towel. Once upon a time, the thick humidity hadn't bothered Brandon. He'd basked in it like a
sauna. It sweated the anger and booze out of his system. By
the close of an Indian summer afternoon, every pore in his
body felt purged. But now it gave him a headache and poked
at his temper, thanks to Dickhead Dillman and some woman
with a sultry mouth and eyes that could jar a man right out
of his Nikes, were he so inclined . . . which he wasn't.

Ticky Creek town square hummed to the tune of hammers,
shouts, and laughter. The locals busily decorated the street-
lamps with giant cutouts of jack-o'-lanterns and witches on
broomsticks—all in preparation for the thirty-first of October,
when every little hobgoblin in the area congregated on the
square to reap sackfuls of candy from the businesses. It was
also the culmination of the Yamboree. Farmers trucked in
yams by the bushel. They would be weighed, measured, and

rated; fried, stewed, mashed, and molded into pies, cakes, loaves, and burgers.

The carnies, having taken a break from erecting their rides and game booths, sat on the street corner, smoking cigarettes and making obscene comments to the cheerleaders who were busy hanging banners and doing handstands in the middle of the street.

Brandon watched it all from behind his Ray-Bans, his anger at Dillman still like a wad of cotton in his throat. He needed a drink. Desperately. Just one. To replace the fire of temper in his gut with the fire of alcohol. Get his mind off his immense desire to drive his hand into Jack Dillman's mouth, wipe the grin off his face once and for all. Hell, the pleasure he'd experience feeling Dillman's teeth shatter would almost be worth spending the next three years back in Corcoran.

He shifted his focus from the short-skirted pom-pom queens to the red Ford Escort hitched to the wrecker just pulling into the impound lot behind the hardware store. His mouth curled at the thought that the pretty lady snoop with a camera would pay a hefty fee to Juaquin Gonzales to get her car back, especially when he discovered she was an out-of-towner.

Freelance writer, my ass, he thought. The female smelled of reporter. She reeked of it. They had a way of carrying themselves, like they were soldiers in God's army, ready to strike a blow against any man or woman who saw fit to fight his or her way out of mediocrity.

That's all he needed, some young, hungry reporter blowing the whistle on his whereabouts. Every freaking rag in five countries would be swarming through Ticky Creek within a week. Barbara Walters and Oprah would engage in hand-to-hand combat to be the first to pin his back to the wall with questions like "So what would drive a man who looks like you and who is as successful as you—desired by women the world over—to subject himself to the perversions of a woman like Emerald Marcella?"

Then Sam Donaldson, looking like a Vulcan from *Star*

Trek, would elbow his way between the women and demand: "How could you do it, Carlyle? You had it all. Fame. Fortune. You blew it, and the world deserves to know why!"

He fished a cigarette out of his pocket, held it between his teeth as he flipped open his lighter, and cupped his hands around the flame, drawing in the smoke as he glanced back at the carnies. Sliding the lighter into his pocket, he wove his way between several parked cars, paused at the intersection long enough for a powder blue Impala with tinted windows to crawl around the corner, muffler scraping the brick street and exhaust spewing out the back in a acrid black stream. The car stopped in front of him, rumbled like a tank, muffler tap-tap-tapping on the pavement. He moved around it, flicked his cigarette ashes onto the street as he ran toward Juaquin Gonzales, who looked up from locking the impound gate, his expression registering surprise.

"Hey, man." Juaquin grinned. *"Como esta?"*

"Not too bad, Juaquin." Brandon pointed his cigarette toward the Ford Escort. "I wanna have a look at that car."

Juaquin looked back at the Ford. His heavy black brows drew together. "I can't do that, man. Dillman will have my ass."

"So don't tell him."

Brandon shoved the gate aside and slid past the nervous man. The car was still attached to the wrecker, front end in the air. He opened the door, climbed onto the front seat that was littered with Twinkie wrappers and an empty Diet Dr Pepper bottle. Nothing on the floor. He opened the glove compartment. A map fell out, along with a partially melted Hershey bar and a small bag of Fritos. Damn, for such a junk food freak, the woman had a hell of a body. Not that he was in the least interested in her body. . . .

He grabbed the keys from the ignition as Juaquin shook his head and splayed his arms. "Shit, man, you're gonna get me fired! Don't be fuckin' with dem keys! Are you loco?"

"As a loon, Juaquin. Haven't you heard?" He flashed the man a smile. "Dillman gives you any grief, you tell him I said he can kiss my butt."

"I don't see what kinda good that's gonna do me." Juaquin walked to the closed gate and looked toward the courthouse, mumbling to himself and shaking his head. He glanced back at Brandon as he shoved the key in the trunk lock and turned it. The lid popped loose with a thunk, exposing a black canvas bag and a pair of muddy Ropers. He opened the bag, turned it upside down, and shook it, spilling an array of socks, panties, and bras onto the trunk bottom.

Jesus, the woman was a walking advertisement for Victoria's Secret. He hooked a pair of red satin thong panties on one finger and held them up, stared at them through the stream of smoke curling up from his cigarette. The earlier image of her in jeans dissolved into one of her wearing nothing but a sliver of red satin and a smile, her thick, dark hair the color of cherry coke seductively shading her big eyes.

He shook off the thought. The idea of slowly peeling her out of satin thong panties had as much appeal as curling up in a nest of scorpions.

"Hurry!" Joaquin shouted.

Brandon took one last drag on his cigarette, then tossed it to the ground. He riffled through the underwear again to make certain he hadn't missed anything: a gun, a knife, a small explosive device—even worse, press credentials. He wondered which was worse. One way he died by wounds; the other, by words. At least a bullet in the brain got it over quickly.

He turned the canvas bag inside out and ran his hand into the side pockets, finding a single tampon and a couple of lambskin condoms. Trojans. Ribbed for Her Pleasure.

His face turned warmer, and something down low began to stir.

Don't even think it, a voice in his head whispered. *The woman is trouble with a capital T. She represents everything you hate. Everything that dragged you down into the filthiest gutter. Her presence in Ticky Creek threatens your peace and harmony. And safety. Hell, she could be Anticipating, making plans to creep into your bedroom tonight and blow your brains out with an Uzi.*

Brandon imagined his poor uncle Henry stumbling into his nephew's bedroom in the morning and finding Brandon's brains spattered over the striped and flowered wallpaper. He suspected it would take more than a nitroglycerin tablet under Henry's tongue to prevent another heart attack like the one that nearly killed his uncle shortly after Brandon's arrival in Ticky Creek.

Behind him, Juaquin let loose a string of expletives. Brandon gathered up the underwear and shoved it back into the bag—all but the red satin thong, and one of the condoms. He tucked those deep into his jeans pocket.

There was something about small town drugstores that had always fascinated Alyson. There was a certain smell that she could never quite put her finger on. Perhaps it was simply so many items crammed so close together: over-the-counter medications, greeting cards, toiletries, makeup, and knockoff perfumes. She always felt like tiptoeing up and down the aisles, as one does in a hospital.

Today she tiptoed down the candy aisle and grabbed up a bag of Kandy Korn and one of miniature Snickers, then, to balance her diet, she selected a can of Pringles. Alyson made her way to the rack of disposable cameras and film. She had tons of film back at the motel, but they weren't going to do her any good at that particular moment. No respectable photographer would ever be caught without film in her camera— Brandon Carlyle or no Brandon Carlyle. She wondered what he had done with the canister he had confiscated from her earlier that day. Thinking of the shots she had gotten and would never see, she felt queasy.

At the checkout she collected copies of the *Gazette*, the *Enquirer*, the *Sun*, and the *Globe*. The woman behind the cash register regarded Alyson over the tops of her thick glasses. Alyson smiled and shrugged. "I buy them for the crosswords."

A chubby blond in a bright red smock with a name tag emblazoned

HELLO I'M IRIS.
Ask about our one hour developing

moved behind the counter at that moment, her arms full of
envelopes of recently developed photographs. Pulling out a
drawer, she proceeded to file them in alphabetical order.

"Oh, my gosh!" Alyson slapped her forehead, causing Iris
and the tabloid-disapproving woman to stare at her. "I totally
forgot what I came in for in the first place. What a doofus.
I'm supposed to pick up some photos for Carlyle if they're
ready."

Iris narrowed her eyes.

Alyson smiled pleasantly. "Or maybe he hasn't gotten by
to drop them off yet. In that case—"

"They're ready," Iris offered, slowly withdrawing the
package from the drawer, suspicion forming deep lines across
her brow. "Mr. Carlyle didn't say nothing about somebody
else picking these up. Said he'd be back in a while to get
them himself."

"Ah . . . I bumped into him earlier. At the sheriff's office.
We're supposed to meet at the café in a little while. He's at
Doc Simpson's office. With his uncle. Henry. Got to get his
blood pressure checked, you know. Henry, that is. Actually,
they're shots of Brandon I took this morning. With this." She
held up her camera and smiled again. "If you don't believe
me, have a look for yourself."

Iris and the checkout woman looked at one another. Finally, Iris shrugged and hesitantly slid the package across the
counter to Alyson and went back to the sorting and alpha-
betizing of the remaining envelopes.

Alyson waited, holding her breath as the cashier totaled
the items and with the speed of a snail, dug under the counter
for a sack in which to put them. The front glass doors slid
open . . . her heart shuddered—a man she recognized as one
of the carnies walked in and moved behind her, his gaze
scanning the collection of cigarettes on the wall beyond the
counter. His body odor washed over her so thickly she

couldn't breathe, then he glanced down at her and smiled, revealing two missing front teeth.

"Something I can do for you?" The cashier looked up from her search for a sack, pinning the man with another of her disapproving glowers.

Come on. Come on. Alyson tapped her foot, glanced again at the door, expecting Carlyle to come breezing in at any minute and nail her for stealing his photos—only they weren't his photos, they were hers. But she suspected he and Mack the Truck Dillman wouldn't see it that way.

"I need me a carton of Pall Malls," the man said. "Soft packs." He jutted one greasy finger toward the packs near the bottom of the shelf.

The cartons were locked behind a glass case.

Apparently losing track of her priorities, the cashier began shuffling through a drawer for a key to unlock the case.

"Ah . . . I'm really in a hurry," Alyson pointed out, smiling apologetically as the cashier glared at her again over her glasses. Finally, she stooped to snatch a brown plastic sack from a box and stuffed the purchases into it. Alyson grabbed it and made her way out of the store as quickly as possible.

Once outside, Alyson looked around and focused on the Dime A Cup Café:

SPECIAL OF THE DAY

Meat Loaf Turnip Greens
Mashed Potatoes Sweet Potato Pie

$4.99 ALL YOU CAN EAT

She moved to the plate-glass window and, cupping her hands around her eyes, peered into the café, which was mostly empty except for a pair of stoop-shouldered farmers wearing John Deere caps and conversing over cups of coffee and plates of pie.

Stepping back, she refocused on the reflection in the glass:

not her own, but Brandon Carlyle's, staring at her with a murderous expression.

Spinning on her heels, she looked up into his eyes and backed against the wall, her heart sinking and jumping at the same time. She clutched the Discount Drugs sack to her chest and released a sharp breath. "Don't tell me there's a law against peeking into café windows. I'm not sure I can stomach another half-hour in Dillman's company—as pleasant as it was, of course."

"We need to talk." He took a hard grip on her arm and ushered her through the café door, which jangled with what looked like big brass Christmas bells. The farmers glanced around. A waitress sitting at a table and staring up at a small black-and-white television anchored near the ceiling, shifted in her chair and turned, her face brightening.

"Hey, Mr. Carlyle. You want a menu?"

"Just coffee, Janet. Thanks." He gave Alyson a sharp shove into the booth seat, then slid into the seat, across from her. His eyes were piercing, his jaw clenched, as were his fists. He looked on the verge of exploding. But then, he always did. It was what made him so appealing to the female masses. He was a man on the edge. Dangerous.

"Who are you, and what do you want?" he demanded before she could totally collect her sensibilities.

"Nothing like getting right to the point, is there?" She attempted to smile, and failed. Clearing her throat, she extended her hand across the table and did her best to recall all the pat words and phrases she had rehearsed in preparation for this moment. "How do you do, Mr. Carlyle. I'm Alyson James. I'm greatly honored to meet you at long last. I'm a huge fan, of course. . . ."

He ignored her hand.

"I apologize for the earlier fiasco. It was stupid of me. I'm usually smarter than that."

He still ignored her hand.

"Just for revenge you could stake me out spread-eagled on the courthouse lawn and subject me to twenty-four hours of Sheriff Dillman's good humor." Curling her arm back into her lap, she sank deeper into the booth. "You're not going to make this easy for me, are you?"

"No." He shook his head, spilling strands of dark brown hair over his brow.

Janet ambled to their table with a cup of black coffee in each hand. Dishes rattled as she placed them, then dug into her pocket for a handful of individual creamers. She sized up Alyson speculatively before turning her attention on Brandon. "How's your aunt Bernice, Mr. Carlyle? Any improvement at all?"

Brandon turned his blue eyes up to Janet and smiled. The woman's face went a little slack, and color crept up her neck. "No improvement, Janet. Thanks for your concern. I'll tell her you asked about her."

"Henry dropped in earlier. On his way to Doc's office. Mentioned you had a little trouble at your place earlier. Everything okay now?" Her gaze shifted again to Alyson. The flush had crept over Janet's cheeks.

"Everything's fine," Carlyle assured her.

Nodding, Janet withdrew a check from her pocket and slid it onto the table, facedown. "If you need anything, Mr. Carlyle, just let me know." She turned away, glanced once over her shoulder before wandering across the room to see to the pair of farmers.

"It's obvious the people of this town think very highly of you—aside from the sheriff, of course." Alyson reached for a couple of creamers and did her best to focus on something other than the fact that he still looked as if he fully intended to reach across the table and choke her. Lord, why couldn't she ignore the idiotic thrills shooting from one throbbing nerve to the other? "I suppose that's not surprising, since you were born here. Still, small towns have a way of being very narrow-minded when it comes to scandal. You must have encountered some resistance when you returned here after your release from prison."

"Who do you work for?" he asked, nudging his coffee aside.

"I told you—"

"You're lying."

"I want—"

"What do you want? Or rather, how much?"

She blinked, frowned, and forced herself to focus on his sharp eyes again. "Sorry. I don't follow you."

"What's it going to cost me for you to drive out of this town and forget you saw me here?"

"Ah." She poured a stream of sugar into the beige coffee. "You think I'm into blackmail." She stirred the beverage with a spoon. "Don't get your BVDs in a twist, Carlyle. Your bank account doesn't interest me. Neither does your body, as gorgeous as it may be. I'm not Anticipating, if that has you worried. I have more interesting things to do with my life than tag along after narcissistic movie stars and besiege them with gooey love letters."

"Like climbing trees in order to take photographs of them." His gaze cut to the Discount Drug sack. He grabbed it before she could react, and dumped it out on the table, spilling the contents in a heap. His face grew dark at the sight of the yellow and black envelope. Ripping it open, he spread the photos, all filled with his image, across the table. Anger radiated from him like shock waves. His hands opened and closed. Then he began to collect them and tear them into minuscule pieces while she watched.

What could she say? Nothing, of course. He had every right to be angry. Every right to rip his images into shreds. And he did a good job of it, much to her great disappointment. Jaw locked, the muscles of his face so tense that its every angle and hollow were exaggerated, Carlyle purposefully tore each and every photo of his face down the middle, right between his exceptional blue eyes, as if he were a psychopath intent on the mutilation of some hated enemy—or a man intent on self-destruction.

When the photos lay in a pile like discarded confetti, he reached for the negatives and lighter in hand, touched the flame to the dark strips one by one, watching as they curled and melted.

Finally, he pocketed the lighter and sat back, pleased with himself. Smug.

Doing her best to relax and to keep her focus, Alyson sipped her coffee, decided it needed more sugar, and reached for the dispenser. "You know, your attempt to camouflage your identity by becoming Mick Warner from *Dark Night in Jericho* is ridiculous. There isn't anyone, aside from a few tribes of Zulus on the African plains, who hasn't seen that movie at least a dozen times. Still one of Blockbuster's most rented videos. The poster of you in black leather pants, shirtless, and wailing into a microphone is still selling fifteen years later. Sexy. So was Mick Warner."

He said nothing, just stared at her so coldly she expected her coffee to ice over.

Alyson sipped her coffee again and tried to keep her hand from shaking. Still, the cup clattered against the saucer as she set it down. "Funny. Or maybe it's not so funny. Your life has mirrored Mick Warner's. He was a rock star whose career was nearly destroyed by drugs. You're a movie star whose career began to erode because of your alcoholism. But, unlike you, Mick didn't bury himself away in B.F.E. after he hit rock bottom. He overcame the obstacles that life threw in his path. I think that's why the moviegoers loved him so. He represented everyone who ever found himself beaten down by life and circumstance. He rallied. Like Rocky Balboa. An underdog who fought his way back to win the hearts of all disbelievers."

"Only to have a fan blow out his brains in the end," Carlyle pointed out in a monotone, his expression unchanging. "Life's a bitch, and then you die."

"Another parallel. Someone who calls herself Anticipating is sending you love letters. And you're afraid that if you crawl out of this town, she's going to put a bullet in your head."

"Obviously I don't have to crawl out of this town for her to put a bullet in my head. She's here already. Somewhere." His eyes cut to the front window, as if expecting to find Anticipating peering in at him through the tinted glass.

"And you don't want to end up like Mick Warner, bleeding to death on a dark, rain-slick street, Technicolor life fading to black and white as he dies." Narrowing her eyes, Alyson added, "Or maybe you really don't care if your existence fades to black and white. Maybe your only concern is for your aunt and uncle, and how your death would affect them."

His brows drew together. "I won't talk about my family."

"What will you talk about?"

"Nothing. Not to you."

"I can help you. If you let me."

"That's a lot of bull crap. No one does anyone a favor without getting something in return."

"I never said I didn't want something in return." She reached for her purse. He tensed, and for an instant looked as if he might bolt. But something kept him from it. Perverse curiosity, perhaps.

She dug into her big, deep bag and withdrew the hardcover book with his photograph on the cover. She slid it across the table, next to his forgotten cup of coffee. An expression of surprise momentarily replaced his stony anger as he stared at it, his face at first turning bloodless, then as dark red as it had in Sheriff Dillman's company.

Brandon Carlyle
HOLLYWOOD HELLION
an
Unauthorized Biography

Alyson frowned, a sick realization spreading through her chest. "You haven't seen it? You didn't know . . . ?"

He swallowed and closed his eyes tight for a moment, shook his head.

She took a deep breath and sank back against the booth. "It's been number-one on the *New York Times* best-seller list for the last eight weeks. I can't believe no one told you. Your agent—"

"Is going to die," he said through his teeth as he reached

for the book, as cautious as if it were a pipe bomb.

"Your manager—"

"Gone. All gone. Fired them. Mildred's next." He flipped through the pages, his expression growing darker. Alyson wondered if he was reading the interview with his mother: how Cara slaved and sacrificed so that her son could become the world's most recognizable face, only to have him disown her, ignore her as if she were a nonentity.

"I'm sorry. It isn't very pretty," she told him, turning her gaze to the pair of farmers who were slowly moving toward the door.

The sympathy she felt for Carlyle annoyed her. She had always reasoned that if people in high places were stupid enough to wreck it all with bad behavior, they deserved to drown in the muck of rotten publicity. The country, indeed the entire world, had elevated Brandon Carlyle to something just short of the Pope after the release of *Jericho*. They had made him the highest-paid actor in Hollywood. In return, he had smashed their fantasies, not to mention their respect, by scandal and, ultimately, crime.

"This is neither the time nor the place to submerse yourself in a lot of b.s. that is probably untrue anyway. Besides, I want to be across town when you explode. I really don't care to pick little pieces of you out of my hair."

He didn't look up, just continued to turn the pages, his expression shifting from simmering fury to disbelief to shock. His lips thinned and pulled back from his teeth as he growled, "Bitch. Lousy, stinking bitch."

Leaning toward him, Alyson lowered her voice. "Don't get mad, get even. There's nothing wrong with standing up for yourself. If this book is all a lie, then say so."

With effort, he forced his gaze from the book and back on her. "What are you getting at?"

"My reason for coming here. To help you write your own book. An autobiography. Carlyle on Carlyle."

"What makes you think you can write a book?"

"I'm published. Freelance stuff mostly. I can provide you with copies of some of my articles." She shrugged and mentally bolstered herself for the next lie. "I need a break. Pitching ideas to *Reader's Digest* just isn't cutting it anymore. I help you. You help me. We both get something out of this."

"Why should I use you? There are a hundred other established authors who would happily take this on, and they already have a track record in the business."

"And they'll take control. Steal your thunder. My name and reputation can't get in the way of what you have to say."

His eyes narrowed. "And if I say no?"

Her eyes narrowed. "What do you think?"

"You blow my cover. That's blackmail."

She smiled. "I hadn't thought of it like that."

4

The rush of anger that had ignited in him when he first saw
the book, settled someplace deep inside him as Brandon
looked hard into Alyson James's eyes. Wide eyes. Shadowed
by dark lashes, even darker than her hair, which was a blend
of rich brown and red. The scratch on her pale cheek stood
out in contrast and had begun to scab over.

There was something much more troubling snapping at
him than anger over the unauthorized biography. He felt
compelled to listen to what Alyson James had to say. He
wanted to trust her. He didn't want to think that if he told
her to stick her proposal, she would walk out the door and
announce to the world that Brandon Carlyle had taken up
residence in a logging mill community where the harvesting
of sweet potatoes was celebrated as reverently as Christmas.
And he sure as hell didn't want to consider that she might
be Anticipating. Perhaps in that deep canvas bag of hers,
formerly tucked beneath the twisted speculation about his life

in hardcover, was a Glock 9 mm with a loaded clip—sixteen bullets with his name engraved on each.

"Of course it would mean your trusting me," she said, her long fingers bothering the spoon near her cup and saucer. "Might do you good, actually. The purging, I mean. Imagine regurgitating all the garbage you've had to swallow over the years. Be a little like getting your stomach pumped after eating a can of bad Vienna sausages. Think how much better you'll feel."

"And what do you get out of it?" he asked, already knowing the answer but wanting to hear her admit it.

"Money and acclaim, of course. I'm not so altruistic as to do it for nothing. Being associated with a book that will blow the lid off the best-seller lists will open doors for me."

"Not to mention get your pretty face on *Late Night with David Letterman*."

She raised her eyebrows and tipped her head. One corner of her mouth lifted. Not a smile, exactly. "You think I'm pretty, huh? That's quite a compliment, coming from you."

"Yeah, well, don't get carried away. I've seen a lot of pretty faces, and they were usually attached to big trouble. Let me rephrase. They were *always* attached to trouble. Trouble is the last thing I need right now."

"Do you intend to hibernate in Ticky Creek forever? Don't you entertain the thought of at least attempting a resurrection of your career?" She shook her head, and her fine, arched brows drew together. "You're a brilliant talent, Carlyle. I can't see you wasting your life growing hay and watching afternoon reruns of *Ma and Pa Kettle Do Hawaii*."

"You're hardly in a position to speculate on my emotional fulfillment. You don't know me."

Her gaze shifted to the book under his hands, and her expression became hard. "I know what I've read. That you're a self-centered egomaniac who drinks too much, emotionally abuses his mother, and spends his nights cavorting with S&M porn queens. You get off on whips and bondage, and occasionally experiment in bestiality. All evidence points to your raping and murdering Emerald Marcella, and the only reason you got off with manslaughter was that the District Attorney owed your mother a favor—Cara to the rescue once again, despite having been used and so heartlessly tossed aside when you no longer needed her influence to get you movie roles."

He almost laughed at the ridiculous accusations, but her expression and the steely intensity in her hazel eyes told him that she was dead serious. Cold nausea rolled inside him. Fear clamped around his throat—as suffocating as it had been the morning he woke up in a hospital emergency room to learn that Emerald Marcella was dead. First there had been the despair over Emerald's death—which had quickly become terror over how the news would affect his already tarnished reputation.

His image on the book jacket glared up at him, his own eyes, angry and razor sharp, mocking him. "That's sick. That's just . . . sick." He gave a short laugh and rubbed one hand over his forehead, which had begun to sweat. He wanted like hell to howl at the absurdity of it all, but his throat remained closed so tightly he could hardly breathe.

"Jesus, I thought the nightmare of rumor and speculation after Emerald's death left me impervious to shock and humiliation. I buried myself in obscurity to avoid confronting the nastiness of people who get their jollies eviscerating celebrities. Now here it is again. Lies. Sick, perverted lies spewed by so-called acquaintances who're simply using a book to grab their fifteen minutes of fame."

The woman across from him frowned and leaned toward him. Her eyes were no longer accusatory, but showed concern. She reached across the table and laid her hand on his, the contact like a warm shock to his raw senses. The touch traveled up his arm and slammed into his chest.

"Carlyle, are you all right? You look like—"

"Can't breathe." He waved her away, jerked from her touch, and slid out of the booth, swaying to his feet and focusing on the distant door emblazoned "Gents." He wondered if he'd make it that far before he vomited on the Dime A Cup's floor.

Out of the corner of his eye, he saw Janet hovering near the cash register, a pencil tucked behind one ear, her fists planted on her ample hips as she watched him cross the room.

"You okay, Mr. Carlyle?"

He ignored her, slammed his hands against the bathroom door, and shoved it open, enclosing himself in the six-by-six space with yellow walls of unfinished pine and air that smelled of sickeningly sweet strawberry-scented Glade.

Sinking back against the door and closing his eyes, Brandon did his best to force down the disgust and panic rising in his throat, not to mention the anger—the explosive fury that came from total helplessness.

How the hell was he supposed to defend himself? How could he shout to the world that he didn't murder Emerald Marcella when he couldn't remember anything beyond his car sliding out of control on a dark, rain-slick highway?

How the hell had he gotten out of his car before it plowed through a guardrail and rolled a hundred feet to the bottom of a cliff?

And as far as all the other accusations: Bestiality? Whips and bondage? What kind of sick minds sat around and thought up that kind of perversion?

Moving to the sink, he turned on the water, cupped his hands beneath it, and splashed his face until the shock of the cold water evened out his breathing. Alyson James was right. The reflection staring back at him from the mirror belonged to Mick Warner, hero of *Dark Night in Jericho*: bone-weary, disillusioned, stressed-out drug addict with long, unkempt hair, unshaven jaw, and eyes red and swollen from lack of sleep and substance abuse.

During one of Mick's more memorable scenes, he had excused his bad behavior by replying to the question "What kind of satisfaction do you get from killing yourself with drugs?" with "When life gets too difficult, we have to have someplace to go."

For Mick, that had been shooting up heroin. For Brandon Carlyle, his place of escape had been booze. After the booze had come Ticky Creek. As long as he didn't know about the ugly stuff that was being said about him, he could pretend it didn't exist.

But reality had just clubbed him between the eyes again, first in the form of a maniac who called herself Anticipating, then of a beautiful stranger with a Nikon camera and a telephoto lens who could be Anticipating, as far as he knew. Instead of using an Uzi to do him in, she would simply point her camera at him and fire. Her arrival in Ticky Creek was a harsh and sobering reminder that Brandon Carlyle, movie star and big-time fuckup, could run but couldn't hide forever from his past. And with her came the brutal monster of innuendo and false accusations in the form of an unauthorized biography that portrayed him as some kind of sicko.

He splashed his face again, and watched as the water ran in beads down his cheeks. Frown lines etched his forehead. Grooves bracketed his mouth. Mildred was right. His prime had come and gone. Soon he would be relegated to second-billing character roles—if he was lucky. With the publication of that book, he'd be lucky to get anything outside of porn work.

Thinking of Alyson James, he grew angry again. Despite the fact she had sexy eyes and a mouth that would tempt a monk, she was just like the smut rakers in that book: a vulture eager to pick his bones of the last shred of meat in order to make a buck. He'd tell her to get lost. But how the hell was he going to do that without risking her blowing his cover? Money, of course. Although she claimed she wasn't interested in his bank account, she'd change her mind fast enough if he offered her a few hundred grand. Get her and her satin thong panties the hell out of Dodge before her plump lips and bedroom eyes encouraged another awakening in his jeans.

Brandon turned off the water and dried his face and hands on a brown paper towel. He took a deep breath and slowly released it, counted backward from ten, forced the tension squeezing his temples to relax. Everything was going to be fine. He'd pull out all the stops if he had to, in order to get Alyson James out of his life. He hadn't met a woman yet who couldn't be bought and manipulated by money and charm. Then he'd decide how to deal with the book.

At the door of the "Gents," he hesitated. Alyson still sat in the booth, staring down into her coffee cup. Janet was pointing a remote control at the TV and flipping through channels while someone in the kitchen began humming the theme from *Jeopardy!* A customer had entered the restaurant during his sojourn in the toilet and sat with her back to him, her arms clasping a big straw purse to her breast as she studied a menu.

As he crossed the room, Alyson looked toward him, her expression concerned.

Alex Trebek's face filled the TV screen as Janet shouted for Carolyn to hurry or she was going to miss her show.

The customer rose from her chair and turned toward him in one fluid motion. The menu flew one direction as her purse hit the floor with an odd, heavy clatter. Her hands like claws, she flew at him, lips pulled back from her teeth.

"Bastard!"

The woman hit him with the force of a Dallas Cowboy tackle. He flew back, sprawled across a table, crashing salt and pepper shakers and a sugar dispenser to the floor. She crawled on top of him, dishwater blond hair streaming wildly around her head, her fists swinging at his face as he attempted to deflect the blows.

"You can't do that to me!" she screamed. "I'll show you you can't use me and get away with it. Stinking liar!"

Janet hooked one big arm around the woman's waist, hoisted her into the air, and flung her away. She landed on the floor on her backside, knees splayed, skirt hiked to the tops of her thighs, revealing a flash of yellow nylon panties.

Carolyn ran out the front door, yelling at Sheriff Dillman, who was harassing the carnies lined up along the curb.

Alyson positioned herself between Brandon and his attacker, her arms stretched out before her and her palms up;

she looked a little like a harassed traffic control officer. She glanced over her shoulder at Brandon as he rolled off the table and onto his feet, one hand clutching his chest where the lunatic had hit him with the force of a battering ram. He bent over, hands on his thighs, as he tried to get his breathing back to normal.

"Are you okay?" she asked, her eyes wide with concern.

He nodded, unable to get enough air in his lungs to respond.

The woman slowly raised her face to glare at him through her hair. Then recognition struck him.

Narrowing his eyes, he asked, "Mitsy?"

Showing her teeth, she raised one hand and shot him the finger.

Janet grabbed Mitsy by one arm and hauled her to her feet just as Dillman and Carolyn entered. Carolyn jabbed her finger toward Mitsy, declaring, "She assaulted him, Sheriff."

Mitsy scrambled across the room and snatched her purse off the floor as Dillman, his gaze still locked on Brandon, slid a toothpick into his mouth, then thumbed his sister toward the door.

"Get lost," he told her. "I'll deal with you later."

She hustled out of the café, brass bells clattering her exit.

"She's crazy," Brandon said to Dillman as he finally got his breath back.

"I wouldn't go so far as to call her crazy, exactly." Jack gave a short laugh and tongued the toothpick to the other side of his mouth. "She sure don't think a lot of you, does she? Then again, who does?"

"Maybe I'll press charges against her."

"You don't want to do that, Carlyle, I promise you. You think you're in hot water with me now, you just make more trouble for my little sister, and I'll haul your ass back to Corcoran myself."

Brandon moved toward Dillman. Alyson stepped between them and locked one forearm across Brandon's chest, her legs braced in her attempt to push him back. He looked around her and pointed one finger in Dillman's face.

"You keep her away from me and away from my family. If she so much as sneezes in a threatening manner, I'll go over your head and see she's put away for the rest of her life."

Dillman's yellow-brown eyes narrowed as he removed the toothpick from his mouth. Dark color crawled up his cheeks. "Punk. It's just a matter of time 'fore your ass is mine. You're just this close." He held up two thick fingers pressed together. "You so much as jaywalk, and you'll be back writin' letters to your uncle on prison stationery. Now if I was you, I'd crawl back to that cozy little farm and stay out of my sight." He glanced toward Janet and Carolyn, touched the brim of his hat with one finger. "You ought to be more discriminatin' about who you serve, ladies. Have a good afternoon."

Janet waited until Dillman exited the café before she released her breath in a huff. "Can you believe that guy?"

Brandon shifted his attention to Alyson, her arm still locked across his chest, her serious eyes fixed on his. Forcing an unsteady smile, she said, "Carlyle, he's bigger than you. In fact, he's bigger than two of you. If I'd let the two of you go at it, there wouldn't have been anything left of you except a greasy spot on the floor."

"I might surprise you," he said through his teeth.

"First you'll have to convince me that all the chop socky shenanigans you performed in your last movie weren't done by a stunt double." She backed away and rubbed her hands up and down the butt of her tight jeans. "You'll thank me later when you've had time to reminisce on your Shangri-la days in Corcoran."

"Mitsy Dillman should've been locked up years ago," Janet declared as she picked up a chair and shoved it against the table, which was leaning precariously to one side. "That woman is crazy as a betsy bug."

Carolyn shook her head and stooped to collect the salt and pepper shakers from the floor. "I was sorry to see her come back to Ticky Creek. She'll have everybody's husband howling at the moon, including mine."

Brandon forced himself to look away from Alyson, to Carolyn, who was sweeping spilled salt off the table with her hand. "Where's she been?"

Carolyn shrugged. "Who knows? She floats in and out of Ticky Creek whenever the whim hits her."

"Heard she lived in New Mexico awhile." Janet straightened the red-and-white-checked tablecloth, then bent to retrieve the TV remote she had dropped in order to help Brandon. "Then she strayed out to California. Said she wanted to become a movie star. I thought to myself, *And pigs might fly.* Marla Shaffer got a postcard from her once that said she'd landed the starring role in a Cecil B. DeMille movie. We all had a good laugh—Cecil B.'s been dead over thirty years."

Carolyn and Janet giggled.

Brandon didn't. Even if Mitsy hadn't just knocked him off his feet, the news that she had found her way out to California was enough to bother him.

"Obviously you and Mitsy share a history," said Alyson near his ear. As he looked into her amused, inquisitive eyes, she whispered, "Let me guess. The two of you were an item once. Young love. She thought when you whispered 'I love you,' you really meant it."

"Close, Miz James, but no cigar. I've never in my life told a woman that I love her."

"Never?" She grinned skeptically.

"Never." He looked at her mouth. "You have an attitude toward actors. Why is that?"

Her eyes narrowed and her voice took on an edge. "I haven't met one yet who didn't believe he was God's gift to women."

He dug a cigarette from his pocket and studied her eyes, which were shadowed with emotion. "You dated an actor, right? Or married one."

A thin smile curved her mouth.

Taking a deep drag on his cigarette, Brandon shrugged. "Yeah, well, it's those women who make us into gods, isn't

it? Then they take pleasure in crucifying us just as soon as
we show the slightest hint of being human."

"So what about the book? Do we have a deal?"

"No. I don't think so." He walked to their table and tossed
several dollar bills next to the check. Alyson moved up beside him, leaned one hip against the table, and stared up at
his profile.

"You'd risk my breaking the story of your whereabouts?"

"I'll give you a hundred thousand to keep your mouth
shut."

"No."

He turned toward her, expecting her to back off. She
didn't, just lifted her chin and met his eyes with a look of
total willfulness. "One million, Miz James, to go away and
forget you ever saw me."

That one rocked her. Disbelief widened her eyes; her lips
parted. Sinking against the table, she blinked and blew out a
quick breath. "Jeez, I wasn't expecting that. One million,
huh? That would sure tide me over for a while."

She laughed and crossed her arms over her waist. "I never
thought blackmail could turn out to be so lucrative. After all,
I'm just a lil' ol' writer of no consequence. That kind of loot
would allow me to spend the rest of my life writing articles
with a five-minute life span. Just imagine how fulfilled I'll
feel when I'm seventy, rocking away my golden years and
reminiscing on that unforgettable article that won me a Pu-
litzer: 'I Am Joe's Kidney Stone.' "

"Writing about my life is hardly going to win you a Pu-
litzer, Miz James."

"No, but it's a better start in that direction than writing
about the life journey of a kidney stone down a urinary tract."

Despite the ache in his chest where Mitsy had slammed
him, not to mention the nervousness caused by the incident
and the possibility that Mitsy might well be his stalker and
she was obviously just short of insane, he felt a smile tug at
his lips. At another time he might have considered a relationship with Alyson James. She was certainly desirable. And
given other circumstances, he would've found her tenacity

and sauciness humorous. But not now. She fully intended to turn his life upside down. Not just his, but his family's. And not just his family's, but the entire town of Ticky Creek.

She picked up the book and shoved it against his chest. "Once you've read what your closest acquaintances have to say about you, give my offer a bit more consideration. I'm staying at the Pine Tree Lodge. Room ten." She smiled. "You'll call."

"No." He shook his head even as his hands closed around the book. "I won't."

"You will." She thumped the book. "You will."

For thirty-eight dollars and fifty cents a night, the room at Pine Tree Lodge on Highway 59 just outside the Ticky Creek city limits wasn't so bad. Certainly Alyson had stayed in worse—lived in worse, if one wanted to bow to reality. Aside from the hint of stale cigarette smoke permeating the avocado green carpet and drapes, she could almost feel snug. The air conditioner worked, even if it did sound a little like a bulldozer in fourth gear. The room had a fairly comfortable queen-size bed, a kitchenette with a small fridge, a coffeepot with a half-dozen plastic-wrapped Styrofoam cups, and a microwave oven. There was television with HBO and pay-per-view raunchy movies, which she intended to check out later.

Propped against her plumped bed pillows, Alyson thumbed through her copy of the *Galaxy Gazette*, and with cell phone pressed to one ear, listened as an answering machine clicked on:

"This is Dr. Alan Rodgers. Leave a message and I'll call you back."

"Alan, pick up if you're there." She turned the page and frowned at a picture of Goldie Hawn picking her nose. "Alan, it's me. I have to talk to you. It's urgent."

There came a click as Alan Rodgers shut off the machine and picked up the receiver. "A. J., your timing sucks. I just saw the man of my dreams in-line skating down the sidewalk. This better be good."

She grinned. "I take it you and Chip haven't kissed and made up yet."

"He can kiss my butt. That's the only thing of mine he's going to kiss from now on." He laughed. "So tell me all about it. I assume you made contact today, or you wouldn't be sounding so stressed."

"I don't sound stressed."

"Babe, you're tight as a piano wire. I'm a shrink. And I know wired when I hear it. Besides, I'm your best friend, remember?"

"Alan, he's not at all what I expected."

"Okay." There came a squeak and a click as Alan changed over to the speakerphone. Alyson pictured her best friend getting comfortable in his chair, feet propped up on his disorganized desk, no doubt expecting another marathon conversation where Alyson droned on about how another one of her life fantasies just got crushed like a bug.

"Shoot," he told her.

"First of all, let me say that this town is *weird*. They have one of the world's most famous men living here among them, and it's as if he were simply another Joe Blow bubba. It's like they've all joined forces to protect him, with the exception of the sheriff and his crazy sister. He's lived here for *months*, and not a soul—aside from my cousin Sally, who was just passing through—has breathed a word of his being here to the outside world." She sighed. "God, Alan. I thought he was going to cry. Can you imagine how I felt when I realized he was totally unaware of the biography? The man looked as if I just castrated him with a dull knife."

"I take it you didn't exactly hit it off."

"He thinks I'm a stalker who calls herself Anticipating."

Silence. Then in a voice shaded with caution: "Explain, please?"

"Some woman is writing him letters."

"I thought you said no one knows where he is."

"*She* obviously does. She somehow found him out and followed him from California. I saw the letter. Something about *I've been watching you. When the time is right, we'll be together. I didn't follow you from California to let you slip through my fingers."*

"Not good. Definitely not good. Is he nervous?"

"Yes, especially after he walked out of the men's rest room and was flattened by an old girlfriend whose elevator stops shy of the top floor. According to the waitresses, the woman spent some time in California. Carlyle thinks she might be Anticipating. Then again, he thought *I* was Anticipating."

"If this cat followed him from California, then she's obviously tiptoeing on the high wire of erotomanic delusional disorder, and if that's the case, he could be in for a time of it. These patients, even when faced with substantial evidence to the contrary, remain convinced that their fixated object passionately loves them in return. It's quite common with celebrities. Has he discussed this with the police?"

Thinking of Dillman, Alyson grinned and shook her head. "They go way back. The sheriff here would arrest Carlyle for sneezing if he could. He's made it pretty clear he isn't the least interested in Anticipating . . . which would make sense if his loony sister is involved."

"Most of the time these people don't get violent. They're just a pain in the butt, but there have been occasions when they go over the top. If she's getting nasty, then he's got a big problem on his hands."

"Just what he needs . . . more trouble. The man buried himself in Ticky Creek in the hopes of healing and forgetting, and what happens? Some nut named Anticipating followed him here, and now I show up. I feel like a worm."

"You're not a worm, but what you're doing isn't nice either. Why don't you just tell him the truth?"

"That I'm a tabloid writer—*the* tabloid writer who eight years ago first broke the story of his alcoholism—and gee whiz, I'm sorry about that, but I need another big story that will make some respected magazine sit up and take notice so I can tell the *Galaxy Gazette* adios—and you're it? I think he'll go for it, don't you? I just wish he wasn't so vulnerable. And sad. And scared. I can deal with arrogant. And angry. And even mean. But I can't deal with looking into his incredible eyes and seeing pain. He was so hurt by what he read in that book."

"Stop looking into his 'incredible' eyes and remind yourself that Brandon Carlyle was a bad, bad boy with an obvious need to self-destruct. God, what I'd give for the opportunity to have a peek inside his head. It's so obvious he hates his mother, but the mother-child bond he feels as her son won't allow him to strike out at her the way he'd obviously like to. Instead, he turns it in on himself. She screwed him up big time."

"Thanks a lot. That really helps to ease my guilt."

"You're welcome. What are you going to do tonight in bright lights, big city Ticky Creek, Texas?"

"Cruise the Wal-Mart and dine at the Dairy Queen."

"Charming. Hurry home. I miss you."

5

*Brandon gently lifted his aunt's frail body out of the wheel-*chair, taking care not to displace the nasal cannula, two short prongs inserted in her nostrils to feed her oxygen continually. It was attached by a long plastic tube to a portable oxygen tank beside her bed. He placed her in the hospital bed situated near a window overlooking the cluster of red rose-bushes she had nurtured for thirty of the forty years she had been married to Henry Carlyle. Her blue eyes stared up at him, bright but distant, as if she were focused on something or someone in another dimension.

Bernice had been a vibrant, beautiful woman until she had suffered a brain stem stroke, known as "locked-in syn-drome." When word of Bernie's stroke reached Brandon in prison, he'd lost it. He'd blamed himself—her heartbreak over his trouble had brought on her illness.

Brandon could still recall the only time Henry and Bernie had visited him in prison. Through a glass barrier he had watched his aunt and uncle weep, though they had tried hard to be strong for his benefit. Speaking to Bernie through a phone, his hand pressed to the glass barrier, he'd pleaded, "I'm so damn sorry. *Please* don't stop loving me."

She hadn't, of course. Until her stroke, not a day passed that he didn't receive a letter—always cheery, the day-to-day ritual of her and Henry's life together in Ticky Creek, and how they looked forward to his coming home upon his release. They strongly believed, as they always had, that life in Ticky Creek would offer him a spiritual rebirth; they were fully convinced that Satan and psychosis never could, and never would, stick so much as a toe over the town's city limits. Brandon's thought on that was *They wouldn't dare. Not with Jack Dillman as sheriff.*

He tucked the quilt around her and brushed a strand of gray hair from her forehead. There had been much speculation among Henry, himself, and the doctors over whether she could comprehend anything of the world around her. The doctors said she would remain a vegetable, incapable of understanding or communicating. He and Henry refused to believe it. Perhaps it was just mule-headed stubbornness and the inability to let her go, but as long as she drew a breath on her own, they chose to hold on to the faith that somewhere inside her head she understood them.

Brandon bent and lightly kissed her cheek, smiled into her eyes. "I've got a date tonight. Charlotte Minger from Wal-Mart. She's young. In fact, if Betty's right, I'm probably old enough to be her father. That's pretty depressing to think about . . . that I'm getting to be such an old fart. I know I should be focusing on someone closer to my own age. Yes, yes, I want to settle down and get married. Absolutely, I want kids while I'm still young enough to play ball with them. But we have to ask ourselves just what sort of role model I'm going to make. I'm really *trying* to be good, Bernie. Ask Henry and Betty. I haven't had a drink in years, and I haven't hit anyone recently. Close calls don't count, right? Because I have to admit, I came close today. A woman photographer fell out of a tree on top of me. Thought she was a guy at first."

He gazed out the window at the deep red roses, and thought of the satin thong panties in his pocket. He'd forgotten them until now. "Definitely not a guy," he repeated, vaguely aware that his voice sounded a bit rough and the air felt a touch warmer on his skin. "She wants to help me write a book. An autobiography." Looking down at his aunt again, he shook his head. "I'm not sure I'm ready for that." *At least not as long as you and Henry are still alive,* he thought, as he closed his fingers around Bernice's frail hand. Because the reality of it was just too horrifying for a couple of old people who had spent their entire lives cocooned in the innocence of Ticky Creek, Texas.

Once upon a time, Bernie would have drawn him near and held him tightly. He'd close his eyes and allow his starving senses to swim in her closeness. She'd always smelled of bleach and lemon furniture oil with the faintest underlying scent of Estée Lauder's Youth Dew cologne. Her hands had been strong but achingly gentle. With words that were whisper soft and trembling with compassion, she would have encouraged him to talk about the fears buzzing around inside of his head.

Eventually, she would have drawn the truth out of him: how he was afraid that Mildred Feldman was right; he was getting old, and maybe the success he had known as an actor had everything to do with his looks and nothing to do with actual talent. Or maybe he would confess that the paranoia he felt over some nut named Anticipating was beginning to make him feel shakier than he wanted to admit even to himself. Hell, he might even admit that the idea of going out on a date for the first time in four years made him feel sick with nervousness. He hadn't been alone in a room with a woman since Emerald Marcella stuffed white powder up her nose and became such a sex-crazed maniac he'd felt like an unwilling gang bang victim. He could almost hear Bernice, her unplucked eyebrows lifted, eyes twinkling with amusement, sternness, and understanding:

You're a good boy, Brandon, and intelligent. Think with

*the head on your shoulders, and not with the one in your
pants, and you'll do just fine.*

Smiling down into her staring eyes, Brandon whispered,
"Ah, Bernie, you always had a way with words."

Henry entered the room, mopping his washed face with a
paper towel. "Betty says to tell you that if you want to have
dinner here, there's plenty of food. It's about ready. I think
she's still in a fluster about you going out with Miss Yamboree." He walked to the bed and smiled down at his wife.
"How's my girl? Her color looks good today, don't you
think, Brandon?"

Brandon turned away. He would never grow accustomed
to witnessing the pain on Henry's face every time he looked
at his wife. It filled Brandon with fresh anger. Such tragedy
should be heaped on sinners like himself—hell, he deserved
the very worst of God's wrath—but Henry and Bernice were,
or had been, the most spiritual, kindhearted human beings on
the face of the earth.

Betty stood over the stove, prodding cutlets of breaded
steak around in a skillet. Her eyes brightened as Brandon
entered the kitchen. He moved beside her and slung one arm
around her shoulders, lifted the lid on a saucepan of peas,
and inhaled deeply.

"If Charlotte hadn't looked so damn good in that short
skirt, I'd be real tempted to stay home tonight. Of course,
we could always invite her to dinner here. You could sit
between us and make certain she doesn't get fresh." He
grinned, and hugged Betty more tightly.

"Go on and make fun, Mr. Brandon. But that girl is trouble. No decent young woman would go out with a man your
age."

"What is this? Let's All Gang Up on Brandon and Convince Him He's Old as Methuselah Day? Jeez, thanks to you,
Mildred, and Alyson James, I'm ready to check myself into
the Shady Pines Retirement Home."

She stopped poking and turned her eyes up to his. "You
pressed charges, right?"

"No."

"Why not?" she asked.

He shrugged. He'd asked himself the same question at least a dozen times. "Maybe I liked the way she looked in her jeans or something. Don't worry. I offered her a million bucks to take a hike. I suspect once she's slept on the offer, she'll grab it."

Betty blinked and stared at him. "A million . . . ?"

"What else am I gonna do with my money?"

"There are charities—"

"The last year I've financially supported the American Heart Association, cancer and AIDS research, and fed half of starving Mongolia, not to mention too many politicians to name . . . and I can't even vote anymore. Sometimes it's *okay* to do something extravagant with money."

"Fine," she said. "Then I could use a new car."

He grinned and winked, and turned for the door. "You got it. What's it going to be, a Rolls-Royce or an Aston Martin?"

"You're being very congenial tonight," she called after him. "And I'd settle for a Ford Taurus with leather seats and a CD stereo with Bose speakers."

"You're too cheap, Betty. When a gift horse presents itself, you gotta go for the gusto. A Ford Taurus just ain't gonna cut it."

"Fine," she shouted. "I'll take a fire engine red Dodge Viper. Make it a convertible while you're at it."

"Ooh, hot mama! Next you'll be slipping into black leather and changing your name to Bambi. I'm not sure I want to contribute to the delinquency of a babe. Maybe we should stick with a Taurus."

He heard her giggle, and he imagined her complexion turning red as apples.

Congenial wasn't exactly how he was feeling. More like wound up. Uptight. On the edge. It had been a long, eventful day, not to mention upsetting. His chest where Mitsy had battered him hurt like hell.

He checked his watch. Charlotte was due to pick him up in half an hour. He still needed to shower and shave. If he wasn't so pressed for time and Betty wasn't busy with cook-

ing, he'd ask her to give him a massage. She had the best
hands he'd ever lain down for, as good as or even better than
the masseur he'd employed in California.

Reaching his bedroom, Brandon tugged the T-shirt off
over his head and threw it on the bed, then removed his shoes
and socks, unsnapped his jeans and began to unzip when he
looked around. Betty stood in the doorway, a collection of
plastic-covered starched shirts on hangers in her hand.

"I picked up your laundry at the cleaners." She extended
the shirts toward him and smiled. "Thought you might need
a clean shirt for tonight."

He crossed the room and took them from her. "Thanks."
He turned toward the closet.

"You sound tired, Mr. Brandon."

"I am, a little. It's been a long day."

"Perhaps you should stay home tonight. I'm sure Miss
Minger would understand."

Shaking his head, he pulled out the top drawer of his
dresser and searched through his socks and briefs, all folded
neatly and placed precisely, thanks to Betty's meticulousness.

Betty stepped hesitantly over the threshold, her hands
gripped together under her breasts. "You seem stressed. Would
you like a treatment? A short one, just enough to relax you?"

Brandon checked his watch again, and grinned. "You must
have read my mind."

Her face brightened, and she motioned toward the bed.
"Where is the oil?"

"Top shelf in the bathroom closet."

As Betty disappeared into the bathroom, Brandon peeled
out of his jeans, at the last minute remembered the panties
and condom in his pocket, and dug them out. He frowned a
little as the thought occurred to him that stealing a woman's
panties was maybe a little too kinky even for him. He
couldn't imagine why he'd done it, except for spite. As Betty
reentered the room, he tossed the condom on the bedside
table and curled his hand around the minuscule panties, hid
ing them within his fist.

Dressed only in his Y fronts, Brandon stretched out, facedown across his bed. Betty kicked off her shoes and mounted him, straddling his hips. Her weight rested on her knees as she poured a thin stream of oil over his back. Normally she would have heated it slightly. The coolness of it made him catch his breath.

Her broad hands slid over his skin, pressing. Like a slow heat wave, the beautiful torment rippled through him. His fingers curled more firmly around the satin panties, and as he squeezed his eyes closed more tightly, the image of Alyson James wearing those panties and nothing else suddenly winged at him, her body stretched out over a bed with black sheets, her skin very white in contrast, her long, pale legs spread wide as her mouth smiled and taunted him. He imagined himself burying his face in the red satin and drinking in the scent of her.

Charlotte Minger drove a 1991 Pontiac Firebird with a crunched right rear fender. The front bucket seats were covered with fuzzy leopard-print fake fur that made Brandon sweat—there was no air-conditioning and the temperature outside hovered close to ninety degrees. There were sticks of Big Red chewing gum scattered over the dashboard, along with several tubes of lipstick, and a five-inch cardboard tree swung from the rearview mirror, turning the car's interior into a cedar forest. 'N Sync blasted from the tape player, adding to the oppression that pressed against his temples.

It hadn't taken Brandon long to surmise that Charlotte Minger's idea of a Beltbuster for dinner had nothing to do with a hamburger from the Dairy Queen. Her skirt barely covered her crotch. Braless, she wore a skintight tank top that left little to the imagination. She had bathed in Red Door perfume, curled her silver hair into sexy ringlets around her face, and accentuated her full mouth by lining it with black, then applying dark brown lipstick. Henry's face had turned white at the sight of her. Fortunately, Betty had left by the time of Charlotte's arrival. Otherwise, Brandon suspected, she would have locked him in his room and thrown away the key. Perhaps that wouldn't have been such a bad idea. He was trying very hard to focus on anything other than the skirt inching up Charlotte's thighs with every bounce of the car. Not so very many years ago he would have suggested they pull over to the side of the road, then hauled her onto his lap and got on with the business of cooling their lust. But that was then and this was now. He was infinitely wiser . . . not to mention older . . . and feeling older by the minute.

He smoked and tried to think of a topic of conversation to which they could both relate.

"Oh, my God!" she suddenly announced, her voice raised to be heard over the wind rushing into the car through the open windows and the boom-boom of 'N Sync blasting from the speakers. "I can't believe I'm on a date with Brandon Carlyle!"

He glanced at her legs again and shrugged. "Get over it, Charlotte. It's no big deal."

"Right. Sure. You're only the sexiest man alive."

"Don't believe everything you read. And besides, that was a long time ago."

"Whatever. God, you're better than Brad Pitt ever thought about being. Then again, I don't like blond guys much, and he started wearing that goofy beard thing that makes him look like a goat. And Ben Affleck is pretty awesome. Do you know him?"

"No."

"What about Matt Damon?"

"No."

"Course, they're lots younger than you, huh?"

He cut his eyes to hers and blew out a stream of smoke. "Right."

"I don't care much for DiCaprio either. I read once that you were considered for his part in *Titanic*, but the producers decided they wanted someone younger."

"Could we please talk about something besides my age?"

"I suppose if you're like twelve or something, you'd find DiCaprio sexy, but when I fantasize about a man, it's gonna be someone like you. Tall, dark, and dangerous. A real bad boy. Know what I mean?"

He nodded and reached for the cigarette pack in his shirt pocket, dug out a cigarette, and used the stub in his mouth to light the fresh one. No doubt about it, he was a card-carrying bad boy.

"I used to be in love with Johnny Whitehorse. God, that Indian was so sexy. I have his poster right next to yours on my bedroom wall. You know the one where he's standing on a street in New York with his jeans unzipped?" She fanned her face with one hand and squirmed in her seat. "Then he had to go and get married. And if that wasn't enough, he quit acting and went into politics. Do you know Johnny Whitehorse?"

Brandon grinned and nodded. At one time Johnny had been a fierce competitor in the business. But his being a Mescalero Apache had limited his opportunities. Johnny had been bright enough to branch into business, and from there to politics. He was now Senator Whitehorse, married, with three kids—all boys—and there was buzz of his running for president before the end of the decade. During Brandon's trials and tribulations over the Marcella fiasco, Johnny had been the only one of his peers to call and offer not only his support but his law expertise.

"I really loved *Dark Night in Jericho*. I heard you did all your own singing. Is that true?"

"I feel like I'm being interviewed by *Rolling Stone*. Could we talk about something other than me?"

She shrugged and reached for a stick of Big Red. "The girls at Wal-Mart didn't believe me when I told them you asked me out."

"You asked *me* out, Charlotte."

"Oh. Yeah, I guess I did. Oh, well, it doesn't matter. We're together, huh?" She gave him a tight smile and unwrapped a second piece of gum. "I have a surprise for you," she said as she chewed.

Brandon didn't much care for the sound of that. The last time someone declared "I have a surprise for you," Emerald Marcella had whipped out a pair of handcuffs and a torture device.

He flipped his ashes out the window and, with a sigh of relief, fixed his gaze on the Dairy Queen in the distance. Dusk was just settling, and the lights on the big red DQ sign were just sputtering to life. A dozen or more cars had already congregated in the parking lot. He wondered if maybe they shouldn't get their food to go. The idea of strolling into the burger joint arm in arm with Miss Yamboree made him a little nervous.

Charlotte hit the directional signal and turned left on Highway 59, away from the Dairy Queen.

A flush of color crept from beneath her tank top as he turned to look at her. "What are you doing, Charlotte?"

"I told you; I have a surprise for you."

He looked down into the sideview mirror and watched the DQ sign disappear as they rounded a bend in the highway. "Where are you taking me?"

"It's—"

"I know: a surprise."

She nodded, again with the tight smile that looked disconcertingly like guilt. By now the hot color had crawled up her neck and was bleeding onto her cheeks. "I figured you'd be more comfortable someplace more private. So I packed us a picnic dinner." She thumbed toward the backseat. Turning, he noted the foam cooler and paper sack from Piggly Wiggly. "I hope you like fried chicken," she said.

Sinking back into the seat, Brandon watched the countryside slide by as daylight waned. The relief at not having to make an appearance at the DQ was surpassed only by his hesitancy over Charlotte's surprise. If he was smart, he'd demand that she take him home immediately; that was the rational part of his brain thinking. Unfortunately, it was another part of his anatomy that had an armlock on his reasoning at the moment.

He glanced again at Charlotte's legs, noted that she wasn't wearing hose. He'd never cared for the overt, choosing instead to direct his attention to the more wholesome sort—discounting Marcella, of course, but that had been nothing more than a romp brought about by curiosity and too much booze. He'd never cared much for casual sex, perhaps because of his own disgust with his mother's promiscuity. Not that he hadn't had his stupid moments. Seeing Mitsy Dillman today drove that point home with a vengeance. As Henry had pointed out throughout Brandon's coming of age, you better be damn certain when you climb into bed with a woman that you like her looks enough to want to gaze into her face for a long, long time, because if you knock her up, you're going to be spending the rest of your life paying for it one way or the other.

That had happened twice. First with Mitsy. At seventeen he had not had a lot of say in the decision that was quickly made by his mother, who financed Mitsy's abortion.

The second time with an up-and-coming actress he had dated just short of a year. He had already won his Oscar. She wanted still to win one. He offered marriage.

Do you love me, Brandon?

I care for you, baby. I care a lot.

Brandon, people care for pets. They care for a comfortable pair of shoes. They care for an old sweater knitted by some elderly aunt in a rocking chair. Do you love me?

I don't know.

Perhaps he was simply expecting too much from love. He wanted to feel gut-punched. Knocked out. Obsessed. He wanted to be so swept away with intense love and desire that he'd throw himself in front of a train to protect his beloved . . . after he had sent her into orbit with the best orgasm she had experienced in her life.

Beautiful and career driven, his girlfriend got an abortion and told him about it afterward. He never spoke to her again.

It occurred to him in that moment that if Mitsy had had their baby, the kid would be seventeen . . . not much younger than Charlotte, trusting that Charlotte had been honest about her age. Studying her in the dim dashboard lights, he began to suspect that she just might have lied.

Thick pine forests crowded the two-lane highway. Charlotte turned the car up a gravel road that Brandon recognized. It led to the quarry, Ticky Creek's infamous make-out spot. Once excavated for sandstone, the place had been closed

once the government had declared the surrounding countryside a national forest. For years people used it as a landfill.
Then Smokey Bear had decided to divert murky Ticky Creek
through the old quarry, believing the large, creepy lake
would attract locals and tourists to fish and swim and picnic.

Charlotte stopped the car thirty feet from the water, shifted
into Park, and killed the engine. She left the ignition on so
the headlights and stereo remained working. She smiled at
Brandon, then reached over into the back and dug into the
cooler, extracting two icy beers, one of which she pushed
into Brandon's hand.

Sinking back against her door, one leg partially propped
on the console between the seats, she tipped the sweating
beer bottle up to her lips and drank deeply. He watched her,
his mouth dry and his fingers gripping the bottleneck. The
scent of the beer made him dizzy.

One beer isn't going to kill you. It's not as if it's Chivas.

"You bring any Cokes?" he asked, aware of the tightness
of his voice.

"Nope. Don't you like beer?"

Just a couple of sips. To cool you down.

He lifted the bottle and pressed its cool, wet surface to his
forehead, tried to focus on the pool of illuminated water up
ahead and not on the fact that his hands were trembling. In
the car's headlights the water looked green and bottomless.

"My old man once caught a catfish out of this place that
weighed fifty-five pounds," Charlotte informed him as she
stretched out her legs and kicked off her shoes. Her feet,
with black-painted toenails, rubbed against his knee. "If
you're hot, you can open the door."

"Good idea." He shoved the door open. He planted one
foot on the ground. If worse came to worst, he could jump
and run.

"Aren't you gonna drink that?" She pointed to the bottle
in his hand.

"I don't drink," he admitted without looking at her.

She giggled. "Come on. You're joking, right?"

Shaking his head, he handed her the bottle.

"I thought you were a real boozer."

"I got well."

She shifted and shoved the bottle back into the cooler. When she straightened, she held an ice cube in one hand. She leaned so close he felt her body heat. The ice melted and dripped through her fingers onto his shirt. "Open up," she told him softly and placed the ice against his lower lip, slid it between his lips as she nestled closer. "You don't mind me getting a little cozy, do you? I mean, it isn't every day a girl gets to spend time with a movie star." Her hand slid across his chest and toyed with the shirt buttons. "Do you ever get turned on when you're doing love scenes?"

"No." That was a lie, of course, but he didn't want to encourage her.

She wiggled closer. Her breath smelled like cinnamon, and her skin radiated Red Door. Her breasts pushed against his arm. Her hand slid down his stomach toward his crotch. He grabbed her wrist.

Her eyes widened and her mouth pouted. "God! I hope the rumor I read about you isn't true."

"Which one?" he asked through his teeth. Her lips were an inch from his; her fingertips felt hot through his jeans, which were growing tighter by the second.

"That you're really gay."

"I'm not gay, Charlotte. I promise."

"Then prove it." She slid her left leg across him and settled onto his lap. Her skirt slid up around her hips, revealing the fact that she hadn't bothered to wear underwear. In one swift move, she pulled her tank top off over her head and threw it over the steering wheel.

He stared at her breasts as his body broke out in a sweat.

Charlotte lifted her breasts as if showing off two prize melons. "Nice, huh? And they're real."

"Congratulations." Gripping the sides of the car seat with both hands, Brandon attempted to take a deep breath. Impossible. The heat of her crotch had begun to melt through his jeans. If she so much as wiggled, he was going to explode.

Forcing a smile, he looked into her eyes. "You have lovely breasts. Tempting as hell. But I don't operate well on an empty stomach. Maybe we should eat first."

She took his face between her hands and kissed him, wringing a groan from his throat. Pulling away, she smiled and said, "You just think about that for a while. I'm gonna take a little dip. I'm just so hot, if you know what I mean."

With that, she slid off him, exited the car through his door and strutted into the headlights' twin beams. She unzipped her skirt and allowed it to fall to her ankles, kicked it aside, gave her blond hair a shake so it tumbled in a mass around her face and over her naked shoulders. She ran for the water, her nice round ass reflecting the lights like a glowing celestial body.

He punched the Off button on the stereo, filling the car with the sudden sound of croaking night creatures. A bullfrog bellowed as Miss Yamboree sank to her breasts in the green water. She bobbed up and down and shouted, "The water's great. Take off your clothes and join me!"

In your dreams, he said to himself, smiled, and waved.

The walk back to town was roughly ten miles. If he started now, he might make it home by just after midnight.

Resting his head against the seat, he closed his eyes. He didn't really want to walk back to town. He wanted to spend a semi-pleasant evening someplace other than his aunt's room, staring at television, making conversation with his uncle—whom he loved more than life but who, like clockwork, fell asleep in his chair at precisely eight-thirty and proceeded to snore loudly enough to shake the windows.

Opening his eyes, he focused on the illuminated pool and listened to a lone bullfrog *garump* someplace in the dark. Where the hell was Charlotte?

He got out of the car, squinting to see beyond the circle of light. His heartbeat accelerating, he moved toward the water, his hands on his hips and his senses expanding.

"Charlotte!" he shouted as he stopped at the water's edge. He listened harder, but all he could hear was the roar of his blood in his ears.

A flash of light made him turn. High-beam headlights beyond Charlotte's Firebird crawled toward him up the gravel road. Now what the hell was he supposed to do?

The pickup lumbered out of the dark, windows rolled down and a man's scruffy face grinning out at Brandon. Most of the logo on the door had peeled away, but there was enough left that Brandon could just make out the words Carnival Rides. Beyond the man at the steering wheel were two more faces, both craning to see him where he stood in the stream of light from the Firebird's headlamps.

The driver braced one greasy arm on the bottom of the window space and raised a Coors can to his lips. "How's it goin'?"

"It's going," Brandon replied, making a point to keep his voice as neutral as possible. The last thing he wanted was the truckload of creeps to misconstrue his words as an invitation to hang around.

"Havin' fun, I see."

Brandon followed the man's gaze to the ground near his feet. Charlotte's skirt. Christ!

The man grinned and put the truck in Reverse. Brandon watched as the truck rolled off through the dark, its red taillights disappearing beyond the trees. Releasing his breath, he turned back to the water—

Charlotte hit him with enough force to stagger him backward. Laughing and wrapping her wet arms around his neck and her legs around his hips, she squeezed him fiercely and planted another kiss on his mouth before sliding to the ground and prancing again toward the water.

"Did I scare you?" she called, splashing into the water.

"You've got a sick sense of humor," he yelled after her. Returning to the car, he dropped down into the seat and reconsidered the possibility of walking back to Ticky Creek. He was too damn old for kid games.

"Hey, Carlyle. Fancy meeting you here."

Startled from his thoughts, he looked up, straight into Alyson James's amused eyes.

Grinning, she said, "I can't begin to tell you how relieved I am to find you with your jeans still zipped."

6

"What the hell are you doing here?" Carlyle demanded.

Alyson watched the look of dark anger and suspicion slide over Brandon's features, which were made sharper by the overhead lamp. The amber light made his eyes look green instead of blue. His mouth hooked down at one corner. She didn't want to acknowledge to herself that his animosity bothered her. But it did. For the last ten minutes she'd stood in the distance and watched him with Miss Yamboree, and while a great many emotions had crossed his face, none of them had been anger. Now he virtually simmered.

She looked toward the water where Charlotte Minger floated on her back, her nipples bobbing in the water like two fishing floats. "Let's just say that I'm here to save you from yourself."

"Who died and made you my guardian angel? And how the hell did you know we were out here?"

"Lovely Rita from Wal-Mart. I happened to drop in to the DQ for dinner, and she and some boy had worked themselves into a lather over the prospect of Charlotte tempting you with southern fried breasts and thighs here at the quarry." Hooking one arm over the top of the car door, Alyson grinned, reached out with one finger and slid it over his bottom lip. "Either you've been sucking up close and personal to a Hershey bar or Miss Yamboree put a Mocha Bronze liplock on you."

He turned his face away and ran the back of his hand over his mouth, smearing lipstick across his cheek.

"Actually, Carlyle, I'm quite proud of you," she said, shifting her weight so she leaned against the car and crossed her arms over her chest. "You've got self-discipline. I don't know many men who would just say no to such a generously endowed temptation as our Miss Yamboree. Then again, I suppose you've had the pleasure of spending time with some real doozies, haven't you? Of course, I have to question the wisdom of a man who'd put himself into this situation in the first place, considering it could send you back to prison for another three years."

"What's that supposed to mean?"

"Check her driver's license. Not the fake I.D. she uses to gamble at the Horseshoe in Shreveport. She keeps the real one in the glove compartment, just in case she gets pulled over by one of the local black-and-whites who knows her."

He glared at her before opening the glove compartment, which was stuffed full of miscellaneous paper, chewing gum, hairbrushes, and a pair of foam rubber shoulder pads. Under them was a Texas driver's license.

Gazing over his shoulder at it, Alyson said, "Nice picture. Don't care much for the birth date, however. It just screams statutory, doesn't it?"

He flung the I.D. into the glove compartment and slammed it closed.

"And I hate to be the bearer of more bad news, but according to lovely Rita, our Miss Yamboree had a long talk this afternoon with Dillman. Now maybe I'm letting my writer's fanciful imagination run away with me, but I'm thinking that if Dillman wants to nail your cute butt for something other than a traffic ticket, how better to do it than to catch you in a compromising situation with a minor?"

Grabbing the tank top from the steering wheel and swearing under his breath, Carlyle unfolded out of the car, his shoulder ramming her aside as he stalked toward the water, pausing only to sweep up Charlotte's skirt from the ground. Bathed in light from the headlights, he looked as if he were on stage. He focused on Charlotte breaststroking her way toward him.

"Get out of that damn water, Charlotte, and get dressed."

The smile on Charlotte's face evaporated as Alyson sat on the Firebird's front fender. As Charlotte stood and waded toward shore, her hands doing a pitiful job of covering up her feminine assets, Carlyle flung her clothes at her. "You want to tell me what you and Dillman have cooked up to put me back in jail?"

Charlotte dragged the tank top down over her wet shoulders and stepped into her skirt. She glanced toward Alyson, her expression sullen. "I didn't want to do it," she declared, hopping up and down on one foot. "I just wanted a freakin' hamburger and to get to know you better, but Dillman said he'd forget about my shopliftin' a lipstick from the Discount Drugs if I saw my way to get you out of your pants." Her eyes widened as Carlyle turned his back on her and started toward the car. "What are you gonna do now?" she yelled as she zipped up her skirt.

He moved past Alyson and said, without looking at her, "I assume you rode here in a car and not on a broomstick."

"And here I thought you'd get all mushy with appreciation over my saving your tush."

With a curse, he kicked the car door closed and started down the road into the dark. Alyson ran after him, deciding that the less said, the better, at least for the moment. Carlyle had every right to be angry, but she didn't want to take any chances that he'd turn a fraction of that infamous anger her direction.

Suddenly, from up ahead, headlights flashed on, bright and blinding, bringing Brandon and Alyson to a stop. They raised their hands to shield their eyes.

Dillman climbed out of his cruiser, one hand resting on the butt of his revolver, and sauntered toward Carlyle, looking like Gary Cooper in *High Noon*.

"Oh, boy," Alyson muttered, "here we go again."

She ran to Carlyle's side as Dillman stopped, looking surprised to see her. "Ignore him, Brandon. He's bad news."

"Get out of my way." He nudged her aside, his gaze still locked on Dillman.

"He's not worth going back to prison. You're playing right into his hands. If he pushes you hard enough, you're going to push back."

"What's wrong, Carlyle?" Dillman called. "You look like a man who was almost caught with his pants down."

"Charlotte told me about your plans, Dillman. It didn't work. I've got a witness here who can testify that I didn't touch the girl. She also heard Charlotte admit you coerced her into setting this whole thing up, so maybe you should *fuck off* before I decide to call the State Police and inform them that Ticky Creek's sheriff dabbles in collusion and blackmail."

Alyson elbowed him in the ribs. "Cool it."

Dillman advanced slowly, gravel crunching underfoot. His face, backlit by the cruiser's headlights, looked sinister, almost inhuman. His teeth showed a little under his yellow mustache.

He moved up against Brandon, butting him with his body. Carlyle set his heels and didn't so much as stagger, just looked straight into Dillman's eyes with a "go to hell" intensity that made Dillman's jaws knot.

"One of these days," Dillman drawled, "we're gonna meet when I ain't in this uniform. And when we do, I'm gonna take great pleasure in rearrangin' your face. There won't be a plastic surgeon in this country who'll be able to put you back together."

"Did that sound like a threat to you, Alyson?" Carlyle said as he continued to stare into Dillman's eyes.

"Sure sounded that way to me," she replied.

Dillman cut his eyes to her then, but as he made a move

toward her, Brandon shoved her back and stepped between them. The belligerence that had earlier made him stand his ground in the face of Dillman's hostility suddenly turned into something more threatening.

Brandon shook his head and said in a low voice, "You don't want to go there, Jack."

For an instant—so quick that Alyson might have imagined it, the expression on Dillman's face faltered. His mouth moved nervously; he licked his lips and slid his hand down over his pistol grip. Alyson sensed she should do something to stop the impending disaster, but she was afraid to move for fear the slightest provocation would cause the combustible moment to erupt.

"Get in the car," Brandon ordered her.

She backed toward the Escort she had parked in the trees. Her brain scrambled over what she would do if Dillman decided to pull his gun and pop a bullet between Carlyle's blue eyes. Dillman might be a bully, but he wasn't stupid, she told herself, swallowing her panic.

Alyson crawled into the Ford and turned the ignition, holding her breath as the engine choked, then started. She flipped on the lights, shifted the transmission into Drive, and eased the car onto the road. Reaching across the passenger's seat, she shoved open the door. Staring out at the men standing toe to toe in her lights, she said to herself, *Come on, Carlyle, stop being a tough guy and get in the car before you get yourself killed.*

At last, Carlyle turned away and walked toward the car. Alyson kept her eyes on Dillman, determining that if he did go for his gun, she'd hit the accelerator and flatten his broad backside into the gravel.

Brandon dropped into the seat beside her and slammed the door. Carefully, she steered the car around Dillman, who remained in the middle of the road, as if daring her to hit him.

She didn't relax until turning left onto Highway 59, back toward Ticky Creek. Still, she kept glancing into the rearview mirror, expecting to see the flash of red and blue lights in the dark. Carlyle dug into his shirt pocket and extracted a cigarette. He lit it with a disposable lighter and inhaled deeply. The red-orange glow of clean ash momentarily brightened his angry face.

"Carlyle, you're a study in self-destruction. I'm not sure I've ever met anyone who so dared the world to take a punch at him."

"I don't want to talk about it."

"Maybe you should. You might feel better. It might even save your life—unless, of course, you don't really give a damn about that. Is that it? You haven't got the balls to blow your own brains out, so you try to bully someone else into doing it for you?"

"Why don't you mind your own business, Miz James?"

"If I minded my own business, you'd be bare-assed and boffing to the tune of statutory rape. Tack on another four years to the three you still have left to do in California, and you'll be collecting Social Security by the time you get out again."

He sucked hard on his cigarette, then looked at her. She kept her eyes on the road, her hands on the wheel, palms sweating and heart hammering. She realized that her anxiety had nothing to do with the fact that she had nearly witnessed his murder, and everything to do with the lightning-hot tension suddenly charging the air between them.

"Pull over," he told her, his voice rough and semi-mean.

She frowned and gripped the wheeler harder. "Why?"

"Just shut up and pull the damn car over."

Slowing, hesitant, she eased the car onto the shoulder of the road. He reached over and shifted the car into Park.

"What are you doing, Carlyle?"

He didn't respond, just opened his door and got out. She watched as he walked around the front of the car, the cigarette hanging loose from one corner of his mouth. Reaching the driver's side door, he waited until an eighteen-wheeler roared by, blowing his hair over his eyes and scattering glowing cigarette ashes into the dark, then he flung the cigarette onto the road and jerked open her door, took her arm, and hauled her roughly out of the car.

Shoving her against the car, he took her face in his hand and kissed her. Hard. Forced her lips apart and slid his tongue inside her mouth while he pressed the length of his body against her, moved his hips into her so his erection felt like a crowbar digging into her stomach.

A startling response ignited inside her, as shocking and confounding as his actions. He tasted like cigarettes and something else, something musky and erotic that made her go liquid, despite the wall of denial that her heart struggled to erect in those first blinding seconds that his tongue slid against hers and a groan rumbled deep in his throat. The heat from his body turned the air into steam. His cotton shirt felt damp with sweat, and so did his face. Her first instinct was to wrap her arms around his neck and kiss him back, forgetting who he was and what she was and why she had come to Ticky Creek. Hell, if she wanted to be absolutely honest, she would admit to herself that her reasons for butting in on Charlotte Minger's action had more to do with green-eyed jealousy than with saving Carlyle's butt from Dillman.

But she wasn't about to be honest with herself. She'd been down that road before, swept away by looks and charm and celebrity. Steve Farrington might not have been in Carlyle's league, but he was certainly enough to make a naive, starry-eyed, small town girl from Longview believe in happily ever after.

Still, in the two years that she and Farrington had shared the same name, he had never kissed her like this. And her body had never reacted like this, as if every nerve had been electrified, so that the very brush of Carlyle's breath against her cheek made her skin feel on fire. Then she reminded herself that this unsettling turn of events had nothing to do with any real or imagined attraction; it was just another infamous Carlyle tantrum.

She turned her face away, gasping for air and sanity and control over the rush of white-hot lust that made her hurt between her legs. "Back off, Carlyle."

She gave him a shove, then planted one hand against his chest to keep him at bay. She felt his heart beating fast and hard against her palm, the hot dampness through his shirt that seemed to seep into her flesh and ooze through her bloodstream like steaming molasses. Damn, if he kissed her again, she'd be helpless to stop him. She wished she hadn't stopped him in the first place, and that made her mad. She'd convinced herself before she ever crawled into that tree with her trusty Nikon that she wouldn't allow herself to be influenced emotionally or physically by Hollywood's beloved bad boy, yet here she stood in the dark with the taste of him in her mouth and her legs feeling as if they would give out at any minute.

Drawing herself up, she gave him a sarcastic grin and shook her head. "What's wrong? Couldn't take a punch at Dillman, so drilling me with a kiss that's rough enough to remove the vinyl from siding makes you feel better? Or maybe you've just lost your touch, lover boy. Either way, I'm not much impressed."

The heat of the night and moment weighed down on them as they stared into one another's eyes, breathing hard, sweating . . . aching.

Gradually, the sexual intensity on Carlyle's face metamorphosed into something else—just a flash of pain, perhaps regret, certainly a vulnerability that was gone as quickly as it had appeared, then shaping into a look that was sharper and almost cruel. His mouth curled up on one end as he planted a hand on each side of her and leaned in close, almost as if he intended to kiss her again, lips parting, eyes narrowing. His voice a razor-edged whisper, he asked, "Just how badly do you want that autobiography, Miz James?"

She frowned, confused and wary.

With one finger, he traced the curve of her cheekbone down to the corner of her mouth. "What, exactly, are you willing to do to convince me I shouldn't call up Andrew Morton to write my story?"

His meaning struck her, and new anger flared. "Are you

suggesting that I prostitute myself to you? And if I don't, you'll take my proposal to Morton?"

"What do you think?"

Raising her chin, she did her best to ignore the sudden sting of tears in her eyes. "I'm sure you're well acquainted with prostituting yourself to get what you want in Hollywood, Bubba, but my name on your book isn't worth a pile of fresh horse manure compared to my self-respect—of which you must have little, or you wouldn't have to bully women and blackmail them into having sex with you." She shoved both hands against his chest, knocking him back, then dropped into the driver's seat and slammed the door, locked it, and rolled up the window as he bent to look at her through the glass.

"Hey," he said, and tapped on the window, his expression no longer angry or mean, maybe chagrined. She couldn't tell, exactly, because her eyes were so blurry that the world had turned into hot, salty water. "Alyson, I didn't mean—"

"Get stuffed, Carlyle!" She shifted into Drive and stomped the accelerator. He jumped back as the car leaped forward, tires squealing, rear end fishtailing as she sped toward town.

Charlotte Minger watched the red taillights on the sheriff's cruiser disappear beyond the distant pine trees, leaving her standing in the yellow pool of illumination that spilled out her open car door. "Creep," she said aloud as she shoved three sticks of chewing gum into her mouth and looked around her, into the pitch-black beyond the car light. Night creatures whirred and croaked. Something splashed, causing her to focus hard on the green water where she had swum half an hour before.

If Dillman hadn't interfered with her plans tonight, she would have spent a pleasant time with Carlyle at the Dairy Queen, showing him off to her friends, all of whom had hinted that she didn't stand an ice cube's chance in hell with Ticky Creek's resident movie star hunk. Right about now she would be dropping casual hints that she might like to try her hand at acting: she'd won the lead in her sophomore play, and her drama coach had gushed over Charlotte's potential.

Now Dillman was ticked off with her, as if she'd been the one to spill the beans that he wanted to nail Carlyle. Well, she was glad his plans had been blown to smithereens. While she wouldn't have minded locking her legs around Carlyle, she didn't want him to go back to jail, even if she might have gotten her picture in the *Galaxy Gazette*.

"Charlotte?"

Charlotte looked around, into the dark near the water. "Is somebody there?" she called.

Nothing.

She eased nearer to the car, focused on the black shapes of trees and brush, a prickle of uneasiness forming goose bumps on her arms. No doubt she had just imagined someone calling her name; frogs, probably.

"You've been a naughty girl, Charlotte."

Her heart slammed against her chest wall. She backed toward the car seat, turned her foot on a rock as she tried harder to see in the dark. "Who's there?" She gave a nervous laugh. "Cy Ricky, is that you? 'Cause if it is, I am really gonna be pissed."

Her gaze swept the black perimeter around the car. She couldn't even be sure where the voice had come from. It seemed to float, first near the water, then near the rear of the car.

A noise, like a stone clattering.

The intensity of the night sounds magnified, pulsed in a singsong rhythm, growing louder so they seemed to press in on her.

"This isn't funny," she said in a dry voice as her legs started to shake and her entire body began to seize up with fear. Stupid time for her grandmother's old spook tale of the Baygall Bogeyman to come crawling out of her subconscious: story about a young girl left home all alone in a house buried deep in a forest not far from here. As she lay in her bed in the dark, she asked herself aloud, "Who will stay with me this long, lonesome night?"

And a voice from under her bed whispered, "I will."

*   *   *

Humphrey Bogart, looking like a hungover derelict, snarled
an insult to prim and proper Kate Hepburn as they trudged
through swamp water and swatted at mosquitoes. With the
volume muted and her arms wrapped around a pillow, Alyson fixed her gaze on *The African Queen* and tried to block
out the rain and wind driving hard against the window. She
didn't want to think that because of her immature temper
tantrum, Brandon Carlyle might be out in the tempest.

She had driven down Highway 59 a second time, after her
phone conversation with Alan's message machine. The night
beyond the two-lane, twisting highway had been black as tar,
the forest lining the shoulder so dense a coyote would be
hard-pressed to weave its way between the towering pine
trees. She'd slowed once, seeing a car pulled over, but the
owner, changing a tire and not too happy about it, had glared
like a hoot owl into her headlights and shot her the bird.

She'd even thought of returning to the quarry, which was
the likeliest place for Carlyle to have gone—back to catch a
ride with Miss Yamboree. She'd driven right up to the entrance of the gravel road and stopped, sat there with the engine running, Trisha Yearwood warbling about a heart in
armor on the radio, and convinced herself that Miss Yamboree would be the last person Carlyle would go to if he
valued his freedom. So she'd returned to the motel, finished
packing, and crawled between the sheets, hoping to fall
asleep so the morning would arrive quicker and she could
bid Ticky Creek a relieved fare-thee-well.

But she hadn't slept.

At twelve-thirty-five the predicted front had moved
through, dropping the temperature by thirty degrees in a matter of half an hour. She'd stood at the window and watched
the wind drive dust and leaves and paper cups across the
parking lot that was empty except for her rented Escort and
an old Volkswagen Beetle straddling two spaces near the
office. Lightning had danced in yellow streaks across the
black sky.

At one-fifteen the rain hit. Gray sheets rattled the window and turned the parking lot into a lake. Sudden memories had come knocking: of green, turbulent skies and whipping winds; of curling up under her bed with a lot of dust bunnies, her eyes squeezed closed, feeling the old building sway; and of thinking that at any minute a tornado would suck up her and the Three Forks Café, the way it had Dorothy and Toto, and plopped them down in Oz.

Bogart and Hepburn exchanged droll banter. The sexual chemistry between them contradicted their sarcasm and dislike for one another. The relationship between the two had always left her wound up and aching a little by the time *The End* materialized across the screen. Maybe it was from watching the evolution of unlikely love transform two stubborn people into compassionate and trusting equals. Who didn't leak a few wistful tears over happily ever after? Or maybe it simply left her frustrated that the few times she had allowed herself to become involved beyond the fringes of infatuation, the relationships had stopped short of maturing into anything closely resembling fulfillment.

She pointed the remote at the screen and hit the Off button. The light from the neon Pine Lodge Motel sign filtered through the unlined drapes and painted the walls in a pink and green haze, despite the rain. The room that had seemed so comfortable and functional earlier now felt shabby and bleak.

As a teenager, she and her friends had nicknamed such establishments Ram-it Inns, for obvious reasons. To that very day she couldn't pass one without torrid, clandestine fantasies burning as brightly in her imagination as the flickering neon sign in the distance. Lying in the bed with her arms wrapped around a pillow, she really didn't care to think about all the others who had burned up the mattress before her. The idea only made her feel all the more isolated.

Alyson tried to think back to the last time she had spent an intimate night with a man. There had been only one since her divorce from Farrington. David something . . . a reporter for the *Los Angeles Times*. Athletic. Witty. Not particularly good-looking but with a line of schmooze that could charm the buttons off a rattlesnake. He had not called her again; she had not expected him to. The sex had been mildly enjoyable, like drinking Coke after it had sat open a bit too long. A little fizz but mostly flat.

No one had flipped her switch in a long, long time . . . until tonight. Damn Carlyle in his tight, faded jeans and chambray shirt. Damn him for tasting like smoke and smelling like raw, sweaty sex. Damn him for his smoldering eyes and his mouth that made her ache even now. Damn him for being better-looking in person than he did standing twenty feet tall on a movie screen. And damn damn damn him for occasionally looking like a lost, vulnerable little boy who needed someone to protect him.

Throwing back the blanket, Alyson sat on the edge of the bed and focused on the dark shape of her suitcase on the floor by the door. She tried to think of her life as it had been before Sally called, informing her that the missing-in-action Brandon Carlyle was hidden away in Ticky Creek, Texas. Had she actually been content with her life? No. Not content. The stirring of career frustration and steely ambition had been there, scratching at her subconscious for some time. The Carlyle opportunity had only kick-started her into action.

This whole idea was stupid, now that she allowed herself to think about it. Brandon Carlyle was about as likely to spill his guts to her as O. J. Simpson was to admit that he liked to play with knives.

Running one hand through her hair, Alyson reached with the other for her watch, squinted to see the fluorescent hands. Two o'clock. If she took off now, she could be at DFW by eight. There was a flight leaving for San Francisco at nine-thirty. That would give her time to turn in her car and grab breakfast—she was starving, all of a sudden.

Wearing black leggings and a Forty-Niners jersey, she pulled on her socks and Ropers, grabbed a Twinkie from the bedside table, and scooped up her purse and camera bag, hefting both onto her right shoulder as she bent for her suitcase.

The phone rang.

She jumped and turned, stared at the phone as if she must have imagined it rang at two in the morning.

It rang again.

Alan. The dork finally got in and got her message.

Wincing from the weight of the camera and purse, she grabbed the phone as it rang a third time. "Alan!" She laughed into the phone. "What timing! I was just on my way out the door, and was going to call you. . . ." Her voice faded as silence echoed back at her. "Alan? Is that you?"

Again silence. Then, "Alyson James?"

The voice was deep and husky, a touch of smoky drawl that was familiar and yet unfamiliar. It made her heart squeeze a little. She frowned and held her breath.

"Alyson James?" he repeated.

"Yes." She nodded, and her frown deepened.

"Brandon Carlyle."

He sat in the dark on the bench swing on Henry's front porch, his hair and clothes dripping water, his shoes covered in mud. Shivering, he held the cell phone to his ear as rain ran in sheets off the eaves and formed large puddles at the base of the house. He listened to the sudden silence and waited, teeth clenched to keep them from chattering. In his other hand he held Alyson's red thong panties twisted around his fingers.

"Ah . . . well, Carlyle, this is a surprise. Gosh . . . I'm glad you're okay. For what it's worth, I went back twice to look for you. . . . I guess you got a ride . . . ?"

Shouldering rain from his cheek, he took a deep breath and slowly released it. "About that book. I'll do it. But on my terms. Understand? We talk about what I want to talk about, and if you get pushy, I'll walk away."

"Right. Okay. Gosh, I'm just so shocked. After tonight I thought—"

He hit the End button, hanging up in her ear, then sat back in the swing and closed his fingers tight around the panties in his fist.

7

The Escort's heater didn't work, and for the third time in as many minutes, Alyson was forced to roll down the window and punch the call button on the Carlyles' security gate, allowing cold, wet air to invade the car. Damn Texas weather. Hard to believe this time yesterday she'd been swearing at the heat and humidity. Hard to believe that less than twenty-four hours had passed since she'd first climbed a tree in order to invade Brandon Carlyle's privacy. She felt a decade older. Not having closed her eyes all night didn't help. Having to look into Brandon Carlyle's eyes again after what had transpired between them the night before didn't either. She didn't much want to try to convince herself that her body had not reacted to his kiss, or that the memory of his kiss had not kept her up all night, staring at television and entertaining fantasies involving a motel room. If she was smart, which she obviously wasn't, she would have taken off for the airport regardless of Carlyle's phone call hours earlier.

When she hit the security buzzer again, she held it a good

ten seconds before releasing. Finally, the low, smoky voice came back, tweaking the same vague recognition that had unsettled her at two that morning.

"What?" it drawled.

She stared at the speaker while her checks grew colder and damper from the rain and her heart did a slow somersault in her chest. "Alyson James," she finally replied.

"Who?"

Her eyes narrowed, and she stuck her tongue out at the dripping black box. "Cute, Carlyle. I'm freezing my butt off out here, thank you very much."

"So? Nobody told you to show up here at the butt crack of dawn, did they?"

Sarcasm and derision again. God, she must be nuts to put herself through this. "Instead of hanging up in my ear last night, you might have given me a clue as to when to come calling. I'm not a mind reader."

Silence.

She rolled up the window and hugged herself to keep warm. To think that she could be home now, in bed, warm and dry. Why couldn't Sally have called one of the *Gazette*'s competitors? Let them get verbally bashed by Hollyweird's bad boy.

Finally there came a hum, and the gate began to slide open. Alyson blew into her hands to warm them, then shifted into Drive and eased the car forward, up the crape myrtle-lined drive.

The day before, she had paid precious little attention to the house, much too busy focusing her telephoto lens on Carlyle. As the neat, white frame house with its blue shutters and wraparound porch materialized through the rain, she got the impression of permanence and warmth. "Charming" was the only word to describe the scene. There were flower beds with a splash of red roses—late stragglers that were bowing heavily from the bombardment of rain. There were other flower beds as well. Irises, by the looks of the brown spear-tip leaves clustered behind stone and railroad-tie borders.

Giant azaleas and dogwood trees would no doubt give the grounds a parklike appearance during late spring.

Beyond the house were the outbuildings. A large, weathered barn looked like something out of a painting, slightly lopsided with a high-pitched roof and a hayloft. An ancient well house, once painted bright red, was now mostly hidden behind a hedge, and near it was a newer double garage painted to match the house. A beat-up Chevy truck circa 1975 was parked beside the house, as was a rust-colored sedan with a crunched fender and a University of Texas decal on the rear window.

Alyson parked the Escort behind the truck, collected her purse and camera bag, checked the side pocket to make certain she had not forgotten her microcassette recorder. Forcing herself to take a deep breath, she slid out into the rain, catching her breath as the wind drove a cold fist into her face. She mounted the steps at a run, drew back her shoulders, and banged on the door with her fist. And waited.

A pair of muddy boots sat on the porch near the door.

On the far end of the porch a bench swing with peeling paint shifted with each gust of wind, as if occupied by ghosts.

Finally, the door slowly opened and Carlyle filled the threshold, staring at her through the screen door with a smug curl to his mouth. His hair was shaggy and mussed. He wore baggy jeans and a Hard Rock Café sweatshirt, socked feet, no shoes. Warmth and light rushed over her, as did the smell of frying sausage and coffee, a cup of which he held in his left hand. The heat of it rose from the hot liquid in a gray curl of humidity.

"Cold?" His mouth curved with spitefulness.

"Carlyle, you have a mean streak a mile wide in you."

"I wasn't expecting you so early."

"This is what you get for calling at two in the morning."

"You weren't asleep. You told *Alan* that you were just leaving the motel." He nudged the screen door open with his fingertips and stepped aside, allowing her to enter. She was forced to brush against him as she stepped into the warm, fragrant house. "So who is Alan?" he asked in a flat tone, and closed the door against the cold and rain.

"My best friend." As she did her best to ignore the heat and smell of him standing so close behind her, her eyes scanned the rooms to her right and left: homey, nineteenth-century antiques—no knockoffs here. There was a fortune tied up in furniture and lamps, not to mention rugs.

He caught her arm and directed her down the long hall, toward the smell of food and coffee. "I'd invite you to break-fast, but I'm afraid we're all out of Twinkies."

"Not to worry." She patted her purse. "I brought my own." Frowning, she risked a glance at him, noting the glint of amusement in his eyes. "How do you know I eat Twinkies?"

"There are no secrets in Ticky Creek, Miz James."

"I beg to differ. The CIA could take lessons from Ticky Creek residents on how to keep a secret—at least where you're concerned."

"Mind divulging how you found me?"

"My cousin Sally saw you at the Dime A Cup."

"Figured as much. How did you find the farm?"

"It's called ears. These folks might not blab about you to outsiders, but they flap to one another ninety to nothing. I just dropped into Redneck Feed. You know no one likes to talk like men at the feed store—those bubbas put gossiping women to shame. They know everybody's business in three counties. While Bubba Junior was helping Modeen load feed into the back of her truck, I flipped through the card file to find your uncle's address."

His blue eyes fixed on hers and his eyebrows lowered. "That kind of nosiness can get you in trouble around here. People's privacy is just short of sacrosanct in Ticky Creek."

"Which is why you've lived here for months without the rest of the world finding out."

"People here like to feel they've got one up on the world. If they blow my cover, then I have to go away and maybe not come back. Besides, most people don't really think of me as Brandon Carlyle the movie star. Hell, most of the people here probably have never even seen my movies. I'm just John Carlyle's boy and Henry's nephew, who drops into

Ticky Creek occasionally to spend a little downtime from his West Coast job."

She flashed him a skeptical smile. "You're joking, right?"

"I'm just a country boy, Miz James, whether you want to believe it or not."

Right, and Queen Elizabeth was formerly a Rockette at Radio City Music Hall.

She stopped abruptly as they reached the kitchen threshold. The large room glowed with warm yellow walls and white woodwork. Here, too, antiques filled the room with character. A sideboard displayed blue and white dishes and jars of pickles, relishes, and fruit. A massive harvest table sat in the middle of the room. A realistically painted, life-size cast iron rooster served as a centerpiece surrounded by clusters of oat straw and miniature gourds.

A man she assumed was Carlyle's uncle sat at one end of the table, glasses perched on the end of his nose as he read the morning paper. A red-haired woman in black slacks and a tight black turtleneck sweater stood at the stove, pouring Egg Beaters into a skillet. They each looked at Alyson as she stepped into the room.

"Don't be shy," Brandon said quietly but firmly.

"I—I don't like to intrude," she replied as quietly.

"Since when?" He directed her toward the table. "Henry, I believe you recall Miz James from yesterday?"

Henry had twinkling blue eyes—the color not so intense as his nephew's, but certainly friendlier. There was a depth of compassion there as well; humor, kindness, understanding. He had bright pink cheeks that turned redder as he tossed down his paper, smiled, and, rising partially from his chair, extended his hand.

"You're just in time for coffee and breakfast, Miss James. Please, sit down and join us."

As Alyson put her hand in his, big and rough as old leather, she felt those blue eyes drive right through her. Compassionate as they were, they were also shrewd. She suddenly felt as if he were staring right into her soul.

He gave her hand a quick shake and turned to the cook. "Betty, you remember Miss James?"

Betty glanced over her shoulder, striking Alyson with her intensely green eyes that weren't nearly so welcoming as Henry's. "I remember. The young woman with the camera. *That* camera, I presume." She pointed a plastic spatula toward the bag hanging from Alyson's shoulder.

Alyson took a deep breath and forced a smile. "I owe you an apology for yesterday. I appreciate your not pressing charges, Mr. Carlyle. You had every right, of course."

"Water under the bridge, dear. Betty, get Miss James a coffee. Will you join us for breakfast? There's plenty. Betty always cooks enough for an army." Henry slapped his round stomach and chuckled. "And I eat enough for an army."

As Alyson sat in a chair, Brandon moved around the table to take a chair next to Henry's. "You're supposed to be dieting. Doctor's orders. Take off twenty pounds or else."

Henry grunted and reached for his coffee. "Hell, Betty's got me on those damn fake eggs in a box, not to mention fake bacon and sausage. I don't care if it *is* spiced to heaven and back, you're never going to convince me that turkey sausage tastes the same as a good thick patty of fried pork."

Alyson smiled her thanks as Betty plunked a mug of black coffee in front of her. Betty raised one eyebrow in response and turned back to the stove.

"My nephew tells me you want to help him write his autobiography, Miss James."

As she reached for a creamer that looked like a miniature black and white spotted cow, Alyson glanced toward Brandon. His eyes narrowed, and he gave her an almost imperceptible shake of his head. So, he hadn't told Henry about the unauthorized biography yet.

"There are a great many people who'd like to read Brandon's life story—straight from the horse's mouth, so to speak. There's been so much . . . speculation, of course, about his career, not to mention his personal life."

"Mostly a lot of hogwash," Henry declared with a frown, his face turning dark. He reached over and slapped one hand on Brandon's shoulder, gave it a squeeze. His voice grew heavy with emotion. "I couldn't love Brandon any more if he were my own son. But that doesn't color my perception of his character. He's made a few life choices that weren't particularly bright—but don't we all, occasionally? Hell, nobody's perfect. But the important thing is, Miss James, he never set out to hurt anyone. Sometimes fate deals us a lousy hand, is all. We deal with it. Brandon's dealt with it the best he can, and he's bounced back stronger than ever. We believe he's on the right track now. All the garbage of the past is exactly that. The past."

Alyson smiled and stirred sugar into her coffee. Her gaze slid to Brandon, whose face had colored slightly with Henry's words. Keeping his eyes downcast, Brandon raised his coffee to his lips. Perhaps he felt a little embarrassed that his uncle would be so straightforward with a stranger. Or maybe the flush on his cheeks was due to raw emotion. Whatever, he looked like a kid who had been both praised and chastised in one breath.

As Betty sat a plate of turkey sausage and scrambled Egg Beaters in front of Henry, she looked at Alyson. "There's plenty if you want some, Miss James."

Odd woman. Blunt features, not totally unattractive. Her voice sounded as if she were struggling with a throat infection—a bit scratchy and breathy. It made Alyson want to clear her own throat. "No, thank you. I have something in my purse. I'm really not much on breakfast, actually. Just makes me want to go back to bed—especially on a morning like this."

Henry reached for his fork and knife, eyes fixed on his plate of steaming food. "So what's your slant on his story, Miss James? A positive one, I hope. God knows we've had enough of that tabloid trash to last us a lifetime."

All eyes came back to her, perhaps not so friendly as before. The subtle message was *If you have any plans to do the dirty on Brandon Carlyle, you can take a hike off a tall cliff.* She tried to ignore the spear of guilt that stabbed at her conscience, then mentally reminded herself that her reasons for being here might be a lie, but that didn't necessarily mean her slant on Carlyle's story would be anything but positive.

"Of course this is Brandon's story," she replied. "I'm just here to get the details on paper and put it all into some kind of order that people can follow easily."

Satisfied with her answer, Henry refocused on his food, Betty dropped the frying pan into a sink of soapy water, and Brandon put his coffee cup down and stood up. For the first time Alyson allowed herself to look at him directly. He looked tired, eyes a bit droopy and red. Hungover was what he looked. Like he'd spent the night on a real bender. Not the case, of course, unless he'd tied one on after she'd left him beside the road. When he'd called her at two that morning, he'd sounded sober.

He glanced at Betty. "Is Bernie ready to get up?"

Betty nodded and dried her hands on a dish towel, her green eyes drifting back to Alyson. "Fed and bathed. I'll do her hair once she's situated. The room is cold, so you might want to put that plaid lap blanket over her legs."

"I'll get a fire going in the fireplace soon as I finish up here," Henry announced, then smiled at Alyson. "I'll get one started in the den as well. I guess you kids will want some privacy while you talk. Den's a good place for that."

"We'll talk after I finish chores," Brandon declared as he disappeared into a room off the kitchen.

"I'll be happy to feed for you this morning," Henry called. "Nope."

Henry chuckled and shook his head. "Boy spoils me rotten. Since he moved home, he's taken over the running of this place like it was the most natural thing in the world for him. Does him good, I guess. Keeps his mind off other things. He was never one to sit around idle, even when he was a youngster. His mother would let the boy come home frequently, but there was hell to pay when he did. She was on the phone three, four times a day, checking on him. God forbid that something should happen to him. Then her source of income would dry up and she'd be forced to get her lazy tail out there and earn her own keep."

"Henry!" Brandon barked from the other room. "Behave."

He forked a sizable chunk of turkey sausage and pointed it at Alyson, lowered his voice. "Woman's a witch. Spawn of the devil. I use to tell John, Brandon's father, that Cara was going to blow his chances for a baseball career. John had one of the best pitching arms in the country. There wasn't a major university that wasn't prepared to finance his education if he'd play ball for them. Problem with John was he was just too damn good-looking. Women wouldn't leave him alone. You can't expect a man to concentrate on baseball when gals like Cara are shaking their fannies at him every chance they get."

"Henry!"

"It's the truth, and you know it," Henry shouted, the chunk of sausage bulging his cheek. "You've got the same problem. Too damn good-looking for your own good."

Brandon stepped into the room and glared at his uncle.

Alyson tried to hide her smile behind her coffee cup as Henry sat back in his chair and chewed, not in the least affected by Brandon's visual warning. "Remember when you used to come home and Cara'd send a list of things you weren't allowed to do: no mowing, something might get cut off; no swimming, you might drown; no fishing, you might drown or hook an eye or something; no biking, you might get hit by a car; no horseback riding, you might get thrown and bust your head. She'd even send a list of foods he couldn't eat. No fried foods or desserts. No colas or Kool-Aid. No candy." Turning his eyes back to Alyson, he said, "You remember that movie *Boy in the Plastic Bubble*? Well, it might as well have been about Brandon. He wasn't ever allowed to be a kid."

"So I take it you always followed Cara's orders." Alyson suspected she knew the answer before Henry swallowed his sausage and replied with a wide grin:

"Me and Bernie stuffed Brandon so full of fried chicken, pie and ice cream, and cherry Kool-Aid it was a wonder he survived it without rupturing."

Alyson laughed, as did Betty. They looked at Brandon,

leaning his left shoulder against the doorjamb, fingers slid into his jeans pockets, mouth curled up on one side as he watched Henry bounce up and down with laughter. Something in the way the two men looked at one another made Alyson feel as if she were trespassing into sacred territory—the same way she'd felt stepping into this kitchen. The package was one of comfort, safety, and stability, not to mention love as deep as an ocean. Henry Carlyle and this house were Brandon's port in a storm, and she, the outsider, was invading it. In truth, the atmosphere disoriented her. Family wasn't something she had ever known outside reruns of *The Waltons* and *Ozzie and Harriet*. Being suddenly dumped into the midst of such warm, loving energy made her breathless and dizzy.

Henry finished his food and shoved his plate back. His face looked serene as he rubbed his belly and regarded Alyson with a smile. "You're from around here, Al?"

She was warmed by his familiarity, as if his calling her Al was a form of acceptance. Somehow acceptance by this man felt inordinately important to her. "Longview," she replied.

"What school?"

"Pine Tree."

"Go to college?"

"Briefly. Two years at Stephen F. Austin."

"And then?"

"I moved to California."

"L.A.?"

"For a while."

"Acting?"

She smiled and shook her head. "No."

Silence filled the room as Henry watched her, waiting.

"I waitressed for a while. Freelanced with my writing. Took night courses in photography. This and that." She glanced at Betty, who leaned back against the sink with her arms crossed over her chest. Her face was emotionless. Her eyes, however, looked hard as jade.

"You still have family in Longview?" Henry asked as he removed his glasses and cleaned them with his napkin.

"No."

"Are your parents living?" He replaced the glasses on his nose.

The room closed in on her suddenly. The air felt hot and difficult to breathe. She got the impression that the kindly man staring at her through the thick lenses of his glasses would somehow know if she lied. Though she had become adept at keeping her life a closed book to the world, something about Henry Carlyle invited her confidence. She wanted to crawl into his lap, lay her head on his shoulder, and spend the next hours revealing her greatest fears and secrets. She realized in that moment that the farm and its peaceful solitude weren't what had lured Brandon back to Ticky Creek. It was the old man with his ruddy cheeks and twinkling blue eyes that had the ability to turn a person's insides to butter.

"My grandmother raised me, actually." She glanced over her shoulder, straight at Brandon, who continued to watch her with his sleepy eyes and a lazy curl on his lips. Wrapping her fingers around her coffee cup for security, she took a deep breath. "My mom took off for better places when I was six. Last time my grandmother heard from her, she was living in Vegas, had just married some gambler named Bill or Bob or something, and was relocating to L.A. I was thirteen at the time. And my dad. . . ." She shrugged. "I never knew him."

Henry pursed his lips thoughtfully. "And your grandmother?"

"Died my first year in college."

"So you went to L.A. to find your mother. Did you find her?"

"No."

He smiled. "Well, you seem to have done all right for yourself, Al. You're pretty, intelligent, and ambitious And honest for the most part, although I sense you're holding a lot back. Understandable. You don't know me from Jack

Adam. Are you married?" His eyebrows lifted as he waited for her reply.

"No."

Smile stretching, he shoved back his chair and stood. "Would you like to meet my better half, Al?" He offered her his hand. She took it, and he helped her out of her chair, directed her toward the door where Brandon had earlier been standing. Reaching the threshold, she stopped while Henry moved ahead. He moved the empty wheelchair beside the bed where Brandon stood, holding a woman's gray hand.

Like the kitchen, the room held a certain kind of magic that evoked security in Alyson. The air smelled of jasmine potpourri. The walls were dusty rose; the hardwood floor, covered with an Oriental carpet. Boston ferns crowded the corners, Victorian knickknacks cluttered every square inch of the antiques hugging the walls. There were stacks of old paperbacks piled on a short table near the television.

"This is my wife," Henry declared. "Bernice. We call her Bernie." He locked the chair and smiled at his wife. "Bernie with laughter like birdsong. Isn't that right, Brandon? When Bernie laughed, anyone in earshot would stop and listen."

Brandon gently shifted Bernie to the chair. He moved carefully because there were tubes attached to her nose from an oxygen tank by the bed. Henry wrapped a shawl around her frail shoulders while Brandon covered her lap with the plaid blanket. His movements were achingly gentle, and the fondness in his eyes as he regarded the tiny woman made emotion rise up inside Alyson so that she was forced to look away, toward the collection of framed photographs crowding the top of the fireplace mantel.

There were images of Brandon smiling back at her—not black-and-white glossy head shots, but life moments frozen in time: a child lazily sunning on the steps of Henry's front porch, another of Brandon and Henry carving a jack-o'-lantern from a massive pumpkin, both child and adult covered with pumpkin slime and seeds. Still another showed a much younger Bernice with flowing brown hair and sparkling eyes perched atop a big, shaggy plow horse, young Brandon sitting behind her, his arms wrapped around her waist and his cheek pressed against her back. He looked sublimely content.

Henry bent over and smiled into his wife's eyes. "We have a guest this morning, Bernie. A young woman is here to see Brandon. She intends to help him write his autobiography." Henry looked up and smiled at Alyson. "Come here, dear, so she can see you."

Alyson moved to stand beside Henry while Brandon backed away just enough to allow her room. She felt him at her back. The scent of him made her heart do a queer missbeat that was beginning to annoy her. The last thing she needed was to become emotionally involved with Brandon Carlyle and his family. Then she reminded herself that the stirring going on inside her had nothing whatsoever to do with emotion. It was physical, pure and simple. There wasn't a woman born who could stand in the man's proximity and not feel her body heat up. There was something to Henry's observations about women and good-looking men. *It's all chemical*, she repeated to herself. *The heart has nothing whatsoever* to do with it.

A. J., just continue to remind yourself that the last time chemicals and chemistry entered into the love equation, you married a jerk you didn't love any more than he loved you.

The woman's pale blue eyes stared up at Alyson from a slack, expressionless face that had once been beautiful. The laugh lines bracketing her mouth were evidence that once she had been the vibrant, smiling woman in the photographs. Although the hair was gray instead of brown, the natural waves were still there, soft around her cheeks that looked as delicate as a flower petal. A sense of loss tugged at Alyson, yet she couldn't help but smile into the blue eyes that looked into her own in a way that unbalanced her. There was emotion there—warm and convivial. Or was there? Whatever, it was gone as swiftly as the brief brightness of a firefly's flicker.

She reached out and placed her hand on Bernie's, which

felt cold and lifeless. "Hello, Bernie. I'm very pleased to meet you."

Henry turned on the television while Brandon moved to the fireplace and began stacking wood inside. Betty entered, collected a silver-backed hairbrush from the dresser top, and moved up behind Bernie. She rested her hands on the chair grips, and focused on Alyson, who was still smiling down at Bernice.

"It's time to do her hair," Betty explained, allowing Alyson a tight smile.

It was there again, the flicker of emotion in Bernie's eyes. Only not so warm this time. But . . . something else—gone too quickly to interpret it.

Forcing her gaze up to Betty's, Alyson asked softly, "Can she hear us?"

"No."

"Are you certain? It almost seems like—"

"No, Miss James." Betty's expression softened and saddened. She gently stroked Bernie's hair. "There's something about the dear woman that continues to inspire hope in us. But the doctors have assured us that what's left of Bernice is little more than a shell." Lowering her voice, she looked directly into Alyson's eyes. "She won't last much longer. I simply do all I can to keep her as comfortable as possible. And to support her family, of course. This tragedy has been draining and painful for them, as you can well imagine."

"Obviously they're very lucky to have you," Alyson said.

A smile turned up the corners of Betty's red mouth. "Miss James, I'm the one who's lucky. They've become like family to me. Their generosity has been a gift from God." She placed one hand on Bernice's shoulder, which looked exceedingly fragile under Betty's fingers.

Alyson backed away and directed her look toward Brandon.

He sat on the hearth, his back to the sputtering flames, elbows on his knees, watching her.

Just what the hell was he doing, bringing this stranger into his home? And what had prodded him to call her at two that morning, to agree to her idiotic idea of an autobiography? She'd left him by a highway in the dark. No way in hell would he have thumbed it home: the last thing he needed was to be picked up by someone who might recognize him. So he'd trudged ten miles along back roads, was drenched and partially frozen by the time he got home. He felt numb from lack of sleep, and a cold had begun to scratch at his throat and eyes. By nightfall Betty would be forced to infuse him with hot Thera-flu—after he turned her loose on the muscles in his legs that cramped like hell.

Yet, there she stood in leggings, Roper boots, and a football jersey, hair slightly disheveled, eyes sleepy. Mouth still so red it looked as if he'd just kissed it . . . again.

Maybe you've lost your touch, lover boy.

Henry sat down beside him and adjusted his glasses on his nose. He, too, focused on Alyson James as she spoke quietly with Betty, her gaze frequently shifting between Bernie and Brandon, dodging his eyes, which apparently made her nervous.

"Nice-looking woman," Henry commented under his breath, his words diluted by the Weather Channel.

Brandon shrugged. "I hadn't noticed."

Henry chuckled and handed Brandon his glasses. "Then you need these more than I do."

"She's too full of sass," Brandon commented, watching Alyson continue to avoid his gaze. She attempted to focus on Betty, who had begun to brush Bernie's hair.

"Sass is good. Bernie had sass."

"Yeah, but there wasn't a dishonest bone in Bernie's body."

"You don't trust our Miss James, I take it."

"Not as far as I can throw her." He glanced over his shoulder at the fire. It was finally catching, throwing minute amounts of heat against his cold back.

"Then what's the point?" Henry asked, frowning.

Exactly, Brandon thought. If he didn't trust her motives, why the hell was she standing there now, looking like she wanted to throw herself out the window and run as hard as she could down the road?

"The point is, I offered her a million bucks to get lost, and she didn't take it. Money obviously doesn't mean a hell of a lot to her. But her career does. Maybe I'm just curious to what lengths she'll go to get her name on a book."

"You serious about this book?" Henry regarded Brandon's profile, his brow creased. "You know how you've always shied away from interviews. Could stir up a lot of hornets again. Are you sure you're ready for it?"

"Serious?" Brandon shook his head and ran one hand through his hair, massaged the back of his tense neck. "I'd rather crawl into a bed a fire ants."

"Then why put yourself through it?"

Looking into his uncle's concerned eyes, Brandon said, "I haven't actually decided to do it yet. I'm thinking about it."

"Which brings us back to why she's here." Henry nodded toward Alyson, who appeared to be focusing on the stack of romance paperbacks. She was bent at the waist, butt toward Brandon, as she searched through the books, flipping them over to read the blurbs on the back. His mouth went dry, and while he wanted to think it was because he was growing more ill by the minute, he suspected cold germs had nothing to do with it. Undoubtedly every cold germ squirming in his system right now had just got a hard-on at the site of Miz James's tight tush.

"I haven't figured that out yet," he finally replied. "The woman abrades my nerves like sandpaper. Every time I look at her, I want to do something evil."

A slow smile curled Henry's mouth. "I can't say I'm not pleased that she's here. She's a hell of a lot better for you than Charlotte Minger."

Brandon winced and groaned, and again attempted to block last night's fiasco from his mind. He sure as hell didn't want to think about what might have happened if Alyson hadn't shown up when she did. If nothing else, he owed her for that. "We don't want to go there, Henry. Trust me, it wasn't pretty."

"That bad, huh?"

"Let's just say that while I was spending my days counting the cracks in the ceiling of my cell for three years, I vowed strict celibacy for the rest of my life, because women were, and had been all my life, misery and trouble. A flash of Charlotte's legs obviously confused my reasoning. Last night was a brutal reminder that women are nothing but worry. In fact, I'm convinced there was no serpent in the Garden of Eden at all. There was only Eve with triple D boobs and temptation winking out of both flirtatious eyes."

Before Henry could respond, Brandon stood, arched his stiff back, and moved across the room, his gaze fixed on Alyson's butt as she shifted from one foot to the other while she perused the paperbacks. He eased up behind her as the naughty image of her bent over with thong panties around her ankles slid into his thoughts. No doubt about it, she was just the right height to—

She turned around suddenly, plowing into him, dropped the book in her hand, stumbled back, her eyes flying wide and her lips parting as she found herself against him and no place to go but over the stack of books at her back. She didn't retreat. It wasn't in her to back down if she thought she was being harassed or bullied.

"Time we talk," he told her, took her arm, and turned her toward the door, aware that Henry and Betty were watching; aware, too, that, judging by the color on Alyson's face, she had a few words to say herself, but wisely kept her trap shut in front of witnesses.

He walked her through the kitchen, down a short, dark corridor, and opened the den door. They moved down several steps, his fingers still gripping her arm—uncomfortably, he suspected. He ushered her to the plaid early American sofa situated before the fireplace, and shoved her down onto it. She glared up at him, her eyes narrowed and her face in full flush, darkening even more as he leaned over her, forcing her to sit back against the pillows and hold her breath, her eyes dropping to his mouth, then back up again.

"Let's get something straight from the beginning, Miz

James. If you want to make idle chitchat about the weather, fine and dandy. If you wish to elaborate on your choice of Twinkies over Ding Dongs, then be my guest. But never, under any circumstances, question Henry about my life. Do we understand one another?"

She nodded.

"I have a few chores to do. Can I trust you to behave while I'm gone?"

Her lips curved and her eyelids drooped. "I guess you're gonna have to, Bubba."

"I don't gotta do nothin', Cupcake. I can toss your cute butt out in the rain and tell you to take a hike back to Alan, God help him, and you can spend the rest of your life languishing in obscurity."

Eyes narrowing, she said, "You're an ass, Carlyle. Anybody ever told you that?"

"Yeah, a few agents and a dozen or so directors." Pushing away, he backed toward the French doors across the room. "And another thing. I won't be so nice to your pretty camera next time you take a photograph without my permission."

"Oooh, I'm scared." She relaxed against the pillowed sofa arm in a half-reclining position, crossed one booted foot over the other, and stifled a yawn. "My best to Dolly if you see her."

8

The rain fell in sheets, the sound on the roof and windows
like a lullaby that made Alyson drowsy. Having removed her
boots, she curled her legs under her and sank into the sofa,
her head resting on the pillowed arm, and tried not to think
about how good the Carlyle house felt. It made her melan-
choly. Made her compare this warmth and comfort to the
stark, dreary apartment over the Three Forks Café. There had
been no pictures on the walls. No colorful rugs on the floors.
Instead of frilly country curtains there were brittle yellow
newspapers plastered with Richard Nixon's squint-eyed face
and the bold headlines I AM NOT A CROOK! No harvest
table with a colorful rooster, just an overworked, old-before-
her-time grandmother who slung hash for truckers and, more
often than not, forgot the kid upstairs waiting for her dinner.
If it hadn't been for Twinkies and Moon Pies and Fritos,
she'd have starved before reaching her fourth birthday. And
not to forget the jukebox bumping twenty-four hours a day.
She woke up to Waylon Jennings and fell asleep to Tammy

Wynette with a good dose of Elvis in between.

But this house was perfection, like the ones in the magazines her granny occasionally brought home, bought out of boxes at flea markets for a dime. She could almost hear Granny now, slumped in a chair with her swollen feet propped on a crate, a cigarette hanging slack from one corner of her mouth, her thin gray hair tucked into a hair net. "There's two kind of people in the world, Princess. Trash like us and the others. Have a gander at how the others live. Makes you a little sick, don't it?"

It didn't make her sick. Not at all. It inspired her not to settle.

The aroma of turkey sausage and strong coffee hung in the air, as did the underlying perfume of the scented Tranquillity candle burning on a far table. There was tobacco, too, just a hint, giving the masculine room even more of a male ambience, as if it needed anything to emphasize the air of testosterone and virility. Obviously, this room was Henry's haven. Mounted deer heads and mallard ducks and striped bass graced three of the paneled walls, as did framed photographs like the ones in Bernie's room. A built-in gun cabinet that would rival the United States arsenal took up the fourth wall, along with shelves lined with what appeared to be every *Field and Stream* and *Guns* magazine printed in the last three decades.

"I brought you a blanket in case you're cold."

Alyson opened her eyes and looked up into Henry's smiling face. As he draped the blue and white throw over her body and tucked it around her feet, he said, "Brandon'll be a while. Stock needs feeding. Rain'll slow him a bit. Sure as the devil needed this rain, though. Not that it's goin' to do us hay farmers any good. Could have used it three, four months ago when our pastures were dryin' up."

He took split wood from a stack on the hearth and carefully placed it among the cold ashes of the previous fire, turned the gas key, then tossed in a lit match, stepping back as the whoosh of fire erupted among the oak and pine logs.

Firelight immediately bloomed, giving the dim room a warm, cozy glow.

Henry reached for a pipe on the mantel, along with a bag of tobacco. With his back to the fire, he packed the pipe bowl with something that smelled slightly spicy, his inscrutable eyes coming back to her. "Mind if I smoke, Al?"

"Not at all." She sat up, pulling the throw around her shoulders.

Thunder shook the walls. She glanced toward the French doors, thinking of the cold, damp wind that had rushed through the room at Brandon's exit, and how she had fretted over his being out in the inclement weather. She'd stood at the door, shivering, watching him run toward the barn, his head bowed under the onslaught of rain, and feeling . . . what? Stunned that she'd somehow bamboozled her way into Carlyle's life? Unsettled that he'd trust her with his confidences—not to mention his family? Giddy, like some spacy fan who looks into Carlyle's face and at his body, and sees her ultimate fantasy? Even worse, fantasizes that he's going to find something in her that will magically make him fall in love and desire to stroll hand in hand with her into the sunset? There was that kiss, after all. She could still taste it— smoky, like his voice. She could still feel it, hot and wet and so impassioned that its energy had electrified every erogenous nerve in her body. She wanted to feel it again, because never in her life had she ever been kissed like that.

"Since Brandon's out, I thought we could take this opportunity to get to know one another better. You don't mind indulging an old man awhile, do you?"

She smiled. "You should know that your nephew has forbidden me to talk to you."

Chuckling, Henry lit his pipe. "He'll bully you if you let him. Don't let him, Al. Stand up to him. He likes that. He'll respect you. He also likes discipline. If he acts like a jackass, which he will frequently, get in his face about it. One thing I never did with the boy is pander to him like everybody else—treatin' him like his being on this earth was the Second Comin' or somethin'. If Cara knew how many times I took my belt off to that boy, she would've croaked." He puffed on the pipe and looked thoughtful. "Now Bernie was a different matter. I whupped him, and she cuddled him. I used to tell her that my disciplinin' Brandon for being bratty wasn't goin' to do him any good if she was goin' to coo like some mamma pigeon over him and stuff him full of milk and oatmeal cookies."

Henry moved to a wall and pointed to the collection of photographs. "Have you had a look at my gallery, Al?"

Alyson tossed aside the throw and joined him, comfortable in his company and eager to hear more about the Brandon Carlyle that few people, aside from Henry and Bernie, would ever know. She focused on the black-and-white shot of a young man in a plaid shirt and faded jeans, a baseball mitt on one hand, a baseball in the other.

"Brandon likes baseball?" she asked.

"That's not Brandon," Henry replied. "That's Brandon's father, John."

She stared harder. "My God, they're clones."

He laughed. "If you stood them up side by side right now, you couldn't tell the difference, aside from Brandon's bein' a hair taller." He pointed to others: of John Carlyle with his newborn son; John and a toddler Brandon with a mass of wild, dark curls; another of John squatting beside a two-year-old Brandon wearing a little baseball uniform, the too large cap over one eye. The boy gripped a miniature bat in both hands, as if prepared to take a swing.

"This one here is my favorite." Henry gently touched the glass, his fingertip stroking the image that made Alyson's chest tighten. Father and son sat under a tree, Brandon nestled on John's lap, his head on his father's shoulder as he slept. With his arms wrapped around his child's body, John rested his cheek on Brandon's head, his expression so full of love the image virtually radiated with it. There were toys scattered around them, and discarded wrapping paper and bows. "Brandon's fourth birthday. Tyke was wore out and so stuffed with birthday cake and ice cream he couldn't move. They'd been playin' with the new bat and ball John bought him. Sat down under that old pine out there to take a breather. Brandon fell asleep." Henry looked away, and when he spoke again, his voice was raspy. "Next mornin' John was killed. Freak accident. Load of trees came off the truck on top of him. Hardly enough left of him to bury. He was twenty-three years old . . . gone, just like that."

Alyson slid one arm around Henry's shoulders, her own eyes burning and her throat aching, as much for his loss as for Brandon's.

Henry turned away, reached into the hip pocket of his overalls, and dragged out a handkerchief. He removed his glasses and blotted his eyes, sniffed self-consciously, then walked to the next group of photos. "These here are of Brandon from five to ten years old. Once Cara got ahold of him, he didn't get to come home more than three times a year, so we went a little camera crazy." He put on his glasses and tucked the kerchief back in his pocket. "Tell me what you think."

She scanned the photos, obviously arranged by age, the young images vibrant and smiling, but hauntingly empty after the previous shots of Brandon with his father. She moved down the wall, smiling to herself as she saw him gradually changing from one year to the next, but always with the infectious, engaging smile and twinkling eyes. And then . . .

She stopped. Frowned.

Alyson looked away, then back. Closed her eyes briefly, then focused again. "A different child," she said more to herself than to Henry, who moved up behind her and pointed to the shot of Brandon sprawled on the front porch steps, a hole in the knee of his jeans and his sneakers untied, his face full of sunshine as he laughed.

"He was eight here. Home durin' a break from shooting *Those Foster Kids*. Here he was nine. Just one year later."

She moved back, as if space would somehow give her a better perspective on the boy whose vacant eyes would not look directly into the camera. Where was the twinkle? Where was the smile? His young mouth barely curled up on one end, as if the effort to smile caused him pain. He'd gone from eight to ancient in a year.

"What happened?" she asked softly. She felt cold, drawn into the dark pits of Carlyle's young eyes.

"Bernie and I have asked the same question for the last twenty-seven years. We'd stand here side by side, just as we're standing now, stare at this group of pictures, then at that one, and ask, What happened?"

"You've asked him, of course." Alyson continued to move along the groups of pictures, noting how the vacant eyes metamorphosed into anger.

"Until we were blue in the face." Henry walked back to the fireplace and stood staring into the flames. "Kids change, I guess. Acting is a tough business. Hard on children. His mother didn't help, always pushin' him. He grew up too fast. Hell, he skipped adolescence and went straight to manhood. When he was fifteen, he was playin' adult roles. I use to tell Bernie, Brandon was a kid held hostage by his mother in an adult world. God only knows what happened to him there. Knowin' Cara, it wasn't good. No telling what kind of debauchery she subjected him to."

He set down his pipe and walked to the gun cabinet, opened a low drawer. When he turned again, he held out a copy of the dreaded biography. "Have you seen this?"

Alyson winced and looked past him, at the drawer full of books, all the same: *Hollywood Hellion*.

"Trash. All trash. Grover Comstock, manager over at the Wal-Mart, called me the minute the books showed up there. I beelined it down there and bought ever' last book on the shelf. Now it's one thing if some fruitcake wants to make up a lot of garbage. It happens in this business. But when his own mother starts in on him, then that's somethin' else. What kind of mother does that, I ask you—turns on her own flesh and blood, her own boy, blamin' the failure of her career on him when she's the one who drove him to alcoholism by the time he was thirteen?" He turned and flung the book as hard as he could into the fire. He threw a second book, then a third, his face growing redder, his breath shorter, as the flames leaped higher, devouring the curling pages.

As he reached for a fourth, Alyson grabbed it and threw it in the fire. "Calm down," she told him sternly, taking his arm and squeezing it for emphasis. She directed him toward a chair and made him sit. Dropping to her knees beside him, she took his big hand between hers and patted it. "You shouldn't get so worked up, Henry. It isn't good for you."

He stared at her, his eyes bright with emotion and tears. "I should've fought her. Soon as we put John in the ground and Cara showed up here in her black leather pants and her gigolo boyfriend, I should've told her to her face that no way was she gettin' her hands on Brandon, especially since she hadn't so much as called him in over a year. But I didn't. I didn't. She was his mother, after all."

"What could you have done?" she commiserated, and squeezed his hand.

"Nothin'. I've been able to do nothin' but offer him a safe house from her craziness. Maybe if I could've done more, taken a firmer stand, circumstances might have been different for him. But we were afraid of rockin' the boat, Al. We felt lucky she let him come back to Ticky Creek at all. If we'd raised too much of a stink, she'd have cut us off altogether, and then where would Brandon have been? So we watched him grow angrier by the year, our hearts breakin' for him."

Sitting on her heels, Alyson watched emotion deepen the lines on his face. Gradually he relaxed. His breathing eased. His color returned to normal. When he spoke again, the feistiness was back, as was the twinkle in his eye, though he wouldn't look at her directly, as if embarrassed that he'd confided such personal matters to a virtual stranger.

"Maybe this book will be good for him, now that I think about it." Henry's gaze skipped to her briefly before focusing again on the fire. "Maybe you'll be good for him, Al. He's had no social life since he's been home. Hibernatin' with a couple of sick old folks isn't good for a man his age. He needs a life. He needs a friend. He used to have a lot of friends, before the Marcella thing."

He sank deeper into the chair. "Something just wasn't right about that accident. Just didn't make sense."

Alyson glanced toward the door, where the rain continued to slash against the panes. Opportunity screamed at her. Obviously Henry needed to confide. Her reporter's instinct wanted to dash for the recorder in her camera bag and get every relevant tidbit on tape. A thousand questions burned the tip of her tongue, but Carlyle had warned her. If he were to walk in now and see her with Henry, he'd throw another of his infamous Carlyle fits. He'd personally repack her bags and punt her all the way back to San Francisco, where she'd spend the rest of her life interviewing women who claimed their children were sired by Elvis.

"I'm a good listener," she heard herself encourage him. Standing, she walked to the fire and stared into it, her hands planted on her hips, her heartbeat pumping in her ears. Guilt rapped at her conscience.

She tried to recall the facts of the incident. At the time of Emerald Marcella's death, she'd been bogged down in her own personal tragedy—divorcing a man who'd burned up her savings on self-promotion and wining and dining his bevy of starlet lovers.

According to Carlyle, he and Marcella left a party, where they had met for the first time. He'd been drinking, his blood alcohol level above the legal limit at the time of the crash . . . barely.

They drove to a secluded area. Marcella, who'd been drinking and snorting, got kinky and abusive, and Carlyle didn't like it. They argued, and he decided to take her back to the party. The weather turned bad, and so did Marcella— coke and booze made her crazy. She jumped him while he was driving, which caused him to lose control of his Ferrari. Some time later, he was found beside the road, unconscious. Brandon knew nothing until he woke up in a hospital with no memory of anything beyond his car spinning like a top on the wet road.

"The entire rape issue was beyond idiotic," Henry said in a weary voice. "Hell, the man's had to fight women off since his voice changed. Why the devil would he try to do it with a porn queen if she didn't want it?"

"He admitted they'd had rough sex," she pointed out, still staring into the fire.

"Consensual, Al. And she was the one who instigated the rough stuff. When it got out of hand, he stopped it, which is what pissed her off." Henry shook his head. "That damned district attorney wanted blood. He thought he had himself another Simpson case. Brandon's defense was if the car goin' through that guardrail was premeditated to shut her up about a supposed rape, wouldn't he have made damn sure the woman was dressed before doing it? Hell, she had on panties and a blouse. Regardless that the D.A.'s case was damn weak, the grand jury gave the nod to indict—the D.A. knew well enough that his case for murder wasn't strong enough, so he went the manslaughter route.

"Bernie and I wanted him to fight it. But he didn't. Although he didn't come right out and admit it, I think he decided to plead because he wanted to save us the heartbreak of a trial. And if there's one thing Brandon'll do without fail, it's accept responsibility for his actions. He don't make any excuses, Al. In his mind, he'd been drinkin' and shouldn't have been behind the wheel of a car. A woman was dead. He couldn't prove that Marcella caused the accident any more than he could explain how the hell he got out of that car before it went over the cliff."

"He could have been thrown from the car—"

"No way."

She looked at Henry.

"He had bruises across his chest and hips from the seat belt when the car hit the guardrail, and there were considerable facial abrasions from the air bag. Investigators said if he'd somehow been thrown from the car going at any rate of speed, there'd have been extensive injuries from his hitting the asphalt. There weren't."

"So somehow, between the time the car hit the guardrail and then went rolling end over end down that hundred-foot embankment, Brandon got himself out of his seat belt, and out of the car, all of this with extensive injuries. That's impossible, Henry."

Lowering his eyes, Henry ran one hand over his mouth, and said in a voice barely above a whisper, "Impossible."

Brandon slumped in a chair near the fire, his legs stretched out, socked feet propped on the hearth, one hand wrapped around a mug of hot chocolate as he watched Alyson sleep. He felt hot with fever. His throat hurt like hell. He wanted to climb into bed . . . and take her with him.

He'd come to that aggravating realization at approximately one that morning, somewhere in the dark on a back road between Highway 59 and home, thunder rumbling overhead and rain pounding his shoulders. The taste and smell of her wouldn't leave him alone. The angrier he'd become, the more he wanted her. He'd hurt with wanting her.

Maybe next time he'd kiss her with tenderness. And maybe not. He hadn't so much as touched a woman in four years before last night, so she was lucky to have gotten off with nothing more than a kiss that was—how had she phrased it?—rough enough to remove vinyl from siding. Hell, he'd endured an hour of Charlotte Minger's all but raping him. He could still feel the heat and dampness between her legs burning into his crotch as she straddled him. So maybe he wasn't Don Juan when he kissed Alyson.

Maybe you're losing your touch, lover boy.

He should choke her for leaving him on the side of the highway in the dark. For invading his privacy. For stirring up a hornet's nest of lust that even now made him feel borderline psychotic. He wanted to stretch her out on his uncle's sofa, rip the clothes off her, and bury himself inside her, make love to her luscious mouth, and look into her incredible eyes as she squirmed and bucked beneath him and screamed in pleasure. She would, too. Scream in pleasure. Love him hard. He knew a hot number when he saw one; there was enough smolder behind those sultry eyes, he suspected, that she'd combust the first time he slid his tongue inside her.

Oh, yes, she was going to enjoy it . . . and so was he.

She stirred and opened drowsy eyes; her face was painted gold by the firelight. She raised her head and swung her gaze around to his. She grinned as she ran one hand back through her hair.

"Hi," she said sleepily.

"Hi."

"Guess I fell asleep."

"Soundly."

Sitting up, she knuckled one eye and yawned. "Gosh."

"Gosh what?" He sipped his chocolate, watching her over the rim of his cup. The ache was returning, clenching in his groin, again sending hot shivers to his brain. Apparently barn chores and slugging a hay bale with his fists for over half an hour hadn't remedied them.

"How long have I been asleep?"

"An hour."

Frowning, she regarded him intently. "You sound awful. Are you sick?"

"Getting there." He drank again, the heat intensifying.

She stretched her legs, pointing her toes, bowing her back, thrusting her breasts forward so the jersey molded against them. The shirt had worked up around her waist, exposing a line of skin that looked creamy, soft, yet firm. Tossing aside the blanket, she stood, scratched her head, and started toward the door. "I'll get my equipment and we'll get started. I hope you're not recorder phobic. Are you?"

"No." He watched her butt as she left the room.

In a moment she came back, dropped onto the sofa, and began to extract the camera from the bag.

"No photographs."

She stared at him with annoyance. "We need photographs."

"No."

Alyson shoved the camera back into the bag, then withdrew the recorder, which she placed on the end table. Next came a spiral notebook and a pen. Once settled comfortably, she pointed the recorder toward him, punched buttons. She sat back, yawned again, and said, "We record everything that's discussed between us. I'll supply you with a copy for your records. Agreed?"

He focused on the small machine. "Agreed."

"I've made some notes here; an outline to follow, mostly addressing the issues mentioned in the biography—which your uncle knows about, by the way." She smiled as he frowned. "You don't give him enough credit. He knows it's all a lot of bunk.

"Let's discuss the years you worked on *Those Foster Kids*."

"No."

She raised her eyebrows, shrugged, then looked again at her notes. "Okay, we'll come back to that later. Let's address the comments your mother made regarding your relationship—"

"No."

"Then what about the incident with Emerald Marcella?"

"Forget it."

Biting her lower lip in an obvious attempt to control her mounting irritation, Alyson tapped the notebook with her pen before bringing her gaze back to his. "Fine. You tell me where you want to start."

He narrowed his eyes and curled his mouth. "We'll discuss my sex life."

Not so much as blinking, the woman fixed him with a look that was totally blank. But her body language screamed something different. She sat on the sofa edge as if she were preparing for a hundred-yard sprint. Finally, she took a deep breath and sat back, smoothed the paper on her lap, and clicked her pen. "Okay, Carlyle. Ready when you are."

"I like sex. A lot. I think about the women I've made love to through the years, and of the women to whom I'd like to make love in the future."

"Care to elaborate?" She doodled on her notepad, swirls in dark red ink.

"I don't kiss and tell, Miz James."

"The biography claimed you're into kinky."

He laughed softly and reached for a cigarette in his pocket. "Define kinky."

"Threesomes. Bondage. Voyeurism." She licked her lips, drew a question mark and three exclamation points.

"I wouldn't exactly say I was 'into' threesomes, bondage, and voyeurism."

"Then you're guilty—"

"You make it sound like a crime." Flicking his lighter, he held it to the tip of the cigarette, and watched as she did her best to keep her expression as neutral as possible.

"You acknowledge that you've participated—"

"Yes." He took a drag on his cigarette and put the lighter aside. "I've been to bed with two women. Several times. Did I like myself in the morning? Not particularly, but I won't deny I enjoyed it. I had a girlfriend who demanded to be tied up when I made love to her. It wasn't my thing, it was hers. And as far as the voyeurism . . . I enjoy watching people make love. I don't hide behind walls and peek through keyholes. If I'm invited to watch, I watch. Hell, millions of people a year used to pay money to go to movies to see me lay women. The more raunch, the higher the ticket sales. I did a total frontal nude scene in *Hot Property*, and the movie was number one at the box office for five months, made billions worldwide. It was borderline X-rated because of the love scenes—so don't try and convince me people were interested in the acting or the plot. Let's face it, Miz James, sex sells."

She laughed nervously and averted her eyes. "Yes, but in the movies, you aren't really doing it."

He watched her through a thin curl of smoke. "Surely you're not that naive. Look at me, Alyson."

Slowly, very slowly, she raised her eyes to his.

"Have you seen my movies, Aly?"

She nodded.

"Did you enjoy watching me make love to those women?"

She nodded.

"Did it turn you on?"

She swallowed.

"Did it?" he repeated, his gaze never releasing hers.

She nodded, her lips parting.

"Then I guess that makes you a voyeur, too, doesn't it?"

No response. She just continued staring into his eyes as if hypnotized, her face flushed with color.

"I enjoy oral sex. Getting it, and giving it. I enjoy watching a woman masturbate. I love seeing a beautiful woman in the throes of excitement and ecstasy. A woman's face as she's experiencing orgasm is the most fulfilling part of sex for me. She's vulnerable. Oblivious. In those few seconds I could do anything to her I wanted, and she'd be helpless to stop me."

He inhaled again, then tapped the ashes into a bowl on the table by his chair. His eyes continued to hold hers. He could hear her breathing.

"I like rough sex to a point. I'm not into pain. I'm into passion. I don't normally go to bed with women I don't know, although doing so allows one a certain freedom, I suppose. There's no need to pretend it actually means something other than what it is. You don't wake up in the morning worried that while in the throes of ecstasy you've made promises you don't intend to keep.

"I pride myself on being an excellent lover. I'm good for four, maybe five times a night if I haven't been drinking. I can go as long as my partner needs me to. Some women want it hard and fast. Others take time. I enjoy foreplay. I'm good at it. I'm also a tease. I can do things with my fingers and tongue that will make you delirious." He blew out a stream of smoke that clouded between them. "So tell me, Aly. What do you like?"

The clock on the mantel ticked loudly, suddenly, in the silent room. He crushed out his cigarette and waited.

Finally, as the flush on her face intensified, she replied in a tight voice that quivered slightly with emotion, "This interview isn't about me, Carlyle." She flung the notebook aside and left the sofa, advanced on him, eyes glassy and teeth clenched. Leaning over him, hands braced on the chair arms and her nose nearly touching his, she said, "You're bullying me again. So you can just knock it off. You don't intimidate me in the least, and I find your blatant attempt to embarrass me infuriating and offensive."

"Yeah?" Sliding his thumb over her lower lip, he said softly, "Sweetheart, if I so much as tongued you once, you'd come."

Her eyes widened. She slapped his face—hard.

He grabbed her wrist and twisted, throwing her down across his lap, took her face in his hand. Their gazes locked, hers snapping with surprise and anger, challenging him. The ache between his legs became excruciating, her weight in his lap a catalyst to the hunger that had maddened him since the instant the day before when he'd discovered the body squirming under his wasn't male, since the moment he'd buried his hands in her red thong panties that even now were burning a hole in his pocket.

"Excuse me . . . Mr. Brandon?"

The words came to him through a fog of lust so thick he couldn't breathe.

Alyson shoved his hands away and rolled off his lap, retreated to the sofa.

He redirected his focus on Betty, who stood at the door, her expression frozen in surprise, her posture rigid as a robot's. "What?" he snapped, his face burning like hot needles where Alyson had slapped him.

"I'm terribly sorry to interrupt." She pursed her lips briefly. "There's a Deputy Greene from the sheriff's office here to speak with you . . . about Miss Minger. I'm afraid something tragic has happened."

9

Deputy Tommy Greene wore a slicker over his beige uniform, galoshes that he wiped carefully before entering the Carlyle house, and a cowboy hat with a plastic cover. He studied the spiral notebook in his hand as if mentally rehearsing the questions he was forced to direct to Brandon. He licked his lips and cleared his throat before forcing a smile. Henry continued to stare into his coffee cup, Betty hovering at his side. Alyson loitered in the background with her arms crossed over her chest. Part of her wanted to bury herself back in the den, away from the tension mounting in the room, away from the vision of Brandon Carlyle's white face and shocked expression.

"Mr. Carlyle, I'm one of your biggest fans. I guess I've seen every movie you've made. And my wife—gosh, she thinks you're great. She was gonna name our firstborn after you if it was a boy. It was a girl, though." He cleared his throat again and shook his head. "I don't like havin' to come out here like this. I know how you like your privacy and all, and wouldn't have disturbed you this early but, well. . . ."

"Would you like a glass of water, Deputy Greene?" Betty partially filled a glass with water from the tap and handed it to him, smiling sympathetically. "Or would you care for coffee?"

"No, ma'am." He gulped down the water and handed her the glass. He studied his notebook before focusing on Brandon, who stood in the center of the kitchen, his hands on his hips, looking as if he'd just been informed he had five minutes to live. "At approximately six-fifteen this morning Jim Benton drove out to the quarry to check his trotlines. There he found Charlotte Minger, severely beaten and unconscious. She was transported to Tyler General Emergency and is in critical condition at this time. Sir, it's been reported to us that you were with Miss Minger at the quarry last night. Is that true?"

He nodded.

"Why?"

"She picked me up here at eight o'clock. It was my understanding we were to grab a burger at the Dairy Queen. Instead, she drove me to the quarry for a picnic."

"And what transpired there, sir?"

He shrugged. "Nothing."

"Nothing, sir?"

He shook his head. "I didn't stay at the quarry longer than maybe forty-five minutes—an hour at the most."

"How did you leave—"

"With me," Alyson declared.

Deputy Greene's gaze sharpened as he assessed her. "Who're you?"

"Alyson James. From San Francisco. I'm in town on business with Carlyle."

"Why were you at the quarry, Miss James?"

"To get him." She pointed to Brandon, who didn't look at her.

"Because . . . ?"

What was she supposed to say? The truth? That Brandon had naively believed Charlotte when she told him she was twenty; that Alyson had driven to the quarry to stop him from making one of the biggest mistakes of his life—or, rather, another one? Or that Dillman had used Charlotte to set up Carlyle in hopes of sending him back to prison? It all sounded far-fetched, even to her.

"There were others there as well," she said, avoiding the question. "A truck full of carnies. They were drinking and didn't hang around long. Then there was Sheriff Dillman."

The deputy's brows drew together. "Why was Sheriff Dillman there?"

"I shouldn't speculate as to Dillman's motives, Deputy."

Deputy Greene jotted notes before focusing again on Brandon. "Did you return home immediately, sir?"

Brandon looked at Henry, whose face was pale, his expression, concerned. Henry turned away to refill his cup with fresh coffee.

Something like dread seeped through Alyson, and fear, as the realization closed around her throat that Carlyle had no alibi from the moment she had driven away and left him standing beside the highway. How had he gotten home? And when? She thought of herself sitting in her car at the entry to the quarry, engine idling, speculating on Carlyle's having returned to catch a ride with Charlotte—had convinced herself that he wouldn't be that stupid, not a second time.

"I didn't bring him home," she heard herself explain as her face warmed and her heartbeat quickened. This time Brandon's head slowly turned, and he skewered her with his eyes. "He stayed with me," she lied. "At the motel."

Oh, my God! What had she done? She could hear Alan yelling in her mind: *Are you crazy, A. J.? What the hell were you thinking? I'll send you a care package while you're spending five to seven in San Quentin for aiding and abetting.*

If Deputy Greene doubted her, he didn't show it, just scrawled on the notepad, flipped it closed, and tucked it into his pocket. He smiled his apologies. "With any luck the victim will regain consciousness soon. Hopefully she'll be able to give us a description, if not the identity, of her attacker.

We have a crime unit on the scene now, working the area for evidence. The perpetrator had a hell of a grudge against Miss Minger. He scrawled a note on the windshield with her lipstick, *Back off, Bitch*, then used the same lipstick to paint teardrops on her cheeks. Damn creepy." He smiled toward Henry and Betty. "Sorry to trouble you folks."

"Not at all," Betty said. "I'll show you out, Deputy."

As Betty and Deputy Greene left the room, Henry looked at Alyson and pointed to the chair she had occupied at breakfast. Then he turned on Brandon, and said in a stern voice, "Sit your tail down, boy."

"Henry," Brandon began.

"Shut up and sit."

They sat. Alyson felt that any moment Henry would throw a switch and send several thousand volts through her for lying. Brandon slouched in his chair like a recalcitrant juvenile who'd been caught smoking behind the barn.

Henry walked to the door through which Betty and Deputy Greene had left the kitchen, waited until Betty closed the front door behind the officer, then turned on Brandon. Pointing one finger at Alyson, he said, "Did you spend the entire night with this woman, Brandon?"

"No, sir." Brandon flashed Alyson a look. "Apparently I was an ass to Miz James and she dumped me out on 59. I walked home."

Henry's eyebrows raised. "You walked? From the quarry?"

Brandon nodded.

"What was Al doing there in the first place?"

"Saving my neck. Seems Betty was right about Miss Yamboree. She's one week shy of being legal."

"So you have no alibi once Al deposited you on the highway. Did you go back to the quarry, Brandon? You look me right in the eye, boy, and tell me the truth."

"Come on, Henry. I don't beat up little girls."

"You didn't think she was such a little girl when you left here with her, did you? God almighty, Brandon, you didn't fool with her, did you?"

"No." He shook his head. "Henry, I told you; I walked home. I took the back road, the one I used to bike on when I rode to the quarry to swim. I can't believe we're having this conversation. I can't believe you'd question me about this."

Henry dropped into his chair and wiped the sweat from his brow. Brandon stood and moved around the table, stooped beside his uncle, took Henry's hand and held it. "Don't do this, Henry, get yourself worked up over nothing—"

"Nothing!" Henry's voice cracked, and he turned his face away, refusing to look at Brandon. "If you're sent back to prison, it'll kill me. You're all I've got, you and Bernie . . . I won't have her for much longer. If I lose you, too, it'll be the end of me. I wouldn't want to go on."

As the sound of rain filled up the silence, the image of Carlyle on one knee, holding the old man's hand, rattled Alyson, made her feel alien again. She wanted to go to her knees beside Brandon and comfort Henry, too. He'd welcomed her into his home and his confidence like a long-lost member of his family, a family that was eroding around him. His love for Brandon showed in every seam of his face, as did his fear of losing him; suddenly she didn't care that she'd lied to Deputy Greene if it meant Brandon wouldn't be hauled off to jail again, breaking Henry's heart.

She returned to the den and collected her recorder and notes, mentally reminding herself that her reasons for coming to Ticky Creek did not include becoming emotionally involved with an infuriating bad boy with a kiss that could melt iron and an old man who epitomized the ideal parent.

"Miss James."

Alyson turned.

Betty stood near, her eyes friendly for a change, and a faint smile on her lips. "That was a very brave thing you did for Mr. Brandon, although not very wise."

"You can say that again." She slid the camera strap over her shoulder.

"I'm certain Henry and Brandon will be indebted to you."

"That's not necessary, Betty. Brandon wouldn't be in this pickle if I hadn't driven off and left him by the highway. It's the least I can do."

Betty regarded her closely. "I couldn't help but notice earlier, when Deputy Greene arrived . . . and I found the two of you. . . ." Her voice dropped off, and she averted her eyes.

Alyson tried not to think about what might have happened if Betty hadn't made her entrance when she had. Carlyle had been on the verge of either breaking her neck for slapping him . . . or something else altogether. The something else would have been more likely, because his assessment of her heightened sexual state had been right on the money.

"It was nothing, Betty. There's a power struggle going on between us. Carlyle is accustomed to getting his way with women, and I'm not . . . interested."

Betty's eyebrows raised. "That'll be a first. He came to Ticky Creek to get away from the bimbos who constantly made themselves . . . available, like that dreadful Marcella person. That Mr. Brandon has had to endure the shame of that catastrophe is a crime, but I suspect it taught him a valuable lesson. He'll be more discriminating about the company he keeps."

"I don't call Charlotte Minger discriminating, do you?"

Betty's smile widened. "Touché, Miss James."

The wind whipped rain through the pines as Brandon sat on the porch swing, smoking and shivering but unwilling to go inside and face the fear and disappointment on Henry's face. The front door opened and Alyson stepped out, burdened by purse and camera bag. She looked surprised to see him there, as if she were attempting to make a quick getaway before he noticed.

"Leaving so soon?" He gave her a cryptic smile.

"Henry's upset. I shouldn't be here now. Besides, I get the impression you aren't serious about this book. Unless you're ready to talk about something other than your five-star sex life, we're not going to get very far."

"In case you haven't noticed, sex is what I'm about." He shook his head and looked away. "It's all I'm good for, isn't it? All I've ever been good for. I won an Oscar for my acting in *Jericho*, yet all the producers, directors, and moviegoers are interested in is my bare ass and how many gratuitous sex scenes they can get for their money. Let's face it, I'm a piece of meat, Aly. I'm a commodity. Or was." He laughed and tapped the ashes off his cigarette. "I ceased being worth a plugged nickel the instant Emerald Marcella went through that guardrail."

She crossed the porch and sat down beside him, camera bag and purse on her lap. They swung back and forth while the swing chains creaked with their weight and thunder rumbled in the distance.

Brandon took a deep drag on his cigarette and thought of the panties in his pocket. Thought about how good Alyson had felt in his lap earlier. Thought about how badly he wanted to take her in his arms right now, not for sex but for human contact, just to feel another's arms around him, as if that would assure him that the Minger issue would disappear along with the fear of his being hauled back to California and buried in a prison cell.

"Henry's pissed," he said in a tight voice.

"He's afraid."

"Sometimes I get the impression that he isn't very confident of my innocence regarding the Marcella accident. Now this deal with Charlotte." He glanced at her. "You shouldn't have lied for me, Aly. The last thing I need on my conscience is for you to get involved in my problems. Maybe you should leave town, get out before this thing gets ugly."

"Is that what you really want? Do you want me to go away and leave you alone?"

He considered the question before looking into her eyes. "No," he replied, and shook his head.

"I can't float forever, waiting for you to make up your mind that you're going to cooperate on this project."

He swallowed and nodded in understanding. "It isn't easy.

It's not like I had a normal childhood. When I think about it, I get. . . ."

"Angry?"

"Angry is a gross understatement." He closed his eyes as the fury roused, as it always did if he so much as teased the recollections of his childhood. "I can't define what I feel when I visit those memories. I start unraveling, and get scared that I'm going to lose control and totally disintegrate."

"Maybe disintegrating would help. Get it out and over with."

"There wouldn't be enough left of me to put back together." He shrugged and tossed the butt of his cigarette into a puddle. "I have to think about Henry. His health isn't good. He beats himself up because he feels he could have done more to help me. That was impossible, of course. Cara wasn't about to let anything or anyone come between her and the lifestyle my success afforded her."

"She had her own career."

"What career? A lot of B movies, cheesy commercials, and on-again, off-again soap opera roles. Cara enjoyed Hollywood glitz and glitter, but the only way she was going to afford it was through me. Nothing was more important to Cara than power and money, and I was her source. She sold my soul to the devil more times than I care to remember."

"Maybe that's where we should start. The story, I mean. Discuss exactly how she used and abused you, and what price you paid to keep her pacified."

Brandon stared at the unlit cigarette between his fingers, then crushed it in his hand.

Jack Dillman watched Deputy Greene splash through rain puddles as he returned to his cruiser, then, as calmly as possible, considering his anger, closed the door and turned to find Mitsy plunked in his chair, skirt barely covering the tops of her thigh-high nylons. He'd been cleaning his gun before Tommy came beating on his door with news of Charlotte Minger's assault, followed by an interrogation regarding his motives for being out at the quarry last night.

Mitsy had Polaroid sunglasses on, a cigarette in one hand, a beer can in the other, and a shit-eating grin on her mouth. She was in her Marilyn Monroe mode, right down to her blond wig, push-up bra that made her tits look big enough to topple her over, and a mole near her mouth. Ten in the morning, and she looked like she'd just stepped out of *Some Like It Hot*.

"If I was you, I'd get the hell out of my sight, Mitsy. I ain't in the mood to look at you right now. It's too damn early to have to tolerate an idiot."

"You're just pissed 'cause you got caught doin' the dirty on Carlyle."

"I ain't done the dirty on nobody, and if I hear you say somethin' like that outside this house, I'm gonna make you regret it."

"No? Then what was you doin' out at the quarry last night?"

"You heard what I told Tommy."

"That you was on your way to the River Road Honky-Tonk after work and just decided to swing into the quarry to make sure there wasn't no nekkid teenagers doin' the hokey-pokey in the backseat of their daddies' cars. You're lyin, Jack. I can always tell when you lie. You know why? 'Cause your eyes go all squinty and your nose starts to sweat. It sweated big fat drops the whole time Tommy Greene was here."

"Well, ain't you a Miss Smarty Pants all of a sudden? Get out of my chair and sashay your butt into that kitchen and fry me some eggs, Smarty Pants."

"Fry your own damn eggs. Do I look like a wife to you?" She swigged her beer.

"You look like a nut." He grabbed her arm and hauled her out of the chair, nearly upsetting her crown of platinum curls. "This is my goddamn day off, and I intend to enjoy it without havin' to listen to you smart off. I said eggs. And biscuits, too. Not them shitty canned things. I want you to make 'em fresh. And while you're at it, fry me up some ham. I want red-eye gravy with them biscuits."

Mitsy rubbed her arm. "I ain't makin' you squat. If you want a slave then get married again—that is, if anybody'll have you."

He took a swing at her. She ducked and knocked over the table where the pieces of his Ragin' Bull were laid out, cleaned and well oiled. They hit the floor, sounding like a hod of tumbling bricks. "Goddammit!" he roared as Mitsy ran for the kitchen, wobbling on her high heels that were a size too large; she got them in a two-for-one deal at Shoe Saver, so it didn't matter. The silly bitch would buy used underwear from a whorehouse if she thought she could save a nickel.

"You want to tell me where you were at midnight last night?" he yelled over the sound of clattering pans. "The way you went at Carlyle at the Dime A Cup, I'm just liable to think you'd beat the shit out of Charlotte just on principle."

Mitsy appeared at the kitchen door, an iron skillet in one hand, her beer in the other. Her wig had slipped low on her forehead, so she was forced to stare at him through her coarse blond bangs and askew sunglasses. "I was fishin', if you want to know."

"Fishin'? Since when do you go fishin' at night?"

"I got a hankerin', okay? I took the boat up the creek and fished for crappie. You can ask Frank Fleming down at Wonder Worms Bait and Tackle. I bought three dozen minnows and a cooler of Budweiser. I loaded up with a couple pimento cheese sandwiches, some pork rinds, a kerosene lantern, and fished until the winds came up around one or so."

"Yeah? Then where's the fish?"

"I didn't catch none."

She turned back to the kitchen, and Jack shook his head. Son of a bitch Carlyle'd been a thorn in his side since they were kids. Ever' time Carlyle came back to Ticky Creek, the town acted like Jesus Christ Himself had floated down from Heaven. It was Carlyle this and Carlyle that. Carlyle with his mug a gazillion times on *People* magazine. Carlyle winning a stupid Oscar. Let Carlyle come to town back in their high school days, and Jack might as well kiss his chances of getting laid after the football game good-bye, because all the decent-looking bitches were wagging their butts at Carlyle. Hell, Jack had thrown a Hail Mary pass for a touchdown during the Homecoming game, securing divisional first place, and nobody was paying attention 'cause Carlyle was in the stands, signing autographs and having his picture made with the pom-pom queen, Geena Beckett. Jack had stood a good chance of becoming her hero after that freaking touchdown— and, as usual, Carlyle had ruined it. Hell, Geena had been the only decent girl he'd ever stood a chance with—his heart still ached with the disappointment when he allowed himself to think about it . . . which was ever' time Mr. Hollywood came to town. After his football-ending injury, Geena wouldn't so much as give him the time of day.

Then there was the issue of Carlyle's knocking Mitsy up and the abortion that left her plumbing screwed. Jack considered the botched abortion had been a miracle, not a tragedy. Mitsy was crazy as a rabid coon, and had no business with kids. They'd have had the IQ of Silly Putty and the disposition of Cujo. It was the principle of the thing that made Jack's brain buzz like a hornet ever' time he heard Carlyle's name. If Jack hadn't ruptured his back in the final football game of his senior year, he'd have gone on to college ball, and from there maybe even had a chance at pro ball. He might have become another Joe Montana or Troy Aikman. Then the Ticky Creek bitches wouldn't be so quick to ignore Jack Dillman when Carlyle strutted into town.

Jack collected his gun pieces from the floor, dropped into his chair, and carefully reassembled the weapon. The Taurus Model 444 Ragin' Bull .44 magnum was a five-pound monster with an eight-and-three-eighths-inch barrel, a six-bullet cylinder, blued finish, and a 1.5-4X Burris EER scope sight that could magnify the nose hair of a field mouse to the size of an elephant. Jack's penis got hard as he stroked the weapon, then he raised the Bull, aimed it at the framed painting of a matador on black velvet, looked through the scope, and imagined the face on the painting was Carlyle's.

Leave it to Charlotte Minger to screw up ever'thing. If the bitch regained consciousness and revealed he had coerced her into doing a number on Carlyle, his job was toast. Then again, if that James bitch hadn't butted in when she had, Carlyle'd be waking up in a jail cell this morning.

The happiest day of Jack's life had been the morning he'd flipped on *Good Morning America* to discover Carlyle's life and career had just gone up in smoke because some porn whore had died in a car crash. He'd jigged in glee when the District Attorney announced he'd pursue criminal charges against America's dream boat. He'd howled with laughter while Court TV broadcast Carlyle's image in a courtroom, his head bowed as he pled guilty to manslaughter charges in an emotion-choked voice. He'd wanted to shake his fist in the face of every Ticky Creek resident who'd ever put Mr. Hollywood on a pedestal. Surely folks would see that Brandon Carlyle was nothin' more than a too-big-for-his-britches fraud whose country boy charm and manners were just another Oscar-caliber act.

No such luck. After the initial shock wore off, the townspeople had actually rallied to form a support group. They'd sent him enough mail while he was in prison to pave the highways from Texas to California.

"You gonna shoot somethin' with that cannon or make love to it?"

Jack looked up at Mitsy, who stood by his chair, a soiled apron tied around her waist, her hands white with flour. He swung the barrel her way and, pointing it at her face, said, "Bang."

"Your nose is sweatin' again," she said. "I wonder why."

"What's that supposed to mean?"

"Maybe you was the one who beat the hell out of Charlotte. That's what I mean. Maybe you wanted to shut her up about somethin'. Or better yet, maybe you figured you'd implicate Carlyle and get his tush sent back to prison."

"Think again. The son of a bitch left the quarry with that California bimbo. He has an alibi."

"You gonna deny you wanna get rid of Carlyle?"

"Hell, no, I don't deny it."

"Why don't you just call up the *National Enquirer* and blab that he's here in Ticky Creek? Once word hits the press, this town'd be overrun with reporters and fans. He'd get out of town so fast, his leavin' would cause a sonic boom."

"I don't want no strangers in this town causin' havoc."

"You're afraid somebody'll find out that Ticky Creek's sheriff is about as worthless as spit. Or maybe you're afraid that if somebody got wind of your blowin' the whistle on Carlyle, you'd be workin' crossin' guard duty at James Bowie Elementary School for the rest of your redneck life."

"You're startin' to piss me off, sister." He put aside the gun, stood, and thrust a finger at her. "Let this be a warnin' to you. If you got some cockamamie idea of callin' up the tabloids about Carlyle, thinkin' to grab yourself a little publicity cuz you think you're reincarnated Marilyn Monroe, think again. I'll institute your ass in the Terrell loony bin so fast, you won't know what end's up."

She backed away, her eyes widening as he glared at her, his teeth showing behind his ratty mustache, and his nose sweating. "God," she muttered. "Chill. I ain't about to call no tabloids, Jack. I want Carlyle exactly where he is for the time bein'. I've got plans for the bastard."

"Yeah? Well, I don't wanna know about it." He shoved her aside and started toward the kitchen.

"Well, you're gonna know about it," she yelled after him. "The whole goddamn world is gonna know about it by the time I'm done."

10

"It's been days. I haven't heard a word from him. He said he'd call when he was ready to discuss the book further, but so far, nothing." Alyson looked out the motel window. Thank God the rain had finally stopped. The dreariness remained, however. The low gray clouds turned the afternoon dark as dusk—like her mood. Ticky Creek and room number ten, Pine Lodge Motel, were beginning to feel claustrophobic. "I drove into Tyler and bought a VCR, and found a Video Classics store at the mall that had an entire collection of Carlyle's works, including the complete *Foster Kids* series." She picked up a videotape box and grinned at the image of a cheeky eight-year-old with a twinkle still in his eye. "Wow. Was he precocious or what? Eight years old, and he makes my stomach do flip-flops."

"He must be doing more than making your stomach flip-flop if you were stupid enough to lie to an officer about his alibi. A. J., what am I going to do with you?"

"Alan, you're right. I'm too stupid to live. But so was he,

for going out with Charlotte in the first place." She punched
the VCR remote, kicking on a tape that filled the screen with
the muted image of Brandon, not as an eight-year-old but as
a naked Army captain putting it to a general's wife while the
wife-negligent general ate eggs Benedict in the next room.
She sat down on the bed, her mouth going dry and her body
warming. His naked buttocks pumped like a machine between the actress's spread legs. Every well-defined muscle
in his back strained and flexed. His lover twisted her hands
into the sheets, her eyes glazing and her mouth falling open
in a silent scream.

Yes, but in the movies you're not really doing it.

Surely you're not that naive.

"A. J., the man is a magnet for trouble. Stay away from
him. Pack your bags and come home. Besides, what makes
you think he didn't walk back to the quarry and do a number
on the Minger girl? I can quote you a textbook full of cases
where men with a mother hatred take out their anger on
women."

She hit the Off button, stared at the blank screen while the
heat between her legs began a slow throb.

I guess that makes you a voyeur too, doesn't it?

"I don't think so," she finally replied, stretching out on the
bed. She tried to rid her mind of Carlyle's image, naked and
thrusting, driving the actress mindless.

*I love seeing a beautiful woman in the throes of excitement
and ecstasy. A woman's face as she's experiencing orgasm
is the most fulfilling part of sex for me. She's vulnerable.
Oblivious. In those few seconds I could do anything to her I
wanted, and she'd be helpless to stop me.*

"Alan, regardless of the stories we've read about his temper, he's not a loose cannon. He doesn't just explode. I've
seen him pushed. While he might stand up to it, he doesn't
push back on a whim. I think it'd take a lot more than some
horny teenager to push him beyond his ability to contain his
anger. He strikes me as the kind of person who doesn't get
hostile unless he's backed against a wall."

"But you've never seen him angry, A. J."

"I've seen him frightened. Shocked. Severely miffed. Distraught over the welfare of his uncle. So gentle and loving to his invalid aunt that I felt like crying. But you're right. I haven't seen him really angry."

"And you won't until it's too late. Guys like that spontaneously combust. You won't see it coming."

"He didn't spontaneously combust when Emerald Marcella angered him. Or when Charlotte Minger tried to seduce him. Driving his car through a guardrail in order to murder Marcella, and returning to the quarry to beat up Charlotte would indicate premeditation."

"Are you losing your objectivity? Because if you are, I'm coming down there and drag your butt home. Hey, the D.A. knew he had a weak case, which is why he went the manslaughter route. Carlyle pled guilty."

"How did he get out of the car before it went through the guardrail, Alan?"

"This conversation is giving me a headache. Look, you went to Ticky Creek to get a story on what has become of Brandon Carlyle since he left prison. You got it. So come home."

"I came to Ticky Creek for more than that. I want an inside peek at the real Carlyle, not just what we've fed the public and what's been fed to us by the media. I'm dancing on the edge of something here. He's close to opening up, Alan."

"He's close to getting in your panties, I think."

She pointed the remote at the television and clicked. Carlyle rolled from the bed and walked toward the camera. She hit the pause button, freeze-framing the image. The heat returned, making her skin sweat and the air too thick to breathe.

"What's the difference between perversion and voyeurism?" she asked.

"Nothing. Why, A. J.?"

"Because." She sighed. "I'm feeling a little perverted right now."

*   *   *

Dressed in starched bib overalls over a plaid flannel shirt, a red, sweat-stained Texaco cap on his head, Henry smiled down at his generous slice of coconut meringue pie. "I don't know why I haven't thought of this before. Hell, I can't stop in at the Dime A Cup and just smell the grease without Betty or Brandon finding out. If this pie tastes as good as it looks, I'm liable to become a frequent patron of the Pine Lodge Café. How's your chocolate pie, Al?"

Alyson licked her fork and closed her eyes. "Awesome. Rich as fudge. I give it five stars. Want a bite?" She shoved her plate toward Henry. He dipped his fork into the chocolate, then ate, his eyes slowly rolling back in his head as he savored it.

"There ought to be a law against something that sinfully delicious. Maybe when I finish my coconut, I'll have a piece of chocolate."

"I think if I let you get away with that sort of indulgence, Betty and Brandon would run me out of town on a rail. One piece only, Henry. You promised. There's enough cholesterol in that pie to clog up the entire New York City sewer system." Sitting back in her booth seat, Alyson smiled as Henry dug into his pie like an eager child. "I take it you don't get pie much at home."

"Are you kidding? You saw what Betty was feeding me for breakfast—fake stuff dressed up to taste like sausage and eggs. Once a week she lets me eat a fried meal. The rest of the time, it's baked this and broiled that. Even tried to feed me baked catfish." He pointed his fork at her. "I wouldn't eat it. God made catfish to be rolled in cornmeal and deep-fried with a side order of french fries and a dozen hush puppies."

"Do you take medication for your heart?" she asked.

"Nitro." He patted the pocket of his overalls. "In case I have a spell. Keep a bottle in my pocket, one on my bedside table, another in the glove compartment of my truck in case I forget to put them in my pocket. I don't forget, but it makes Brandon feel better." He chewed and watched her. "You haven't asked about him. I figured that'd be the first thing out of your mouth."

"I'm still trying to figure out why you've come to see me. I'm sure it wasn't simply to buy me a piece of pie and a cup of coffee."

"I've got good news, Al. Deputy Greene dropped by the house this afternoon. Charlotte got a brief look at her attacker. Bald guy. Stocky. Grabbed her from behind as she was getting in her car."

Alyson sank back in relief. "That's great news. Brandon must be hugely relieved."

"Brandon hasn't been up to feeling much of anything the last few days. Been sick in bed with a cold and sore throat. Betty's been clucking over him like a mother hen." He took a drink of his coffee and regarded her over his cup. "He'll want to see you. Soon, I suspect. Unfortunately we have a . . . situation that's kept him buried in his room as much as possible. His agent is in town. Mildred Feldman. Staying here at the Pine Lodge, I believe."

"Judging by your tone, you're not pleased."

"Woman's a snake. She and Brandon had a thing for a short while. Ever since she's acted like he owes her something."

"Why doesn't he fire her?"

"There's not a decent agent out there right now who'll give him the time of day. He may have pled guilty to manslaughter, but people remember that the damn District Attorney originally wanted to get him on murder, the idiot." He drank again, then set the cup aside. "Al, I believe this autobiography you want to help him write will remedy that. There's things I want people to know about him—good things. He anonymously financed the pediatric wing of the medical clinic out on Gunther Road. Before that, parents had to drive their kids to Tyler for decent doctor care. In memory of his father, he founded the John Carlyle Fund to help those who've been disabled on the job at the mill. Then there's the Little League ballpark. Kids were playing ball on what amounted to a cow pasture. Brandon bought land just outside of town and built an entire ballpark—even pays the utilities so the teams don't have to. And personally? I can't even begin to tell you what he's done for me and Bernie. Back when meat prices went to hell, I about lost the shirt off my back. I had to mortgage the farm to pay my creditors. Without my knowing, Brandon went in and wiped out my debts, got me my farm back. And as far as Bernie is concerned, anything that insurance don't cover, which is a hell of a lot, Brandon picks up. There wouldn't be no full-time nurse care if it was left up to the HMO. I got a fifty thousand-dollar van in the garage that he bought so I can transport Bernie around in her wheelchair. Now I ask you, does all that sound like a man who'd kill somebody?"

"It's impossible to help someone who's unwilling to help himself," she pointed out.

Henry nodded and refocused on his pie, his face darkening. His voice took on a rough tone. "When he was a kid, nine, ten years old, and he came home to visit, he'd sit on the front porch and cry. When Bernie or I'd try to get him to tell us what was wrong, he'd run away into the woods and stay there for hours." Putting down his fork and shoving his empty plate away, Henry turned his blue eyes to Alyson. "He still cries, Al. In his sleep. Sometimes it's all I can do not to go in his room and comfort him. But I figure he's a grown man now and won't appreciate my treating him like a kid. He'd be embarrassed. I don't think Brandon'll ever open up to me because he's trying to protect me. He needs a confidante he can trust. He likes you, Al. For the last days he's found every excuse under the sun to bring up your name. He's starting to sound a little like a broken record, and a man with more than a casual interest in a woman."

She looked away. Her face warmed and her heartbeat accelerated as she perused the café: the silent jukebox against the far wall, the half-dozen empty tables decorated with vases of red plastic roses. She thought, *Don't Henry. Don't plant that seed*. If he did, she might not be able to deny the niggling emotions that had bothered her the last days and nights as she hovered near the phone, waiting for Brandon to call.

It was hard enough hearing Henry go on about trust and confidences . . . not to mention an autobiography that was no more than a figment of her imagination.

It was then she noticed the woman sitting alone at a table near the kitchen. Perhaps thirty. With hollow eyes and gaunt features. She stared at Alyson with an intensity that made her frown. Made a shiver run through her.

The front glass door opened. A woman walked in, dressed in a teal leather skirt and a cream silk blouse. Coal black hair framed a sharp-edged face that was beautiful enough to stop traffic. She stared at Alyson and Henry from behind the mirrored lenses of her sunglasses. Alyson knew instantly who she was. The chocolate pie in her stomach slowly turned over.

"Don't look now," she said, shifting her gaze back to Henry, "but I think your snake just slithered in."

Henry mumbled under his breath as Mildred crossed the room, the steel caps on her heels sounding like tap shoes on the tile floor. As a waitress hurried to greet her, Mildred waved her away.

"Henry, dear. Fancy meeting you here."

"Get tired of harassing Brandon so soon, Mildred, or did he finally throw you out on your keister?"

She gave him a flat smile. "How sweet, Henry. I can certainly see where Brandon gets his charm." Her head turned toward Alyson. "And you must be Alyson. James, is it? Our little stalkarazzi with a Nikon. Considering Brandon's immense dislike of anyone invading his privacy, I'm surprised there was enough left of you to haul into jail." She slid into the booth beside Henry and removed her glasses. Her eyes were hard and cold and black as charcoal. Her mouth was the same Passion Red as her long fake nails.

Alyson had seen a thousand just like her while married to Farrington: mean and hungry as a junkyard dog for power, money, and recognition. As she returned Mildred's direct stare, the desire to protect Carlyle roused in Alyson.

"I understand you're interested in helping Brandon write his autobiography," Mildred said. "Who's your agent?"

"I don't have one . . . yet."

"Who's your publisher?"

"Don't have one . . . yet."

Mildred raised one eyebrow, and all pretense of pleasantry disappeared from her voice. "Who do you work for?"

"I freelance."

"My dear, no one pays their bills by freelancing in publishing. Where do you live?"

"San Francisco."

Her eyes narrowed. "Sweetie, you could sell articles to *Reader's Digest* every day of the week and still not afford to live in San Francisco—unless, of course, you live under a bridge and eat scraps out of trash bins. You look healthy enough. So I'll ask you once again. Who do you work for?"

"That's enough," Henry declared, pointing a finger in Mildred's face. "Alyson doesn't owe you a detailed résumé of her work history."

Mildred rolled her eyes and sat back. "Sorry, Henry, but I have every right to protect my client's best interest."

"Since when have you had my nephew's best interest at heart, Mildred? The last job prospect you presented him was a hemorrhoid commercial."

"That's what he gets for making an ass out of himself."

"Brandon never made an ass out of himself. The media made an ass out of him. Other actors can throw hissy fits and we never hear a word about it. Let Brandon sneeze, and they hear about it in Mongolia."

"With one of the most recognizable names and faces in the world, he has an obligation to live up to his fans' ideals."

"Nobody can live up to everyone's ideals, Mildred. Not if they're human. Besides, there are individuals out there who want to rip an artist or his work apart because it makes them feel better about their own miserable lives."

As Henry's face turned red as the plastic roses, Alyson reached for his hand, which was clenched on the table. "Enough," she said sternly. "I'm sure Brandon appreciates your enthusiastic defense of his character, Henry, but not at the expense of your health. Take a deep breath and relax. Do you need a pill?"

He shook his head and looked away, attempting to control his anger. Alyson shifted her gaze to Mildred, who obviously didn't share Alyson's concern for Henry. Mildred's focus was still on her.

With her red mouth curled at one end, Mildred relaxed against the back of the booth and drummed the table with her fingernails. "Convince me that I should agree to this project. Why should I? You're a nobody, Miss James. Your name won't sell a solitary book."

"But Brandon's will," Henry said, his face growing redder. "This story is going to show Cara Carlyle for what she is. And isn't. And for your information, Mildred, we don't give a dizzy duck whether you agree to this project or not. You're not agenting this project. Keep your nose to your own business, and maybe Brandon won't fire you."

She laughed. "Brandon won't fire me, Henry. He's burned too many bridges. If he ever hopes to get a job in front of a camera again, he'll need an agent. We both know Brandon's made enough money to last him very comfortably through the next ten lifetimes, but we also know he's a workaholic. I'm sure he'd like nothing more than to be on location this very minute, spitting obscenities at the director and telling the producers exactly where they can cram their budgets."

Henry's face turned darker, and his voice began to shake. "Are you insinuating that he's unhappy living here with me and Bernie? That we're somehow cramping his style?"

Alyson slid from the booth and took hold of Henry's arm. "Time to go. Will you walk me to my room, Henry?" She tugged on him, bringing his attention reluctantly back to her. His face looked pinched, and he was sweating. She felt him trembling under her hand. "Time to go," she repeated, smiling as calmly as possible, considering her mounting concern. The color was leaving Henry's face. His eyes were glazed.

He stood unsteadily. She turned him toward the door, gave him a little nudge, and watched as he moved slowly across the room, his broad shoulders rounded and his heels dragging slightly.

Alyson dug into her pocket and withdrew a ten-dollar bill that she tossed on the table, then focused on Mildred. "I don't profess to know Brandon well, but I do know how he treasures Henry and Bernice. I suspect that if he knew you'd caused Henry distress in any way, there wouldn't be enough left of you to box up and ship back to Hollywood. Henry said you were a snake. Obviously, he overstated your character."

She ran after Henry, catching up to him outside the café. He leaned against his old pickup, his face colorless as he struggled to breathe. He clutched at his pocket. "My pills," he barely managed before sliding to the ground, landing hard on his backside, his legs outstretched and his hands falling helplessly at his side. Alyson dug in his pocket, extracted the medicine bottle, fought, cursing, with the cap while attempting to read the directions on the label. Her hands shook so badly that the words blurred.

Finally, she poured the pills into her hand, took one small pill from the heap, grabbed Henry's chin, and slid the pill under his tongue. "I'll call Brandon," she told him.

He shook his head and grabbed her hand. "I'll be fine in a minute. Don't want him bothered."

Taking his face between her hands, she shook her head and did her best to blink back the tears of worry and anger that burned her eyes. "Pay no attention to what Mildred said, Henry. Brandon adores you, and he's exactly where he wants and needs to be. You and Bernie are the most important treasures in his life. He's told me so."

His eyes closing, Henry rested his head back against the truck. Gradually, his color returned and his breathing evened. Sinking down beside him, limp as a rag doll as the fear and adrenaline subsided, Alyson buried her face in her hands and willed back the swell of emotion in her throat.

*   *   *

In the Pine Lodge parking lot Brandon sat in his car that purred like a contented cat. From the CD player Garth *Brooks* sang about wolves at his door while the darkening sky drizzled slow rain on the windshield. There was just enough light left for him to reread the letter in his hand—bold, angry print in red ink.

YOU'VE BEEN BAD BAD BAD. I WON'T TOLERATE THIS BEHAVIOR. YOU'VE SUFFERED ONCE FOR YOUR STUPIDITY. DON'T FORCE ME TO PUNISH YOU AGAIN. THE TIME IS COMING FOR US SOON VERY VERY SOON. NOW MORE THAN EVER IT SEEMS RICH TO DIE, TO CEASE UPON THE MIDNIGHT WITH NO PAIN. UNTIL THEN, I AM STILL . . . ANTICIPATING.

He hit the stereo Off button, then turned off the car ignition. Silence filled the Jaguar's interior as Brandon stared through the rain-speckled windshield at room number ten. Even before the arrival of the letter in the late afternoon mail, he'd been planning to come here. He'd rehearsed a thousand excuses; now he had a legit one. Going to the sheriff with the letter was a waste of time. Jack's own sister could be Anticipating. She could be sitting in her car watching him at that very moment. A shudder ran through him as he glanced in the rearview mirror, as if expecting to find the eyes of a lunatic staring back at him—like something out of *The Twilight Zone*—an entity that could materialize itself in glass.

No supernatural entity this, however. No figment of a horror writer's imagination. Anticipating was real, and somehow he had majorly pissed her off.

Tucking the letter into his shirt pocket, Brandon got out of the car and glanced around the parking lot, which was empty except for Alyson's car and a couple of trucks parked outside the café. Looking for what, he wondered. He could be looking Anticipating square in the eye and he wouldn't know it. She could have him focused in the crosshairs of a rifle scope, and what the hell could he do about it?

His hand dropped to the pager on his belt—a habit he had established over the last months. If there was trouble at the farm, Henry would alert him.

He knocked on the door and waited, listened to the television chatter from within. The television shut off, and her voice called out:

"Who is it?"

"Brandon."

Silence.

He grinned. "Come on, Aly, open up. The last thing I need is for someone to see me skulking around a tawdry motel. They'll think I'm into cheap hookers."

The door opened, slowly. She peered up at him with swollen, red-rimmed eyes. "So what else is new, Carlyle? According to the biography, you were Heidi's best customer."

"The key word here is 'cheap.' " He frowned, and said in a softer voice, "If you'll let me in, we'll discuss why you're crying."

"It's none of your business why I'm crying." She sniffed and propped her hands on her hips—a defiant stance that said, despite the tears, she wasn't a pushover when it came to sweet talk and charm.

"Okay, then I'll appeal to your guilt. If you let me in, I won't die of the pneumonia I nearly caught when you left me by the road in a thunderstorm." He shouldered the door open, forcing her to step back so he could enter. "FYI," he added as he spotted the partially packed suitcase on the bed, "I never bought a hooker in my life. Are you going someplace?"

She closed the door and leaned against it. "Home. And it wasn't raining when I left you. Not that it would have made any difference if it had been. You were being a jerk."

Sliding his hands into his pockets, he glanced around the shabby room. It smelled like sex. Hers, maybe. More likely the hundreds who came before her—cheating lovers who drove in from surrounding towns to scoot boots and binge-drink at the River Road Honky-Tonk before finding their way to the Pine Lodge. It sure as hell wasn't tourists that kept the place in business.

"Why are you leaving?" He turned his gaze back to her. Her hair was mussed, as if she'd been sleeping. She wore a mid-thigh green T-shirt that hung off one shoulder, and bright yellow kneesocks imprinted with tiny Bugs Bunnys. "Why?" he repeated, watching her mouth and trying to ignore the desire the sight of her always evoked in him. Bugs Bunny looked sexy as hell on her.

Averting her eyes, she shrugged. "Something happened today that made me realize this entire idea was stupid. I've got no business here, Carlyle. I'm losing my objectivity. I came here to do a job, and suddenly I can't . . . rationalize my reasons for doing it any longer."

"Think money." He smiled.

She didn't. "That just makes me another bone picker. I'm taking advantage of someone's misfortune to line my own pockets."

"There's a difference. I've invited you to pick my bones."

"Well, don't. I'm a hack, okay? Today I realized and accepted that you—your family—deserve better. Call Andrew Morton. You have my blessings." She moved to the bed and continued to shove jeans and T-shirts into the case. Brandon watched her, unsettled by the idea of her leaving. Sick and running a fever the last few days, he'd spent most of his miserable hours thinking about her—how good she'd tasted when he kissed her. How the compassion in her eyes made him want to confide. How the scent of her made him ache.

Christ, he ached. Badly.

"Aly." He reached for her.

She stepped away and shook her head. "Don't. Just don't. In fact, I want you to get out of here."

"What the hell are you afraid of?" he asked, angry with frustration. "Me? Do you think I'm going to do a Marcella number on you or something?"

"Brother, do I wish it were that simple." She tunneled her hands through her hair, sweeping it back from her pale and flawless face. "I wish you were the ass I expected when

I came to Ticky Creek. I didn't want vulnerability, Carlyle. I didn't want tenderness. I didn't want to see so much love in your eyes when you look at your family that I want to cry. I didn't need to know the sort of pain you feel over your mother's betrayal. And I sure as hell didn't want to know that you cry in your sleep at night."

His face turned hot. "You've been talking to Henry."

She nodded, refusing to look at him. "He came to see me today. Dammit." She kicked the nightstand by the bed, knocking the telephone receiver off the hook. The dial tone filled up the heavy silence.

Brandon stepped around her and hung up the phone. His face still burned, and he couldn't quite catch his breath. Because he was embarrassed that Henry had shared one of his most intimate secrets with a virtual stranger? Or because the smell and closeness of Alyson James's body was like slow torture to his senses, and had been since the instant he'd stepped into the room? Or, worse, because the thought of her walking out on him now seemed as bleak and unsettling as spending years in a prison cell?

"Why do you cry in your sleep?" she asked softly behind him.

He shrugged, but didn't look at her. "Hang around awhile longer, and you might find out."

"You think?"

Finally, he turned his eyes back to hers. "No promises. You'll have to take your chances."

She moved away, putting space between them. "Good news about Charlotte."

"Relieved that I'm not an assailant after all?"

"If I thought you were guilty of beating up a teenager, I wouldn't have offered you an alibi."

His eyes narrowed and his voice lowered. "By now everyone in town thinks you and I are sleeping together."

She backed against the dresser, sending a stack of video boxes tumbling to the floor, scattering around her feet. Images of himself stared up at him.

"Why are you here?" she asked, bending to collect the tapes and replace them on the dresser.

Ignoring the question, he picked up the remote from the bed, aimed it at the television, clicked, and watched as, naked and sweating, he made frantic love to a woman whose gasps and whimpers of ecstasy filled the sudden silence in the hot motel room. A grin curled his mouth as he shifted his gaze back to her red face, which had begun to shimmer with moisture and complete humiliation. Yet she didn't so much as blink, just raised one eyebrow and said, "Research."

"Research for what?"

"Your . . . growth as an actor."

"Sweetheart, acting isn't the 'growth' you're interested in here." He hit the Fast Forward, to the point he rolled out of bed and walked, stark naked, toward the camera. He hit the Pause button, freezing the image, his grin stretching. "If it's really research you're after, why sweat over a videotape when you've got the real thing right here? I'll be more than happy to oblige any way I can."

Irritation flashed in her eyes. "You're bullying me again."

"No, I'm not. I'm just wondering why you'll work yourself up over a stupid movie when I'm more than willing to give you the real thing."

Looking at her feet, she shook her head. "I'm not interested in you that way, Carlyle."

Tossing the remote onto the bed, he moved toward her. "You're lying, Aly. A man knows when a woman wants him. Right now you're aching so badly that I could breathe on you and you'd come."

"God." She moved away, toward the kitchenette, one long sock creeping down her leg to bunch around her ankle. "Do you always have to be so crude?"

"I'm not crude. I'm honest. Which is more than you're being with me and yourself right now."

"I'm trying to avoid complications, Carlyle. Mixing business and pleasure doesn't work."

"So we'll forget about the business aspect and focus totally on the pleasure."

Rolling her eyes and shaking her head, she continued to back toward the kitchenette, the other sock now halfway down her calf. "You're incorrigible."

"Thank you."

"And you're too damn used to getting your way with women."

He laughed and shrugged. "You're right. I can't recall a time since I was fourteen that I've had to pursue a woman."

"Yeah?" She backed against the kitchenette counter and stopped. "Is that when you lost your virginity?"

"That's when my mother invited a friend of hers into my bed to initiate me in the fine art of pleasing women. As I recall, the lady was forty-five, had memorized the *Kama Sutra*, was double-jointed, and could unhinge her lower jaw in a way that would make Linda Lovelace of *Deep Throat* envious."

Her eyes widened, and for an instant her nervousness was replaced by angry disbelief. "My God, that's horrible. How could a mother do such a thing?"

The memories tumbled in on him, suddenly, igniting the old fury and the almost suffocating desperation that made the walls close in. A long time had passed since he'd last visited that dark place of images that popped like flashbulbs before his mind's eye. What the hell was it about Alyson James that made him want to go there, to dig up the skeletons and rattle them before the entire world—no, not the entire world, just her?

He tried to swallow the tightness in his throat. Impossible. As impossible as willing back the rush of heat through his body that made him sweat as he heard himself explain. "I soon became the party favor. If there was anyone left standing after a night of boozing and snorting at my mother's drug and orgy fests, and the lady was still capable of clawing her way up the stairs to my bedroom, I was expected to amuse her. Of course, by then I was plastered myself, so any normal hesitance I might have had while sober was lost in a fog of Chivas."

Oh, my God, her lips formed silently, and for an instant she appeared to struggle not to reach out.

"I never knew whose face would be beside mine on the

pillow when I woke up in the morning. Sometimes there wasn't a face. Sometimes there was just money." Narrowing his eyes and curling his lips, he stepped closer. "Are you shocked yet, Aly? Are you taking notes? Will the readers who buy my autobiography throw the book in the trash because I've shocked their sensibilities? After all, everyone wants to believe in the fairy tale, don't they? My fairy tale was a little like Hansel and Gretel. Only forget Gretel. Hansel was kept captive in a pretty gingerbread mansion by a witch who threatened to eat him if he wasn't a good little boy."

He took a deep, steadying breath. His eyes held hers, which were wide and distressed and as red as when she first opened the door. "I didn't keep the money, of course. Hell, I was the highest-paid young actor in Hollywood. I flushed the money. Literally. Down the toilet. By the time I moved out of my mother's house at eighteen, there was probably enough money in the sewer system to pay off the United States debt."

Cupping her cheek, he gently stroked the corner of her mouth with his thumb. "So you see, Aly, I've known for a very long time exactly what I'm good for, and good at. What intrigues me is why you aren't interested."

For a moment she didn't reply, obviously too shocked to respond. Or perhaps she was simply disgusted. Her skin felt warm and moist against his palm, and smelled like the soap she'd bathed with earlier. He wanted to draw her close and hold her. Just hold her. Maybe then the memories would go back into the dark, closeted places in his mind and stay there until they could squirm their way back out into his dreams—when he was helpless to stop them.

Finally, with an effort, she stepped away, her voice thick when she spoke. "Believe it or not, Carlyle, I'm interested in what's in your head and heart, not what's in your pants. Besides, I don't care much for recreational sex. Call me old-fashioned, but I like to think I mean more to a man than a way to alleviate years of repressed sexual urges."

She sidestepped around him, leaving him staring down at the microwave oven.

"Let's try this again," came her unsteady voice as she

turned off the television. "Why are you here?"

With a sigh of resignation, he returned to the main room and sat on the bed by her suitcase. He pulled Anticipating's letter from his pocket. "This came this afternoon."

She took it and read it. Her brows drew together, and her gaze came back to his. "What's she talking about? What does she mean by *punishing again*?"

"Hell if I know."

Sitting beside him, she continued to read and reread the message. "She's very angry. Why?"

"Obviously I've done something to piss her off."

"Obviously she's watching every move you make."

He left the bed, walked to the window, and nudged aside the drawn curtain. The wet parking lot glistened under the burning streetlights. His car was the only one in sight.

"How long have you been getting letters from Anticipating? And have they always been so threatening?"

"Five, six years maybe. I got a great many letters, Aly, from different nuts. Most of them my employees screened. If the letters were too crazy, I'd hear about it. Advice mostly to watch my back. Eventually I was forced to hire bodyguards when I went out in public. Nothing ever happened. Then letters from Anticipating began coming directly to my house, sometimes with no postmark. At first they were never directly threatening or sexual. Just the typical *I love you, I love your work, blah blah*. Then it became apparent that she was watching me whenever I left the house. Annoying, but such is the life of a celebrity, right? We're going to be watched."

Returning to the bed, he sat beside Alyson again, his thigh pressing against hers, took the letter from her, and reread it before continuing. "Once I came home from a shoot in Wyoming—I'd been on location for six weeks—and discovered someone had been living in my house, sleeping in my bed. Personal belongings were missing: clothes, jewelry, photographs. I had a girlfriend at the time and kept her framed picture on my bedside table. The photograph had been destroyed and a note left on my pillow: *Leave her alone, if you know what's good for you.* The police dusted for prints, but there were only the prints of regular visitors that would naturally be found in my house. There was nothing the police could do unless she presented herself. Then I could have put a restraining order on her, for whatever good that does."

"Do you still have the letters?"

"Most of them. Once they became threatening, I decided to save them. I expected they'd stop when I went to prison. They didn't. I expected they'd stop when I came home to Ticky Creek. I've never, in any interview, mentioned Ticky Creek, so how the hell did she find me?"

"What about Cara? Perhaps something she's said—"

He shook his head. "Cara would never admit to coming from some small East Texas town, Aly. God forbid the world should know she was nothing more than poor white trash who didn't finish high school because she got pregnant. As far as the world knows, Cara was born and raised in Dallas."

Brandon folded the letter and returned it to his shirt pocket. "Henry doesn't know about this. He's not ever to know about it."

"What are you going to do now?"

"What can I do?" He grinned at her. "You ever eat anything besides Twinkies?"

"Occasionally." She grinned back.

"You like greasy hamburgers, cold beer, and loud music?"

"Are you asking me out on a date, Carlyle?"

"Nope. This is strictly business, Miz James. I'll even let you bring your recorder, as long as you keep it turned off and in your purse."

She chewed her lower lip in contemplation, an action that he had come to recognize as part shyness, part nervousness, thoroughly sensual, as was the way she looked up at him from under her lashes. Not for the first time he felt a surge of need rush through him, razor-sharp and painful, made all the more fierce by her earlier rejection. An ache deep inside pressed against his ribs as he waited for her response. Christ, he needed to be with her tonight.

Finally she shrugged and nodded, her sensual mouth curling up ever so slightly. "Why not?"

11

Alan Jackson's "Don't Rock the Jukebox" blasted from the
megaspeakers that hung from the old pine beams overhead;
each twang of the steel guitars and bump of the drums vibrated Alyson's inner ear. Communication with Carlyle was
next to impossible, but she got the impression that he hadn't
brought her here to communicate. What communication he'd
shared with her at the motel had come to a complete stop
the instant they'd settled into his Jaguar and headed down
Highway 59. She'd read about his love of fast, expensive
cars. Obviously his years spent in prison hadn't dampened
his enthusiasm.

Throughout the drive her mind had drifted to Anticipating's letter. What was it Alan had said about such letters?
Most of them were harmless, but a very small fraction were
not, and one of the first indications of big trouble was threats.

Occasionally she'd glanced toward Carlyle, doing her best
to ignore the sudden jump in her heartbeat and idiotic gid-
diness. Since her up close and personal nightmare of life and

marriage to a Romeo actor who thought he was God's gift
to women, she had believed she was immune to men like
Carlyle—all looks and no conscience, and no feelings in their
hearts for anyone but themselves. Then she'd reminded herself that Mother Teresa would have had a hard time looking
at the man and not appreciating him for what he was—even
now; no *Gentleman's Quarterly* model in a Versace suit tonight, but a pair of thin, faded jeans that accentuated his
privates, scuffed Roper boots, and a blue and green plaid
flannel shirt with sleeves rolled halfway to his elbows. He
might have been one of the good old boys down at Red Neck
Feed if not for the stainless steel Rolex on his left wrist and
the eighty-thousand-dollar machine wrapped around her. And
God Almighty, he smelled good. That, and the hint of rich
leather from the car seats, had made her dizzy and invited
video images of him buck naked with his tight butt driving
like a well-oiled piston between a woman's legs.

These last days, while waiting for his call, she'd fantasized
every time she hit the Rewind button on the VCR that the
woman spread across the red satin sheets was her. She'd
closed her eyes and imagined that the dirty words he whispered in the actress's ear, he was whispering to her. She'd
imagined the hand between her legs was his . . . and not hers.
Then she'd lain aching and throbbing with her legs wrapped
around a pillow and cried a little because she was falling for
him, just like the other hundred million women in the world
whose reality became confused by the fantasy that he could
somehow turn their staid and boring lives into a fairy tale
with one kiss of his sensual mouth. Damn it, she hadn't come
to Ticky Creek to get sucked into that delusional vortex of
fantasy.

Damn it, until Brandon showed up at her motel door tonight, she'd had every intention of leaving Ticky Creek at
first light because, once again, her conscience was getting in
the way of her goal—to get the scandalous goods on Carlyle
and beat it back to San Francisco; to break the gossip story
of the year so every respectable magazine on the planet
would scramble to hire her. Only now, she wasn't simply

dealing with guilt over deceiving Brandon, but over breaking an old man's heart that was already so crippled it could physically shatter with the least provocation. Dear God, she adored Henry Carlyle.

And what, she wondered, was she feeling for Brandon?

The River Road Honky-Tonk was twelve miles out of Ticky Creek, perched on a dogleg of the creek itself, raised high on piers in case the creek rose—which it inevitably did once a year, during spring rains, according to Brandon. The building was massive, built out of pine logs. The vast parking lot could accommodate five hundred cars and ten eighteen-wheelers.

Groups of mill workers, still wearing their sweat-stained khaki uniforms, clustered around the half dozen pool tables, and like jackdaws on a high wire, young men wearing too-tight Wranglers and oversized cowboy hats, elbows planted on the bar, perused every female in the joint with hungry, hunting eyes. Waitresses, trays balanced on their hands, hurried to refresh drinks and deliver plates heaped high with burgers and ribs—the River Road specialties.

Alyson tapped one foot in time to the music as a skinny waitress with orange hair in pigtails, and wearing a cowgirl waitress uniform—denim blouse emblazoned with lone stars over her breasts, a red handkerchief skirt, and boots that nearly reached her knobby knees, plunked a platter on the table in front of her. The Texas-shaped name tag pinned to her shirt declared: *Howdy, I'm Ruth.*

Ruth bent toward Alyson and shouted over the music, "There you go, hon. Hamburger nekkid and still mooin'. Mayo only. One cold long-neck Budweiser. I got it from back of the cooler, so it's a little frosty." She then gave Carlyle a platter heaped with barbecued brisket, potato salad, and a massive stack of battered onion rings. Then came a tall iced tea. Then a glass of Chivas.

Tucking the tray under one arm, she grinned at Carlyle. "You got this whole damn honky-tonk buzzin', Brandon. This the new girlfriend I've been hearin' so much about?" She turned her smile toward Alyson before waiting for Carlyle's response. " 'Bout time he got himself a girlfriend. Nice lookin' one, too. Welcome to Ticky Creek, hon. Name's Ruth Threadgill." She extended her hand to Alyson, her smile stretching as Alyson took it, thinking she should nip the rumor of her and Carlyle's relationship in the bud. So why didn't she?

Giving Brandon a sideways nod, Ruth said, "Course there's gonna be a lotta heartbroken women 'round here. Me included. But I'll say this, the two of you look damn good together. First time I've seen Mr. Hollywood smile since he come back to Ticky Creek. Clyde, he's the owner of this joint, says to tell you dessert is on the house. We got Mount Fudgiama tonight." She winked at Alyson. "Enjoy your meal." Turning on her boot heels, Ruth dissolved into the crowd.

Alyson studied the two-inch-thick meat patty on her plate before looking at Brandon. He regarded her with a half-grin on his lips. "Good thing I got it nekkid," she yelled. "I'd never get my mouth over it."

He said nothing, just continued to grin, his eyes holding hers.

She glanced at the glass of Chivas, then back at him. As she focused intently on his blue eyes, suddenly the din didn't seem so loud and his grin didn't reflect as much flirtation as it did strain. Forcing a lightness that she didn't feel into her voice, she joked, "You're not headed for another of your infamous Chivas fogs, are you?"

"Relax. I don't drink it. But I could if I wanted to. Not that I don't want to. I'm an alcoholic, and have been since I was thirteen. I'm going to want it for the rest of my life. But trying to ignore the need is harder than confronting it and conquering it. Every time I walk away from it, I feel a little stronger. Each time walking away gets a little easier."

She wondered just how easy the walking away had really become for him. She suspected it wasn't as easy as he pretended, even to himself. As he turned his attention to his food, his gaze slid frequently to the glass of Chivas. Occasionally, it drifted to her beer. More often, his gaze lifted toward the bar, where men sucked beer from frosty mugs or tossed back straight shots of tequila and lime. Neither did she miss the sheen of perspiration that came and went on his brow or the sudden trembling of his hand that forced him to put down his fork and concentrate on the couples line-dancing across the floor.

As she studied his profile, his earlier confessions came back to her. Thirteen and an alcoholic. Fourteen and a boy toy for his mother's friends. She got the gut feeling that there was more, so much more, darker and more disturbing lurking under the surface.

So much for fairy tales.

That old, annoying need to comfort and protect roused in her again, making her reach for her long-neck bottle and force her attention on the River Road patrons and not on Carlyle. But even as her gaze shifted from one face to the other, mounting suspicion scratched at her. Behind every glance and smile hid a possible threat—and if she sensed it, imagine what Carlyle must be feeling.

Yet, as the evening progressed, there was no doubt in Alyson's mind that Carlyle was much adored by the River Road regulars, who made their way over to chat with Carlyle and introduce themselves to her. The men flirted outrageously. The women smiled at her with a ghost of envy in their expressions. And as Alyson knocked back her third long-neck, she decided to relax and allow herself to go along with the crowd's assumption that she and Carlyle were an item. She began to feel a little like Cinderella at the ball, and her prince was, or had been, the most eligible and desirable bachelor in the world. Now, however, he didn't look much different from the good old boys with whom he played pool, arm wrestled, and exchanged bawdy jokes. They talked about guns and the local drag races, and debated over the best fishing holes. Occasionally, a woman would work up the courage to ask him to dance, careful first to ask Alyson if she "mind' to share her boyfriend for a spell."

Alyson, with one ear barely listening to the chatter around her, followed Carlyle with her eyes, watched the women's

faces as they danced, and wondered if her own face glowed
in such a way when he smiled at her. Maybe it was the
sensual backbeat of the music, or maybe it was the beer
sluicing through her system, but she was beginning to feel
as giddy as a groupie, and if she didn't knock off the Budweiser, she was liable to do something for which she'd hate
herself in the morning.

*"I'm just wondering why you'll work yourself up over a
stupid movie when I'm more than willing to give you the real
thing."*

Carlyle moved up behind her, slid one arm around her
waist, and eased his body against hers. He whispered in her
ear, "I think I've danced with every woman in this place but
you. People are gonna start thinking that maybe we're not as
hot together as they'd like us to be. How many more of those
beers am I gonna have to buy before you relax and let me
get to first base?"

As he nuzzled her neck, her eyes drifted closed and her
lips curled. "I guess that depends on what you're expecting
to find at first base."

"Hell, at this point I'll take what I can get."

"Carlyle, there isn't a woman in this joint who wouldn't
provide you with all the companionship you could handle
every night for the next century."

"I don't want them. I want you."

"Only because I'm a challenge."

"Because you're the most beautiful woman in this place.
Because your mouth makes me hurt like hell. And I like you.
A lot. I think you like me, too, Aly. You're just too damn
stubborn to admit it."

He turned her to face him, took the bottle from her hand,
and set it on the bar. "You gonna slap me again if I kiss
you?"

She tried to pull away. He clamped his arm more tightly
around her back and drew her close, against his body that
felt hard and hot, and smelled of arousing cologne and sweat.
Oh, but she wanted him to kiss her, right there in a crowded
room with several hundred pairs of eyes watching them, with

a sensual drumbeat in the background vibrating every nerve in her body and the heat of his gaze making her liquid inside.

He lowered his mouth to hers—lightly brushed her lips with his, testing more than tasting, then drew back, settled against the bar as his eyes held hers and his mouth curled in that way that made women the world over ache to hold him. Her heart swelled with the ache. Damn the music and damn the beer and damn his blue eyes that made her feel as if she were drowning.

"No slap yet," he said, his grin growing. "Guess I'm making progress."

"I figure I'm safe enough with two, three hundred people watching us."

"Since when have I been bashful about making love in front of a few hundred people?"

She laughed. "Good point, Carlyle. I'm starting to think there's a little bit of the exhibitionist in you. Come to think about it, I recall that you and some actress were videoed making love on a beach in broad daylight."

"It was a private beach on a private island."

"As I recall, that honey of a video made Pam and Tommy Lee's home flick pale in comparison. There hasn't been a website hit that hard and fast since the Monica Lewinski deposition was released on-line."

"Judging by your taste in movies, you visited the site a few times yourself."

"Unfortunately I was never able to get on before your actress friend put the kibosh on it. She sued the dude who made the video, didn't she? They settled out of court, and she walked away with a few million in her pocket. I'm just curious why you didn't sue."

"One thing I'm not, sweetheart, is a hypocrite. I could hardly plead humiliation when I've dropped my pants in every movie I've made since I turned eighteen." He looked away, his expression sobering. "I eventually learned it was all an elaborate scheme to get much-needed publicity. She and the photographer were in it together. They split the profits from the website, and she got the notice she needed to move onto the A list. Glad I could help the slut with her career. Every time she has a movie premier, I send her three dozen roses and sign the card *Fuck You. Love, Brandon.*"

A sudden rush of heat through her body turned the air uncomfortably hot, and Alyson sank back against the bar, her gaze fixed on the blur of bodies on the dance floor. There was no denying the hurt she heard in Carlyle's voice, not to mention the bitterness. Disgust over the actress's betrayal made the beer in her system turn sour. But more disturbing and disgusting was the realization that she was just as guilty as that actress who took advantage of Carlyle's name and reputation, not to mention his trust, to gain publicity.

Catching her arm, he backed toward the dance floor, pulling her with him, though she was reluctant to follow. Her legs didn't want to work. Her eyes stung with tears she tried to blink back. Throughout her life she had desperately fought to like herself, yet here she stood with the first strains of Trisha Yearwood's "Without You" wrapping around her, looking up into the eyes of a man she had every intention of destroying for her own gain. She had to get away from Ticky Creek before she hurt him again. Before she hurt herself. Loving a man like Carlyle would be emotional suicide.

Brandon slid one arm around the small of her back, pulled her close against his body that was hard and hot, and already moving to the slow, sensual rhythm of the love song that felt as erotic as his hips swaying against hers. With one hand curling around hers, he rested his cheek against hers and sang softly in her ear.

Her eyes drifted closed as he rocked her, as his warm breath fell softly against her ear, as the touch of his hand on hers felt like slow, liquid fire oozing down her arm and wrapping around her heart.

He lowered his mouth to hers, teased her lips apart with a tentative nudge of his tongue.

The breath left her in a rush; she surrendered, welcoming the invasion of his tongue that slid like warm silk against her own. She became mindless of the people watching them as the floor dizzily tipped and swayed as gently as his body against hers. Whatever resistance might have remained, dissolved in a rush of desire that made her melt into his arms, lift her arms around his neck, and shamelessly draw him more deeply into the kiss. The music faded. The dancing stopped. His arms closed around her, almost crushing, pinning her against his aroused body in so blatant a manner that she would have, at any other time and with any other man, felt shocked and outraged. But not now. Such electric desire vibrated inside her that control felt as impossible to contain as a windstorm.

How long they stood there, embracing and kissing, she couldn't guess. Didn't care. Nor, apparently, did he. But suddenly, at the same moment, they noticed that the music had stopped and the normal ear-shattering din of conversation was silent. With extreme effort, Carlyle lifted his head, reluctant to take his eyes from hers. They each blinked drowsily, shook free of the spell, and looked around them. They were alone on the dance floor. Spectators stood beyond the lights, shadowed faces smiling as they enjoyed the show.

As they burst into applause, Brandon stepped away, leaving Alyson to stand alone under the overhead spotlight, her face burning with embarrassment that mounted as Carlyle, grinning like the cat that swallowed the canary, applauded as well. If she hadn't been so shaken by what had passed between them, she might have formed some saucy retort, but her entire body, including her brain, had become as diffused as fog. Instead, she took a bow, turned on her heel, and returned to the bar, where a smiling Clyde had replaced her empty beer bottle with a fresh one.

As the jukebox blasted again and the crowd surged back onto the dance floor, Carlyle eased up beside her. If she believed the current of desire that had rocketed through her on the dance floor had subsided, she was wrong. One brush of his body against hers cut through her like a raw bolt of electricity. Sweeping the bits of melting ice from the bottle, she pressed them to her forehead and did her best to stabilize her thinking before she embarrassed herself again.

"And here I thought you were shy," he said with amusement. "You've got a lot of nerve calling me an exhibitionist."

She refused to look at him, just took a deep swig of her beer and closed her eyes as it hit her stomach. "Maybe we should make our own video. Might help me pay for that room at the Taj Mahal where I'm staying. Did I happen to mention that I'm burning up my life savings while waiting for you to confide the dark secrets of your life?"

"I'd be happy to move in with you. Share the cost. I might even buy you Twinkies for breakfast." He took the bottle from her and set it aside, caught her chin gently with his fingers and tipped her face toward his, forcing her to look directly into his eyes. "I'd like to spend the night with you, Aly."

She smiled nervously. "You cut right to the chase, don't you, Carlyle?"

"Flirtation has never been my strong point."

"Neither is abstinence, from what I hear."

"Hey, I've been 'abstinent' for four years."

"You mean from the booze, of course, because there's no way this side of heaven that you're going to make me believe you've gone four years without. . . ." Her words trailed off as she searched his eyes, which were unnervingly intense. Realization drove sharp emotion into her chest, and she forced herself to step away, withdrawing from his touch. "I don't believe you," she declared.

"Corcoran didn't provide us women—"

"You've been out eight months." She moved farther away, dragging her bottle with her. "I'm supposed to believe that until now you've had no desire—" She shook her head and drank. "Don't do this to me, Carlyle. Don't take advantage of my stupid weakness to martyr myself for idiotic causes."

Frowning, he leaned against the bar and crossed his arms over his chest. "I think I'm offended. I've been called a lot of things, but never an 'idiotic cause.'"

"Why me?" she demanded, pressing the cold bottle to her hot cheek. "Why not one of them?" She swept her hand toward the dance floor. "They'd take numbers and line up for a chance at you."

"Exactly."

Lifting one eyebrow, she cut him an askance look. "What happens if I give in? Then I'm no better than they are, am I? I'd be nothing more than another notch on your belt." She turned away from his gaze. Forcing herself to smile, she said, "I suspect you want somebody you can pat on the head when it's all over, and wave good-bye and good riddance when I drive out of town. I doubt you want many more like Dillman's sister hanging around to remind you of your past indiscretions."

"I think you need to stop analyzing my motives, Alyson, and just accept the fact that I'm attracted as hell to you and I want to spend the next"—he checked his watch—"eight hours making love to you. I'd be happy to make it longer, but Henry and I have a date to go fishing at five-thirty in the morning."

Her mouth dropped open and her eyebrows shot up. Shaking her head and laughing, Alyson propped one elbow on the bar and tapped Carlyle on the chest with the lip of her beer bottle. "I can see that you're a real sweet talker. And I'm flattered as hell that you want to sandwich me in between a bit of boot scooting and fishing with your uncle, but I like to think that when I cozy up to a man, he's got something on his mind besides dipping his hook in a catfish hole."

His lips curved and his eyes narrowed. He reached for her, slid one hand around the back of her neck and drew her close, lowered his head and whispered in her ear, "Honey, when I'm between your legs, you'll have no doubts where my mind is, and my hands, and my mouth. In fact, for the next few days you won't walk without a reminder of exactly where my attentions have been focused." To punctuate his meaning, he dipped his tongue in her ear. A sudden surge of longing rose like a tide inside her, flushing her skin with such heat that the room and everything in it turned red. "Please," he implored softly, deeply, and with a desperation that vibrated straight to her heart. "I promise you won't hate yourself in the morning."

The ability to reason vanished in a haze of aching need

that she had tried desperately to ignore the last days. As if her bones had turned to rubber, she felt herself sink against him, felt his arms slide around her as she nestled her face in the curve of his throat. Her eyes drifted closed as her every nerve absorbed the touch and smell of him, as his hands rubbed her back and slid down to gently cup her buttocks and tilt her body into his, which was shockingly aroused.

He brushed her cheek with a kiss. Held her close. Breathed in her ear, and repeated, "Please."

She needed air. And space.

Pulling away, planting one hand on his chest, she did her best to collect her scattered senses, knowing even as she looked up into his waiting, wanting eyes that her heart and body had surrendered, regardless of what her mind told her. "I need a few minutes," she said, aware her voice sounded revealingly husky. Plunking her bottle onto the bar, she grabbed up her purse and, without looking at Carlyle, headed for the ladies' room down a long, dim corridor lined with framed yellowing newspaper photos depicting the winners of dance and fishing contests.

Several laughing, chattering women crowded before the line of mirrors on the bathroom wall. They fell silent as she plowed into the room, then stopped short as she was confronted by the intensity of their interest. Then they shuffled out of the room, and the door bumped closed behind them. Silence rang in her ears while the strong scent of perfume lingered in the air so thickly her eyes burned.

Alyson entered the farthest stall, locked it, and dropped onto the toilet seat. Elbows on her knees, she buried her face in her hands and did her best to will the Budweiser out of her system so she could know for certain that the decision she was about to make had nothing to do with inebriation and everything to do with pure, unmitigated lust. No, not lust. At least not for her. God help her, there was more going on here, and she was just too damn proud and frightened to admit it.

A phone rang. A moment passed before she realized the whirring was coming from her purse.

Alan's voice crackled over the line. "Am I catching you at a bad time, A. J.?"

Laughing to herself and rolling her eyes, Alyson leaned back against the exposed plumbing pipes and crossed her legs. Scrawled in Magic Marker across the door in front of her was *FUCK A DUCK IN A DODGE PICKUP TRUCK.* "Just catching up on my reading," she replied. "What's up?"

"Just got back from a symposium on schizophrenics with borderline and schizotypal personality disorders."

"Bet that kept you on the edge of your chair."

"No, but the conversation I shared with one Ronald Peterson did. Name ring a bell?"

"No."

"He was the chief investigator for the D.A.'s office. He worked on the Carlyle case."

Alyson sat up straight, and waited.

"Peterson left the D.A.'s office two years ago. He's started his own security business. Specializes in troubleshooting for celebrities, politicians, and high-powered executives. His expertise is stalking the stalker. Say a celebrity or politician gets harassed, Ron tracks the stalker down, checks them out to determine just what kind of threat they pose. His investigators try to nip the problem in the bud before it gets out of hand. A. J., it seems there was a great deal going on behind the scenes of the Carlyle-Marcella case that we never heard about. Are you sitting down?"

Swallowing, she closed her eyes. The beer climbed up her throat, rancid as bile. "I don't think I want to hear this, Alan."

"Oh, yes, you do. The couple who found Carlyle by the road was ready to testify that as they approached, they saw a car leaving the scene. They couldn't give a description. It was after midnight, black as pitch, and raining. Only one taillight was working. They found Carlyle on the shoulder of the road, lying on his back, legs together and arms crossed over his chest—as if he were laid out in a coffin."

"Someone in the car that drove away must have—"

"Might explain how Carlyle got out of that car before it

went through the guardrail. Somebody removed him from the car."

"Why would someone go to the trouble to remove him from the car, then simply drive away and leave him? It doesn't make sense. How and why did that car go through the guardrail if the momentum of the crash didn't do it?"

Alan remained silent, then, "Perhaps our mystery car shoved the Ferrari and its occupant over the ledge."

A sudden beep warned that the battery was going. Frowning, Alyson clutched the phone harder against her ear. "Alan, is that your hypothesis or Peterson's?"

"Peterson's. But he couldn't prove it to the D.A. any more than the D.A. could prove that Carlyle did a number on Marcella and killed her to shut her up."

"Were these possibilities ever discussed with Brandon?"

"Never. No point. Carlyle rolled over by pleading guilty to manslaughter—which, I learned, went against his attorney's advice. Seems Carlyle didn't want to put his family through the ordeal of a trial."

"But if someone else sent the Ferrari through the guardrail . . . that means Carlyle spent three years in prison for something he didn't do. And if he didn't do it . . . who did? And why?"

"Listen to me very carefully, A. J. This is all conjecture. There isn't one shred of evidence pointing to anyone other than Carlyle causing the death of Emerald Marcella."

"But . . . ? I hear the *but* there."

"I couldn't help but think about one of our previous conversations. As a psychiatrist, I must first examine, then offer the possibility with extreme caution, if not outright reluctance—"

"Get over it, Alan!"

"I feel that I should raise the disconcerting possibility that Emerald Marcella might—I repeat might—have been a victim of someone who was going to make damn sure she wouldn't be putting any more moves on Carlyle."

She stared at the stall door in front of her, the bold black graffiti letters blurring, the air in the cramped space becoming so hot her skin began to sweat.

"A. J., in the most extreme cases, stalkers look at anyone who comes between them and the object of their obsession as an obstacle who must be eliminated."

"Anticipating." She said it more to herself than to Alan. A cold chill shimmied up her spine.

"I'm concerned that Anticipating might be more dangerous than we first believed. And if that's the case, if she suspects that you're bonding to Carlyle in any way—"

The phone went dead.

Alyson stared at it. Shook it. Punched the Power button repeatedly, only to have the battery alarm burp in response.

It was all too far-fetched, of course—some obsessed fan removing Carlyle from the car, then in a fit of jealous rage murdering Marcella.

Perhaps someone happened on the accident and removed Carlyle from the car, simply didn't want to become involved, so drove off into the rainy night—

Alyson sank back against the plumbing again. The earlier buzz of inebriation had vaporized. She felt like Jell-O. Dear God, could Anticipating have killed the woman she considered an obstacle between her and Carlyle by sending the car over a cliff?

If so, then Carlyle was in a lot more danger then he imagined.

And so was she.

The bathroom door opened, allowing music and laughter to boil into the room, then eased closed with a thump. Silence hummed in the air. She listened for footsteps, the opening of a stall door, the jangle of a purse. Nothing.

The lights went out.

Alyson stood slowly, unbalanced and confused by the unexpected blackness.

From her right came the squeak of a stall door slowly opening, and the reality slammed her that she wasn't alone.

Another squeak, closer, as if someone was working their

way down the line of stalls. In the dark. Looking for someone. Looking for . . . her?

Of course not. What idiotic paranoia—

She reached out blindly, found the latch, fingertips ascer-
taining that, yes, she had locked it.

Another door opened. Then another. Then silence again.
Seconds stretched out like an eternity.

As she stared hard through the dark, her senses expanded
to the shattering point. She wasn't a screamer—there wasn't
a reason to scream, because it was all a joke or a misunder-
standing. Besides, she had always been one of those very
weird birds who didn't panic easily; rationalization was as
much second nature to her as breathing.

Alyson backed against the toilet bowl, tottered and threw
her arms out to the stall walls to balance herself—

"Come out, come out, wherever you are," came the singsong whisper.

Okay, so this was no joke. And if it was, it was a damn
sick one. She climbed onto the toilet seat, one hand gripping
the dead telephone so tightly it felt like her knuckles would
pop through the skin. What was she supposed to do now?

Laughter, soft and throaty, sounded near the stall door.

A sudden burst of conversation erupted in the corridor
outside the rest room.

The door blew open, and someone said, "Who turned out
the lights?"

Alyson closed her eyes, relief draining the strength from
her legs as the overhead fluorescent lights flickered on again
and a swarm of women scurried for the stalls. She jumped
to the floor and grabbed up her purse, popped the latch on
the stall door, and stepped out. Her gaze leaped from the
cluster of women crowding the sinks to the line of closed
stall doors. A half-dozen faces turned her way—again with
eyes that were as curious as they were envious.

She left the powder room at a semi run, hurried down the
corridor while the blast of music and the roar of conversation
ricocheted off the walls around her. She came face to face
with Ruth, who grabbed her by the shoulders and laughed.

"Whoa, darlin'. You been shot out of a cannon or what?"

Sinking against the wall, Alyson struggled to take a breath. Air rushed into her lungs so explosively that she wondered just how long she'd gone without breathing.

The smile sliding from her mouth, Ruth frowned and patted Alyson's cheek. "Hon, you ain't lookin' so good."

"Too much Budweiser," she managed, forcing a smile. "I think I need some air."

"The deck is fairly quiet right now. I'll bring you some coffee. Here, Sugar, borrow my jacket. I was gonna take my break, but that can wait another five." Ruth slung the neon yellow parka over Alyson's shoulders and nudged her toward the glass doors that led to a broad wood deck lit by hundreds of red and green jalapeno-shaped Christmas lights twinkling in the trees. "You want me to get Brandon? I think I seen him go into the gents' room a few minutes ago."

Alyson nodded and smiled her thanks as Ruth opened the door to the deck, allowing her to step out into the cool, fairy-like atmosphere. The rush of sharp air momentarily took her breath away. Pausing, clutching the parka around her, Alyson briefly closed her eyes while the serenity of the lights and muted music calmed the frantic pounding of her heart. Only then did she realize that she still held the phone in her hand. When she tried to open her fingers, it was as if they were frozen in a death grip.

What in God's name had just happened?

Surely she'd allowed Alan's phone call to rattle her reasoning. There was absolutely no cause to believe that what just took place was anything other than a mean-spirited prank by one of a hundred catty, jealous females who were pissed over her perceived relationship with Carlyle.

Perceived relationship my tush, she thought. Before Alan's phone call she had been on the verge of giving in to Carlyle's seduction. They had practically made love on the dance floor.

Light laughter drew her focus to a couple standing together at the far end of the deck. They touched and snuggled and kissed. Ordinary people doing ordinary things. Suddenly Alyson's once ordinary existence felt as conspicuous as King

Kong in a china shop. She suspected that if she looked over her shoulder, she'd find people with their noses smashed against the windows as they watched and waited for her next move.

Alyson walked to the deck railing and looked down on the creek, dimly lit by the overhead twinklers. The murky water shifted and coiled around the mossy pilings, carrying debris into the dark like silent sailing vessels. A shiver ran through her, and she took a cautious step back from the railing. She'd nearly drowned when she was a child. Since then she'd had an unreasonable fear of wading into water that was more than knee deep.

There was a sound behind her. She turned, pulling herself back hard against the deck rail as Marilyn Monroe came flying at her, teeth bared and fists raised.

She hissed, "Stinkin' home wrecker! I'm gonna kick your ass!"

12

Brandon slammed his fist against the condom machine, then jabbed the unresponsive button below a photograph of a buxom redhead in a black garter belt and lacy bra. Nothing. He slammed it again as the bathroom door opened and several men walked in. They crossed the room to stand beside Brandon, their attention focused on the machine that ate another two of Brandon's quarters and responded with nothing more than a whir and click.

"Damn," Jim Benton said as he thumbed back the brim of his cowboy hat. "This ain't good. Move over, Carlyle, and let me try." Jim blasted the machine with his fist. Nothing.

Gordon Franks, wearing a Mesquite Rodeo cap and a Horseshoe Casino T-shirt, swore under his breath before saying, "Somebody call nine-one-one. I just spent half my week's salary on freakin' strawberry daiquiris to get some sweet thang in the mood, and now I can't get no damn rubber? Move over, boys, and let me at her." Franks pounded the row of buttons, swearing louder with each punch until he grabbed the machine with both hands and tried to pry it off the wall.

Raymond Melroy had come to the River Road straight from work. Still wearing his greasy Econo Lube 'N Tune uniform, he shoved through the group of men and waved a screwdriver that he'd extracted from his hip pocket. "Let me at that som'bitch, but if there's anythang in there, I got first dibs on it."

"No way," Carlyle argued. "I've fed that damn machine three dollars—"

"I got fifteen dollars invested in daiquiris," Franks argued.

"I haven't been with a woman in four years," Brandon shouted back. "Cut me some slack here."

The men stared at him, mouths open, eyes wide with shock. His face warming, Brandon gave them a weak grin and a shrug.

"Hell," Raymond said, slapping Brandon on the shoulder, "I'm sensin' some desperation here. You got it, Carlyle. In fact, if this som'bitch is empty, I'll drive down to the Texaco myself and buy you a box of rubbers. Any man who's gone that long without gittin' any probably can't think straight enough to drive."

"What the bejesus is goin' on in here?" Clyde yelled as he stormed into the room. Six-foot-five and weighing in at nearly three hundred pounds, he lumbered toward the men with a dark expression on his face. "What the hell are you boys doin' to my damn rubber machine?"

"It ain't workin'," Raymond declared, pointing at the machine with his screwdriver. "We got an emergency here. Carlyle's about to git him some for the first time in four years, and this baby ain't cooperatin'."

Clyde dug in his pocket and withdrew a ring of keys. He opened the machine and stood back. With a collective groan, they all stared at the empty compartments. Scratching his head, Clyde offered, "Sorry, boys. Guess we had a busier weekend than usual."

The door opened again and Ruth Threadgill ran in, waving

her arms. "Carlyle, you better get out here quick. Somebody's done jumped your girlfriend."

At first, Ruth's meaning didn't sink in. Brandon stared at her. "What?"

"Hon, get your brain outta your pants and get out here. Some loony's tryin' to claw Alyson's pretty eyes out."

He ran out of the gents' room and into a wall of bodies, all moving toward the deck doors. Brandon attempted to shoulder his way through the crowd as his panic mounted. Clyde came up behind him and began grabbing people, flinging them away so Brandon could get through.

With a final surge, he broke through the mob, stumbled onto the deck as, in the distance, a man tackled a blond woman and sent her careening to the deck. Looking around at Brandon, he shouted, "She's in the water! She's gone under, and she ain't come up!"

Fear surged through him, seizing up his body for an eternal instant so that he couldn't move. He stared at the shattered deck rail that gaped like a hole to perdition. Then, as if from some inner source, a momentum pushed him forward, carried him across the deck toward the splintered rail.

Atop the dark water floated a bright colored parka. He dived toward it.

The black water sucked him deep, cold enough to drive the air from his lungs. He kicked out with his feet and struck at the water wall with his fists. Above him, floodlights cut through the dense water, and he clawed his way toward them until his head broke the surface and he gasped for air. People shouted and pointed. To his right, Alyson thrashed at the water before going under again.

She clawed at his face and grabbed his shirt. They sank again, drawn under by the weight of their clothes and her flailing. He beat her hands away and managed to grab her hair, pulled her to the surface as Clyde flung a life preserver to them. A group of men slid down the muddy banks of the creek, and as Brandon managed to heave Alyson onto the life preserver, they were hauled into the shallows.

Wrapping his arms around Alyson, he dragged her onto

the bank, sinking to his shins in mud. They sprawled, she clutching at his shirt and retching water out her mouth and nose.

"I—I can't swim," she choked, her face buried in his shoulder.

"I noticed." He stroked her hair and gasped for breath. His pulse hammered. He hadn't felt such terror since his Ferrari had careened out of control and into a guardrail.

Catching Alyson's bruised and lacerated face in his hands, he tilted her head back and forced himself to smile—a task, since the last thing he felt like being was cordial. "I was going to take you fishing with me and Henry in the morning, but now I don't think so. You've come as up close and personal to a catfish as I'm willing to allow in a twenty-four-hour period." Her right eye was swollen, and her lip bleeding. When she attempted a weak smile, she flinched in pain. "Aly, the next time you find yourself in over your head, try to relax and roll to your back. Whatever you do, don't fight the water, because the water will win every time. Got it?"

She nodded.

Like a yowling cat, Mitsy Dillman attempted to escape the men who fought to control her. With her blond wig on the deck and her lipstick-stained teeth bared, she flung herself wildly from side to side and screamed, "You sons of bitches, let me go! You got no right to keep me from my husband! Filthy, two-timin' son of a whore, cheatin' on me with that hussy while our kids are home cryin' for their daddy, and me with another young'un under the belt. I'll kill the bitch—and him, too. Git your hands off me! You can't treat me like this. Do you know who the hell I am? I'm a frickin' movie star, you sad sack of pig dung. I'll club you over the head with my damn Oscar if you ain't careful."

Brandon helped Alyson to her feet. Someone else flung a jacket around her shoulders. From the distance came the shrill call of a siren.

*   *   *

Deputy Greene shook his head as his partner wrestled a handcuffed Mitsy into the cruiser. "She's nutty as a fruitcake. I don't care if she *is* Jack's sister." He turned to Alyson and Brandon. "Ma'am, I'm awful sorry about this. If I was you, I'd go to the clinic and have that cut looked at. Might need a few stitches. Don't much like the look of that knot on your head, either. Could have a concussion."

Alyson, wet and shivering, shook her head and continued to hold a bag of ice against her lip. Brandon held her against him, his arms offering her strength and his body warming her. A spasm ran through her, and she buried her face against his shoulder until it passed. His clothes clung to his body, and there was mud in his boots. He did his best to ignore Mitsy's ranting, but that was no easier than containing his mounting anger.

Deputy Greene said, "She'll be transported to Tyler General for assessment, to see if she's mentally competent enough to go to jail. I'll give you a call tomorrow and let you know. I'll do my best to keep her away from you, sir, but there's no guarantee. You might try having a restraining order put on her, but as crazy as she is, I don't know that it'll do you a lot of good. Ma'am." He touched the brim of his hat and turned away.

Ruth and Clyde had done a respectable job of dispersing the crowd. Now Ruth put a foam cup of hot coffee in Alyson's hand, and smiled encouragingly. "You'll have a real shiner in the mornin', and I suspect you'll feel a few muscles that you didn't realize you had. That dimwit must have hit you like a bull to knock you through that deck rail. Course, it don't help that the rail needed replacin' anyway. I told Clyde not two weeks ago that it was rotten, and if he didn't do somethin' about it soon, somebody was gonna take a dive and wind up suin' him. Drink your coffee, hon. Might chase away the shivers."

Alyson smiled her thanks. "Sorry about your coat, Ruth."

"Aw, hell, I've had that old thing for years. We're just grateful the creek was relatively calm. It can get pretty nasty after we've had a lot of rain. Clyde's cousin drowned in it

last year. Fell out of his boat, and that was that. Currents
sucked him under and didn't spit him out for two weeks.
Found him down near Nacogdoches, or what was left of him
that the catfish and gar hadn't eaten." She smiled up at Brandon. "Hon, you handled that like a character right out of one
of your movies. Now when somebody says, *Aw, he's just
playin' a role and he's probably a wussy in real life*, I can
say *Not even.* You went into that water like a freakin' Navy
SEAL. Kinda romantic, ain't it?" She nudged Alyson and
winked.

Paying little attention to Ruth, Brandon watched the
cruiser pull onto the highway and drive off into the dark.
Mitsy's white face stared back at him as she continued to
rant.

"I think she intended to confront me in the ladies' room,"
Alyson said as she sipped her hot coffee. "Someone came in
and turned off the light—"

"Wasn't her," Ruth said, shaking her head. "I kept my eye
on Mitsy soon as she come in. She's always makin' trouble
for somebody. We got to throw her out of the place at least
once a week when she's in town. Few days ago she came in
announcin' she was gonna have Joe DiMaggio's baby. Few
nights ago Jim Benton was upcreek checkin' his trotlines at
midnight, and who comes by him but her in her brother's
bass boat, lookin' like Marilyn Monroe in a poodle skirt and
high heels, and swiggin' vodka straight out of a bottle. She
pulled her sweater up and flashed her boobs at him. Said he
almost tossed his dinner."

Ruth patted Alyson on the shoulder. "Get you some rest.
Have Mr. Hollywood bring you back in a couple days and
dinner'll be on me. And if you need a friend to hang out
with while you're in town, just give me a call. I'm in the
book."

Alyson rested her head against the car seat and closed her
eyes as Brandon drove back to town. The temperature had
plummeted the last hour, so he turned the heater on, as well
as the overhead lamp, so he could better see Alyson's face.
He glanced at her frequently, fresh anger, as well as frustra-

tion, surging through him. The aftershock of what had happened left him physically numb, not unlike the morning he had awakened in a hospital and learned that Emerald Marcella was dead.

The dim overhead light did nothing to alleviate the extent of the injuries to her face. There was a swelling over her right eye that gave her the appearance of a prizefighter after a particularly punishing round. Her lower lip looked swollen, and there were smears of blood on her chin. Yet, since he'd pulled her out of Ticky Creek, she hadn't made so much as a whimper. Her composure had extinguished his own barely contained fury—if she'd shown the slightest emotional or physical distress, he'd have been hard-pressed to keep his hands off Mitsy. An emotion washed over him, unfamiliar and as shocking to his senses as his dive into Ticky Creek's cold waters. Alyson James had become important to him.

"Do you think she's Anticipating?" she asked, looking at him with concerned eyes.

A couple of times he'd reached for Anticipating's letter in his pocket, only to recall that it was now nothing more than a soggy mess. "Maybe. If it's Mitsy, at least Anticipating has an identity and I can deal with it—I can't deal with an unknown who's nothing more than a name and threat on a piece of paper." He reached for her hand and curled his fingers around it. "I'm sorry you got caught up in this, Aly. I'll do whatever I have to, to make certain she won't hurt you again."

"I want to talk about Emerald Marcella."

Frowning, he withdrew his hand. The statement had come out of left field, unbalancing him. It wasn't a topic he allowed himself to visit often. The guilt, not to mention the unsettling memories of that night, rushed through him in a black wave. "No." He shook his head as his hands gripped the wheel almost convulsively. "I don't want to go there. Not tonight."

She studied him silently. "It's important that you do, I think. A woman is dead—"

"And buried." He took a deep, steadying breath. "I accepted the responsibility for it. I'm attempting to put it behind me. Stirring up the memories and regrets won't help me forget it."

"What if someone—not you—killed her?"

He hit the brake, causing the car to fishtail across the double yellow lines. Both hands gripping the steering wheel, he stared through the windshield at the twin shafts of headlights disappearing into the dark ahead. Familiar raw emotions shot through him: anger, frustration . . . helplessness, and confusion—everything he'd experienced during those horrifying days following Emerald's death.

Forcing himself to look at Alyson, he said through his teeth, "Obviously Mitsy hit you harder than we thought. You're hallucinating."

"What if Anticipating was there?"

He stared into her eyes, a sudden rise of unreasonable anger directed at her for prying open his Pandora's box of memories. Now Alyson James and her writing aspirations had opened that box just enough to allow the sound of clattering bones to remind him that he could run and he could hide, but inevitably the past would come tapping him on the shoulder.

When he spoke again, his voice shook. "There were only two people in that car, Alyson. Me and Emerald—"

"And only one of you went through that guardrail." Her voice remained soft, calm, reasonable, as if she realized that she had just wandered too close to a land mine and one wrong move meant disaster. Shifting her body toward the door, her hand dropping toward the handle, she continued to hold his gaze with hers although the swelling of her eyelid made her squint and the puffiness of her lip gave her a slight lisp as she continued.

"The D.A. would have had the entire world believing that you somehow purposefully sent the car careening over the cliff, hurling yourself out of harm's way the instant before the car and Emerald went airborne. What if . . . someone removed you from the car, then sent the car and Emerald over the cliff? Who would have a motive to do such a thing . . . except someone who considered women in your life as competition to be eliminated? Carlyle, the letters she's sent you have made it crystal clear that she watches your every move. What if she followed you that night? She witnessed the accident, removed you from the car, then eliminated Marcella from your life by using her own car to shove the Ferrari through the guardrail."

His jaw tightening, he glanced away. The unwelcome memories rushed back to him, closing off his throat, making him sweat.

Mr. Carlyle, Emerald Marcella is dead. . . .

Mr. Carlyle, you're under arrest for the death of Emerald Marcella. You have the right to remain silent. . . .

Brandon Carlyle, on behalf of the State of California, I hereby sentence you to six years in the Corcoran State Prison . . . .

Alyson touched the lump on her forehead and sank against the seat, closed her eyes, and sighed wearily. "A car was seen leaving the scene of the accident, according to the D.A.'s investigative officer, Ronald Peterson. He considered the possibility that someone in that car removed you from the vehicle then did a number on Marcella, but he couldn't prove it any more than he could prove you intentionally killed her."

"How the hell do you know all this?"

"I got a call from Alan while I was in the ladies' room. He met Peterson at a symposium. Your name came up or something, and Peterson was apparently more than willing to discuss the case."

"Who the hell is Alan? And what business am I of his?"

"He's my friend—"

"Boyfriend? Lover?"

"Don't change the subject, Carlyle."

"Considering we would have ended up in bed tonight if it wasn't for Mitsy, I think I have a right to know if you're involved with someone."

A grin toyed with her swollen mouth as she regarded him. "Jealous?"

As bright car lights appeared on the road behind them,

Carlyle stomped the accelerator on the Jag. They sped down the black road as if by doing so he could outrun the images materializing before his mind's eye.

Fifty, sixty, seventy miles an hour—

The rain-slick highway curved like a serpent's back in the Ferrari's high beams. Heavy metal music screeched with ear-shattering volume from the radio. He turned it down. Marcella turned it up, higher. The crazy bitch had hit him. There was blood in his mouth. Blood seeped through his shirt and pants: dark, thin stripes where her fingernails had torn his flesh. She gyrated in her car seat, swinging her head from side to side with the guitar crescendo, her eyes rolling and her nose running. She flung herself across the console, buried her face in his crotch. He grabbed a handful of her hair and hauled her back, shoved her into her seat and shouted, "Enough! Stay the hell away from me!" She tore at her hair as her mouth spewed obscenities. Her hands came at him; her jagged nails ripped at his face, then she went for the steering wheel. He hit the brakes, felt the car surge sideways as he fought for control—losing it, losing it—the guardrail loomed ahead, reflectors glowed red like devil eyes—going over, they were going over—Jesus, oh Jesus, they were going to die—

Perhaps bringing up the topic of Emerald Marcella at that point in time hadn't been the smartest move on her part, but considering what had happened at the River Road, Alyson felt the topic should be broached. Obviously, Carlyle didn't agree. For the remainder of the drive he stared straight ahead while the car's speed crept faster and his expression turned darker.

He did not slow as they neared the motel. As they flew past the entrance, she sank deeper in her seat. "I trust you aren't intending to ride me out of town on a rail."

"You're going home with me. You'll be more comfortable there, and I can better keep an eye on you. I'm still not convinced that I shouldn't take you straight to the clinic. You look like hell."

"There you go, smooth talking me again. I'm not sure how much more of your charm my heart can take. I'd feel a whole lot better if you didn't look as if you're about to explode."

"Don't get involved in my business, Alyson, and we'll get along just fine."

"Mitsy just shoved me headfirst into your business." She pointed to the knot on her forehead. "This baby is throbbing involvement. At this very minute she's no doubt fantasizing ways—very messy ways—of assuring that our relationship ends before it can begin. If you want to ignore the possibilities I've mentioned and stick your head in the sand, fine. But I can't help wondering if she's capable of more than punching my lights out. If she's Anticipating—and she was following your Ferrari the night Marcella was killed—then I have a right to suspect that she'll stop at nothing to make certain you and I have no future together, be it business or pleasure."

She watched his jaw work. "I only want to help," she added more softly.

"You want." He gave a cold laugh. "I want a lot of things, Alyson. I want to pull this car over and make love to you until you scream in ecstasy. I want you to give me a blow job until I scream in ecstasy." His head turned, and he skewered her with his eyes. "I want Bernie and Henry to be well again. I want to play ball with my dad again. Sometimes I want to never have been born. But we can't always get what we want, can we?"

Brandon lifted Alyson out of the car seat and into his arms. Straightening and stumbling back a little, he attempted to shift her weight as he kicked the car door closed.

Wrapping her arms around his neck, she said, "Ah, come on, Carlyle, in movies I've seen you heft at least half a dozen women up entire flights of stairs."

"They were anorexic with the bone density of sparrows.

Christ, I'm trying to be chivalrous here, and you weigh a ton."

"I'm one-twenty, soaking wet."

"Bullhockey. You're one-forty, easy."

"It's muscle mass. I work out."

"You eat too damn many Twinkies."

Pooching her swollen lip out, she attempted to look pitiful. "Are you calling me fat?"

Gritting his teeth, he mounted the porch steps, staggered sideways before righting again.

"I wear size six jeans, sucker. I'm telling you, it's muscle. All muscle. I have an incredible metabolism. Twinkies don't stand a chance at my thighs."

"Yeah? Wait until you hit forty, cupcake—or, better yet, drop three or four babies. Every Twinkie you've eaten since you cut teeth will be riding on your butt."

Since she'd last visited Henry's farm, great care had been taken to decorate the porch for Halloween. A giant jack-o'-lantern perched on the top step. Ghosts dangled by fishing line from the rafters, shifting and spinning as the night breeze teased them. Alyson caught the screen door handle and flung it back so Brandon could manipulate the doorknob with the hand hooked behind her knees. With an exaggerated grunt, he stepped into the house, and came face to face with Mildred.

Brandon set Alyson on her feet. "What's this, trick or treat already? I like the mask, Mildred. Very scary. What the hell are you doing here this time of night?"

She ignored him as she stepped closer to Alyson. "My, my, looks like you forgot to duck, Sweetie. What happened? Lover's spat?"

Brandon brushed Mildred aside as he caught Alyson's arm and propelled her toward the kitchen. "I'm not in the mood to forgive your cattiness tonight, Mildred." He glanced at Alyson and said, "Mildred is my agent. She'll try and convince you we were madly in love. Don't believe her. I allowed her to seduce me once when I was stinking drunk. I don't remember anything beyond waking up the morning after. As I recall, I reacted as if I just woke up in a rattlesnake pit. It hasn't happened since, and it will never happen again. Did you hear that clearly, Mildred? Never again."

"Do you hear me complaining, darling? I'd have experienced more satisfaction with something battery-powered."

He pointed his middle finger at her.

The door to Bernie's room was open, allowing Jay Leno's monologue to spill into the kitchen. Henry lay on his roll-away bed next to Bernie's. Propped up on pillows, his glasses askew on his nose, Henry slept deeply, his snores resonating behind the high-volume laughter of Leno's audience.

Brandon closed the door, then sat Alyson in a chair by the harvest table. Spread over the surface were several dozen fishing lures, an open tackle box, a shoe box of red-and-white bobbers, and reels of fishing line. There was also a clear plastic bowl full of miniature Halloween chocolates, and a dozen or more discarded wrappers scattered among the lures. Obviously Henry had not begun playing with his fishing toys until Betty had left for the evening. The diet watchdog would not have approved of Henry's bingeing on milk chocolate Krackles.

Brandon walked to a cupboard where he located a bottle of peroxide, cotton swabs, and Band-Aids, all of which he moved to the table where Alyson remained, her gaze locked on Mildred, who returned her stare with eyes as cold as marbles. Even if Mildred hadn't caused Henry's old heart to go haywire, and even if Mildred's energy wasn't so overwhelmingly acid that Alyson felt like her skin was going to melt from the bone, she wouldn't have liked Mildred just on principle. Her appearance made Alyson think of something reptile. All that was missing was a long black tongue to slither through her lips.

Brandon pulled a chair up to Alyson's and sat. He reached for a cotton swab and peroxide. "What are you doing here, Mildred, besides reminding me why I should fire you?"

"Waiting for you, dear."

"Where's your car?"

"Seems the alternator is sick. I dropped by to see you

earlier, and when I tried to leave, the car wouldn't start. Someone named Joe Bob or something hauled it away behind a wrecker. Henry offered to drive me back to the motel, but I declined. I said I'd wait for you. I didn't realize I'd be forced to endure an education on jigging spoons and crank-baits and the pros and cons of baiting fishing holes with soured corn."

Brandon caught Alyson's chin with one finger and tipped her face toward his. His eyes said, *Ignore her*. Gently, he touched the cotton swab to the cut above her eye. She winced and jerked away. He blew on it lightly until the burning eased, then he carefully cleansed the cut again.

Mildred dug a cigarette from her purse as she watched the procedure. She was extraordinarily beautiful, a petite package wearing jade capris and a cropped black off-the-shoulder angora sweater that accentuated her slender, pale throat, as did the upswept raven hair. Jade and diamond earrings glittered on her lobes. If Carlyle never worked again, Alyson suspected that Mildred would fare just fine. More than fine. She'd buy more overpriced baubles for her ears and in another three, possibly four years she'd splurge on another face-lift. Alyson suspected that Mildred Feldman was every bit of fifty-five, because though a surgeon could yank up face flab until the client talked out her scalp, the hands didn't lie. Mildred had the hands of a woman who'd lived the better part of half a century.

Brandon threw the used cotton swab toward the sink. He drenched another in peroxide and dabbed it lightly against the swelling near Alyson's lip.

Mildred smoked and watched the proceedings. Her lip curled as Alyson flinched at the sting of antiseptic. "Are you going to enlighten me as to what happened to this woman?" Mildred sucked harder on her Virginia Slim. The air in the room suddenly felt charged, like those seconds before a storm erupts.

"A crazy woman under the delusion that our brief moment of passion meant more than it really did," he said pointedly as he looked at Mildred over his shoulder. "Why are you here, Mildred?"

"I spoke with Scorsese today." She paused, allowed the weight of the director's name to fill the room. "He might have a part for you in his upcoming work. It's a Clancy film. The kind of story that will drown the audience in testosterone. Harrison Ford has committed. He suggested to Scorsese that you might be good in the role of the turncoat CIA agent who's married to Ford's character's sister. I could get you five million."

"I'm worth twenty. And I don't take second billing to Harrison."

He stood, collected the first aid items, and returned them to the cupboard. Mildred stared at him through the curling thread of smoke from her cigarette. "You're not worth twenty anymore. You're not worth five. In fact, at this stage of your career, you should be offering Scorsese that much to allow you on the set."

Carlyle opened the fridge and withdrew two cans of Pepsi, one of which he handed to Alyson. His cheeks looked red, and when he ripped back the aluminum ring on the can, Alyson got the impression he was fantasizing it was Mildred's throat. She wouldn't have blamed him. That old protective surge flooded her. She was forced to sink back in her chair before she pulled a Mitsy and shoved the Pepsi can up Mildred's carefully constructed nostrils.

"Seven," Mildred went on. "At the most. And possibly a percentage. Baldwin, Pitt, and Damon have expressed extreme interest, but Scorsese feels your reputation would give you the harder edge. You'd have to read for the part, of course." Twin streams of smoke slid from her nostrils, making her look like a bejeweled incense burner. "After all," she added, "they'll want assurance that you can still act, not to mention that you're sober enough to remember your lines. Did I mention that they'll be shooting the first half of the movie in Singapore? Then Paris and finally back to D.C."

He set his Pepsi can on the table and reached for a miniature Krackle, unwrapped it, and fed it to Alyson, his eyes narrowing slightly as he laid the chocolate on her tongue. "No," he replied simply as he allowed his thumb to stroke her swollen lip.

"What do you mean, no?" Mildred demanded. The ash on her cigarette was becoming long and bent and white.

"I stopped auditioning for parts when I was fifteen. So, no, I won't read for the part. No, I won't accept seven million, and I won't bill below Harrison. No, I won't fly off to Singapore, Paris, and D.C. Even if I thought I was ready to allow some director to dictate to me when I can breathe, belch, or pick my nose, I wouldn't at this point. My family is ill, in case you haven't noticed."

Mildred crushed the cigarette out in the sink. Alyson got the impression that if she weren't sitting there as witness to any scandalous unprofessionalism, Mildred would have blown her cranial gasket and told Carlyle exactly what he could do with his contrary bullheadedness. Then it occurred to Alyson that perhaps her earlier assessment of Mildred was wrong. Perhaps despite the Rodeo Drive lode on her ears and the extravagantly expensive threads she was wearing, Mildred desperately needed to make this deal rock and roll all the way to the bank.

Crossing her thin arms over her bosom, Mildred put on a mask of indifference and said, "I think our business should be discussed in private. After all"—she redirected her marble eyes to Alyson's, and one black eyebrow arched—"there's no telling who this woman really is. She's a writer, and writers are trouble. Their insecurities are surpassed only by their conceited belief that the world actually gives a damn about what they have to say." She turned back to Carlyle. "At least drive me back to the motel."

"Fine." He slammed the empty Pepsi can down on the table.

"I can smell trouble a mile away, and I'm telling you, Brandon, that woman is trouble. I don't care what sort of stories

she's fed you. She's lying. She's up to something, and if you aren't careful—"

"Get out of the car, Mildred. In fact, get out of Ticky Creek. When I'm ready to work again, I'll call you."

As the motel's neon lights reflected in red and yellow streaks off the Jaguar's hood ornament, Mildred shook her head and laughed in exasperation. "You think I'm being a jealous cat, don't you? Well, maybe I am . . . a little. You have an opportunity to bounce back from the fiasco you've made of your life; let some mystery hussy wag her ass at you, and you fall right back into the same old sexual cess pit. Are you screwing her, darling?"

"Get out, Mildred."

He reached across her lap and shoved the car door open. She caught his hand and gripped it, hard. "I took you on when no one else in the business would return your phone calls. I held your head when you were puking up Chivas and couldn't remember your name, much less your script. Didn't I tell you that that dreadful little gold digger DeAnna What's-Her-Name was using you to get herself publicity? And didn't I warn you that if you didn't stop running with that particular party crowd you were going to find yourself in deep trouble? There's nothing I wouldn't do to protect you, darling, but you continue not only to ignore me, but to defy me."

"You're my agent, Mildred, not my keeper. And whatever happened between us one dark and stormy night was nothing more than a bad combination of alcoholism and a death wish—both of which I've kicked. Let it go. What I do and who I do it with outside of a movie contract is no business of yours."

"I won't allow another bitch to get in the way of your career again. What hurts you, hurts me, baby." She swung her legs out of the car, stood, and slammed the door. Leaning partially through the open window, she said, "You owe me, Carlyle. Big time. I've kissed a lot of ass for you over the last few years. While you were walking the line in prison, I was moving heaven and earth to get people to forget you'd been a belligerent bully who couldn't spit out his lines without first taking a drink. They all think you're going to cave again, that something or someone is going to send you back to that bottle, and then you'll be right back where you were before Marcella led you down a perverted path. Who else will be willing to hold your hand and convince you again that you're actually worth something? That you're more than Cara Queen Bitch Carlyle's spoiled brat whose claim to fame isn't how well he can act, but how good he looks with his clothes off."

Carlyle looked through the darkness at her, his eyes dimly illuminated by a streak of yellow-green light from the Café Open Twenty Four Hours a Day sign. He didn't look pissed, but resigned and tired. He was thinking that she was right. She knew that look well enough. When he didn't have the ammo to fight, he simply stared with those eyes that turned women into puddles—herself included, and that was saying something. Mildred Feldman prided herself on having ice water for blood and a sump pump for a heart.

"Good night, Mildred," he said calmly, then hit the Up button on the electric window.

She stepped back as he drove away. The taillights flashed briefly before he pulled out on the highway and streaked off into the night. Her face burned as she thought of the woman waiting for him back at his uncle's house. She'd watched women come and go in Carlyle's life—all beautiful, rich, talented, and driven by ambition—but he'd never looked at them the way he looked at this one. She'd recognized it the moment he'd slid the candy into her mouth: how his eyes had appeared to absorb the woman's body and soul, how his fingers had touched her so gently. Deep in her gut, Mildred had always known what sort of woman it would take to capture the emotionally elusive Carlyle, even if he hadn't. The girl next door, that's what he wanted. A scrubbed-face tomboy who'd be more than happy to shovel horse shit and raise half a dozen brats with snotty noses. For that sort of woman he'd turn his back on his career and walk off into the sunset.

Still, while on the surface this particular chick might appear to be "the one," there was something rotten about her.

She had the look of someone who expected to see her face crop up on America's Most Wanted. The autobiography ploy just didn't ring true. Mildred was a master of intuition, and right now it was glowing hot enough to blow out a Geiger counter.

Digging in her purse for her crumpled pack of Virginia Slims, Mildred entered the motel office, where a gnome of a woman in black spandex pants sat at a desk with a phone to her ear. Mildred would check for messages, then pop into the greasy spoon café for a diet whatever, something to wash down a few sleeping tabs—she wouldn't be able to sleep tonight without them, not with the image of Carlyle's name on a Scorsese film fading to black and her one big chance to shoulder her way into the big time going with it.

The night clerk scrawled on a pink While You Were Out pad and nodded as she glanced up at Mildred. "Yes, sir, I got it. I'll see Miss James gets the message soon as she gets back to her room." The woman listened with a bored expression as the caller rattled on. She held up the pad and squinted at it. "Yes, sir, I'll be happy to read it back. A. J., call Alan as soon as possible. I spoke with Peterson again, and he's willing to help us dig further into this Anticipating matter." She nodded. "You have a good night, sir."

The gnome hung up the phone and smirked a little as she turned her fleshy face toward Mildred. "That guy's as queer as a three-dollar bill. You can just tell, y'know? But what do you expect when he's livin' in San Francisco with the Golden Gate to Fairyland, as my husband says." She covered her mouth with a chubby hand and giggled.

Mildred hardly heard her. Her eyes were still focused on the pink message pad on the desk.

"You ain't had no calls," the gnome informed her.

Turning on her heels, Mildred left the office, stood on the sidewalk beneath the flickering neon, and lit her Virginia Slim. The message from Alan kept replaying in her mind. *A. J., call Alan . . . A. J., call . . . A. J.* Where the hell had she heard that before? *A. J. Alyson James. A. J.*

Forgetting about her diet whatever, Mildred went to her

room. As the door shut behind her, her gaze swept the interior as if she expected the A. J. secret to materialize on the dingy walls. Then her gaze snagged on the *Enquirer* and *Gazette* she had earlier deposited in the trash can.

She dug them out and spread them over the bed, finding what she was looking for in the *Gazette*.

DOG SAVES BABY
THEN IS SHOT BY CRUEL NEIGHBOR!
By A. J. Farrington

Mildred straightened. With her hands on her hips, she smiled and said, "Bingo."

13

Alyson stood beneath the showerhead, eyes closed, the steaming water pouring over her sore and throbbing body. Still, she shivered. It was as if the cold, murky creek water had soaked through her pores and turned her blood into mud. She couldn't shake the feeling.

Ruth had been right. There were bruises and abrasions across her back and between her shoulder blades. She had a vague memory of Mitsy driving her knee into her leg, followed by a right slug to her eye that had made the red and green jalapeno Christmas lights look as vast as the Milky Way.

This'll teach you to spread-eagle under another woman's husband!

She saw herself in the Jaguar, staring over at Carlyle and asking, "Do you think Mitsy's Anticipating?"

That would tie things up very nicely, wouldn't it? She could go on with her plot to bamboozle Mr. Hollywood, as Ruth called Carlyle, without a worry that some loony tune

with a personality disorder was going to attempt to claw her
eyes out . . . or worse, send her through a guardrail to die in
a mishmash of crumpled metal.

Mitsy was obviously delusional. Anyone who walked
around believing she was Marilyn Monroe one minute and
Mrs. Brandon Carlyle the next was a few bricks shy of a
load. But Mitsy didn't feel sinister. She was a nut, but she
didn't feel . . . evil. Pathetic, perhaps, but not evil.

Anticipating, on the other hand, felt very evil. The difference between the two was as great as walking through a
cemetery during daylight and dark.

Alyson turned off the water and stood with her head down
and eyes closed. She wanted to believe that Mitsy Dillman
was Anticipating . . . but she didn't.

The shirt Carlyle had given her to wear to bed smelled like
him. The scent curled along her bruised nerve endings, which
were sensitive enough to react with painful little pricks of
sensation, like static electricity.

The soft flannel caressed her body the way his hands had
done on the dance floor. The shirttails hit her mid-thigh, just
enough to hide the fact that she wore no underwear. Hers
was wet still with creek water. If she'd thought of it, she'd
have given him her room key and asked him to bring her a
change of clothes, but she'd still been a bit shell-shocked
after being pummeled and nearly drowned by Mitsy Dillman.

She wondered if he'd come back from delivering Mildred
to the motel. She'd noted the time when he left . . . nearly an
hour ago. Fifteen minutes to the hotel, fifteen minutes back
home . . . unless Mildred talked him into staying.

No chance.

Brandon had put her in Henry and Bernie's old room, the
bedroom they'd shared for thirty-eight of their married years.
It was a time capsule of their lives. The walls were covered
with photographs, mostly black and white: a beautiful, beaming Bernice in a poodle skirt and sweater, short pearls around
her throat; a tall, thin Henry at her side. Moving along the
wall, she watched them age through birthdays, anniversaries,

and Christmases. In the final photograph, they sat together on the porch swing, holding hands, Bernie's head resting on Henry's shoulder. It must have been taken shortly before Bernie's stroke. There was something in her eyes that looked sad, as if she knew the end was near.

Alyson forced herself to look away.

There were mementos of Brandon as well: finger paintings and connect-the-dots framed and hung in a cluster above the bed's headboard—obviously a place of honor; bouquets of Kleenex flowers that looked like pink and white carnations; a jewelry box made from a cigar box, covered in macaroni shells, birdseed, and glass beads, spray painted gold and trimmed with multi-colored glitter. Smiling to herself, Alyson carefully lifted the lid. On the inside of the lid, scrawled in a child's writing, was *BRANDON LOVES BERNIE FOR-EVER.*

The bottom had been covered in purple velvet. On the plush bed were numerous pieces of jewelry: a heart-shaped brooch of diamonds and sapphires, a bracelet of rubies, a necklace with an emerald pendant the size of a quarter. All gifts from Brandon.

There was a ring, a thin gold band, caught within a coil of the ruby bracelet. She picked it up and cradled it in the palm of her open hand. The lamplight glinted on it. Bernie's wedding band, perhaps too large now for her wasted finger. She imagined Henry's heartbreak at having to remove it, as if he were severing one of the last, most important threads of their life together. He might have even imagined that the removal would release her spirit, which most surely must be imprisoned by her broken body. That would have been the hardest part, she thought, letting her go.

Yet, Bernie remained. Something was holding her here. Something far more powerful than her freedom from pain and physical bondage.

Put it on.

No. She couldn't.

Go on. Try it on for size. Might look good on your finger. You never know—

Her fingers closed around the band as she frowned. *Don't even go there*, she thought.

Why not? Why continue to deny that since she zoomed that telephoto lens up close and personal on Mr. Hollywood's twenty-million-dollar bod, she'd toyed with the possibility that they might stand a chance at happily ever after. The morning she walked into this house, and into this family, she felt as if she'd come home at long last. She knew it the minute Henry showed up at the Pine Lodge and the two of them shared coconut and chocolate pie—he knew it, too, or he wouldn't have been there. She knew it by how the River Road patrons regarded her—resignation and envy on their star-struck faces. They all knew. Not by looking at her, but by looking at him. What had Ruth said? *First time I've seen Mr. Hollywood smile since he came back to Ticky Creek.*

She slid the ring onto her finger. It fit. Perfectly.

Alyson lay down across the bed. Tired. Sore. Beaten. The bed was comfortable, much more comfortable than the Pine Lodge bed. This one felt a little old and soft, and creaked a bit with her weight. She imagined that for thirty-eight years Henry and Bernie had held one another in this bed, experienced passion and heartbreak.

You know Anticipating is the least of your roadblocks to happily ever after. If he learns you've been lying to him about your reasons for coming to Ticky Creek (and God forbid he discovers you're THE A. J. Farrington who broke the nasty news of his alcoholism), any hope you have of happily ever after is going to incinerate in a mushroom cloud.

Closing her eyes and pressing her hand with the ringed finger to her heart, she said aloud, "I don't want to talk about it." She was even beginning to sound like Carlyle. They could both give lessons on denial.

But you're going to have to talk about it. All of it. Confession time. If you're going to lie here on his family's bed and fantasize that you're going to "drop him three or four babies" and fill up these walls with another generation of Carlyles, then you must prostrate yourself before him and beg him to forgive your underhandedness.

"He'll never forgive me, and I won't blame him. I'm having a hard time forgiving myself."

You're not a worm, A. J., but what you're doing isn't very nice.

What if—

You turned the lie into a truth?

What if—

The autobiography became a reality?

Forgetting the hot poker of pain jabbing at her back, she sat up. Her heart gave a quick kick at her ribs as the illumination of possibility made the room shimmer. She expected a chorus of angels to crescendo above her head, *"Hallelujah, she has seen the light!"*

She stood at the top of the stairs and gazed down into the ocher haze of the kitchen night-light. Carlyle had silenced Jay Leno's banter with Rosie O'Donnell before he left to take Mildred to the motel. She'd watched Brandon carefully remove the glasses from Henry's nose and place them on a table near the bed, close enough so when Henry awoke in the morning, he could easily find them. He'd tucked a blanket under his uncle's double chin, then walked around the bed to press a kiss on Bernie's cheek.

To her left now, a square of light spilled into the hallway through an open door. She moved to the threshold and peered into the room. Brandon sat on the edge of the bed, his elbows on his knees. His head was tipped down and his damp hair spilled over his brow. He'd showered. She could smell tangy soap and a touch of the same cologne that had made her senses go muzzy. His jeans were clean, as was his shirt. He was barefoot.

He looked like a kid, set against a backdrop of a boy's playhouse. The walls were lined with black-and-white photos of baseball players, all autographed. There were baseball bats propped in the corners and autographed baseballs lining shelves on the walls. Several glass display cases held baseball cards and game programs.

This had been John's room, she realized.

Brandon looked up.

He showed no surprise at finding her standing in the doorway, wearing nothing more than his flannel shirt. She supposed he was accustomed to half-naked women prowling his space, while she, on the other hand, was not accustomed to prowling even fully clothed. Yet, here she stood, shivering a little. From cold, perhaps. Perhaps not. Perhaps from the realization that something emotionally intense was happening here. Or perhaps it was simply those bruised eyes, so full of turmoil, looking at her with a hunger that made her knees weak.

"I was about to check on you," he said in a rough voice, then cleared his throat. "I thought you'd be asleep by now."

She shook her head. "No."

His gaze took a slow journey down her body.

Alyson stepped into the room and closed the door behind her. She leaned against it and tried to will the strength back into her legs. When he looked in her eyes again, his expression had turned dark. His eyes were black. His body radiated a sort of heat that made his face and chest and hands appear to glow in the white lamplight.

He straightened as she crossed the room, unbuttoning the shirt that slid open, exposing a pale valley of skin between her breasts, and down . . .

"Jesus," he whispered, sounding a little drugged.

His long legs were spread; she moved between them and took his face between her hands, tipping his head back so she could look down into his eyes. "Still want to make love to me?" she asked, smiling a little, deliriously nervous and disbelieving that she had come to him like this. She had never been so forward, even with her husband.

His eyes drifted closed, and he nestled his cheek against her palm. "Why are you trembling?" he asked softly.

Until that moment she hadn't realized that she was trembling.

"Are you afraid of me?"

The odd question stunned her, then she realized what he

meant. The Marcella thing. The D.A.'s idiotic statement declaring Carlyle capable of rape and murder. "I'm only human," she tried to tease. "You're Brandon Carlyle, God's gift to women, according to *People* magazine."

Shifting his cheek away, he bowed his head. "Wrong answer, cupcake. This is where you're supposed to convince me that you want me for me. That you would desire me just as much if I were Klem Kadiddlehopper with a harelip."

"But you're not," she replied seriously, and stroked his hair. "You are who you are, and what you are. Maybe I'd eventually come to desire you if you were Kadiddlehopper with a harelip, but it would take a while longer."

She felt a shudder pass through him, then he reached for her, slid his hands up the outside of her thighs and the shirt she wore. His warm fingers spread around her buttocks, and he pulled her close, pressed his face against the hollow just above her navel. The moist heat of his breath on her skin sent rays of bright pain streaking through her. Pressure mounted between her legs, and she suddenly felt liquid and heavy, as if every drop of moisture in her body had pooled between her thighs.

He moved his face and tongued her navel. Just a dip. A taste. Fingers drifted along the crevice of her buttocks, sliding low until touching—

A groan turned over in his throat and he withdrew his hands, curled them into fists and buried them into the soft mattress at his sides. He breathed hard. Sweat made his hair moist and her fingers damp as she continued to stroke him, to trail her fingers along his nape to linger on the skin of his neck.

Resting his forehead against her belly, he squeezed his eyes shut. "God, I need a drink," he murmured, more to himself than to her.

"Why?" She massaged his tense muscles through his shirt, then nudged the cloth down over his shoulders, baring his skin and the line of muscle that flexed beneath her fingertips.

"I'm scared shitless." He tried to steady his voice, failing miserably.

She bent slightly and kissed the top of his head.

"It's been a long time, Aly. Four years of nothing but memories. Hollow memories. Blurred faces and lost names. Nightmares, some of them. Christ, I think I'm falling in love with you."

His arms encircled her again, tightly, as her heart turned over and tears flooded her eyes. They trickled down her cheeks; she shouldered them away.

His hands clutched fistfuls of her shirt as he lifted his face, the motion shifting the shirt off her breast. His lips parted, and he drew the tip of her breast into his mouth, deeply, as if he would nurse the very essence of her into him. A sound escaped him. His body shook.

The shirt swagged off his shoulders as he stood, his arousal straining within his jeans. He would have kissed her, but her mouth was swollen and sore. So he pressed his lips to her forehead, her temple, took her lobe gently between his teeth before whispering her name in her ear, a flutter of sound that stole through her like feathery heat.

One hand moved between her legs, parted her, slid inside her—she opened her thighs and gasped softly, surprised at how swiftly the ache had become unbearable.

He nestled his mouth against the pulse beating wildly in her throat, slowly withdrew his finger and eased it, little by little along the wet cleft of her until she thrust herself into his hand again and made a whimpering sound that caused her face to heat. She had never ached so badly. Hungered so badly. Perhaps it was the images of him with other women—actresses—that had become burned in her memory over the last days, inviting fantasy. But this was no fantasy. What his hands were now doing to her body made her fantasies pale in comparison. The arousal she had experienced alone in the dark did not shake her. Make her sweat. Make her ooze.

Like warm chocolate.

His lips brushed her ear, and he murmured what he would do to her. How he would do it. Crude words. Love words. Blistering and shocking and stoking the fires until she reached out and tore at the snap on his jeans, the zipper that was pulled so taut he was forced to slide his hand into his jeans to shift his erection so she could drag the zipper down—it made a labored grind in the quiet—the denim peeled back and he caught her wrist, pressed her hand against the massive bulk of him that felt damp and hot through his thin underwear. The scent of him washed over her. Maleness. Musk. It sluiced like alcohol through her blood.

His breath on her neck made her breathe in little gasps, and she wondered if she might faint.

The jeans inched down his hips. He took her hand and put it through the slit of his Jockeys. There was crisp, thick hair there and—

"Oh, God," she heard herself whisper. "Oh, God."

Her fingers closed around him. Not fully around him. That was impossible. A flicker of anxiety bit at her as she thought of him inside her, wondered if it was possible—of course it was—but oh, God—

He trembled at her touch.

His fingers closed around her hand and removed it from his underwear, then with a graceful, skilled action, he pushed the garment down, allowing him to drop heavily against her. That part of him felt hot and silken, and it moved like a muscle flexing as it touched her lower belly. Again his hands slid around her hips, cupped her buttocks and drew her close, loins pressed against loins so she could not tell where her body ended and his began.

The organ thickened, hardened, the delicate skin flushed more deeply, and the veins of it began to pulsate like tiny bursts of fire, like her own heartbeat. The heat felt like a brand against her.

"Undress me," he whispered.

Her hands pulled the shirt down his arms and tossed it to the floor. She caught the waistbands of his jeans and underwear and eased to her knees, drawing them down his thighs, which were rock hard and sprinkled with coarse hair, like the dark thatch at the root of his organ that heavily arced over her shoulder, brushing the side of her cheek. He stepped out of the clothes and kicked them aside.

She allowed her gaze to climb his body slowly, to worship every ridge and bulge, the taut golden flesh that looked slick with sweat, the narrow hips and flat belly, the broad, clean chest, and his developed arms. Her sex felt swollen and hot and wet, throbbing and painful, and the sensations mounted as he shifted his legs apart, inviting her to touch him—the tight purple sacks nestled between his hard thighs.

Not sure if the scent of a man had ever so inebriated her blood—but then she had never experienced this sort of erotic aroma. She felt mad with it, as if what little restraint or shyness was holding her together was snapping like rubber stretched beyond its endurance.

His hands touched her face, and she looked up into his eyes. He slid his thumb between her lips, and she closed her mouth around it, swirled her tongue around it, and sucked it as she took his organ in her hand and gently stroked it against her face.

A groan came from him, and he clenched his teeth. His eyes closed. A pulse throbbed beneath the smooth skin held against her cheek, and he buried his fingers in her hair, as if by doing so, the contact would somehow keep him from falling over the edge.

Four years. She wanted to make this special. She wanted to please him, to chase away the pain in his eyes, to obliterate the nightmares.

Her hand reached out for him. Cupped him, felt the weight of him in her palm, closed her fingers carefully around the tight sacks. His breath caught, and his body jerked. He took his erection in his own hand and gripped it tightly as his body, flushed and beaded with sweat, reflected the lamplight like minute chips of glass.

Her tongue traced the full blue vein that was hot and swelling, tasting slightly of salt, smelling of maleness that made the fullness between her own legs grow excruciating.

His head was broad and smooth, and there was a glistening white pearl of moisture on it. She licked it away, and a spasm flashed through him. He moved, just slightly, as if he were attempting to control himself. His hands fisted, opened, fisted. They shook. His body shook, but when she reached for him again, he succumbed with an exhalation of breath that seemed to rise up from deep inside him.

As if his legs would no longer hold him, he dropped onto the bed, thighs falling open, fingers twisting into the blue sheets as she took him with her mouth and tongue, drawing him in as deeply as she could manage though her lips, though they were sore and she was certain that she could taste her own blood amid the salty sweetness of his skin and fluids. Sweat ran into her eyes as his guttural groans and his rising hips turned the air thick, until the windowpanes became gray with condensation, until the sheets beneath him turned dark with dampness and he tore them from their moorings and clenched them in his desperate hands as he fought to contain the orgasm that was building.

With every flinch of his body, her hunger mounted, fueled her passion and the need to drive him mindlessly to the edge. She felt every throb and pulse upon her tongue deep between her legs until the slightest movement of her own body threatened to shatter her, and a voice in her head chanted *No No No Not yet*—the pain was too splendid.

A rough, fierce curse slid through his lips; his shoulders curled upward and his hands clawed for her, tunneled into her hair and curved around her scalp, lifted her head from him so he could look into her face. "Christ," he hissed through his teeth, and his dark eyes narrowed in concern. "You're bleeding. Your lip is bleeding." Sliding his hands under her arms, he raised her as he rolled and pressed her down into the mattress, drew his tongue over her lip and washed the blood away, slid down her body, fingers pressing into the soft inside flesh of her pale thighs, lifting them toward her chest and spreading her wide.

His face buried there, at the hot wet, apex, making her gasp and jump and quiver uncontrollably, helpless to stop the escalation of the climax that surged as his breath scalded her. His lips enclosed her even as his tongue sank deep into her, as if he wanted to devour her, to drink her—

The pressure exploded outward, lifting her, bowing her;

shot like electricity through her legs that would have kicked
and thrashed had his hands not gripped them firmly, fingertips lightly bruising the velvety skin as he held her in place,
allowing her warm, rich nectar to quench him.

Before the last spasm subsided, he slid his hips into place,
hooked her knees into the crooks of his arms, lifting her,
spreading her wider, and crowned her opening with his throbbing head. Their eyes met and his mouth curled, then he
probed her, little by little, sinking deeper with each small
thrust as if he knew that no matter how wet and slick and
aching she already was, her body would not be completely
prepared.

And it wasn't. The stretch burned, like the first time, and
with a trembling of panic she felt as if she were being im-
paled. Deeper. Deeper. Pausing. Easing, allowing her body
to grow accustomed to him, though the effort must have been
superhuman for him.

With a last sudden drive, he sank into the heart and heat
of her. His eyes rolled closed. Pain and pleasure filled his
face, turned his body hard as stone. The cords in his neck
and shoulders expanded. His jaw worked. The breath shuddered in and out of his mouth, and when he looked at her
again, his eyes were like blue glass.

He ground his body against her, as if he could not go deep
enough. She felt fused to him by heat and pressure. A second
climax made her shudder. He pumped his pelvis against her,
frantically, driving her shoulders into the mattress so she was
forced to turn her face into the pillow to stifle the cry working up her throat.

He growled a four-letter word. Several of them, then let
himself go, head falling back and his mouth opening in a
silent cry. She felt him inside her, pumping and flooding her
with hot semen. With the last throb, he sank onto her with
his face buried in the crook of her neck. Shudders racked
him. A deep moan vibrated his chest and fell warmly upon
her flushed flesh.

He entwined his fingers with hers.

They lay with their arms and legs tangled, their bodies

joined, their hearts pounding together. Neither moved, nor wanted to.

Finally, Alyson opened her heavy eyes and turned her head. He blinked at her, an exhausted grin on his lips.

Smiling, she said, "So, Klem . . . I think I might love you, too."

He watched Alyson sleep, wanting to sleep himself, but already the ache inside him had risen again. His body hurt with it. The smell of her made him drunk, desperate to be inside her. That he had suffered four long years without a woman had nothing to do with it, he realized. Abstinence had not been easy or pleasant, but it had not been hell, either. After the Marcella tragedy, he'd needed time to heal emotionally and get his head straight. The shrinks in prison had helped him to understand his self-destructive behavior. Not that he hadn't understood already, on some level. He'd just learned to stop despising himself—blaming himself—for all that had happened during his youth.

Rolling to his back, he stared at the ceiling. The old heat roiled in his chest. Fear . . . that had not gone away, perhaps never would. It too often surged up from nowhere, unexpectedly. Mostly at night, when he was hovering in that disjointed and confusing place between wakefulness and sleep. Sort of a dream purgatory where his mind couldn't determine if what was happening was real or not. The fear would wash over him like waves of fire that he couldn't stop, igniting the images and sounds in his brain.

He drew in a long, shaking breath and looked toward the window. Rain ran in dark rivulets down the panes. He was nine years old again. . . .

"Mama, don't leave me here. Please. I want to go home. I don't like Mr. Reilly. He's creepy. And Bobby told me—"

"Bobby is a jealous little shit who despises you for your talent, darling. Keep your voice down. It's thanks to Mr. Reilly that you're working on Those Foster Kids. *Do you*

want to spend the rest of your life doing those tacky commercials?"

"I want to go home!"

"Soon, darling."

"I mean, I want to go home to Ticky Creek. I don't want
to live here anymore. I don't want to be an actor. I want to
play baseball like Dad. Where are you going?"

"I'll be back soon. Now behave yourself, Brandon. You
do whatever Mr. Reilly asks you to do. And remember, as
producer of Those Foster Kids, he could have you written
out of the show, and then where would we be? I'd be humiliated, Brandon. I couldn't show my face in this town
again. You love Mama, don't you? You want me to be happy,
don't you?"

She stood in the doorway of Reilly's penthouse apartment,
looking back at him, cold and beautiful as a porcelain statue.
"And if you're very, very good, darling, he'll give you star
billing next season. That means more money. More power.
More prestige. There won't be a door in Hollywood that
won't open to me. To you. To us." Her coral-pink lips
curved. "Think how happy you'd make me, darling."

Then she was gone.

He turned woodenly and stared through the sliding glass
doors at the sheets of rain skittering down the big panes.
There was a balcony with pots of yellow petunias that were
being pounded by the rain. He could just make out the roofs
of buildings beyond, and the thought scuttled through his
mind that there was no escape unless he could fly like Superman.

"Hello, Brandon."

Ralph Reilly walked into the room wearing a red silk robe.
Reilly was enormously fat, with skin white as Elmer's School
Paste. And he smelled. Something like fish. His eyes bugged
a little like a fish, too. He had full, flabby lips that looked
unnaturally red, and there were tufts of gray hair protruding
from his ears. His big belly jiggled under the silk when he
walked, and he wheezed when he breathed.

His lips curved as he padded barefooted over to Brandon.

His fish eyes looked wide and watery, their color a muddy brown. "So glad you could join me this evening, Brandon."

"My mom brought me," he managed in a dry voice. "I didn't want to come."

"No? Why not?"

Brandon looked again toward the glass doors. Where was Superman when you needed him?

Reilly touched him with his sausage fingers, and Brandon stumbled back. "Don't do that."

"What's wrong?" He wheezed.

"Bobby told me . . . what you do to boys. What you did to him. . . ."

His lips curved more. "Bobby is a foolish boy, Brandon. Bobby won't be back next season. You, on the other hand, are a very, very bright boy. Your mother told me so." He caught Brandon's chin, and the clamminess of his fingers made Brandon shiver. "You're a beautiful child. Exquisite. I'm going to make you a superstar. Think how happy that will make your mother. Think of all the pretties you can buy her. A big house. Fancy cars. Expensive clothes. Someday you'll be worshiped by the entire world."

"I don't want to be rich. I don't want to be worshiped. I want to go home to Ticky Creek and play baseball."

"You want to break your mother's heart, Brandon?"

"No." He glanced toward the door again. The rain fell harder. He could barely see the petunias now.

"Just think how much she'll love you. You owe her, you know. She gave up her career to devote her life to your success. If you were dropped from the show, imagine what that would do to her. I don't think she'd ever forgive you. . . ."

He walked to a bar and poured liquor into a glass, then he returned to Brandon. "Drink this. It's a magic elixir. Happy juice. Amnesia in a bottle. It'll relax you, and you'll feel better soon. That's a good boy. Chivas is your friend, Brandon. It chases the fear away. Blurs the memories. Erases the pain. There's more where that came from. Much more. Oh, yes. You'll be my shining star. My finest creation. The

*entire world will love you. Your mother will live like a queen,
and she'll adore you. . . ."*

*. . . Naked, he crawled into the rain that fell stinging and
cold against his bruised flesh. He collapsed by the petunias,
whose yellow blooms were torn and battered, lying in a sodden heap in their pots. Curling his knees into his chest, he
closed his eyes and willed himself not to puke again. Willed
the pain to stop. And the horror. Too late for Superman.
Brandon Carlyle was going to be a superstar. And a god.
The whole goddamn world was going to love him. Including
his mom.*

*He'd simply drink the magic elixir. His happy juice. Am-
nesia in a bottle. Maybe if he drank enough, he'd cease to
exist. Poof! Bye-bye, Brandon. And maybe when, or if, he
woke up again, he'd be home in Ticky Creek, safe with Bernie and Henry, who loved him just because. . . .*

*Looking back through the rain and up into Ralph Reilly's
eyes, he thought, Too late for Ticky Creek. Poof! Bye-bye,
Brandon.*

Alyson opened her eyes, heard the rumble of thunder and
the rattle of hard rain against the window. The bed was shaking.

Brandon sat on the edge of the bed, his back to her, shoulders curled in and his head down.

She sat up and reached out. Body trembling and sweating,
he groaned at her touch.

Crawling to his side, she took his face in her hands.
"What's wrong? Tell me what's wrong."

"Nightmares. I . . . need a drink, Aly. I need it bad."

"Why do you need a drink when you've got me?"

He flashed her a weak smile. "Wanna be my happy juice?"

"I've been called stranger things. Come here. Lie down."
He slid down beside her, and she wrapped her arms around
him, felt his intense heat and the tension in his body that
continued to shake. She held him fiercely to her and kissed
his face, smoothed his hair, slid her legs around him and

invited him in, gasping as he breached her with a forceful thrust that drove white pain up her back.

Joined, they lay motionless, Brandon's hammering heart beating against her, and inside her. Little by little, his shaking eased, his breathing quieted, his body cooled.

"Better now?" she whispered in his ear.

"Hold me," he said. "Just hold me."

14

Alyson looked up into Betty's face, pinched with something just short of fire-and-brimstone condemnation. Matters weren't helped by the fact that during her sleep the sheet and blanket had worked down around her waist. She snatched up the rumpled top sheet to cover her breasts, and smiled weakly.

Until that moment Alyson hadn't paid a lot of attention to Bernie's hired caretaker, but as she studied the woman's coarse features, she realized that most of the makeup on her face was the permanent sort: tattooed eyeliner, blush, and lipstick. And not to forget the eyebrows, black as the ace of spades, arched a little too high, making her green eyes look a bit bulging. There were a few dark hairs sprouting above her upper lip.

Betty, wearing a starched white uniform, drew in a deep breath, as if to calm the anger that was flushing her face. "This is a Christian home with Christian values, young woman. You might at least have had the decency to return

to the other room when you were finished with your forni-
cations."

She thought of spitefully explaining in graphic detail to
Betty just where Brandon's "values" had been located last
night. Pulling the sheet up to her chin, Alyson allowed her
smile to go flat. "Good morning to you, too, Betty."

Betty tossed a box wrapped in Christmas paper onto the
bed. "Mr. Brandon asked me to give you this when you woke
up, and to tell you that he and Mr. Henry will be back by
noon. They've gone fishing. He's left you the keys to his
car. Your clothes have been laundered, so you may leave at
your first opportunity."

She turned on her white, rubber-soled shoes and marched
to the door, then paused and looked back, one tattooed eyebrow rising like some strange bird's wing. "I knew what you
were after the minute I saw you. What women like you are
always after. I'll pray for you at Bible study tonight."

"Thanks," Alyson replied with a wide smile that made
Betty's face go even darker. "And while you're at it, you
might reread the part of the Good Book that says something
about 'Judge not, lest ye be judged.' "

She blinked as Betty slammed the door. Her heavy footfalls vibrated the room as she stomped down the stairs. Another door slammed.

In that moment Alyson realized that she didn't care much
for Betty. In fact, she didn't care for her at all.

Sinking back into the pillows, Alyson focused on the gift
Betty had delivered. Santa's elves, looking like the dwarfs
Dopey, Sleepy, and Doc, smiled up at her from slick, brightly
hued paper. She carefully peeled it away to reveal a twenty-
four-count Twinkie box.

"No doubt about it, Carlyle, you sure know the way to a
woman's heart," she said aloud and reached inside, pulling
out two spongy cakes. She tore open the wrappers and settled
back to enjoy the treats as much as her sore mouth would
allow.

Only then did the memories of the previous night intrude,

as well as the aches and pains that, suddenly awakened, shot like nails through her.

Perhaps the rest room incident at the River Road had only been coincidental to the Mitsy debacle. She mustn't allow paranoia over Alan's suppositions about Anticipating to cloud her judgment. Mitsy was disturbed, but disturbed enough to actually kill a woman?

She touched her lip, then her eye. Certainly disturbed enough to assault her. Disturbed enough to believe she was a dead movie star. Disturbed enough to believe she was married to Carlyle.

Finishing one Twinkie, she started on the next.

Her thoughts drifted to Carlyle, and she smiled.

*Alyson showered and dressed in the clothes Betty had laun-*dered for her. They were heavily starched and abraded her skin. She descended the stairs feeling like Daniel entering the lion's den. From below came the sounds of television interspersed with Betty humming a familiar tune. Pausing on the stairs and cocking her head to one side, Alyson listened hard, her mind trying to place the tune that dissolved behind the fiery Say Yes to Jesus or Go Straight to Hell preaching of Rod Parsley.

She moved through the kitchen to Bernie's door. Betty was in the process of hefting Bernie's frail frame out of the bed and into the wheelchair without so much as a grunt of effort.

Betty looked up and saw her. Her mouth pursed. Straightening, she planted herself between Alyson and Bernie. "What do you want, Miss James?"

"I'd like to say hello to Bernie."

"I told you. She can't hear you."

Alyson forced a smile. "We don't really know that, do we?"

"Certainly we do. The doctors—"

"Aren't infallible. I watched a PBS special on stroke victims not long ago. The brain's a mystery as vast as the universe. As long as there's some sort of brain function, which there obviously is in Bernie's case, or she'd be on total life support, there's a remote chance that she can see, hear, and understand us."

Alyson entered the room, her gaze locked with Betty's. "Brandon and Henry obviously continue to hold on to the faith that she's aware of her surroundings. Why else would they insist on providing her the stimulation of television, even reading to her?" Her smile stretching, Alyson added, "Certainly you're aware of those possibilities. You're a nurse, after all, and judging by what Brandon and Henry have told me, a very responsible nurse. They adore you."

He is the provider of miracles. Ask, and they shall be delivered! Seek Him, and His blessings will abound!

Betty looked away. Her shoulders relaxed a little.

"In fact," Alyson added as she moved past Betty, "they'd be quite lost without you. They've come to think of you as a member of their family."

"They *are* my family," she said in her scratchy voice. "They're all I have in the world."

"Then you'll be understandably cautious about me. I'm certain Brandon is like a son to you."

Betty's head slowly turned, and her eyes met Alyson's again. The color was back in her face, watermelon red. "A son? My dear Miss James, I'm hardly old enough to be Mr. Brandon's mother."

Cast out the demons of vanity and humble yourself before Him. Dooown, I say, dooooown on your knees, I said dooooown on your kneees, and cast out that devil conceit who burns in your heart! Say Hallelujah Jeeeeeesus!

"I'm sorry. A sister, then."

"I'm only forty-five."

"Certainly a sister."

"What I feel for Mr. Brandon, and Mr. Henry as well, is deeper than words can convey. I thank God every night that I've been blessed with the friendship and, yes, love of these wonderful, wonderful men."

Plant the seed and prepare for the harvest. Send whatever you can afford. Five dollars, ten dollars, ten thouuwzand—

"I'm sure. You're very fortunate, Betty. You'll be devastated when Bernie passes away. Then you'll be forced to find another position, won't you?" Alyson placed the lap blanket over Bernie's knees. "Do you live alone?"

Betty nodded.

"Do you work for a service?" Alyson rested on one knee beside Bernie's chair, smiled into Bernie's staring blue eyes. She reached for her hand.

"No." Betty clasped her hands together beneath her breasts.

"Then how did you happen to land this position?"

"As luck would have it, I rented a room from their previous nurse. I had met the Carlyles on occasion, through Johanna—"

Say goodbye to debt and hello to heavenly prosperity!

"What happened to Johanna?"

"Dead."

Alyson's gaze went back to Betty. "What happened?"

"She drowned in Ticky Creek. A boating accident. Mr. Henry was devastated, naturally. I volunteered to step in until the service could provide him a replacement, but we clicked, and here I am."

"Lucky you."

"Yes. Lucky me."

Hallelujah!

Curling her fingers around Bernie's cold hand, Alyson asked, "Where did you get your training?"

"Kansas City. I'm a licensed registered nurse."

"So you moved here from Kansas City?"

". . . Yes."

"What brought you to Ticky Creek?"

"What generally makes a woman pick up and leave home to relocate?"

"A man?"

She nodded.

"A husband?"

"No." She shook her head and averted her eyes. "I've never been married."

"Are you still together?"

"No."

"I'm sorry."

"I don't dwell on what might have been, Miss James. Rather I choose to focus on the present. I'm happy and content with my life, and those with whom I choose to share it."

Amen, Brothers and Sisters. Amen.

The clouds were dark and low, the air thick and cool, and growing cooler by the minute. Calm before the storm, Alyson thought as, settling behind the Jaguar's steering wheel, she glanced up at the towering pine trees with their limbs, saturated by the night's rain, drooping motionless toward the ground.

She punched the remote on the console and watched the giant black iron gate roll to the right. She knew the Jaguar's engine was running, but she couldn't feel it. Or hear it. Not like the Rent A Heap with the broken heater that was waiting for her back at the motel. She glanced into the rearview mirror, knowing what she would see there. Betty, standing picture-framed behind the screen door, arms crossed, face expressionless. Well, not exactly expressionless. If looks could kill, Betty would have had her dead and buried within five minutes of finding her, naked, in Brandon's bed.

The heater automatically kicked on and breathed a warm stream of air over her feet. She shifted her gaze away from Betty and back toward the gate.

A woman was there, just beyond the gate, at the verge of the highway. Alyson blinked and looked harder, thinking that her eyes were playing tricks on her. The figure stood in the middle of the drive just beyond the opening gate, her white legs spread a little, looking like a gunslinger preparing to draw and fire. She wore baggy flowered pants, a pink tube top, and blue and white flip-flops on her feet. After her initial jolt of fear passed, it occurred to Alyson that the woman had to be freezing. For an instant, she'd thought the woman was Mitsy Dillman, but her hair was longer and not as blond as

Mitsy's. And she was thinner. Too thin. She stared back at Alyson with dark, liquid eyes that looked too big for her gaunt face. Alyson recognized her then ... the odd woman she had seen at the Pine Lodge Café the day of Henry's attack.

Alyson shifted the car into Drive and eased off the brake. The Jag crept forward while the woman continued to watch her, her arms hanging limply at her sides and her face a blank stare. Alyson allowed the car to move within three feet of the woman, and still she didn't budge. She braked and opened her hands as if to ask, "Are you going to get out of my way?"

A smile touched the woman's lips, and she raised one hand like a traffic patrolman, indicating that Alyson should stay where she was. Then she moved toward the car.

Alyson hit the locks, and although instinct shrieked at her to floor the gas pedal, she could only grip the wheel and watch the woman move up to the driver's window and stoop slightly to look in at her. She was still smiling a genuinely warm smile, which helped to alleviate some of Alyson's tension.

Alyson touched the window button, allowing the glass to slide down a few inches.

The woman's smile widened. "I have to speak to you," she said in a pleasant voice, a voice that one would use with an old friend—certainly not with a stranger who must have been looking at her as if she would, at any second, produce a butcher knife out of her flowered pants.

The woman tucked an errant strand of hair behind her ear. She glanced toward the house, and the smile disappeared, replaced by a deep furrow between her eyebrows. "This is where he lives, isn't it?" she said in a dreamy voice. "Mick Warner. That rock singer guy. The one I saw on HBO last night."

Oh, boy, here we go again. Alyson jabbed the remote, and the gate began to slide closed.

"It's okay," the woman said. "I didn't come here to see him. I came to see you. We really have to talk. I promise to be brief." She looked away, as if she were listening to something or someone, and having a hard time hearing them. Again she frowned and rubbed her temple with two fingers. "I'm really rusty at this. In fact, I'm not even sure if I'm getting the messages straight. But I must be, mustn't I, or I wouldn't have found my way here? Sometimes there are just too many talking at once. It's a little like radio interference. It takes a while to tune in just right, and like I said, I'm really rusty. Do you mind if I get in the car? I've been walking awhile. My car is a couple miles up the road. I ran out of gas. Forgot to fill up before leaving White Sands. Dumb, dumb, dumb. And I didn't even bring my purse." Again with the smile. Only it was tired now, and the look in her eyes suggested that she knew the thoughts in Alyson's head.

"I'm not a nut," the woman tried to assure her. "And I won't take up much of your time." She flinched and straightened, cocked her head a little to the right, and pressed her flattened hand against her ear, as if she had a severe earache. She squeezed her eyes closed. Between her teeth, she said, "Buddy says the band was Dessie Anne's."

Alyson stared at her.

The woman shrugged and opened her eyes. Her face appeared whiter, if that was possible, and she sank against the car as if exhausted. Her dark eyes puddled with tears. "God," she sighed, "this sucks."

Alyson eased the window down a few more inches. "What sucks?" she asked.

"I forgot how exhausting it all is. And painful. Sometimes you feel as if you're going insane. Think of it this way. Imagine yourself surrounded by a dozen televisions and radios all tuned to different channels or stations, and the volume is turned up all the way. That's what if feels like inside my head right now. Everyone is trying to speak at once. It's INFURIATING!" she shouted as she stared off into space.

It occurred to Alyson that there were certainly a lot of nuts in Ticky Creek. Then again, why was she surprised? The way the citizens sheltered Carlyle wasn't exactly normal. The whole town and its atmosphere were starting to feel a little cultlike.

"Who are 'they'?" she asked hesitantly, expecting her to respond something like "The Mother Ship, of course. Who else?"

She shrugged and rubbed her temple. "I've always called them Watchers. Because that's what they do. Maybe I should have called them Screamers, because they do a lot of that as well." Looking down again at Alyson, she said, "If you'll take me back to my car, I'll tell you all about them. I promise you're in no danger from me. I'm here to help."

Alyson looked the woman up and down. Her flip-flop-adorned feet were partially submerged in a puddle of muddy water, and there were drying bits of mud on her shins. Rain began to fall in big drops, spatting against her naked shoulders, yet her eyes regarded Alyson with an intuitiveness and kindness that made Alyson think of a painting she had once seen of Jesus laying hands on a crippled child.

She'd be stupid to allow the woman in the car, of course. But there was something about her—fascinating as well as disturbing. The reporter's instinct that had made her the sharpest in the business kicked in. That instinct had seldom steered her wrong.

"Fine," Alyson said with an exasperated sigh. "Get in."

The woman rounded the car, opened the door, then removed her flip-flops, which she cradled against her stomach, smearing her tube top and pants with mud. Yet, she didn't get into the car immediately. She stood looking back at the house while rain fell harder and a sudden wind kicked up, rocking the car.

"Excuse me?" Alyson leaned over the console and looked at her, intent on explaining that the owner of the Jag would not appreciate his car seats getting wrecked by rain, but words left her. The woman's expression was blank again, her eyes glazed and lifeless like a doll's as they focused on the house.

Then her head turned slowly, cocked a little, and a frown

creased her forehead. "Watch out for Billy Boy, says Buddy."

"Who is Buddy? And who is Billy Boy?"

The woman sagged against the car door and released her breath. She hesitated before answering. "I don't know. It's not like they introduce themselves. It's not the messenger who's important. It's the message." Dropping into the car seat, her shoes in her lap, she slammed the car door and sank back against the seat, as if her head was suddenly too heavy to hold up.

"Are you ill?" Alyson placed her hand against the woman's damp forehead. She felt frighteningly icy, as if there was no body heat in her at all.

"I suppose that's a matter of opinion," the woman replied in a thin voice, then she looked at Alyson directly, her eyes the same murky brown as Ticky Creek. "I'm very hungry. Would you lend me a few dollars so I can buy gas and something to eat? I promise to pay you back. You're staying at the Pine Lodge, right? I'll send the money to you there."

"How do you know I'm staying at the Pine Lodge?"

"The same way I know everything else, I guess. One of the Watchers told me." Smiling, she wrapped her cold fingers around Alyson's wrist and squeezed it reassuringly. "Drive. I'll try to explain. Besides, the energy here isn't good. And the air smells a bit like sulfur. Do you smell it?"

Alyson shook her head.

"No, I suppose you wouldn't. Trust me, it isn't a good sign." Her stomach growled. She pressed her hand against her flat belly and smiled in chagrin.

Alyson pulled onto the highway and headed toward town. Rain fell harder. She turned on the wipers; they bumped back and forth—the only sound for a long minute.

"My name is Nora," the woman said. "Nora Allen. Actually, it's Nora Jewel Allen. I was married for a while. Three years exactly. His last name was—is—Preston. But I didn't want to keep his name after the divorce. I didn't want anything to do with him—no reminders."

Alyson drove, staring straight ahead through the rain and

feeling as if reality had taken a strange detour into the surreal.

Nora carefully balanced the muddy shoes on her knees, pulled the bottom edge of her tube top up and the elastic waistband of her pants down, exposing the skin below her navel. "This is what he did to me."

Alyson stared at the red, puckered flesh as wide as a fist with threads of blue and pink scars radiating like sunbeams from it. "Oh my," she said, her attention focused on the healing injury and not on the road. The car suddenly shimmied onto the rough shoulder, forcing Alyson to jerk the wheel hard to regain control.

"He shot me," Nora explained, staring down at the scar. "Walked right up to me in the Neiman Marcus parking lot on Christmas Eve, pointed a gun, and pulled the trigger in front of twenty-five witnesses. Then he turned the gun on himself. Unfortunately, he was shaking so hard the bullet only grazed his temple. Three men tackled him and took the gun away."

Sighing, she adjusted her clothes. "I died on the operating table. It was like watching one of those *Unsolved Mysteries* segments where the storyteller describes leaving her body and floating overhead, watching the whole procedure. Only there was no tunnel with a bright light. Just doors, and as I watched, each door blew open. I expected to see long-dead relatives rush out to greet me—welcome to Heaven, and all that—but no. Nothing so grandiose. There was nothing behind the doors. At least nothing I could see. Then there was this roaring, like loud, powerful winds, only I couldn't feel the winds. And then I realized the roaring wasn't wind; it was voices all shouting at once. They were filling up my head."

She touched her temple again and closed her eyes. "Boy, were they pissed. You see, they weren't strangers. Not that they're friends by any stretch of the imagination. They'd been there at my birth—well, not that I can remember anything before my third year, but I do remember the first time I really came to understand that I was different.

"I was three years old. We lived in a house overlooking

Ticky Creek. The woman I thought was my mother was sitting a neighbor's baby—he was toddling around in this droopy wet diaper, and I was on a blanket on the floor in front of this buzz fan, coloring, thinking how bad the baby smelled and wondering why no one else noticed. The stink made me want to puke, and I thought it must be his wet diaper.

"Out of nowhere these voices showed up in my head. One was saying, *Get rid of the kid. Do it. Do it now. Open the door and let him out. He must die.* And the other voice was saying, *Don't do it. Don't you dare do it. Your mother will spank you hard if you do it. Just keep your nose to the coloring book, Nora Jewel, and mind your own business.*"

Nora looked out at the drenched countryside, her face moist with sweat. Rivulets of rain reflected off her cheeks. "I remember looking over at my mother, who was busy preparing dinner and paying me and the boy no attention whatsoever. I wondered why she couldn't hear the voices or smell the stink.

"*Get rid of the kid*, the voice continued to shout. *Time is running out. Almost too late. Do it now. Open the door and let him out!* This voice was very loud and frantic, and the other voice, the one that kept chanting *No no no*, was dwindling, like its volume was slowly being turned down. So I threw down my crayon and ran to the door, barely able to reach the knob, and I opened it and watched as the boy ran out into the yard and toward the creek. *He's going to die*, the voice said, *and that's good. You did very, very good, Nora Jewel. They'll be angry, but you're a child, so what are they going to do?*

"Then suddenly, with no warning, my mother turned toward me and her face was white as the flour on her hands. The voice in my head, said, *Fuck!* and I could hear the other voice, laughing hysterically and shouting, *Got her! The silly bitch was listening for a change!* My mother looked out the window and saw the baby—by then he was nearly to the water—and she screamed and ran for the door. She knocked me aside as she ran from the house and toward the creek.

She tripped and sprawled on her hands and knees while she screamed at the kid—and the voice in my head began to scream, *Let him go!* and it was screaming so loud, I began to scream as well, 'Let him go!' She caught up to him just as he reached the water and toppled facedown into it. I can still see her standing shin deep in the dark water, her knees bleeding and grass-stained, clutching the sopping baby with hands gooped with damp flour. She was horrified and furious, and when she looked at me, she said, 'What are you, a monster?'

"The voices were suddenly silent, and I realized just how frightened I was. And ashamed. And confused. I actually pissed on myself. Then the solitary voice came back, *We tried, Nora Jewel. We did our best. Better luck next time.*

"I tried to explain to my mother about the voices, but she only whipped me, hard, with a thin leather belt, and kept calling me a monster and a devil child. It certainly wouldn't be the last time. Oh, no. Hardly the last time.

"Finally, on my thirteenth birthday, I was sitting in front of the television doing my homework and the six o'clock news was on, a Shreveport channel—a story about a six-year-old missing boy, and suddenly the voice spoke up, *Caddo Lake, Cypress Point. Pier fifteen. The Mona Lisa. Hurry!*

"I ran to the phone and called the local police. Of course I didn't tell them I heard voices, at least not then; I'd learned to keep that little secret to myself. My butt couldn't stand too many more whippings, let me tell you. So I just put on my most adult-sounding voice and told them I overheard a conversation regarding the boy. They didn't believe me, of course. So I was forced to get on my bike and ride to the police station myself. I still remember the police chief's face as I told him about the voice. He howled in laughter, pointed a finger at the tip of my nose, and said, 'What are you, a goddamn psychic?' I'd never heard the word 'psychic,' but I sensed it wasn't something I should feel proud about, not the way he was laughing and pointing. Then the voice piped up, furious, and through me shouted, *If you keep screwing*

Thelma May Stewart, her husband's gonna blow your Wie-nerschnitzel away with his Colt .45!"

Nora turned her smile on Alyson. "You see, it wasn't the Thelma May part that convinced him I had the sight; it was the Wienerschnitzel part. That was Thelma's pet name for his pecker. You should've seen his face. Went white as a sheet. He grabbed up the phone and called the Shreveport police. An hour later they located the boy exactly where I told them, hidden away in the cabin of a cruiser called the *Mona Lisa*. Fifteen minutes later the kidnapper showed up packing a duffel bag containing a hacksaw, a bunch of sexual devices, and a folder of child pornography. Eventually they tied him to ten other missing children throughout the state.

"My sense of satisfaction was short-lived. People knew then, about the voices. Suddenly I was a freak. Weirdos started showing up at our house. My friends would have nothing to do with me. I even had a teacher refuse to come in the classroom until I was removed. Suddenly everyone thought I knew all their dirty little secrets. But the voices didn't work that way. I couldn't read people's thoughts. The voices came out only in a crisis situation.

"Then I overhead my mother on the phone, and she was screaming at someone, 'The girl is a freak. I want her out of my house. I should sue you for this. She's obviously pos-sessed, and I want you to come get her right now.'

"I learned then that I was adopted. Two weeks later my parent dropped me off at a baby-sitter who took in foster children who couldn't be placed for one reason or another. I decided at that point that I was going to closet the voices. I wasn't going to risk another occurrence like the *Mona Lisa* thing, and although it was very hard work, eventually I man-aged to barricade them away, or most of them.

"There were others. Different voices. Late at night they'd come to me with soothing tones. I called them the Storytell-ers. I suppose they'd been there all along, but the Watchers had drowned them out.

"I soon learned that the Storytellers had their own agenda. They drove me to write, and write I did. By the time I was twenty-two, I'd sold my first novel. I wrote three books a year. Or rather, they did, I suppose. I hesitate to take credit for it. I just put my fingers on the keyboard and out came the words. My eighth novel hit the *New York Times* best-seller list. I was living in Dallas then, and making very good money. Then a friend introduced me to Paul Preston. He was a stockbroker. Very successful. . . .

"The Watchers tried to warn me. I could hear them banging on the doors I'd erected, but my ability to contain them had grown powerful over the years. Paul and I married, and the trouble began on our honeymoon. We went to Hawaii. He wouldn't let me wear a bathing suit. Then my skirts were too short. I had to wear long sleeves so my arms wouldn't show, and blouses with high collars. He told me how to wear my hair, and what to eat. When we returned to Dallas, he forbade me to write. He contacted my agent and editors, and announced my retirement.

"I spent our first anniversary in the hospital. He'd beaten me black and blue. I took it for three years only because he threatened that if I left him, he'd kill me. I'll never forget the moment I realized he'd kill me, regardless. I was watching the news about a man who murdered his wife in front of their three children. He choked her, then stabbed her in the throat with a pair of scissors, and proceeded to try and cut off her head. All while the children were on the phone to the police, begging for someone to help their mother. That afternoon I learned I was pregnant, and all I could think of was the recording of those children screaming into a phone, 'Someone stop my daddy, he's hurting my mommy.'

"So I moved out of the house and filed for divorce. He came after me, of course, and though I begged the police to help me, they could do nothing unless he actually threatened me verbally or physically. Which brings me to the Neiman Marcus parking lot on Christmas Eve, the Parkland Hospital ER, and my floating over my body, watching those long-barricaded doors fly open. The Watchers are back, more powerful than ever, but I'm having a very hard time understanding them now. My focus is off or scrambled, like radio interference. I'm going to have to learn how to listen all over again.

"Oh, and that toddler who smelled like urine—only I later realized it wasn't urine I was smelling, it was sulfur—the baby I let out the door when I was only three, who would have drowned if my parent hadn't saved him? Two years ago he was arrested in Florida. He'd murdered sixty-three women and buried their bodies in the Everglades."

Alyson remained in the car as Nora went about the business of filling a plastic jug with gasoline. Part of her wanted to drive away and put the last half-hour out of her memory, but simply driving off into the rain wasn't going to accomplish that. If one could believe the woman's story, then she must also believe that Nora Allen had searched her out for a reason. A very important reason. But did she believe the woman's odd story?

While working at the *Galaxy Gazette* she'd had at least a dozen such tales cross her desk every day. Twice a week she and her peers met in the coffee lounge and shared the stories—reading each aloud to a chorus of whoops and giggles, not for a moment considering that any of them could have been true.

Who the heck was Buddy? And Dessie Anne? And Billy Boy?

Alyson smiled to herself, feeling embarrassed that she'd allow herself, even for an instant, to be enticed by such a ruse.

Nora capped the gas jug and walked to a snack machine, fed it money, and punched a series of buttons. She peered off into space again, obviously listening to her companions, then moved to a newspaper rack, collected a *Tyler Herald*, which she tucked under her arm, then returned to the car. As she dropped into the seat, she tossed a Twinkie package into Alyson's lap. "Here you go, cupcake. And by the way"—she turned her doll's eyes to Alyson's, and a flat smile stretched her mouth—"Klem is crazy about you, in case you harbored any doubts."

The blood rushed from Alyson's head as she stared back into Nora's dark, glazed eyes.

Nora positioned the gas jug between her feet, closed the door, then sank back into the seat. She regarded the collection of snacks on her lap and reached for a Slim Jim.

The idea that Nora Allen was not a kook sank, along with Alyson's heart, to the pit of her suddenly nauseated stomach.

Nora's eyes drifted closed in apparent pleasure and relief as she chewed the spicy beef stick. "God, I'm trying to remember the last time I ate. Yesterday at lunch. I was trying to write last night, and forgot about food. Except I couldn't write. The Storytellers are still brooding, I think. They've been angry since I married Paul. Perhaps he frightened them. That makes sense, doesn't it? Perhaps they were simply trying to protect me, because when they spoke, I was compelled to write. I mean, I had to write. It was a compulsion. But it's been ten months since Paul shot me. Eight months since our divorce was finalized. Seven months since he was incarcerated in Huntsville Prison. So why haven't they returned? I don't know what I'll do if they don't do something soon. I can't exist on air, for God's sake."

She chewed the beef stick and looked thoughtful.

Alyson's blood felt like cold jelly in her veins.

Then, as if waking from her thoughts, Nora handed the *Tyler Herald* to her. "I'm not sure why," she explained with a shrug. "But obviously there's something there that might help you."

"I don't understand why you've come to me like this," Alyson said, finally finding her voice, which sounded tight and dry.

"I don't know either. All I know is that I fell asleep watching *Steel Magnolias* on HBO. I awoke suddenly, around three A.M., with a Watcher shouting in my head, *Wake up, wake up! If you don't do something soon, it's going to be too late!* I was staring at Mick Warner shoving a hypodermic needle full of heroin into his arm."

Alyson shook her head. "There's no such person as Mick Warner, Nora. He's simply a character in a movie, *Dark Night in Jericho.*"

"Jericho, Texas, right?"

"Fictitious. Like Mick Warner."

Nora frowned. "Are they? Fictitious?" She shrugged and shook her head. "Let's look at it rationally. Small town boy moves to bright lights big city. He becomes a superstar. Loved by the world. No, not simply loved—worshiped. Remember a comment John Lennon made once in the sixties, when the Beatles skyrocketed to fame? He said they were worshiped more than Jesus, or something to that effect. He didn't mean it literally, of course, but in a way it was true. When was the last time you saw millions of people fall to their knees in the presence of a solitary man—discounting the Pope, of course? Then the burden of superstardom becomes too much. His image begins to crumble, and people get a glimpse that he's not a god. Not Jesus or Buddha or whatever. And they're angered by his humanity. Angered by his lack of perfection. They feel as if they've been duped.

"The more the worshipers turn on him, the more he disintegrates. It's a vicious cycle, isn't it? He can't scream out his anger and frustration—that's biting the hand that feeds you, so to speak, if you'll pardon the dreadful cliché—so he turns the anger in on himself. He begins to believe their bullshit: that he's not worthy, or that it was all a stupid fluke.

"Superstar returns to his hometown in Texas, where on some level people still worship him and he can begin to feel good about himself again. He heals, grows strong, reinvents himself. Throws a free rock concert for his hometown to say *thank you for your support*. It's a magnificent success. He's back on top. Then some asshole walks up with a gun and puts a bullet in our superstar's head. He's sprawled on rain-slick asphalt at midnight, illuminated by a streetlight while his brains run out in the gutter. Certainly a *Dark Night in Jericho*, Texas . . . and then the Technicolor image fades to black and white."

Wind slammed the car and drove spikes of rain against

the windshield. Alyson looked out at the blurry Conoco sign, feeling as if the temperature had dropped fifty degrees in the last five minutes. "Is someone going to kill Brandon Carlyle?" she asked in a shaking voice. She no longer doubted the haunting young woman—she had been convinced of Nora Allen's gift the moment she said, "Here you go, cupcake. Klem is crazy about you. . . ."

Her cheeks colorless, her hands resting limply in her lap, Nora looked through the windshield, her gaze directed upward. She released a heavy sigh. "Don't look now, but the skies are looking pretty damn dark over Jericho."

The rain abated, but the clouds continued to roil and growl and occasionally lash at the earth with lightning. As Nora funneled gas into her car, a Honda Civic that had seen better days, Alyson stood beside her, unable to walk away. Not yet. Desperation tied her to the pale, thin woman like a chain. The rational part of her mind refused to totally buy Nora Allen's story. The irrational part wanted answers.

"If you're capable of knowing intimate conversations between me and Carlyle, why aren't you capable of telling me who Anticipating is?"

"I might, eventually. I'll try harder. But like I said, I'm rusty." She smiled at Alyson and shrugged. "The voices are quiet now, so they must be satisfied that I've done what I was sent here to do."

"Which is? I mean, you didn't really tell me anything more than I already knew. Someone who calls herself Anticipating is a threat to Carlyle. Is it Mitsy Dillman?"

"I don't know. I'm sorry." Nora screwed on the gas cap and leaned against the fender. "There has to be some message in what they've told us. They don't usually pipe up that loudly for no reason. Could be you're looking the answer square in the eye and you just don't know it. You know that old saying, You're standing too close to see something clearly?"

Nora put her hand on Alyson's shoulder. "The Watchers

are with you as well, Miss James. They're with everyone. Call them what you want—conscience, intuition, angels—all those voices rattling around in our heads from the moment we're capable of understanding language are there to guide us. Listen and trust. Occasionally the choices we make might not seem the wisest or most popular, but ultimately they prove to be right. Like that toddler. If he had died that morning, there would be sixty-three women alive today—"

"But there were also voices who told you not to let him out of the house. The ones who alerted your parent."

"I never said all of the Watchers are good. The gift is in learning which voices to follow. Eventually you recognize the difference." Nora hugged her, held her close. When she stepped away, she looked concerned. She reached for Alyson's hand and lifted it to her nose, shook her head, then bent and sniffed her blouse, pulling away sharply as her eyes came back to Alyson's. "It's the clothes. They smell of sulfur."

Alyson frowned and looked down at her laundered blouse and jeans. "They've just been washed. And what's the deal with sulfur anyway?"

"It's the stench of evil," Nora replied. "I suspect it's closer than we thought."

Henry's face was pale as he looked at Brandon through his rain-speckled eyeglasses. Water dripped off his rubberized hat and pooled in the bottom of the boat where a string of catfish lay.

Brandon hadn't wanted to tell Henry about Anticipating, but the incident with Mitsy the night before left him little choice. Gossip traveled through Ticky Creek like a grass fire in August. Better that Henry hear about it from Brandon.

"Henry, celebrities get this sort of thing all the time. Normally it doesn't amount to a hill of beans. Mitsy Dillman is a nut, and she's been locked away."

"But for how long? If she's Jack Dillman's sister, she'll be out in days, if she isn't out already. Then what?"

"I'll put a restraining order on her. I'll do that this after-noon."

"You can't discount her, Brandon. If she's crazy enough to attack Al—"

"She thinks she's Marilyn Monroe, Henry. She has issues."

Both men stared down at their red-and-white bobbers float-ing on the surface of the rain-pocked creek. The wind was rising and the light dimming. Thunder rumbled north, fol-lowed by a distant flash of light.

"You're in love with her, aren't you?" Henry asked, lifting his line out of the water to check his bait. "Al, I mean."

Brandon glanced at his uncle, thankful to put the topic of Mitsy Dillman and Anticipating behind them. He was re-lieved to see color returning to Henry's cheeks. "Yes, I think so."

Henry eased his hook and line back into the creek. "Thought so. A man's got a look about him when he's soft for a woman. Had that look myself not twenty minutes after first layin' eyes on Bernie. At that very moment I knew we were destined to be married. Asked her to be my wife two days later, on our second date. I thought she might try to play hard to get or somethin', but no. She smiled right up into my eyes and said, 'Henry Carlyle, I'd be honored to spend the rest of my life with you.'

"We were married two weeks later. Your dad stood up with me. He was only ten, and had to borrow a suit from a neighbor. It was too big, and the sleeves kept slidin' down over his hands."

Henry turned his blue eyes on Brandon and smiled. "Me and Bernie used to lie in bed at night and conjecture on the type of woman you'd marry. Ever' time we'd hear or read about you dating this or that actress or model, we'd just shake our heads. 'Not his type. Ain't gonna last.' And we were right. The minute Al fell out of that tree on top of you I knew she was the one. Got spunk, that one. I wouldn't mind seein' you married before I croak. I'd rest a little better in my grave knowin' you were happy for the first time in your life."

Brandon frowned. "Don't talk about croaking, Henry. It's not something to joke about."

"Why not? It's gonna happen whether you want it to or not. I'm not a young man, Brandon. I'm tired. This old ticker is runnin' down. Bernie will be gone soon. I just can't imagine a life without her. For forty years she's been my reason to get up every mornin' and my reason for climbin' into bed at night. I won't want to go on without her."

"What about me?" Brandon demanded angrily. "I need you, Henry. You're all I've got in the world."

"You have Al now. That's where your focus needs to be, boy. She's the future. She and the young'uns she'll give you."

A clap of thunder ripped the air and the rain drove harder. The creek stirred under the boat, turning it in a slow spiral like flotsam on an eddy. "We'd better go in," Brandon shouted.

Henry nodded and secured his fishing pole in the bottom of the boat while Brandon began cranking the outboard motor. Once. Twice. The motor roared, then sputtered, died. He cranked again. Nothing. He unscrewed the gas cap and peered down into the empty tank, glanced back at Henry. "I thought you said you filled this baby up on Sunday."

"I did."

"She's bone dry."

"Can't be. I put enough gas in that tank to do us—"

"She's empty, Henry!"

The boat moved along the water, driven by escalating currents from heavy rains farther north. Brandon grabbed for the paddle on the boat bottom just as the sky erupted and the west bank of trees exploded in a crash of white light and fire.

15

Tyler General Hospital was a multistory redbrick building with satellite offices and a helipad marked with a gigantic fluorescent yellow H. Alyson parked the Jag, and reached for the *Tyler Herald* she'd thrown onto the passenger's seat. Charlotte Minger's high school photograph smiled back at her, along with the caption

ASSAULT INVESTIGATION CONTINUES
AS TEENAGER'S CONDITION IMPROVES

With the newspaper tucked under her arm, Alyson entered the hospital lobby, paused long enough to take a deep breath and try to reason one last time why she had come here. No doubt Nora's directives had something to do with it. But as she'd opened the paper and looked down into Charlotte's eyes, a sense of foreboding had come over her so powerfully that she felt close to shattering.

Fear over Anticipating had swallowed her. The stalker had

become, in the blink of an eye, real and threatening.

The idea that Charlotte could have been Anticipating's victim hadn't occurred to her until that moment. Might never have occurred to her if Alan hadn't suggested that Emerald Marcella might, by some unbelievably slim chance, have been murdered by an obsessed stalker. Those "voices" in her head had argued heatedly. Minger had glimpsed her attacker—a white male, stocky build. Bald. But what if . . . she was wrong?

What if the same individual who'd followed Carlyle and Marcella that night had also followed Carlyle and Charlotte? Assuming that someone had followed Carlyle and Marcella, and the car seen leaving the scene wasn't simply someone who didn't care to get involved—

But who would simply drive off and leave a man lying unconscious—perhaps dying—by the side of the road, unless it was someone who didn't want to be found at the scene of the accident?

She stopped in the florist shop and chose a plastic vase of red carnations from the cooler and sprang for a helium balloon emblazoned with *Get Well Soon*.

A police officer sat in a chair outside Charlotte's room, drinking coffee from a foam cup and working on a crossword puzzle. By the looks of the half-dozen empty cups on the floor, he'd been there awhile. He looked at her with a blank expression as she walked up—the certain sign of a man who'd sat staring at the opposite wall for too many hours.

Alyson introduced herself, explained that she and Charlotte were acquaintances. He disappeared into the room, reappeared, wrote her name on a clipboard pad and thumbed toward the door. "Fifteen minutes. Not a minute more."

Charlotte hardly resembled the sex doll who'd attempted to seduce Carlyle. She looked like a horrified sixteen-year-old as she stared at Alyson through the slit of a swollen purple eyelid. The other eye was completely closed, with stitches running from the center of the eyelid through her shaved eyebrow and into her hairline—or what would have been her hairline. The front third of her hair had been shaved to expose the sutures that made her scalp look like a bruised and bloody jigsaw puzzle. Her lips had been sewn into place, her jaw wired shut. Her right ear was an abraded mess. There were yellowing bruises—like dingy fingerprints—on her throat.

Alyson put the flowers and balloon aside, noted the dozens of arrangements crowding the windowsill and dresser. There were stuffed animals, stacks of magazines, and books. She forced a smile, winced at the sting of her own injury, then felt guilty for it. The pain Charlotte Minger was going through must have been excruciating, not to mention her mental horror.

"You probably don't remember me," Alyson said unsteadily. "I was at the quarry that night."

She nodded and uttered something that sounded like "I memer ou."

"I'm so sorry this happened, Charlotte. Whoever did this is a vicious animal."

She nodded as a tear crept from under her eyelid.

What now? Alyson suddenly felt lost, mentally bumping into walls like a blind person in unfamiliar territory. And her desperation mounted. The horror that was Charlotte Minger's face made her reasoning scatter, and she worked furiously to contain it. She thought of Mitsy Dillman and tried to imagine the petite Marilyn Monroe wanna-be inflicting so much damage. The reality of it fell short, despite last night's incident.

"Sorry," Charlotte uttered through the wires on her teeth. " 'Bout Banon. Shou'na done it. 'Swat I get for ben such a bitch."

"You didn't deserve this, Charlotte. No one deserves this for any reason."

"Really nice. Sent me doze." She pointed toward a massive arrangement of yellow roses. "Call my mom tree times." Her battered mouth turned up. "Tol' her he would hep wif bills."

Alyson smiled. "Yes, he's very nice."

"Wish we wen to Dairy Queen instead."

"So do we all."

"Wa happen to ou?" Charlotte raised one unsteady hand and pointed to Alyson's face.

"It's not important, Charlotte." She took Charlotte's hand in hers. "Will you tell me what happened?"

"Dark. Tryin' get in car. Grab me from behind. Hit me side of my head."

"Did he say anything?"

She nodded and briefly closed her eye. "Been naughty. Naughty girl."

"Do you think it was someone who knew you?"

"Knew my name. Call me slut an' somethin' else. Can't memer." She swallowed with effort, then added, "Guess I won' be cwownin' any yams dis year, huh?"

By the looks of Charlotte's face, she wouldn't be crowning any yams ever again, not without a fortune in plastic surgery.

"Do the police have any leads?" Alyson asked.

"No. Queshionin' carnies an' some the guys I work wif at Wal-Mart. Guys I've dated. Can't think of anyone who do this."

She felt ridiculous asking the next question, but it had to be asked. "Are you sure it was a man, Charlotte?"

The eye stared up at her, and Alyson could feel her own heart beating in her temples. The idea that a woman could have inflicted such injuries seemed absurd, and she felt her face warm with embarrassment.

"Big hands, strong. Grab me from behind, hand over nose an' mouf. Saw in door mirror. No hair. Gold stud in left ear. Hand smelled weird. Like . . . baby formula. Then slam face-down on the ground. That's all I memer. Woke up here."

"Baby formula?" Aly tried to imagine some creep skulking around quarries beating up teenagers—and smelling like baby formula.

"My mom baby-sits. Kid pukes on her afer eatin'. Smell sweet. Make me wanna gag." Charlotte sighed wearily. "Guess I won' be eatin' for long time, huh? Seven my teef gone." Holding up her opposite arm, punctured by an IV hooked to a bag of fluids, she added, "Soon I get to suck my food through straw. Yum. Can hardy wait."

The door opened and the officer looked in. "Time's up, Miss James."

Charlotte wrapped her fingers around Alyson's wrist. They felt weak and clammy, and trembled. "Tell Banon sorry. Tanks for the flowrs. See him sometime at Wal-Mart maybe. Owe him Belt Busser."

Alyson smiled. "I'll tell him, Charlotte." She patted Charlotte's hand. "If you remember anything else, let us know, okay?"

Charlotte nodded and made a feeble, pained attempt at smiling.

Alyson stood in the corridor outside Charlotte's room. Closing her eyes, she took a deep breath. She felt disoriented, confused over her reasons for coming here in the first place. There was absolutely no indication that what happened to Charlotte Minger had anything to do with Anticipating, so why did she still feel that there was something there . . . ?

She felt ridiculous.

Sighing, she headed for the elevator, crowded inside with visitors, their arms full of flowers and gifts. There was a new mother in a wheelchair, holding a red-faced infant to her shoulder as new papa beamed beside her and the orderly escorting her out of the building checked his watch. Baby squirmed, and a bubble of formula erupted over mom's shoulder, spattering on the orderly's shoe.

The sweet odor of it filled the crowded space, and Alyson thought of Charlotte. "Smelled weird. Like . . . baby formula. Make me wanna gag."

It occurred to Alyson that perhaps Charlotte's attacker was a new daddy. She imagined a stocky, bald dude with an earring and a weakness for beating up teenage girls burping a newborn on his shoulder.

The elevator doors opened, and Alyson stepped out in front of the reception/information desk. She walked over to the same woman who'd given her Charlotte's room number. "Is Mitsy Dillman a patient here? I believe she was brought in last night."

The woman turned to her computer screen and typed in

Mitsy's name. "Miss Dillman was discharged this morning."

Alyson mouthed a soundless *thank-you*, walked out of the hospital through revolving doors. She sank onto the first bench she came to, oblivious to the crowds moving around her or the stream of cars inching their way around to pick up discharged patients.

No need to panic yet.

Of course there was a reason to panic.

Mitsy Dillman was an A-number one fruit head.

Mitsy Dillman was more than capable of violence. Go look in a mirror.

Just a few hours ago a complete stranger who listens to voices she calls Watchers predicted that someone was going to kill Brandon Carlyle!

The man you love.

Oh, God.

The man to whom you've been lying.

The man you were going to sell out for a chance to better your career.

Sugar, you'd better start focusing less on 1-900-Psychic and more on how you're going to get out of this mess if you have any hope of your relationship with Carlyle lasting more than a couple more orgasms.

The air had grown colder, and although the rain had stopped, the clouds were dark. So dark that the streetlights along the boulevard were flickering on. Settled into the Jag's leather seats, Alyson tossed the newspaper aside and wearily rested her head back and closed her eyes. She thought briefly of calling Brandon to warn him that Mitsy was again a free woman, then recalled that her phone battery was dead.

As Brandon pulled a clean undershirt over his head, he glanced at Alyson, who sat on the bed, hands clasped in her lap, resembling a scolded six-year-old in the presence of an irate parent. The day had gone from bad to worse. Before the crack of dawn, he had to troop out into the cool, damp weather to fish when he wanted to spend the morning in bed

with Alyson. Then he was forced to tell Henry about Anticipating and Mitsy Dillman. Then there was the storm that
had nearly blown them to Kingdom Come, and them with an
empty gas tank and Henry tottering on the verge of a heart
attack—not only had his uncle forgotten to check the gas
level in the motor, he'd forgotten to pocket his medication.

If that weren't enough, Mitsy Dillman had been released
from the hospital. A phone call to Deputy Greene had con-
firmed that Jack had arranged for his sister's discharge. Now
he learned that another lunatic was wandering around like
Chicken Little, predicting the sky was about to fall in on
him.

"Let me get this straight, Aly. You were confronted by a
psychic who hears voices in her head. She calls them Watchers. And you actually allowed her in the car and you drove
her around."

She nodded.

"Jesus." He raked both hands through his hair and took a
deep breath, hoping it would soothe the flurry of irritation
inside him. Not just irritation. Fear. Marrow-chilling alarm.
"I'd think that last night's nightmare would have been
enough to teach you to be on guard at all times. Watch your
back. Don't talk to strangers. Christ, I feel like I'm talking
to a five-year-old. Honey, in case you haven't noticed, I
don't, and can't, live, like a normal human being because
there are fruitcakes out there like Mitsy Dillman who insist
that I owe them my body organs because they slap down
eight bucks to see my movies."

Alyson frowned. "You're right, of course. But to be fair,
Mitsy's problem with you stems from something other than
fan adoration, right? The woman hates your guts. Want to
tell me why?"

"Not particularly." He returned to the small bathroom that
was still steamy from his shower, rubbed the condensation
off the mirror, and regarded the dark stubble on his face.
Alyson's reflection joined his as she moved behind him, slid
her arms around his waist, and propped her chin on his shoulder. Her eyes met his in the mirror.

"News flash. People in love are supposed to confide in one another, Carlyle. Unless, of course, you were just blowing smoke last night. Mixing up lust and love. It happens." She smiled.

He didn't. "I've been in lust enough to know the difference, cupcake. All right. Mitsy and I went at it like rabbits one night. The next day I left to start work on *Jericho*. Two months later I got a letter from her informing me she was pregnant and wanted to get married. Cara went through the roof, of course. She paid off Mitsy's mother; Mitsy got an abortion. End of story." Turning, he took her face between his hands and searched her eyes. "And don't change the subject. You're going to be a target, Alyson. You can't go around befriending weirdos because they have nice eyes or a sob story that tugs at your heartstrings. I've got enough on my conscience without worrying that your association with me is going to jeopardize your life."

Pulling away, Alyson returned to the bedroom. She paced, hands on her hips. "But you don't understand. She knew things—"

"I don't believe in psychics, Aly. I don't believe in things that go bump in the night. I don't believe in Houdini or seances or UFOs. Reality is scary enough for me."

She grabbed up a double Twinkie package from the nightstand and threw it at him. "Nora bought those—"

"The whole world eats Twinkies. It's America's favorite—"

"She called me Cupcake and said 'Klem adores you.' Now, unless you've got a bug under your bed, explain to me how she would know that sort of thing."

He had no answer for that. Leaning against the bathroom doorjamb, he crossed his arms over his chest and watched her face flush with angry color.

With a huff of exasperation, she dropped to her knees and looked under the bed. Her muffled voice said, "No bugs here that I can detect. I do see a pair of dirty socks and. . . ." Her head ducked farther under the bed, leaving her butt stuck in the air. The image made him hard immediately, and refocused his thoughts on something other than the fear and anger that had eaten at him minutes before. He crossed the room in three strides, a grin curling one side of his mouth, and eased to his knees behind her.

"Oh!" she cried, followed by a thump as she hit her head on the bed's underside. "What are you doing?"

"What does it feel like I'm doing?" He slid his hand between her legs and cupped her.

"Carlyle, you're a pervert."

"I thought I'd already established that fact." Sliding his hands around her waist, he unsnapped her jeans.

"Oh my God!" she cried. "What is. . . . Oh, my God, these are my panties! My red thong panties!"

"Oops." He slapped her butt and got up, laughing.

She shimmied out from under the bed, her panties in one hand. "I looked everywhere for these. What the dickens are you doing with my panties?" She glared up at him from the floor, her nose smudged with dust and her eyes wide as saucers.

"You don't really want to know, do you?" He grinned down at her and winked, reached for her arm and helped her up. He planted a kiss carefully on her cut lip and took the panties from her hand. "Actually, what I want you to do is go in the bathroom and take off all your clothes. Put these on—nothing else—and come back out here, where I'm going to slowly peel them down your legs and lick you until you beg me to—"

"Got a thing for women's panties, don't cha?"

"A big thing."

There came a knock at the door. Betty called out, "Mr. Brandon, dinner is ready."

As he tucked the panties into his pocket, giving Alyson as lascivious a grin as he could manage, Alyson backed away with an odd expression on her face. Not dread, exactly, but close.

She thumbed toward the closed door, and said, "Maybe I should leave."

"Why?"

"She's doesn't like me."

He almost laughed, but the look on her face stopped him. "You're serious."

"She doesn't approve of . . . us. Although I suspect the disapproval is directed more at me in general than at what's going on between us."

"You're imagining things."

She looked as if she expected him to say exactly what he'd said.

"What makes you think she doesn't like you?" he asked, trying to keep any tone of incredulity from his voice. She was obviously serious—she looked like if she walked out the door, she'd discover Betty ready to pull a Mitsy Dillman on her.

Sliding her hands into the hip pockets of her jeans, she backed away and shook her head. "Forget it. I'm probably being overly sensitive. I tend to do that."

"Has she said or done something I should know about?"

She shook her head, but didn't look at him.

"Mr. Brandon," came Betty's faint voice from the bottom of the stairs. "Dinner's getting cold!"

Fried fresh catfish, fried potatoes, and hush puppies were normally Brandon's favorite meal. During the years of his incarceration he'd stare at the ceiling and try to block out the howling of angry men by thinking about Bernie's fried catfish and hush puppies. She'd promised, in the many letters that she wrote him, that the first meal she'd prepare for him when he came home would be catfish, with strawberry shortcake for dessert. But he found, as he picked at his food, that he didn't have much of an appetite. Maybe he was just too damn tired. Maybe he was dreading telling Henry that Mitsy Dillman was walking around free as a bird. Or maybe he was simply more interested in watching Alyson bond with his uncle. Each time she flashed Henry a smile, the old man blushed like an infatuated fourteen-year-old.

He glanced at Betty, who sat at the far end of the table—

not her usual place to eat. Normally she sat at Henry's left, directly across from Brandon—where Alyson now sat, at Henry's insistence. Betty barely touched her food as she watched the interplay between Henry and Alyson.

"So tell me, Al," Henry said, "can you cook?"

"Quite well," she replied. "I make a mean fried chicken. And my dumplings aren't too bad, either. And my potato salad? Truckers used to drive a hundred miles out of their way for a serving of my creamy mustard potato salad."

Henry looked at Brandon and beamed a smile that stretched from ear to ear. Brandon raised one eyebrow and grinned back.

"I started working the café when I was twelve. My gran's health had begun to fail, and she couldn't stand on her feet for so long at a time. I worked the first breakfast wave around six—the farmers mostly, up at the crack of dawn, coming in for coffee. Left for school at eight. Got home at four. Rushed through my homework, then took over the kitchen again at six, in time for the dinner rush. By the time I was fifteen, I ran the whole joint on the weekends, planned the menus, did all the shopping. Gran's phlebitis had gotten so severe she could hardly walk, so I pretty much took care of her as well."

"Do you like kids?"

Her cheeks flushed as she sat back in her chair. She ducked her head in that timid way that made him want to crawl over the table and kiss her, among other things. He shot Henry a look and said, "You're embarrassing her."

"It's a perfectly reasonable question," Henry declared, smiling at Alyson. "She's a beautiful woman. She'll make beautiful babies. I'm sure you agree, Brandon, or you wouldn't be so occupied watching her that you've forgotten to eat."

Her clear hazel eyes came back to his. Her mouth curved.

"Do you?" Brandon asked, grinning. "Like kids?"

"Yes." She nodded, grinning back. "Very much."

"I'd like three or four."

"Four. Avoids the middle child syndrome. I'd like all boys.

Names: Bryan, Christopher, John, and ... well, perhaps name one after his father."

Silence filled the room briefly, and the words were on the tip of his tongue. *Marry me*. It made no sense, of course, this emotional upheaval over someone he'd met only days ago. He'd always been pragmatic when it came to his relationships with women, but all that had flown out the window the first moment he'd looked in Alyson James's eyes. Henry's words that morning had continued to play through his mind— Henry's knowing right off that he wanted to spend the rest of his life with Bernie.

Henry spoke again. "Have another piece of fish, Al. And hush puppies. Go on, take two. Bernie's recipe. She won first place at the State Fair one year for her hush puppy recipe. Remember that, Brandon? I believe we've still got the ribbon someplace."

"Buried away in The Shrine, no doubt," Brandon replied as he poked a fried potato into a puddle of ketchup.

"The Shrine?" Alyson forked another piece of catfish and plunked it on her plate. She reached for the ketchup bottle.

Henry pointed toward the closed door off the kitchen. "Every photograph, news article, magazine article, or award he was ever associated with is in that room, including Oscar."

Her eyes got wide, and she smiled at Brandon. "Oscar? Really? Oh, my gosh. Can I touch it?"

"The naked bald guy? The highlight of my illustrious career? Sure, why the hell not?"

Henry chuckled. "Brandon once threatened to make a lamp out of Oscar. 'Bout gave Bernie a heart attack." Henry plucked another hush puppy from the platter, then wagged it at Brandon. "One thing you could never fault my nephew over was his humility. Success never went to his head, despite what you might have read in those damn tabloids. It wasn't arrogance that caused him to behave like a turd on the job. It was the booze. Made him crazy."

"Christ." Brandon groaned and sat back in his chair. Alyson flashed him an amused look, then focused again on Henry.

"Funny thing about Brandon," Henry continued. "Always acted a little embarrassed by his success. As if he didn't deserve it. Cara took more credit for his success than he did."

Henry smiled. "Remember when you were nominated for that Emmy for best supporting actor in a dramatic role? You were . . . eleven, I think. I still recall the show. *Those Foster Kids*. Brandon's character, Jeff—"

"Forget it, Henry," Brandon interrupted, feeling his face start to burn. The little bit of food he'd eaten began to crawl back up his throat. "Let's change the subject."

Alyson turned her eyes on him, regarded him steadily. "Go on, Henry."

"Jeff's father came to see him. Been in prison for a number of years. Started making noises that he wanted his kid back—"

"Henry—" His fists clenched. Planting his elbows on the table, one on each side of his plate of cooling food, he pressed the heels of his palms into his eyes, thinking he'd do better to cover his ears with his hands, but the damage was already done. Henry had peeled the scab off the wound, and suddenly all the old infection was boiling up—

"Jeff got hysterical and furious and tried to kill himself—"

"Stop it." He looked at Henry, at Alyson, who continued to watch him.

"Kid had a total breakdown, and we discover that he'd been sexually abused—"

Brandon stood up suddenly, knocking the chair back so it slammed against the floor. The loud bang popped like a firecracker, causing Henry and Alyson to jump. Betty dropped her fork.

"Jesus Christ, can't you just leave it alone, Henry? It's history." His voice shook, and sweat rolled down his temples. "I'm trying to put those goddamn years behind me, and you keep belching them back up like gas."

Henry put down the hush puppy and stared at Brandon through his thick spectacles, his normally rosy face suddenly pale. "I'm sorry," he offered softly. "I only meant—"

"I know what you meant. We all know what you meant.

I got nominated for a stupid Emmy. So what?"

"You were brilliant, Brandon—"

"I wasn't brilliant, Henry. I was. . . ." He bit off the words *hysterical and furious and on the verge of killing myself.* He swallowed the admission that there had been no acting to it— the emotions had been raw and real, a scream for help. Instead, he'd been nominated for a fucking Emmy.

Brandon left the house through the back door, slamming it hard behind him, sucking in his breath as the cold air smacked him hard. He made his way to the barn in the deepening dusk—sat on the edge of the rusting metal water trough, and dug cigarettes and lighter from his shirt pocket. His hand was shaking as he put the cigarette in his mouth and lit it.

"Tell me to take a hike, and I will," came Alyson's voice behind him.

"Take a hike." He took a deep drag on his cigarette and looked toward the line of trees in the distance. Once upon a time, he would have run there and hidden.

She moved beside him, sat down close, and slid her arm around his shoulders. "You're shaking."

"I want to be alone, please." He forced a flat smile. "I've just acted like an ass to a sick old man, and I need time to relish it."

"You can't keep running from it, Brandon."

"You don't know what the hell you're talking about."

"I watched you as Henry began talking about *Those Foster Kids.* Absolute horror came over your face. It was the same look you had last night when I woke up to find you trembling. Please, let me help—"

He shoved her aside and stood up, walked away. He sucked hard on the cigarette, holding the fire inside until his chest felt as if he might combust.

"I watched the episode only a few nights ago," came Alyson's steady voice. "I bought all the videos—thought I might get to know you better if I watched you grow up. That particular episode was called 'Nightmare.' You were riveting. I wept. I wanted to take Jeff in my arms and soothe away his pain and suffering, and obliterate the nightmares that tortured him. I can imagine that his every waking and sleeping minute was haunted by the fear that he'd be subjected again to the monster who abused him. Is that what you're frightened of, Brandon? That your monster will—"

"He can't come back, because he's dead!" he shouted at her. The words floated over the dark trees and seemed to hang like low clouds above the earth.

Her face hazy in the deepening twilight, she stared at him with wide, unblinking eyes. Her skin looked white with cold, and her hair stirred with the night breeze.

"He's dead," he repeated more softly.

The cold had begun to bite at his skin, and he realized he'd been sweating heavily. "He died of cancer when I was twenty. The son of a bitch had the nerve to ask to see me on his deathbed. I went, not to do him any favors—hell, no. I'd spent the last eleven years of my life fantasizing all the ways I could kill him. I hadn't seen him for seven years, not since the series was canceled. There was this pitifully wasted man hooked up to machines, blubbering in fear—like I used to blubber every time Cara took me to see him. He actually begged me to forgive him—like I use to beg him to leave me alone. Only when I begged, I was on my knees."

He laughed and shook his head. "Can you believe that? As if I'd forgive him. I looked down in his bulging, glazed fish eyes, and I said, 'You'll rot in hell, you goddamn sicko.' And then he died. Right there in front of my eyes, he died. I started laughing and couldn't stop. I was furious. I wanted him to suffer as long as possible. I wanted him to fester in his agony and think about what hell had in store for him when he finally croaked.

"I thought that would be the end of the nightmares. But they didn't end, they just changed. Instead of dreaming of him raping me in his apartment, I dreamed he crawled out of his grave, his skin squirming maggots, and tried to drag me into the grave with him.

"I used to throw myself out of bed and crawl into the shower, spend half an hour trying to wash his stink off my skin. Only it wasn't his stink, it was mine, rank with fear. No, not fear. Fear doesn't describe what I felt. Horror. He was right, though. Chivas was my friend. At least for a while. Amnesia in a bottle. Happy juice. If I drank enough, I obliterated the past and blacked out the present."

He sat down beside Alyson, close, so his thigh and shoulder pressed against hers. She reached for his hand and pulled it into her lap.

"I used to sit for hours and stare at my reflection in a mirror. I'd pore over the magazine covers featuring this image of what millions of people thought was perfection. I'd go to my movies and sit for hours, hoping for a solitary clue that would enlighten me as to what all the idiotic fuss was about. Because all I saw in the mirror, on the magazine covers, on the movie screen, was the kid who used to hide in a closet in a fetal position and cry. . . ."

He coughed into his hand, only it wasn't a cough. It was a sob. The skin around his eyes began to swell and burn, and for a long moment he couldn't speak. All his strength focused on controlling the emotion short-circuiting his self-discipline.

"Why didn't you tell someone?" she asked gently. "Because Cara—"

"Cara had nothing to do with it. Any love or respect I had for her as my mother disintegrated the first time she walked out the door and left me with Reilly." The ache rolled over in his chest, swelled painfully, closing off his throat like a noose. He threw the cigarette to the muddy ground and crushed it out with his boot heel. Only then did he look at Alyson directly, and he curled his fingers more tightly around hers, cleared his throat twice before he was certain his voice wouldn't shake when he spoke.

"It's Henry. I couldn't have him knowing. He and Bernie . . . too damn innocent. The reality would've shattered them. That sort of ugliness doesn't exist in Ticky Creek—at least not out in the open. He'd have found a way to blame himself. Then he'd have despaired that he'd let my dad down. There'd have been legal issues, lawsuits; the story would have been blasted on every television screen and in every tabloid headline in the world. Cara would have found a way to eat him alive. By the time the dust settled, he wouldn't have had a dime left to his name. And there was the show to think about. That kind of scandal would have tanked *Those Foster Kids*— a lot of people out of work. Besides. . . ." He tried to smile, couldn't quite pull it off. "I was Brandon Carlyle. The golden child. Kid Perfect. I clung to the love of my fans by my fingernails because, except for Henry and Bernie, they were my only source of self-worth. If they turned away from me, I'd have been lost."

Taking a deep breath, Brandon turned his face into the chilled breeze. "He can't ever know about this, Aly. I don't give a damn about how the rest of the world perceives me— not any longer. If they want to believe I'm an irresponsible, alcoholic jerk whose arrogance and love for booze ultimately led to self-destruction, fine. But Henry can't ever know the truth about my past. It would kill him."

16

Brandon kissed the top of Henry's bald head and apologized for his earlier tantrum, then he kissed Bernie and settled into a chair next to his uncle, whose attention did not drift from the television. Brandon stretched his legs out and crossed them at the ankles, fixed his gaze on the screen, and stared at it blankly, seeing nothing but the pictures in his head. Alyson watched him from the doorway, trying to keep her own emotions in check. She was having a hard time looking at him and not imagining the horror he endured as a child— lost and helpless, bearing the burden of protecting Henry and Bernie from the horrifying nightmare that was his life. The outrage she felt at Cara Carlyie made her shake. Somehow, she was going to make damn sure the woman paid for her outrageous sins.

The phone rang. Betty put down a stack of dirty plates and answered it. She stared at the wall as she listened to the voice in her ear, then, "Mr. Brandon isn't here at present. I'll tell him you called." She hung up and, without looking at Alyson, stepped to the door and announced, "That was Mildred Feldman. She's called six times today. She says it's imperative that you phone her at once."

"Fine," Brandon responded, but didn't move.

Betty returned to clearing the table. Alyson joined her, stepping over Rufous where he sprawled on the floor near his food dish, hound eyes regarding her dolefully. As she collected the platter of cold fries, Betty snatched it from her hand.

"That won't be necessary, Miss James."

"I'd like to help, Betty."

"This family is my responsibility. Besides—" Her mouth stretched into something vaguely resembling a smile. "You're a guest here. I wouldn't think of allowing Mr. Brandon's visitor to dirty her hands in greasy dishwater."

"I don't mind. Really."

"No."

Betty turned away and, with her hand, raked the potatoes into the dog dish. Rufous sniffed at them and laid his head on his paws.

Alyson followed her to the sink. Leaning one hip against the counter, she crossed her arms under her breasts and focused on Betty's profile. The steam from the hot water caused Betty's mascara to smudge under her eyes, and beads of sweat formed over her upper lip.

"Thought you had Bible study tonight," Alyson said softly, almost conspiratorially, certainly with an edge of spiteful amusement in her tone.

"I do."

"Guess you'll have to pray doubly hard. I'm staying over again."

"I ascertained as much." Betty plunged her hands deeper into the water. Her mouth pursed.

"I would think, as much as you profess to care about Henry and Brandon, that you'd be grateful that Brandon has a girlfriend."

"Is that what you are?" Raising one black eyebrow, Betty looked at her askance.

"So it would seem."

"Well." Betty shrugged and wrung water from the dish-cloth. "Considering his last fling was with a porno queen, I suggest that you not let this little dalliance go to your head. Obviously, good judgment isn't one of his strengths."

Alyson moved closer and lowered her voice. "Are you jealous, Betty?"

Betty's face flushed, whether from the heat of the water or anger, Alyson couldn't tell.

"Worried that I'm going to usurp your position in this house?"

"Nonsense. As far as I can see, Miss James, you've got little to nothing to offer this family."

"Then would you mind telling me why you so dislike me?"

Betty's head turned slowly, and her intensely green eyes fixed on Alyson's face. Her expression was so expressionless that the effect was as disconcerting as a slap. "My dear young woman, I don't care about you one way or the other. You're simply a temporary nuisance, as insignificant in my life as an insect."

Betty threw the wet cloth onto the countertop, spattering dishwater over Alyson's shirt and jeans. Her eyes narrowed and her mouth curved. "If you'd like to help, dear, why don't you take out the garbage? You look as if you'd be very, very good at that." She pointed to the bulging plastic bag near the back door. "The Dumpster is down near the barn."

Betty turned on her heel and left the room. Alyson stared after her, not certain if she wanted to laugh or hurl something, then she chastised herself. What Betty thought of her didn't matter. She was apparently a good nurse. She worked very hard at taking care of Brandon and Henry. No doubt Betty's animosity stemmed from her concern over Brandon's happiness and well-being. And whether Alyson wanted to admit it or not, Betty had a legit reason to distrust her.

That sharp reality filled her with mortification. She'd come to Ticky Creek to get the scoop of a lifetime, so she could put her tabloid days behind her.

Well, you're sitting on one hell of a scoop now, aren't

*you? Brandon Carlyle sexually molested as a child. Cara
Carlyle an accessory to the crime. The woman could go to
prison for what she did to her son.*

*Brandon is eventually going to find out who you are—no
way to hide it, really. Hell, the* Galaxy Gazette *is going to
trumpet its association with you to the high heavens when
they get wind of your relationship with Brandon. Best to get
it out in the open. Beg for mercy, and just maybe he'll forgive
you. That's a big maybe.*

That thought made her want to laugh hysterically.

She grabbed the garbage and dragged it out the back door,
into the cold and dark, trudged down the path toward the
barn. Rufous followed, detoured to a bush, and hiked his leg.
She found the big Dumpster west of the barn, and hefted the
bag into it. She thought of crawling in with it and slamming
the lid closed behind her.

The easy way out would be to return to the Pine Lodge,
pack her things, and drive off into the sunset, never to be
seen or heard from again. There would be no need for confessions. No more concerns about Anticipating or Mitsy Dillman. Face it, Carlyle would never forgive her for what she'd
originally come here to do; she'd never be able to forgive
herself. Every time she looked into his eyes, she'd think
about how her motive might have destroyed a man who'd
been victimized all his life.

She thought, at first, that the brief flash of light in the
distance was lightning. Then she realized that it had not come
from the sky, but from the line of trees stretching across the
east pasture. Perhaps she'd imagined it.

Rufous growled.

And perhaps not.

Squinting, she stared hard through the dark. Blackness
stared back at her.

Rufous waddled that direction, stopped, lifted his nose, and
sniffed the air. He looked back at Alyson, gave an old dog
grunt, then with a chesty bay, took off at a lope.

She ran for the house and met Brandon coming out the

door. Pointing toward the distant trees, she said, "Someone's there. I saw lights."

Brandon turned on his heel and entered the house. Alyson followed, catching up with him as he went into the den. She stopped abruptly as he opened the gun cabinet and reached for a rifle.

"What are you doing?" she asked breathlessly.

"What the hell does it look like I'm doing?" He grabbed bullets as Betty moved up behind Alyson.

"What's happened?"

"Call the sheriff, Brandon," Alyson said. "Don't do this yourself. Please—"

"What the hell are you doing?" came Henry's panicked voice.

"Trespassers," Brandon said, flashing Henry a calm smile. "No big deal. I'll check it out."

"The hell you will," Henry declared.

Brandon slid the bullets into his shirt pocket and returned to the kitchen. He grabbed a jacket off a peg on the wall and started for the back door. Henry tried to stop him.

"I forbid it, Brandon—"

"It's no big deal, Henry," he repeated as he shrugged into the jacket. "I'll be back in ten minutes. It's probably nothing more than some teenagers fooling around in the backseat of a car."

Henry's face drained of color. Betty caught his arm and propelled him toward a chair as Alyson followed Brandon out the door and into the dark. "Don't do this," she pleaded as she ran to keep up with him.

He headed for Henry's old pickup. "Go back in the house and stay there, Aly."

"What if it's Mitsy?"

The truck door squeaked and rattled as he jerked it open. "Then I'm going to make her very sorry for taking a swing at you."

"I'm coming along."

One foot in the truck, he looked back at her, his hair fallen over one eye. The composed facade he'd presented to Henry was gone. He looked a little unbalanced, as he had during those taut moments when he related his nightmarish childhood—as if, with the slightest provocation, he would disintegrate before her eyes.

"No, you're not," he said simply, but effectively enough to stop her in her tracks. His dark eyes held her another second before he swung into the truck and slammed the door.

With a labored whine the engine fired, sputtered, roared, and hiccuped as he shifted into gear. As the truck rolled past her, she threw herself onto the tailgate. He braked so hard she sprawled over the bed on her stomach, the wind momentarily punched from her. Climbing over the side of the truck, he grabbed her by one arm and hauled her to the ground, tossed her into the grass as effortlessly as she had earlier flung away the sack of garbage.

Thrusting one finger in her face, he said, "Don't push me, Alyson. You don't want to see me mad."

"I don't want to see you dead!" she cried at him.

He ignored her and jumped back in the truck. Alyson watched the red taillights bump up and down as he drove off through the dark pasture toward the line of trees. The brake lights flashed like tiny fireflies, then the truck's interior light popped on as Brandon got out of the truck, leaving the door open. He disappeared into the dark, carrying the rifle with him.

Alyson sat on the back porch step, arms locked around her knees, her teeth chattering, not with the cold that was biting her cheeks but with fear. Henry's voice drifted to her, followed by Betty's as she attempted to assure him that Brandon was fully capable of taking care of himself.

Brandon climbed back in the truck. The truck disappeared beyond the line of trees. Alyson stared out into the complete darkness, her ears straining for any sound, her body hard as stone with mounting tension. She kept seeing Mitsy's eyes in her mind—glazed with fury and madness as she launched herself at Alyson. Then there was Charlotte's face, beaten beyond recognition. Suddenly Anticipating was everywhere: the Pacific Coast Highway on a rainy summer night, the

Ticky Creek quarry, the River Road Honky-Tonk, Carlyle's
cow pasture. Not only that, but she was a shape-shifter: Marilyn Monroe one night, a stocky bald man who smelled like
baby formula the next.

Gunfire jolted her from her thoughts. She jumped to her
feet and turned to see Henry sitting in a chair and Betty
standing over him, soothing him. Obviously, they hadn't
heard the shot, or maybe she'd just imagined the sharp re-
port—

Again, a crack like timber snapping.

She ran almost blindly through the dark, down the path
past the Dumpster, the old gray barn, farm implements, and
the water trough. She found the rutted tire path and ran harder, gulping air, thinking that at any minute she'd sprawl hard
on the ground. Yet, as if her feet had an instinct of their own,
they magically avoided the stones and dips in the tracks.

Where the line of trees began, the tire ruts became over-
grown with scrub brush and vines. She stumbled, caught herself, pushed through the undergrowth that raked at her jeans
and made sounds like an animal breathing. The tall pines
formed a cathedral ceiling that intensified the dark and electrified the still air. She almost ran facefirst into a tree before
she realized the path had taken a sharp bend to the left. For
an instant she lost her equilibrium, turned round and round,
panic closing off her throat as she suddenly realized she
could no longer tell where she was going or where she had
come from. Alyson could no longer see the path. Instead, she
jogged down the black tunnel that was treeless, her footfalls
muted on the thick carpet of wet pine needles that was overwhelmingly pungent to her raw senses. Her clothes felt wet
and clung to her skin. Her lungs hurt, and her eyes felt as if
they would bug out of her head as she tried to see through
the dark. One thought pounded in her skull:

What if I find him dead?
What if I find him dead?
What if I find him dead?

Suddenly there was light up ahead. The old truck listed
slightly to one side, its driver's door open, spilling dingy

illumination into the tangle of brush and weeds crowding against the running board. She eased up to the door, held her breath as she checked out the cab—no blood, no body, only Rufous stretched out on the seat, barely giving her a second's notice. She moved into the light from the headlamps, followed her shadow down the path until the light grew dim and dimmer, until the tracks took a sweeping bend to the right and disappeared again into a cave of nothingness.

The figure ahead was nothing but shadow at first, until it was almost too late to stop the momentum of her body at full run. Upon hearing her approach, he swiveled, his rifle set against his shoulder and his eye staring through the crosshairs. She threw her arms up to shield her face—as if they'd stop a bullet from splitting her skull in two—and she dived toward the ground just as Brandon tipped the barrel up at the last minute even as he pulled the trigger, shattering the silence with an ear-splitting crack of gunfire.

Hitting the ground hard, she coughed out a cry of shock, followed by Brandon's curse. She had barely hit the ground before he fell over her, throwing the rifle aside as he reached for her, his fingers digging desperately into her arms as he partially lifted her.

"Are you hurt? Aly, damnit, are you hurt?" Brandon shook her hard enough to make her whimper. "Say something, for God's sake."

"I'm fine!" she shouted, not certain that she really was. If someone could really die of fright, then she expected to kick off at any second. "I'm okay," she assured him, struggling for a breath.

He sat, his head hanging, his hands drooping over his knees.

She had tumbled into a thatch of prickly weeds. They bit through her blouse and jeans. She sat up, wincing at the scratches she could feel burning her arms and hands and the back of her neck. Finally, Brandon raised his head and looked at her through his tumbled hair. Taking a deep, steadying breath, he said, "What the hell did you think you were doing?"

"I heard shots—"

"So you just go barreling into the fray? I nearly killed you, Alyson."

She climbed over his legs and into his lap, took his face between her trembling hands, and began to cry. "I was afraid she'd killed you. I was afraid I'd find you with a bullet hole in your body, bleeding to death."

She pressed her mouth to his, then to his unshaven cheek, which felt abrasive to her sore lip. She kissed him repeatedly: his mouth, his cheek, his forehead where his limp hair clung to his sweating brow. Her eyes closed and burning with tears, she said, "Please, please don't do this sort of thing again. You're so damn vulnerable, so sad, and I don't want to think you'd just walk right through hell's door because some part of you has a death wish."

"I'm sorry," he said softly. "If there was someone here, they're gone. I took a couple of shots at a coyote—"

"Promise me, okay? Promise me you'll be more careful."

His mouth curled up on one side. "Careful there, Miz James, I might start to think you really like me for something other than my cute tush."

"Well." She smiled. "Your cute tush isn't so bad either."

"Know where my cute tush wants to be right now?" He slid one hand between her legs, to her crotch that was pressed against the erection in his jeans. The pressure of his fingers and the tight denim of her jeans made the sensitive flesh that he stroked, swell. She felt as if she were melting into his palm, and the ache made her groan. It overrode the extreme fear that had earlier swallowed her. She covered his mouth with a fierce kiss, opened her mouth to take in his tongue, the smoky taste of him as intoxicating as the smell of him, the feel of his hard body against hers, his hands hungrily sliding under her blouse to cup her breasts.

"I need you inside me," she gasped, clutching at his shoulders and tilting her crotch more closely against the ridge that was distending and lengthening in his pants. Her hands tore at the button and zipper on his jeans as she pleaded, "Hurry."

*   *   *

Mitsy squatted in the bushes, listening to herself breathe, vaguely aware that an insect was crawling up her bare leg and the thorns on the brush around her ankles were drawing thin, deep lines in her pale skin. He'd almost caught her. Another fifty yards into the darkness and he'd have found her car. And then what?

She bit her lower lip hard to keep from laughing. Imagine Mr. Wonderful's surprise if she'd jumped out of the bushes and pointed her brother's Taurus Bull between his eyes. She could still do it. Wouldn't that be funny—nail him and his slutty girlfriend at the same time. Boom boom. Just like that.

She watched them kiss, their mouths locking, moving and sliding, opening, their tongues dancing together—she sat that close. So close she could almost reach out and touch them. She could hear their ragged breaths, their guttural groans, their sharp inhalations when they touched—nasty boy, making the bitch squirm that way, making her pant.

He laid Alyson back on the carpet of pine needles—so close, so damn close Mitsy could reach out and stroke her face—he fumbled with the front closer of her bra and shoved it aside, made a sound as he laved those naked pink points with his tongue, took them deeply into his mouth and sucked so hard she cried out. Mitsy could remember—oh, yes, she could remember—how his mouth felt on her breasts, hot and wet and hungry. Her eyes drifted closed as she curled her fingers around her own breast and squeezed, her thumb stroking the aroused peak.

When Mitsy looked at them again, he was sitting back on his heels and removing his jacket. He tossed it aside and dragged off his shirt, removed her boots, then peeled Alyson's jeans down her legs, flung them over the bush near Mitsy, then tore at his own jeans, shoving them down his hips and releasing his swollen cock.

Mitsy's mouth fell open and the breath rushed from her. She bit harder on her lip, tasting blood, feeling tears fill her eyes.

Alyson spread her legs, and he stroked her with his fingers until Alyson rocked her pelvis in invitation.

Oh, the pain. The excruciating pain between her legs. Mitsy drew her skirt up and slid her finger under the elastic band of her panties. The flesh there was hot and slick and swollen, and the very touch of her finger sent ripples of fresh agony through her.

She could smell his arousal—like no other man she had ever been with before him or since—it made her dizzy. The scent made her throb as she recalled how he'd stretched her body, burned her body with friction, making her mindless as no one else ever had or ever would. She stroked herself with her fingers, teeth clenched, the groan of her own desire swelling in her throat.

With a lithe surge, he moved over Alyson's body, slid into her, slowly, excruciatingly slowly, then withdrew, his fingers curving around her hips and tipping her up so he could drive deeper, harder, until their bodies were locked and grinding, moans shuddering through her mouth, which he kissed with heartbreaking gentleness. He hadn't kissed Mitsy—screwed her, yes, but he wouldn't kiss her, as if the act were too intimate, as if a kiss would magically transform what he'd been doing to her that night in the backseat of her car into something resembling love.

Oh, yes, he'd deserved what he got after that. He deserved what he was going to get very soon now. Because she knew a secret, a very dirty secret. He'd better enjoy the bitch while he could, because it was all coming down down down, and he was going to SUFFER!

Alyson cried out, the sound reverberating through the pitch-black forest.

Mitsy sank to the ground, twitching, as she stared with tear-filled eyes at the trees overhead.

Calming Henry down had taken a while. Betty finally left a little after nine—upset at arriving at her Bible study late. Alyson and Brandon sat with Henry and Bernie for the next hour until, as was routine, Henry fell asleep and began to snore. Brandon turned off the television and caught Alyson's hand. They climbed the stairs to his bedroom.

They showered together. With hot water raining over their heads, they held one another until the water became cold. Alyson felt too tired to think, too weak to move. The earlier surge of fear and adrenaline left her muscles sore and her heart aching.

She blew her hair dry as Brandon fell into bed. He had hung her red thong panties over the medicine cabinet mirror. Smiling, she stepped into them and, with nothing else on, walked into the bedroom, which was lit by several candles on the bedside table.

He lay on his back, naked and aroused, a grin curling his mouth and his eyes narrowing in appreciation as he saw her. She moved to the bed; her gaze drifted from his oddly mischievous eyes, down his perfectly honed body to his. . . .

Her mouth dropped open and her eyes widened.

He was wearing the empty double Twinkie wrapper slid over the end of his penis like a cellophane condom.

She began to laugh, not just a little, but from the belly up. The sensation rolled through her in a wave of relief that made her knees weak.

His grin stretching, Brandon rolled from the bed. "Plenty of creamy filling in this baby, Cupcake. Help yourself. Don't be shy—not that you are, judging by last night's performance—damn, you're good; blew my mind, among other things." He laughed so lasciviously her face turned red. "By the way, you look damn beautiful in those panties. But then, I knew you would. Ever think about modeling for Victoria's Secret?"

"You'd like that, wouldn't you?" She smiled into his twinkling eyes.

"Not particularly. I'm a jealous kind of panty pervert, I guess." He picked up a Twinkie from the table, lifted it to her mouth, and touched it lightly to her lips. "Eat it," he ordered her in a soft, deep voice.

Her eyes never leaving his, she nipped off the end of the

cake, swallowed, then slid her tongue deep into the heart of the roll and scooped out the white cream with her tongue.

His face turned dark; his eyes, sleepy. Lowering his mouth to hers, he swept her lips with his tongue and licked away the sweet filling, setting her senses on fire. Her hand curling around him, she peeled the wrapper off him as he lowered the Twinkie and slid it between her legs, murmuring, "Dessert time."

What, exactly, made her glance toward the wall at that moment, she didn't know. Her eyes fixed on the framed black-and-white photograph of a high school baseball team as Brandon kissed the soft underside of her jaw and breathed warmly against her sensitive flesh. She looked into John Carlyle's smiling face; her gaze dropped to the bold print beneath the photo—names of the players—to Carlyle's name. Only it wasn't *John* that blazed back at her, it was—

"Buddy." She said it aloud. Her universe focused on that one bold word that appeared to pulsate like the heartbeat in her ears. "Buddy."

Brandon lifted his head, frowning. "What?"

"Buddy. His name—"

"Nickname." He glanced at the photo. "It was Henry's name for him as a kid. It stuck."

Fresh fear surged through Alyson as she sat up, focusing her attention again on Brandon. "Buddy said the band was Dessie Anne's."

"What the hell are you talking about?"

"Nora. She said, 'Buddy says the band is Dessie Anne's.' " Staring into his still face, Alyson asked, "Who's Dessie Anne?"

"My grandmother," he replied in a dry voice.

Alyson grabbed Brandon's shirt from the back of a chair and pulled it on. She ran to Henry and Bernie's old room, where she had rested the night before, opened the jewelry box, and grabbed the gold wedding ring. By the time she returned to Brandon's room, he'd put on his jeans and was zipping them as he made for the door. She held out the ring on her flat palm as she searched his face. "Whose is it?" she demanded breathlessly.

His blue eyes came back to hers. "My grandmother's."

"Last night . . . when I was alone in that room . . . I put it on. The ring. I thought it was Bernie's. I put it on, Brandon. Nora said, 'Buddy says the band is Dessie Anne's.' The wedding band is Dessie Anne's." Emotion closed her throat as she curled her fingers around the ring. "Now convince me Nora's a fruit head. Tell me it was all a lucky guess. But if you tell me again to forget her and what she said, I'm going to beat you within an inch of your stubborn life."

She walked away, the ring clutched so tightly in her hand she felt it cutting into her palm. "Buddy said to watch out for Billy Boy. Who's Billy Boy?" When he didn't reply, she turned on him. The color had drained from his face. His eyes looked like bruises against the gray of his skin. "Who's Billy?" she demanded frantically.

He shrugged. "I don't know. I don't know a Billy."

"What if Anticipating is a man?"

She blurted the words before considering their impact. Suddenly Brandon's earlier confessions loomed like a behemoth in the room. His monster was back. She saw it reflected in his eyes—a child's eyes trying desperately to contain their terror.

More gently, she said, "That would explain Charlotte. Her attacker was a stocky white male. Bald. Wearing an earring. He called her a naughty, naughty girl—"

"How the hell do you know all this?" he nearly shouted, anger mixed with his mounting tension.

"I saw her today. Charlotte. I was desperate for any clue that might help us discover Anticipating's identity."

He flashed her a disbelieving smile and raked one hand through his dark hair. "Christ, what are you, a freaking private investigator?"

Opportunity had just presented itself. *No, actually, I'm a tabloid writer—was a tabloid writer until my love and respect for you and your family redeemed me. Ferreting out the nasty on people's lives is second nature to me.*

She opened her mouth but nothing came out. Truth lodged like a bone in her throat as she looked into Carlyle's eyes—imagined his anger at her confession—and experienced a rush of such intense grief and loss that her blood turned cold.

"If Anticipating did follow you and Charlotte to the quarry, if she . . . he was furious enough to beat up a teenage girl, doesn't it stand to reason that he might have been diabolical enough to murder Emerald Marcella?" She held up one hand as he started to respond. "Before you argue that the supposition is ridiculous, remember that John Lennon was murdered by a man. George Harrison was stabbed by a man—"

"They're love letters, Aly, written by a woman."

"We don't know that for certain, do we?" Forcing a smile, she walked to him, cupped his cheek with her hand. "I'd like to see them. All of them. Maybe there's some clue hidden there that might tie Anticipating to Marcella."

He turned away, shook his head. "I don't want to go there again. What the hell good would it do?"

"Prove that your actions that night didn't cause her death. Clear your name and reputation. Maybe stop Anticipating from hurting anyone else. If you won't do that for yourself or for me, do it for Henry."

Sitting on the bed, elbows on his knees, he stared down at the floor, silent, his expression intense. Alyson sat beside him.

"Will you tell me what happened the night of Emerald's death?"

"We met at a party. A friend introduced us. I was drinking. She was snorting, only I didn't know it then. One thing led to another, and we left together. I pulled off the road someplace—hell, I don't know where, just down some dirt road into a secluded area. She was into . . . crazy."

He gave a short, dry laugh. "She was into rape fantasies. Rough stuff. The rougher, the better. Pain turned her on. I don't mean discomfort. I mean major pain. Not just getting it, but giving it as well. I might be a lot of things, but masochistic isn't one of them. I told her enough was enough, and things turned ugly. It was starting to rain. I stuffed her in the car, threw her clothes at her and told her to get dressed, I was taking her back to the party. She began cursing, screaming, and trying to beat the hell out of me. The last thing I remember was her grabbing the wheel and the car sliding out of control."

Finally, he looked at her. "I'd like to think that my stupidity didn't kill Emerald. For the last four years I've reminded myself that if she hadn't grabbed the wheel, the car never would have careened out of control, but the same voice comes back reminding me that I shouldn't have been out there with her in the first place. I shouldn't have climbed into that car after drinking, but it had been a bad day—a bad week, actually. I'd been dropped from the movie I was working on, couldn't get my act together. It was the third project I'd been fired from in the last year and a half because of my drinking and temper, so maybe I was feeling self-destructive."

"You didn't deserve to spend three years of your life in prison for Emerald's death, not if she was the cause of the accident." Alyson slid her arm around his shoulder and kissed his cheek. "It's time to stop punishing yourself for the terrible things other people did to you."

He took the ring from her, turned it over in his fingers so the candlelight reflected off the smooth, worn gold, reached for her left hand, and slid the ring onto her fourth finger. He lifted her hand to his mouth and pressed a kiss onto it.

17

Alyson paced the motel room, her phone to her ear, pausing long enough to glance out the window at the mostly empty parking lot. Halloween Saturday had dawned partly cloudy and warmer—the major cold front had, predictably, stalled at the Red River. At least the trick-or-treaters wouldn't freeze tonight, and the Yamboree carnival goers wouldn't find their sweet potato pies and cotton candy waterlogged by rain.

"I have all of Anticipating's letters, at least the ones he saved. There's absolutely nothing here to indicate these letters were written by a man, Alan. The woman obviously is obsessively in love with Brandon. But then, she'd have to be, to have followed him to Ticky Creek."

"Which brings us back to Mitsy Dillman," he replied. "I can't believe you haven't pressed charges against her, A. J. What were you thinking?"

"She's crazy, Alan. Delusional. She needs hospitalization, but thanks to her idiotic brother, she's already on the street again. It wouldn't have mattered if I'd filed charges against

her, she'd be out on bail within hours. The last thing I wanted
to do was give Jack Dillman another excuse to harass Carlyle. Jack's life ambition is to see him back in prison."

Alan remained silent, then said wearily, "Send me copies
of the letters. Peterson wants a look at them as well. If there's
something there we can tie to the Marcella incident—"

"There were letters written to Carlyle shortly after his incarceration." She picked up the note from the table and
tipped it toward the lamplight.

> *I tried to warn you. You wouldn't listen. You never
> listen. You never see me. Why wouldn't you see me? I
> would gladly give you my heart and soul, but you look
> right through me as if I don't exist. Now look where
> your arrogance and indifference have gotten you. The
> next time we meet, perhaps you won't be so quick to
> ignore me.*

She put the letter aside and picked up another.

> *Are you enjoying your confinement yet? Are you re-
> gretting your promiscuity? I tried to warn you, didn't
> I? I told you something dreadful would happen if you
> didn't behave yourself. I miss you terribly. But this
> brief separation will only bring us closer, eventually.
> I'm going to make myself beautiful for you. So beau-
> tiful. And you'll have no more excuses to ignore me.
> And I'll have no further reasons to punish you.*

"Again?" Alan said. "The last sentence—read it again."

"And I'll have no further reasons to punish you."

"As in *I'm going to punish you for your promiscuity by
shoving your date over a cliff in a car*, maybe?"

Alyson nodded. "Maybe."

"As in *I'm going to dress myself up like Marilyn Monroe,
one of the most beautiful women in the world, so you'll have
no more excuses to ignore me.*" Alan cleared his throat and
did his best to contain his mounting frustration. Alyson could

imagine him staring off into space. "I want you to make copies of those letters. Send me the copies and take the originals to the sheriff. If the sheriff blows you off, go to the State Police. Hell, go to the Texas Rangers if you have to. I want you to file assault charges against Mitsy Dillman immediately. There should be enough evidence between those letters, her recent behavior, and her assault on you to keep her behind bars for a little while, maybe long enough to get something going on this end regarding the Marcella case."

Alyson touched her sore lip and tried not to think of Jack Dillman's reaction if his sister was arrested.

"A. J., just how emotionally involved are you with Carlyle?"

"Very."

"Have you told him the truth—who and what you are?"

"No." She glanced toward the muted television, where the face of a smiling teenage boy stared back at her. Tyler's *Channel Four News* had broken the story an hour earlier—the White Sands resident, quarterback for the Tyler Cougars, was believed drowned in Ticky Creek after his fishing boat had capsized.

"Are you going to?" His voice sounded stressed.

"Yes," she replied with obvious uncertainty.

"When?"

"When I work up the courage, Alan."

"Are you prepared for the consequences?"

"Meaning?"

"My dearest friend, he's going to rock your world. You know you've had trouble in the past dealing with rejection and abandonment. Hell, you spent years dealing with your breakup with Farrington and you didn't even love him. You were glad to be rid of him. I'm simply concerned over how you're going to take Carlyle's punting you back to California—and that's being generous. Judging by his past tantrums, I suspect when he blows over this, repercussions are going to be felt in Bangladesh."

"I can deal with tantrums," she said. "I'm more concerned over how the truth is going to affect him emotionally. He's a lot more fragile than I am, Alan. He's been hurt so damn much and for so long." She covered her eyes with one hand and did her best to keep her voice steady. "If I could somehow undo what's been done—the lies—I would. I'll even deal with the consequences, because I know I deserve them. But the shattering of my heart won't come close to the destruction that the truth would cause him right now. I'm prepared to walk away if I must, when the time is right. But I can't turn my back on him now, when there's someone out there who plans to harm him—not if I can, in some way, help to stop it."

"Christ." Alan released a heavy breath.

She shook her head, gave a dry little laugh. "How is it possible to be so damn blissfully happy and pitifully grief-stricken at the same time?"

A long moment of silence ensued. "You're really in love with this guy, aren't you?"

"Afraid so." She stared at the wall and tried her best to force back the swell of emotion making her throat hurt.

"Walk away, A. J." Alan's voice sounded unusually compassionate, making the pain in her chest more acute. "The longer you stay, the more deeply you get involved, the harder it's going to be on both of you. Aly, I don't want to see you hurt like this."

"I can't, Alan. As long as Anticipating is out there—as long as there's a threat that she might hurt him—I can't walk away. Some voice in my head is telling me I can make a difference in his life. "Hey"—she forced a smile—"would you walk away from me if you thought I was in trouble?"

"You *are* in trouble. You just don't know it yet. And no, I'm not about to walk away. Haven't I always told you that if I wasn't gay, I'd marry you myself?"

She moved to the window again. A pair of lanky teenage boys wearing Halloween costumes were walking down the highway, one dressed like Elvis, the other like Frankenstein.

"He's going to ask me to marry him, I think," she confessed, more to herself than to Alan. She hadn't wanted to acknowledge the thought until now, though it had hovered on the edge of her subconscious since the night before. "He put his grandmother's wedding ring on my finger last night. Then he nervously dropped hints that Henry and Bernie were married less than a month after they met. It was all quite charming, actually. He was like a boy trying to work up the courage to ask a girl out on a first date—terrified of rejection."

"What are you going to do, A. J.?"

"Reject him, of course." She closed her eyes. "What else can I do, considering?"

"He'll want an explanation. He'll demand it."

"Then I'll simply—"

"Lie again?"

"I'll tell him I need time to think about it. Then I'll have to find a way to tell him the truth about what I am—or was when I came to Ticky Creek."

"Sheesh. I feel like a bystander watching two trains on a collision course. A. J., if there are survivors after this catastrophe, it's going to be a miracle."

"I know," she said sadly.

Deputy Greene shifted from one foot to the other as he held his hat in his hand and tried not to wilt under Jack Dillman's stare. Not easy. Jack prided himself on his stares. His peers at the station often joked that his stares could melt titanium— especially after he'd had a few drinks, and he'd definitely had a few drinks that afternoon: a full six-pack of Coronas and three straights of Smirnoff, what with watching college football since noon. In fact, he'd been one drink shy of sloshed when Deputy Greene pounded on his door. But anger had a way of sobering Jack real quick. He could feel his mellow buzz vaporizing like steam from his pores.

His fists planted on his hips, his body blocking Greene's view of his living room, Dillman curled his lip and demanded, "What the hell do you mean you got a warrant for Mitsy's arrest?"

"For assault," Greene replied. "You had to know it was

coming, Jack. Maybe if you hadn't pulled Mitsy out of the hospital so quick—"

"I ain't havin' my sister locked up in no loony ward. And I ain't havin' her locked up in no jail cell. How the hell does that make me look, Tommy? Who the hell is gonna vote come Election Day for a sheriff whose sister is a jailbird?"

Deputy Greene shook his head and looked away—down the street, up the street—his face flaming red and his throat so constricted his Adam's apple looked like a kiwi. "I don't like this any more than you, Jack, but I got a job to do. Miz James has filed charges against Mitsy, and I got to take her in."

Dillman narrowed his eyes, and Greene took a step back on the porch. "That shithead Carlyle put her up to it, didn't he?"

"I don't know, Jack. He wasn't with her when she come to the station this afternoon. Don't matter anyhow. Mitsy punched her lights out. There were witnesses. Dozens of 'em. Mitsy'll be lucky if the D.A. don't hit her with attempted murder."

"What?!" Jack shouted so loudly that the neighbor across the street, who was washing his new red Bronco, looked around.

Greene chewed his lip, then said, "There's somethin' else. We got to question Mitsy about some letters Carlyle's been gettin' from some nutcase who calls herself Anticipating."

"Jeeezus!" Jack slammed his fist against the doorjamb, making Greene jump.

"And that ain't all." Greene's voice trembled and rose an octave, as if Jack had already grabbed a fistful of his testicles. "The lady suggested that maybe we need to look into Mitsy's whereabouts the night of Carlyle's accident—the one that killed that porno star. They've got some P.I. snooping into the case again."

"What's that got to do with Mitsy?"

"Looks like they're gonna try an' tie her to those Anticipating letters, Jack. And maybe even to that woman's death."

The sheriff's head started to pound, and his eyes felt big as Ping-Pong balls, like they were gonna pop out of his face at any minute.

" 'Course, all Mitsy's got to do is prove she wasn't anywhere near the scene of that accident. That should be easy enough, right, Jack? Like she was probably living back here with you then, right?"

Dillman pressed his lips together. "Right," he finally managed through his teeth.

"I got to take her in, Jack. I'm sorry. So if you'll just—"

"She ain't here."

Greene glanced toward Mitsy's blue Impala in the driveway.

"She ain't here," Jack repeated in a tone that made Greene rest his hand on the butt of his Sig 226 9 mm.

"Fine," Greene said with a nervous nod. "Okay. I'm gonna take your word on that, Jack, 'cause I don't want this to get any uglier than it already is. We both know it's gonna be in Mitsy's best interest if she turns herself in. But if she don't turn herself in by six P.M., we're gonna come back, and then it's gonna get real ugly." Mustering up his most official voice, he added, "Understand, Sheriff?"

"Understand, Sheriff?" Jack mocked. "Of course I understand. Do I look like a moron to you?"

"Six o'clock. Not a minute later."

"Kiss my ass," Dillman growled as he stepped back and slammed the door in Deputy Greene's face.

Standing in the center of the room, his arms hanging at his sides and his hands fisted, Jack Dillman stared at the television screen where football players scattered like insects over the artificial turf, the volume muted. This wasn't good. Not good at all. This sort of trouble would land him back in a Caprice cruising backstreets for punk junkies and stinking winos. All because his dizzy diphead of a sister couldn't behave herself.

"Mitsy!" he shouted, jabbing one finger toward the floor in front of him. "Get in here now!"

The bedroom door opened slightly. Mitsy peered out at

him with one bloodshot eye that was ringed by clumps of smeared black mascara.

She skulked into the room, looking at him from behind her tangled blond hair, making certain to keep far enough from him that, if he made a grab, she could dart away. He thrust one blunt-tipped finger toward the plaid sofa. She skirted the braided rug, bumped into the BarcaLounger that was speckled with pretzel salt, nearly toppled the pyramid of empty Budweiser cans from the previous evening's binge, and finally crawled into one corner of the sofa and pulled her knees up to her chest.

"Jeeezus, look at you, woman. You're a freakin' wreck."

"I don't feel good," she whined, wiping her runny nose with the back of her hand.

"Well, there's a news bulletin for you. When the hell do you ever feel good, Mitsy? Jeez, you're always moonin' about somethin'. *My head hurts. My ass hurts. I got the cramps.*"

Pressing her head between her hands, she briefly closed her eyes. "You don't got to yell, Jack, I can hear just fine."

"I don't think you do. No, I don't think you do. Cuz if you could hear worth a piddly damn, I wouldn't have Tommy Greene showin' up at my front door in the middle of the game with a warrant for your arrest. Didn't I tell you to stay the hell away from Carlyle?"

"I ain't gone near Carlyle."

"Oh, no. Just punched out his la-di-da girlfriend is all. Now you got them thinkin' you're sendin' Carlyle a lot of love letters and signin' them Anticipatin'. Not only that, but they're tryin' to place you at the scene of Carlyle's accident." Bending over her, he said through his teeth, "Just where the hell were you on the night Emerald Marcella was spattered like a bug on a windshield?"

"Santa Fe, Jack. I was in Santa Fe."

"Don't lie to me, damnit."

"I was workin' at the Top Burger."

"I'm hopin' you can prove it." Bending farther, he said,

"Can you prove it? You got an alibi for that night? Cuz if you don't, I'm gonna arrest you myself."

"God," she whimpered, and gripped her head. "My head hurts, Jack. It just won't shut up. Just keeps poundin' and poundin'—"

"Cuz you're crazy, that's why. You're nutty as a Payday candy bar."

"Doctors at the hospital say I can get help for my crazies. There's medicine—"

"I told you I ain't havin' no sister of mine on that garbage! You'll be runnin' through the freakin' Wal-Mart, mowin' ever'body down with a goddamn Uzi!"

"Maybe you're just afraid I'll get well, Jack. Then you couldn't bully me no more."

"I'll bully you anytime I want to, and don't you forget it."

"But I need help, Jack. My head's all confused."

Burying her face in her hands, she began to sob, to rock back and forth and talk to herself.

This was getting him nowhere. Mitsy was in another one of her funks, and when she got this low, she was just one rung on the ladder brighter than an earthworm. Jeez, he hated to hear women cry. The mewling drove him crazy. Seems all she'd ever done as a kid was cry, until their mother would stand in the kitchen with an apron on and a spatula in one hand and scream at the top of her voice for God to strike her dead so she wouldn't have to endure another of Mitsy's crying jags.

Dragging both hands through his hair, he sighed and shook his head. "Mitsy, Mitsy, Mitsy, what am I gonna do with you?"

She howled louder, and he realized his choice of words left a lot to be desired. Not that he usually cared. He wasn't exactly politically correct—never pretended to be. But he could understand Mitsy's aversion to that particular statement. Bob Wainwright, stepfather from hell, positively thrived on it. Jack could still recall waking up in the middle of the night and looking out his bedroom door, straight into Mitsy's room, lit by a night-light. And there would sit good old Bob on a stool next to Mitsy's bed, dressed in nothing but polka-dotted boxers, his butt crack smiling above the boxers' waistband.

"Mitsy, Mitsy, Mitsy, what am I gonna do with you?" Bob would say, although he knew exactly what he was gonna do with little Mitsy. What he always did with Mitsy.

Jack sat on the sofa next to Mitsy and counted backward from ten. He knew from experience that when she got this emotional, he wasn't gonna accomplish much. "Mitsy, there are two kinds of people in this world. Those who got and those who ain't got. Those who're born to walk at the back of the line, eatin' other people's dust. I've worked hard to get to the front of the line, and here you come actin' like a numbnut and gonna undo me come election time. Now I want you to march into that bedroom and pretty yourself up. Paint your face and curl your hair. Put on some decent clothes—not that supertramp Wal-Mart bargain rack crap that makes you look like a hooker. And sure as hell not that Marilyn Monroe getup. Jeez, I don't know how many times I told you that you ain't ever gonna be Marilyn Monroe. She's dead! And she's gonna stay dead. And you ain't her reincarnated soul. I don't care if you do got a mole on your face and big tits. So you get yourself lookin' like somethin' besides white trash, and then you're gonna go see that silly bitch who's filin' charges against you, and you're gonna smile real nice an' pretend you're sorry for doin' what you done. Maybe she'll change her mind."

Mitsy wiped her eyes and shook her head. "Please don't make me do that, Jack. Please."

"You wanna spend time in prison?" he asked with as much calm as he could muster . . . which wasn't much.

"But I didn't do nothin'. I didn't kill that actress—"

"Porno slut, Mitsy. She was a porno slut. There's a difference. You can't call what those sluts are doin', actin'. She deserved what she got, but I'd be more than displeased if I learned you was the one to give it to her. There are certain things a sheriff's sister just don't do, and snuffin' porno sluts is one of 'em, especially with re-election approachin'."

He grabbed her by one arm. She felt like the old lady's body he'd discovered lying in a ditch out on Randall Mill Road—just bloated enough to make her wobble like a partially inflated inner tube.

Hauling her to her feet, he declared, "I don't want no more lip from you. If you don't get your butt out there in the next hour and try to talk that bimbo out of pressin' charges against you, I'm gonna run your ass into jail myself. Now git." Planting his foot against her butt, he shoved, sending her careening through the doorway of her bedroom.

"I hate you!" she screamed. He grunted in amusement and muttered, "Dizzy bitch."

Carlyle wore a Fu Manchu mustache, a goatee, a pair of Henry's old horn-rimmed spectacles, and a much abused gimme cap. His clothes were army surplus, grease-stained and tattered. He wore combat boots with his pants legs tucked into them. Alyson thought he looked like a refugee from the Vietnam war, but the costume was most effective. She would have had a difficult time recognizing him if she met him face-to-face on the street. While the Ticky Creek residents would have paid little attention to his wandering the town square with the hundreds of other carnival goers, the risk of some out-of-town visitor recognizing him was too high—so he'd layered on the disguise in order to pass unnoticed.

He'd shown up at the Pine Lodge at six-thirty with present in hand: a pair of very sheer thigh-high stockings and black lace thong underwear. She'd changed out of her jeans and into the only dress she'd brought—a short black knit that clung to her curves like a second skin. He'd sat in the chair by the window and watched her slowly work the stockings up her legs. One thing had led to another, and before she could pull on the panties, he'd perched her on the dresser top, her skirt bunched around her hips and her legs wrapped around his waist. By the time they were finished, she'd been forced to undress and bathe, more in the mood to curl up in the bed and sleep than spend the next hours jostled by trick-or-treaters and yam fanatics. As they left the motel room, she grabbed her camera bag and slid the strap onto her shoulder, flashing a frowning Carlyle a smile that promised she wouldn't point the Nikon at him.

Blazing lights lit the town square, and a brisk, clammy breeze snapped the orange-and-black plastic pennants decorating the game and food booths. The air felt charged with electricity—a front was creeping like cold molasses from the north. The smell of popcorn and corn dogs filled the air, as did the roar of the rides, the spinning Tilt-A-Whirl and the Runaway Mouse that clanked and clattered. Costumed children with goody bags in hand roamed in packs from business to business, begging candy and gum handouts from the owners. A country band twanged from a stage at the center of the square, and game hawkers shrilled, "Step right up and win the lady a prize!" and "Round and round she goes, and where she stops, nobody knows!"

They met Henry outside the Dime A Cup at eight sharp. Alyson was surprised to see Bernie with him. Wrapped in sweater and blanket, her head covered with a colorful scarf, she looked healthy, except for the small oxygen tank attached to her chair and the cannula in her nose. Her bright blue eyes gazed over the bustling crowds, and her cheeks appeared almost rosy.

"Bernie and I haven't missed a Yamboree in forty years," Henry explained, raising his voice to be heard over the music. "She was always like a kid when it came to Halloween. She wasn't satisfied to hand out Goober Bars to the kids. She made brownies and popcorn balls and caramel apples." He patted Bernie's shoulder and managed a watery smile, then looked away and did his best to focus on the Skeeball games while he fought to control his emotions. "We had our first date here. Right here. I won her a pink elephant in a dart game. I think she still has it someplace. I knew that night that I wanted to spend the rest of my life with her. She had this way of smiling, shy-like. Made me want to melt right down to my boots. So you see, Al, coming here is a sort of celebration for us. I just can't imagine a Yamboree without my girl."

As a tear crept from under Henry's glasses, Alyson walked away, tried to focus her attention on the camera in her hands and not the swell of emotion that filled her chest. The reality that this would be Bernie's final carnival hung as heavily in the air as the threat of more rain. Reluctantly, she looked back, as drawn by curiosity as she was concerned over how Henry's grief might affect Brandon. The image stopped her heart, and with a photographer's instinct she swung the camera and focused on two men, the younger with his arms wrapped around the older, whose tired face was streaked by tears—intense grief juxtaposed against a celebration of life. The Nikon whirred.

They ate corn dogs and watched Sally Davenport, runner-up Miss Yamboree, crown the winners of the longest yam, the sweetest yam, the heaviest yam, the yam that most looked like a human head, the yam that most resembled Texas. Then there was the pie contest, winner allowed to keep until next year's carnival the Bernice Carlyle Perpetual Trophy, named for Bernice five years ago because she'd won the contest ten years in a row. She had finally retired to the Pie Hall of Fame in order to give someone else a chance. Henry marched proudly onto the stage, and with Miss Yamboree presented the trophy to the winner, a blue-haired octogenarian whose pie had been sweetened by Kahlúa. Together, they posed for a picture that would be in Sunday's *Ticky Creek Mirror* special Yamboree edition.

Brandon talked Alyson into riding the Octopus—not an easy task, considering the last time she'd climbed on such a ride, she'd spent the next hour hurling the roasted turkey leg she'd devoured for lunch. As they stood in line, tickets in hand, she found herself examining the faces of the carnies, part of her desperate search for a glimpse of the monster who attacked Charlotte, knowing even as she did so that she wouldn't find him there. She wondered if Mitsy Dillman had been arrested, if she was watching them from the jail windows.

And if she wasn't there? If she hadn't been arrested?

Her gaze swept the throng of people moving around the courthouse square, many in costumes, some wearing masks. As if a big fist tightened around her chest, she realized that Anticipating could be among them. Was among them. In her gut, she knew it for certain. Suddenly Brandon seemed as conspicuous and vulnerable as the drenched volunteer fireman who dared those willing to plunk down a dollar that they couldn't hit the target that would send him splashing into a tank of water. She was convinced that every ghoulish carnival goer hid a weapon in his or her bag of treats. She felt terrorized, the emotion exacerbated by the frenetic noise of people and music and the roar of carnival rides. The sudden rata-tat-tat of arcade guns made her jump and catch her breath.

She turned to Carlyle, who was focused on the Ferris wheel, its lights reflected in his eyes. Taking his hand in hers, she said, "Let's leave, okay? I've had enough. I think I have a stomachache and. . . . Please, I think we should go."

He frowned and studied her. "Really?" he asked.

"No." Taking a deep breath, she slid her arms around his waist and rested her head on his shoulder. She thought of Henry and his certainty that he wouldn't experience another carnival with Bernie—how his grief had shown on his face as Brandon consoled him—and she wondered how the human heart could possibly endure such an eventuality. Just the fear of something happening to the man in her arms made her hurt desperately. Made tears burn her eyes. Made swallowing impossible.

Lifting her head, she looked into his concerned eyes. "I love you. I just thought you should know."

"Yeah?" He grinned past his Fu Manchu mustache and pulled her closer. He smelled like the cotton candy he'd eaten earlier. There was still a tiny pink fiber of it on the tip of his mustache. "How much?"

"I don't know how much. It's immeasurable, I think."

"Enough to marry me?"

There it was. She'd known it was coming and until that

moment had dreaded it, had done everything she could to avoid it—then gone and thrown open the door and rolled out the red carpet for it. "You don't even know me, Carlyle. You know nothing about me."

"Yes or no."

That simple. Yes or no. How could it be that simple?

Even before the answer was out of her mouth, her entire body seemed to expand with something just short of raw shock and fear—fear of the idiocy of her decision, fear of the outcome. "Yes," she replied. That simple.

A smile touched his mouth, and for a moment the music and bells and whistles faded into a drone. His eyes were a cavalcade of colors: red, blue, and gold of the Ferris wheel. Then he looked beyond her, to where Henry sat on a bench holding her camera, Bernie at his side. "She said yes!" Brandon shouted, and Henry's face lit like a beacon as he raised both fists in the air in a gesture of triumph.

"Tickets!" the carny cried, momentarily diverting Alyson's thoughts from the fact that she had just committed her life to Brandon Carlyle.

The carny plucked the tickets from their hands, and Brandon and Alyson shuffled toward the sprawling ride with shell-shaped capsules extended on octopus arms that were flashing with red and green lights. By the time the carny came around to lock the security bar across their laps, Alyson was already regretting her decision to climb aboard the intimidating machine. Her life suddenly seemed as out of control as the ride she was about to take. She needed time to regroup and think. How could she think as Brandon slid his arm around her shoulder and pulled her as close to him as possible?

With the first sway and tilt of the car, music blasted from surrounding speakers. Mick Jagger shrieked that he couldn't get no satisfaction loudly enough to make Alyson's eardrums throb. As the slow rotation began, she braced herself and glanced out at Henry, who continued to beam and chatter to Bernie.

What made her lift her eyes a degree in that split second

before the hot pink shell they were in suddenly, whipped around, she would never know, but as if she were looking down a rifle barrel through crosshairs, her vision centered on the man standing a few feet directly behind Henry. He wore one of those idiotic Groucho partial masks: bushy black eyebrows, black-framed lenseless glasses attached to a honker nose attached to a caterpillar mustache that completely hid his lips. He was stocky. And bald. The streetlight reflected in a flash of fire off the gold stud in his ear. He looked straight into Alyson's eyes, lifted one finger, and pointed it at her like a gun.

The world tipped and spun out of control, slinging her against Brandon so forcefully she could hardly lift her head. The music cranked up a few decibels more as their car flung them faster and harder, until she could only close her eyes and pray that their outrageously gaudy shell didn't come unhinged—because if it did, they were going to rocket straight to Mars.

After what felt like an eternity, the ride slowed. With great effort she sat up straight while the world continued to career. Brandon was laughing in her ear—laughing at her, she realized. If she looked as bad as she felt, she must have been a spectacle, but that wasn't what concerned her. As she furiously rattled the bar on her lap, she craned her head around to find Henry. He was gone, he and Bernie, and so was the bald man—

"I saw him," she announced, aware her voice sounded full of sickness. "The bald man with the ear stud. Standing near Henry." She looked around, into Brandon's amused eyes. "He pointed at me. Like this." She made a gun with her fingers.

The Octopus began to move again, this time backward. "We have to get off," she shouted, knowing, even as she did, that her attempt to communicate was useless with the music blaring. Brandon shook his head, laughing again, obviously unable to hear her. Sinking against him and closing her eyes, she began to count back from one thousand, focusing on the numbers in her head and not on the fact that it felt as if every meal she had eaten since she was thirteen was about to spew out her nose.

She didn't even notice when the ride finally stopped. Her eyes were clamped shut and her hands felt fused to the security bar. Brandon shook her, only this time he wasn't laughing.

"You okay? Hey, look at me. You still in there, Cupcake?"

He took her face in his hands. She opened one eye, then the other. "Fine," she finally managed. Not fine at all, but she was hardly going to admit that she felt like roadkill.

Brandon jumped to the ground, helped her down, offered her an arm to cling to as she swayed like a boat on choppy water. As they were ushered through the exit, she tried to breathe evenly. Her face cold as ice, and her stomach resided someplace between her ears.

With tremendous relief, she saw Henry on the bench. She hurried to him, her still unsettled vision sliding over the masses of people moving around them. She dropped onto the bench beside him, mustering up a smile as he grabbed her in a bear hug and held on tightly.

"By God, Al, I can't tell you how happy you've made us. I knew the first time I saw you that you were meant for my boy. Brandon did, too. I saw it on his face—thunderstruck he was, like the first time I saw Bernie. Boom! Like a fist to the gut. My greatest dream is to see him happy, and here you are. This is the grandest anniversary present Bernie and I could have gotten."

Henry bubbled on with enthusiasm as Brandon walked to the nearest concessionaire and ordered colas.

As her stomach settled, Alyson's panic returned. While she did her best to listen, nod, and smile at Henry's chatter about wedding dates and plans, her gaze leaped from one stranger's face to another, her exasperation and chagrin mounting as she found no less than half a dozen bald men wandering the grounds. Two were stocky; both were wearing Groucho masks, and on closer inspection, she realized they were brandishing print advertisements for American Savings and Loan

of Ticky Creek. With a weary sigh, she sank against the
bench back and briefly closed her eyes.

Now he was angry. Not just miffed or aggravated or put out.
He was teeth-grindin', fist-pumpin' P.O.'d. Ever'one in the
five surroundin' counties knew life could, would, become
exceedingly miserable if Jack Dillman got angry, so why
didn't Mitsy? Why the devil with horns couldn't she respect
him?

She'd promised him she'd do whatever was necessary to
straighten out the mess with Carlyle's bimbo before it got
completely out of hand—which it was on the verge of doing.
Had she actually done a face-to-face with Carlyle's bimbo?
He didn't know. And really, it wasn't the issue. The issue
was, she was supposed to walk her saggy ass into the station
house and turn herself in by six o'clock sharp.

But Mitsy hadn't turned herself in, and Tommy Greene
and some cheesy, butt-faced, wet-behind-the-ears Meskin
rookie had showed up on his doorstep at seven-thirty sharp,
looking like the Lone Ranger and Tonto.

Mitsy Mitsy Mitsy, what am I gonna do with you?

There was only one thing to do. The only thing to do.
After an intense, brow-sweatin' discussion with the Ranger
and Tonto, he had convinced them not to put an APB on her
yet. Let him bring her in himself. And bring her in he would,
by God, if he had to drag her by her hair.

No Mitsy at the Dairy Queen. No Mitsy at the Piggly
Wiggly, where she occasionally hung out in the produce department and read the latest *National Enquirer* or *Galaxy
Gazette* without having paid for it. No Mitsy at the Wal-Mart.
Although it was a long shot that she'd show her face at the
River Road after what happened, Jack Dillman drove out
there anyway, only to remember as he pulled into the vast,
empty parking lot that Clyde closed for business on Yamboree night.

He pulled into the quarry on his way back to town. He
wouldn't put it past the local punks to throw an impromptu

beer bash—God, he loved to bust the smart-mouthed, cocky young freak heads. No luck tonight, however, but it was early yet. He'd try back around midnight, just pull the Caprice in with the lights off, like he had the night of Carlyle and Charlotte's date, just pull on in there, roll up real close, hit the lights and siren at the same time, and watch them scatter like cockroaches. If he was real lucky, he'd catch a few nekkid. That was pure icing on the cake.

He made the rounds of the pay-for-parking lots surrounding the town square festivities. No Mitsy, but that didn't surprise him. The carnival was heavily patrolled. She'd take no chance of one of the officers seeing her.

Next he drove to the Pine Lodge. The parking lot was packed with cars, thanks to the out-of-towners who were in for the Yamboree, but Mitsy's old Impala wasn't among them. Options depleted, his patience eroding, he swung the Caprice into the Chevron at 59 and Randall Mill Road. Inside he bought another six-pack of Corona, a bag of hot and spicy pork skins, a giant peanut patty.

At ten forty-five he parked the cruiser just off 59 under a low-growing oak tree. The carnival would be closing soon, and the traffic along this stretch of highway would heat up pretty good. If Mitsy had taken a hike to Tyler for some reason, she'd be coming home this direction. Settling back in his car seat, he opened a Corona and ripped open the bag of pork skins, flipped on his trusty Sure Fire flashlight, and thumbed through the *Hustler* he kept under the car seat.

18

Like a haunting, the front edge of the weather system crept through the empty, brick-paved streets; cold fingers of wind scattered paper cups along the deserted sidewalks.

By eleven the food booths had shut down, the rides were silent, the arcade hawkers were packing up their stuffed animals and ready to call it a night. The trick-or-treaters had long since been hauled home by their weary parents.

Brandon and Alyson sat on a park bench on the courthouse lawn, just beyond the floodlights that turned the town square as bright as daylight. He held her close. Her head rested on his shoulder, and occasionally she gave a sniff and shudder as she attempted to control her emotions.

It had been one hell of a night. Experiencing the Yamboree again after so many years had brought back an avalanche of memories—all of Henry and Bernie—their enjoyment in hauling him, in his exuberant youth, through the carnival, stuffing him with corn dogs and cotton candy, laughing among themselves as they thought of Cara's horror if she discovered her golden child moaning with a bellyache within hours.

Tonight, however, Brandon had been forced, along with Henry, to face the heartbreaking reality that there would be no more Yamborees for Bernie. Together, Henry and Bernie had sat in these very shadows, Henry holding her hand as they gazed out on the twinkling, flashing lights of a bustling, youthful world, a world with hope and dreams and a future, a world that once embraced them. Reluctantly, Brandon realized that tonight was the beginning of many good-byes. But when the hurt rose to close off his throat, he looked into Alyson's eyes and held on to the exhilarating truth that it was also a night of beginnings.

He thought of long, languorous days and nights in Alyson's arms. He thought of children, many of them, some with her sparkling eyes and wonderful lips, some with a burning desire to play baseball. The best thing was that he would be there to play with them. He thought of the years of Yamborees to come, of watching their children wave at them from the top of the Ferris wheel. He thought of sitting here on this bench with Alyson forty years from now, recalling this night when she said she'd marry him.

She nestled closer and turned her face to the curve of his throat. Her cheek felt wet, and the idea that she understood his pain, and Henry's, made him love her all the more.

"I'd like to get married as soon as possible."

She sniffed and nuzzled, wrapped her fingers around his hand.

"We'll have to get blood tests, of course. We'll drive up to Longview on Monday morning and get a copy of your birth certificate. You'll need a ring. I'll call Cartier. I have an account there—"

"I want to wear Dessie Anne's ring," she interrupted. "It's all I need. We'll sign a pre-nup if you want." Lifting her head, she looked hard into his eyes. "I'm not interested in your money. I may be a great many things, Brandon, but I'm not a parasite."

He kissed her, just a soft brush and light molding of her lips with his.

She gently placed her fingertips on his lips and took a shuddering breath. "We have to talk. There are things I have to tell you, I should have told you days ago, the moment I realized or suspected where this relationship was headed—"

"There's time for that."

"But—"

"Are you still married?" He raised his eyebrows.

She lowered hers. "No."

"Are you an escaped convict, mass murderer, drug dealer, or into white slavery as a lucrative sideline?"

"No." She grinned and tugged on the end of his Fu Manchu mustache, making him wince as it peeled painfully off the sensitive skin above his lip. She pressed it to his forehead and began to snicker. Then she yanked off his goatee and stuck it on her own chin. "This is what I'll look like after I go through menopause. Will you still love me?"

"Wasn't it written someplace that I have a fetish for goats?"

"Sugar, I'm fishing for sweet nothings, and you're insinuating that I look like a farm animal."

"A very sexy farm animal."

They smiled at one another.

"Really," she said, pulling the mustache off his forehead and tossing it to the ground, along with the goatee. "It's time to be serious. There's something you should know about me—"

"No." He looked away, not sure why, but feeling unsettled by her insistence on confessing something that was serious enough to make her eyes look fearful. "Not tonight. Hey, I've never asked a woman to marry me before, so don't go and spoil it for me, Cupcake." Catching her hand, he stood up. "Besides, I have a surprise for you."

"Here?" She glanced around. "But everything's closed."

"Not everything. Slip a guy a couple of C notes, and the sky's the limit. Hell, in Ticky Creek, two hundred bucks will buy someone's firstborn."

Tugging her along behind him, he walked toward the ancient redbrick, multistory building, circa 1905, directly across the street from the courthouse. The upper windows were boarded, the facade decorated with garish cartoon faces howling in laughter. JOSE'S HOUSE OF MIRRORS. Jose loitered out front, cigarette drooping from his mouth, hands shoved in his pants pockets as he bounced up and down in an attempt to keep warm. He grinned as they approached, gave an approving nod of his head that scattered cigarette ashes in the breeze, and said, "Go for it, amigo. The coast is clear."

Brandon glanced over his shoulder at Alyson. Her eyes were big and suspicious, her mouth just beginning to curve with amused comprehension. He could feel himself already hard, but then he'd been in a perpetual state of rut all night. The dress she was wearing was enough to make him ache to mount the nearest parking meter, and when he'd allowed his mind to contemplate the stockings and panties she wore underneath the short, tight, black dress, he'd been hard-pressed not to undress her on the Ferris wheel.

The first floor of the building was cold and cavernous, and smelled of old timber and mildewing Sheetrock. Jose had transformed the soon-to-be-demolished eyesore into a maze of high mirrors and red lights that turned the atmosphere hellish. Artificial cobwebs hung from the rafters, brushing their faces as they moved down the narrow passage, feeling their way along the walls in search of the next glass corridor.

Music suddenly blasted from hidden speakers, and with it the disembodied shrieks and tortured screams of Halloween ghouls. The backbeat of the tune rapped sensually against their bodies. The lights dimmed and pulsated. Finally, they stepped into the heart of the maze, a circular room of red reflective glass around them and above them. Suddenly the two of them became a hundred, a thousand, dizzying with their numbers.

Brandon turned to Alyson, slid his arm around her waist, and pulled her to him, roughly. He definitely felt like rough tonight. Not much room for tender foreplay. Wanted her too badly. Couldn't get enough of her if he loved her twenty-four hours a day. She slid her hand between them, down his erection, knowing what he needed and wanted. Her eyes became slumberous in that way that made him crazy. Her lips parted and lifted to his.

Their tongues danced, breath mingled, sighs shuddered with arousal and the frantic need that filled them. His hands fumbled with the buttons on his shirt—tossed it to the floor as he went on kissing her, as she went on stroking him, making him grow, and groan. He caught the skirt of her dress and yanked it up her hips, her ribs, dragged it off over her head and threw it on top of his shirt. She stood before him in her black French bra, thong panties, and thigh-high stockings and heels, her dark hair windblown, her pale skin glowing under the throbbing lights.

He lost his breath at the sight of her multiplied by a thousand surrounding him. The overwhelming pain between his legs made him grit his teeth.

He moved around her, behind her, looked over her shoulder at their reflections bathed in red light. She stood nearly as tall as him with her heels on. Nice. It was going to make what he was about to do to her a whole lot easier. Catching her hand in his, he slid them both into her panties. Her eyes flew wide briefly, and he whispered, "Relax, Baby. You're going to enjoy this almost as much as I am."

He guided her hand deeper, between her legs, stroked her with her fingers and his until she was wet and quivering and her breathing quickened. As her eyes drifted closed, he whispered in a tight voice in her ear, "Open your eyes. I want you to watch."

Slowly, slowly her eyes opened, her lips parted. He felt the heat rise off her skin that became slick and fragrant. The scent of her arousal filled his head and sluiced through his body until the swelling between his legs became both heaven and hell, a sublime pain that beat inside him as red as the bathing lights, as distinct and crashing as the drumbeats pulsing from the stereo speakers. As if sensing his ache, she leaned her butt into him, rubbing up and down so the friction made him groan and grit his teeth and mutter soft curse words in her ear. She liked that, he could tell. She enjoyed dirty talk, just as she enjoyed watching—she was comfortable with her sexuality. Good, very good. He'd take her places that would amaze her.

Her head turned slightly, and she looked at him over her shoulder, her mouth turning up as she said, "Someone might be watching."

He slid their hands deeper, stroked harder, smiled into her eyes. "Hope they enjoy the show."

She laughed, a husky sound, yet the reflection that looked back at him from the glass once again held that shy, little girl innocence that made him feel mad with need. Not just need, but possessiveness. Crazy that he'd never felt possessive over a woman before.

Her body trembled, and a sound like a shudder of pain escaped her lips. He slid his finger, and hers, into the wet, slick folds of her body. The unbearable pleasure and excitement of it made her throb, until the crotch of her panties was heavily damp, until the wetness shimmered down the insides of her thighs, just above the lacy edge of her stockings.

With his free hand he unsnapped his jeans, carefully unzipped them—allowed the tips of his fingers to slide over the taut flesh of her firm round buttocks as he did so—he groaned with the relief of pressure against his cock, allowed the jeans to slide down his hips, to the tops of his thighs, nudged down his underwear so his hard, heavy rod fell against the small of her back. She gasped in anticipation. Her hand beneath his began to tremble.

"Easy, easy," he murmured in her ear, then kissed the moist, soft skin just below it. She smelled of Pleasures cologne—sweetly floral. "Nice," he murmured. "I'm imagining pouring that scent into my palm and slowly rubbing it up the insides of your thighs, filling my nostrils with it, of drowning my senses in your female floral scent. And when I taste you, it'll be like dipping my tongue in a flower, only much sweeter, and hotter. Like thick clover honey heated by summer sunlight."

With a shift of his body, he slid his penis between her legs. It rubbed against the wet silk of her panty crotch. He grew harder, longer; the primitive hunger pumped like a heartbeat inside him.

She swelled around their fingers.

The music beat louder.

The red lights pulsated like blood in his veins, like the mounting pressure in his penis. He was forced to close his eyes in order to avoid the thousand reflected images of her with her head fallen back, lifting the arch of her pale breasts captured within the cups of her black lace bra.

"Your panties." He withdrew their hands from the thong. "Pull them down to your ankles. Hurry."

Almost drowsily she slid her fingers into the airy underwear and eased it down slowly, knees bending only slightly as she bent over, allowing it to slide like a feather down her calves to rest in a dark pool around her ankles. And when she started to straighten, he laid one hand upon the small of her back, stationing her in place, the globes of her buttocks slightly raised toward his crotch. Her head lifted, and she met his gaze in the mirrors. The vision was erotic, and for a moment he couldn't breathe, couldn't move. It seemed his entire existence centered between his legs.

"Don't move," he told her in a hoarse, tight voice, his eyes still locked on hers in the mirror. Then, with a slight shift of his body, he eased inside her, probed, prodded, inched, the slick heat of her reluctantly giving way as he pushed harder and deeper, knowing that soon there would be no more control, not with this madness for her expanding. Curling his hands around her hips, he drew her back onto him; her mouth fell open, her eyes closed. Deeper, then easing away, deeper—the beat of the music drove him.

Their image scattered like refracted light, bouncing from one sheet of glass to the other, every angle of their bodies glowing back at him.

His fingers curved more tightly into her skin, holding her steady as he began the rhythm, pumping and withdrawing, her body shaking slightly with each thrust, her buttocks contracting with each slide, her exquisite face tensing as he pushed her toward the climax. Her hands flailed for something to hold, then lifted back to him, fingers splayed as if she were about to tumble off a precipice and desperate for a lifeline. He offered his hands. She gripped them as she pushed her body harder into him, taking all of him with a low moan of pleasure that rippled like waves of light through his body.

A sound slid through his lips—a helpless cry of a man falling, falling into a whirlpool of immense sensation that sucked him deep, too damn deep to think or care about control. Closing his eyes, his head falling back, he surrendered to the hunger, allowed his body to take her hard and fast until he vaguely became aware her fingers were digging into his as he held on, her own whimpers growing until he felt her body stiffen and the first implosive orgasm swept her up in a wave of pure agonizing pleasure. And still he rocked her, even as her body relaxed and the grip on his hands softened, as her head fell almost wearily toward her knees. . . .

He pulled out of her suddenly, stumbled back, wrapped his fingers around the wet, sticky shaft and held it hard until the piercing pain and fullness subsided enough that he could breathe again. As she straightened, he caught her arm and turned her toward him, took her face in his hand and pulled her to his mouth, filled her mouth with his tongue while his arms encircled her and his penis slid between her legs, stroking her, making her body shiver.

"Say you love me," he whispered against her lips.

"I love you," she managed weakly, looking into his eyes as she took his face in her hands and lightly touched her fingertip to his lips. "I fear you'll never know just how much."

"Show me."

She smiled and brushed the hair from his eyes.

He dropped to the floor and lay on his back, propped up on his elbows as his penis jutted up high and hard from its nest of black hair. She kicked her panties aside and straddled his hips, smiled down at him, then slowly dropped, slid her body onto his, taking all of him at once, instant control. Instant oblivion. Raw pleasure and fiery pain. He focused on the overhead mirrors, watched as she pumped her hips up and down, rode him like a horse, swiveled and ground and drove her pelvis hard against him while the straps of her bra slid off her shoulders—he reached up and unhooked it, freeing her breasts that thrust up in firm peaks that he could close his hands over—and did, gently squeezing each time she humped him. Curling his shoulders up, stomach muscles contracting, he took one breast into his mouth, suckled it as the nipple grew hard and harder against his tongue, spurring her to move her hips faster until the ecstasy became more like pain and he could think of nothing, feel nothing beyond the world of his rising cum. Falling back on the floor, his fingers digging into the flesh of her flexing thighs just above the lace band of her stockings, he clenched his teeth—it was coming, the end; he needed it—was desperate for it—yet wanted this excruciating ecstasy to last forever.

The semen rose in a torrent—hot, thick, pulsing, tearing the soul out of him as he drove his fists into the floor and bowed his back. The cry poured up his throat like sharp glass, a crescendo with the clash of drums and cymbals and pulsating light that turned his hellish, heavenly world into a throbbing, white-hot core.

Collapsing on the floor, his eyes closed, he felt one final shudder ripple through him.

Alyson stretched her body out on his, brushed his lips in a feather-light kiss. When he opened one eye, she smiled into it. "Carlyle, I'm starting to get a clue that you're a little kinky."

"This wasn't kinky," he replied with effort. "Kinky is frozen chocolate-covered bananas and warm raspberry sauce in the last row of the Concorde flying at fifty thousand feet."

Her eyebrows raised. "You haven't, have you?"

"Not yet. But we will. Just as soon as we're married and flying to Paris on our honeymoon."

Her smile widened. "I wonder how the other passengers will react?"

"There won't be other passengers. You forget I'm filthy rich. I could buy a Concorde if I wanted."

"Spend money like that, and you'll be forced to go back to work. Which brings me to another topic. I'm not sure I'll care to watch you making love to beautiful women on the screen."

"Not a problem, Cupcake. I'll do nothing but G-rated movies from now on."

"Promise?"

"Cross my heart and hope to die." He made an X over his heart.

Alyson's expression sobered, and she pressed her cheek to his. "Don't say that," came her urgent, rough voice in his ear. "Don't ever tease me about dying, Brandon. Please. The very idea of it horrifies me."

Curling his arms around her, he held her tightly as she shivered with emotion.

At first the low beep-beep-beep was lost behind the cacophony of steel guitars and drumbeats. Frowning, Brandon eased Alyson aside and sat up, strained to hear the sound, hoping he was mistaken even as his heart constricted in his chest. He dragged his jeans up, grabbing the pager attached to his belt loop. Beep-beep-beep. The red light blinked up at him—a signal of trouble.

"Get dressed," he ordered in a flat, urgent voice.

The wind whipped out of the north, slamming like a fist against the Jaguar as Brandon turned onto 59 and floored the accelerator. The rear end fishtailed before regaining traction, then the car sprang forward like its namesake, a sleek white streak of spontaneous speed through the dark. With Alyson's receiver pressed against his ear, he listened as Henry's phone continued to ring with no response.

"Shit!" He threw the phone into Alyson's lap and gripped the wheel with both hands, eased more deeply into the accelerator as the speedometer inched to the right: seventy, seventy-five, eighty. They passed a slow-moving pickup as if it were standing still, then approached an SUV packed with wide-eyed children in Halloween masks; Brandon blinked his brights several times until the Excursion moved to the shoulder and allowed him to pass. The driver flipped him the finger.

No need to panic yet, he told himself. Henry knew the routine. First he was to beep Brandon, then call nine-one-one.

They were two miles from home when the red and blue lights suddenly flashed in Brandon's rearview mirror. A siren whooped as the cruiser moved swiftly up behind him. At first, he thought the pursuer was an officer on his way to answer Henry's call, but the car tailed him dangerously close and the *whoop-whoop* of the siren sounded again in an obvious attempt to pull him over. Brandon cursed and slammed the wheel with his fist, thought about flooring it anyway. He checked his speed—ninety-five and climbing.

Whoop-whoop.

Damn, he was toast!

He slowed and eased to the narrow shoulder crowded by high weeds and brush that raked the side of his car. He killed the ignition. There was going to be no problem here, he told himself; just as soon as he told the officer there was an emergency, he'd be on his way with no more than a minute or two wasted. Everyone in this town knew Henry; they loved him. As he hit the Down button on the driver's window and dug his wallet out of his hip pocket, the cruiser door opened.

Looking over her shoulder, Alyson made a sound and turned her panicked eyes on him. "It's Dillman." She touched his arm. "Stay cool. For God's sake, don't antagonize him."

Dillman. Damn, could this situation get any worse? Glancing into the sideview mirror at Dillman's reflection painted by red and blue lights, his expression like a man who'd just discovered he'd won the lottery, Brandon suspected the situation was about to get much, much worse.

Brandon kept his eyes fixed on the road ahead, his hands

on the wheel as Dillman moved up to the car window, holding a small flashlight in one hand, the other resting on the butt of the gun on his hip. The son of a bitch was singing to himself, the theme song to *Cops*. Even before he bent over and zeroed the flashlight beam into Brandon's eyes, Brandon could smell the beer he'd been drinking.

Dillman stooped so his face came in line with Brandon's. A broad, unconvincing smile stretched his mouth as he turned the light beam first into Brandon's eyes, then into Alyson's. "Well, well, look who we got here. Twiddle Dee and Twiddle Dumb."

"Look, Jack—" Brandon began.

"Did I tell you you could talk yet, Carlyle? I don't think so."

"I got an emergency call—"

"I said, 'I don't think so.' First thing you got to learn when you get stopped for speedin' in my town, is you got to show respect to the Ticky Creek officers."

"Henry is—"

"That means keepin' your mouth shut while I'm talkin'."

Brandon took a deep breath and did his best to relax. His fingers were starting to ache from gripping the steering wheel so fiercely. Anger and frustration mounted, and as if Alyson could sense it, she reached over and put one hand on his shoulder. The connection helped to ground him somewhat.

Dillman said, "First of all, you can provide me with your license and registration."

"Fine," he said through his teeth and reached for his wallet, which he had put on the console. He removed the license after one fumbling attempt—his hands were shaking, not much, but just enough for him to feel his control eroding. Not a good sign. Once his temper got to the hand-trembling stage, he could pretty much count on the situation combusting unless Dillman backed off, and backed off quick. He handed the license to him, then opened the console to extract the registration.

"Oops," Dillman said as he shone the light on the plastic card. "Seems we have a problem, sir. This license ain't no good in Texas." He smiled again. His teeth looked like piano keys in the dark. "This is a California license, and while that wouldn't be a problem if you was just passin' through, I do believe you are once again a Texas resident, and the law declares that you must surrender your out-of-state license and obtain a Texas license within thirty days of movin' here."

Brandon cut his eyes to Dillman's, wincing from the beam of light in his face. "I guess I forgot."

"I guess you did. Like you must have forgot that the speed limit along here is fifty-five. I clocked you at ninety-three. Like you must have forgot the conditions of your parole. But then it seems you got a long history of forgettin' important stuff . . . like usin' a freakin' rubber when you screwed my little sister."

Brandon closed his eyes and released a weary breath. He did his best to keep the temper out of his voice. "Listen to what I'm saying to you, Jack—"

"Sheriff Dillman, you cocky son of a bitch."

"I got an emergency page from Henry. Something's happened—"

"Sheriff Dillman, asshole. Say it. Sheriff Dillman."

"Sheriff Dillman, I got an emergency page from—"

"Get out of the car, Carlyle."

He glanced down at the keys in the ignition, then toward Alyson. Her face looked white in the dark, her eyes fearful. If he drove away now, he'd play right into Dillman's hands. Evading arrest or detention came with a one-way ticket straight back to prison. But if he didn't do something quick, Henry or Bernie could be dying. . . .

Dillman opened the car door and stepped back. "Out of the car."

He unbuckled the seat belt. "Look, Sheriff Dillman, if you want to run me in, fine, but at least allow me to go to the farm first and check on my family. Something's wrong, and—"

Dillman grabbed a handful of Brandon's shirt and hauled him out of the car so unexpectedly he couldn't find his footing, and slid partially to the ground. Only Dillman's grip on his shirt kept him from hitting the road. He heard Alyson cry out, then Jack shouted, "Stay in the car, lady! I'm gonna deal with you next. I said stay in the fuckin' car!"

Brandon attempted to scramble to his feet. Dillman stuck one foot between Brandon's legs and kicked, causing him to sprawl hard on his side. Dillman laughed.

"Damn, Carlyle, you look like a man who might have been nippin' a bit. Maybe you imbibed too many beers at the Yamboree. Or better yet, a wee bit too much of the Chivas. I believe you have a weakness for Chivas. At least that's what I read in the tabloids. Makes you a touch mean, does it? Makes you a touch stupid. Stupid enough to crash cars and kill people."

Twisting both hands in Brandon's shirtfront, Dillman heaved him to his feet and slammed him belly down across the hood of the car, planted a forearm at the base of Brandon's head and drove his face hard into metal. A serrated flare of pain exploded through his face, and the world turned blinding white and hot. He couldn't breathe as blood filled his nose and mouth, and his body convulsed in a spasm that made him flounder to get his head up. Dillman slammed his face again. This time he heard someone howl in pain and realized it was himself.

"Spread 'em, asshole. I said spread 'em." Dillman kicked Brandon's legs apart. "You move so much as a eyelash, and I'm gonna introduce you to a new kind of lover, Carlyle. I'm gonna shove the muzzle of this 226 so far up your twenty-million-dollar ass, you're gonna spit bullets when you talk."

Pain reverberated through him. The metal under his face felt wet and hot, and in some small corner of his muddled brain he realized he was swimming in his own blood.

"Stop this! Oh, my God—" Somewhere beyond his red haze of pain Alyson began to cry.

"Get back in the car, lady," Dillman snarled.

"You can't do this—"

"I can do whatever the hell I want—"

"This is police brutality. This is against the law!"

"Get back in the car, Alyson," Brandon yelled, although

he suspected he wasn't yelling at all. He couldn't seem to drag in enough oxygen through his congested throat to breathe, much less yell. "Get back in the car and stay there."

"He can't—" she began again.

"Get back in the goddamn car!" he shouted before gagging so hard his entire body felt as if it were drawing in on itself. He thought for certain he would pass out, but he wouldn't. He couldn't. No telling what Dillman might do to Alyson—

"That's right, Miss Bitch, get in the car, cuz you don't wanna see what I'm liable to do to lover boy here. Ain't that right, Mr. Wonderful? Mr. *People* magazine. Mr. *G.Q.*, Mr. *Vanity Fair* and all those other fag rags that once upon a time thought you was such hot snot. They don't anymore, though, do they, pretty boy? Only folks who think you're meat on the hoof are the prison fudge packers, who must have thought you were Prime A Number One beef." He drove one knee hard against Brandon's crotch. A new sort of pain rocketed through him—low, and dull like an old knife blade cutting him in two. It wasn't unfamiliar—too familiar. It made the lower half of his body feel like hot water, and the fear washed over him that he'd pissed himself. No. No, he hadn't. Not yet, anyway. But one more knee in his scrotum, and he suspected he might. He just might. And while he could tolerate a great many things—including the agony in his face—wetting his pants was not going to be one of them.

Lowering his mouth near Brandon's ear, Dillman said more softly, "I don't appreciate your makin' more trouble for my little sister, Carlyle. Fact is, I'm real upset about it, in case you can't tell. I do believe it's thanks to you that she's crazy in the first place, and now here you come stirrin' up garbage again. Now I'm gonna give you fair warnin'. If you keep makin' trouble for Mitsy, I'm gonna bury you so deep in shit you'll be pleadin' to get sent back to the fudge packers."

"Look up here and smile, Sheriff Dillman. I want a real up-close and personal shot of your ugly face."

"Huh?" Dillman raised his head and looked straight at Alyson, straight into the lens of her Nikon that whirred and chirped like a bird. "Son of a—"

"This is going to look real nice on the front page of the *Ticky Creek Mirror*. In fact, it's going to look pretty damn good on the front page of the *Galaxy Gazette*." Whir, whir, click. "I can see the headlines now." Whir, whir, click. " 'Dillman can kiss his job as sheriff good-bye.' In fact, I suspect that after the D.A. presents these shots to a jury, you're going to be spending a little time with those fudge packers yourself, sugar, and from what I understand, they absolutely love to sweet-talk law enforcement."

Dillman roared in rage. He hurled himself over the car hood, swiping his big hand at the camera as Alyson lost her footing and stumbled back into the weed-clogged ditch that was shin-high in murky water. She went down with a splash.

Brandon pushed off from the car—right hand slipping in the streaks of dark blood on the Jag's white paint. He caught Dillman in two strides, twisted his hands in Dillman's uniform shirt, and heaved him back so suddenly and hard that his feet left the ground. Pivoting on his heels, Brandon threw him against the car as he twisted his right arm halfway up his back and jabbed his thumb into his jugular, paralyzing him with the excruciating pain and pressure that, if Brandon applied it any harder, would have brought instant death. Dillman stared up at him with bulging eyes, his face white, his teeth bared like a grinning skull. Blood dripped from Brandon's nose and formed a dark, wet blotch on the front of Dillman's shirt.

"Guess what, Jack? Those fight scenes in my last two movies—I did them myself. No stunt doubles. Now listen to me very carefully. I'm going to get in my car now and go home. If I discover that my aunt or uncle is dead because of this antic of yours, I'm going to come looking for you. And make no mistake—I'll kill you. And another thing. If you ever so much as look at Alyson James again, much less threaten her, I'll rip out your heart while it's still beating. Do you understand me, Sheriff Dillman?"

Dillman blinked and made a gurgling sound.

"Aly, get in the car," Brandon said.

She dropped into the car seat, clothes sodden, body shivering. She clutched the camera to her chest protectively. Slamming the door closed, she locked it.

Brandon released the pressure on Dillman's throat and backed away. Dillman clutched at his throat and hacked, never taking his wide, shocked eyes off Brandon as Brandon moved around the car, stopped to pick his license off the ground, then climbed into the driver's seat.

19

A butcher knife jutted out of the jack-o'-lantern face as if it were a prop to add to the ghoulishness of the macabre atmosphere. Window glass lay in shards on the front porch. The metal mesh of the screen door hung in tattered strips from the frame. Great blotches of red paint streamed down the outside walls, like the blood that continued to drizzle out of Brandon's nose.

Standing in the open doorway, looking down the center hallway of Henry's house, Brandon barely listened to the conversation between Deputies Conroy and Sebastian, and Henry, who sat on the porch swing, face pale, body shaking. Alyson sat at his side with her arm around his shoulders as she attempted to comfort him.

Bernie remained close in her wheelchair. Henry had wrapped a blanket around her to ward off the escalating cold. All Brandon could think in that moment was *thank God she's oblivious*. She would have been horrified and heartbroken at what had become of her home in the last few hours.

As fury crawled in the pit of his stomach, he tried to take a breath. First Dillman, and now this. The best night of his life had been turned into a fiasco—worse, a nightmare. His face throbbed as he wiped his bleeding nose with the back of his hand and recalled just how close he'd come to killing Jack Dillman. But even that combustion of fury didn't hold a candle to what was rolling over in him in that instant. He felt afraid to enter the house—afraid of what he might find, afraid if he found evidence of Mitsy Dillman, his last tenuous thread of control would snap.

His voice unsteady, Henry did his best to answer the deputies' questions. "We left the house around seven-fifteen. Met Brandon and Alyson at the Yamboree at eight. Bernie and I arrived back home shortly before eleven. The front gate was closed. You can't get in without a code." Turning his troubled eyes up to Brandon's, he added, "Rufous is gone. I called and called. . . ."

"Is there another way onto the premises, Henry?" Conroy's voice was patient and sympathetic.

"Back of the property. Beyond the trees. We use that entrance for the hauling equipment: trucks, trailers, tractors. No more than a handful of people even know about the entrance."

"I'll drive back and have a look," Sebastian said, then looked at Brandon, his expression still registering disbelief over Brandon's explanation that he'd bloodied his own face and nose when stumbling in his haste to get home to Henry. "Sir, please don't disturb anything. We have a CSU on route. They'll turn this place over looking for evidence."

"Has Mitsy Dillman been arrested?" Brandon heard himself ask. A hazy memory tapped at his skull—seventeen years ago, his midnight rendezvous with Mitsy, who hid her car in the trees.

"No, sir." Deputy Sebastian cleared his throat. "We have an APB out on her. I'm sure we'll be picking her up real soon. But this incident might be nothing more than a Halloween prank—"

"You call this a prank?" Brandon cut his eyes to the deputy. "Someone's destroyed my uncle's home. I'd say that's a bit more serious than a prank. Wouldn't you?"

Brandon moved down the hallway, stepped over the shattered remains of the Tiffany lamps, splintered antiques, destroyed glassware that Bernice had collected throughout her married life—her mother's china cups and saucers and Occupied Japan statuettes, Bernie's collection of Lenox porcelain figurines dressed in period costumes that Brandon had bought in Boston.

He walked toward the kitchen, avoiding streaks of spilled paint on the floor.

Bernie's room remained untouched—at least he could be grateful for that.

In the kitchen Brandon found the refrigerator door open. Puddles of milk, ketchup, and mustard stained the floor and smeared the walls. Beer had been poured over the countertops and tabletop. Pools of it glistened on the floor like urine. The smell of it made his body ache and his stomach turn. Despite the cold, he began to sweat.

He shoved open the door to The Shrine.

The room lay in shambles: glass cases shattered, magazines and photographs ripped to shreds. He kicked aside crushed picture frames, noted that Oscar was gone, as was the life-size cardboard cutout of him as Jesus that had been leaning against the wall.

Brandon climbed the stairs to his bedroom. Only then did he realize just how tired he felt, depleted of all strength—of emotion other than exploding anger that short-circuited his reason. The pain in his face had become numb, like a deadened toothache. It was there, a low, pulsating pressure, but Brandon couldn't feel it. Aside from the anger there was coldness, like the coldness when he awoke from his coma to be greeted by the news of Emerald's death. Disbelief. Fear. Despair. They all curled chilled fingers around his heart and squeezed. He leaned against the staircase wall and tried to breathe, couldn't manage it through his bloody nose, opened his mouth, and sucked in oxygen like a man on the verge of drowning.

Pausing at the top of the stairs, he stared toward his bedroom, dread resonating like a cathedral bell in his head.
Adrenaline electrified his nerves, and he became aware that
blood had begun to drip more freely from his nose. Again
he wiped it with his hand. It made a bright red smear over
his skin.

Finally Brandon moved to the closed bedroom door. He
slowly nudged it open with his foot, part of him wondering
what he'd do if he came face-to-face with the vandal—vandal shmandal, he knew who the hell had done this. She was
going to pay, and pay big time. It was one thing to threaten
him, but when she crossed the line and included Henry and
Bernie in her dark, twisted little games, she was going to be
made very, very sorry. And if he couldn't count on the goddamn law enforcement to help him, he'd do it himself.

The room yawned dark before him—Brandon recalled
leaving the lamp on, as he always did. He slid his hand up
the wall, located the switch, and flicked it. Harsh, white light
bathed the room.

A groan rumbled in his chest and a fresh spear of pain
shot through his face. *Not now*, his mind pleaded. *Please not
now.* He wasn't certain he could tolerate pain along with the
fury eating into his self-control.

His father's photographs had been removed from the
walls, the glass broken from the frames, the photos torn into
confetti. Brandon stooped to one knee and lifted the ragged
scraps of paper in his hand; puzzle pieces of his father's face
smiled up at him. The blood on his fingers left dark prints
on the residue of what had been all that was left to him of
his parent. His fingers curled around them as he stood.

The mattress and pillows had been slashed. Stuffing billowed out of both, and lay on the floor like snowdrifts. The
dresser drawers gaped open and empty. Except for a few
articles scattered on the floor, his clothes were missing, as
was most of what had been hanging in his closet.

Brandon lifted his eyes to the wall.

**NOW YOU'VE DONE IT
YOU'VE FORCED MY HAND**

"Mr. Brandon?"

His head turned. Betty stood in the door. Tears streamed from her eyes.

"Mr. Henry called me. I came as soon as I could." She crossed the room in choppy strides, hands clasped below her chin. Tears painted tiny dark spots on the front of her indigo blouse. "Oh, what's happened to your face? Your wonderful face? You're bleeding. And your nose. Your poor nose. Sit down, and I'll get a cloth. Perhaps you should go to the clinic. I'll drive you, if you'd like. You must be in excruciating pain." Betty caught his arm and urged him toward the bed, where he sat and listened as she hurried to the bathroom.

Water rushed and splashed.

Brandon looked toward the dresser mirror, and for a confused moment wondered who the hell the man staring back at him was. Certainly not the same man who had earlier combed his hair while looking in that glass and contemplated the idea of proposing to a woman he had met only days ago. Certainly not the same man who naively believed his life was about to take a turn for the better. Certainly not the man who, a few short hours ago, believed Mitsy Dillman and/or Anticipating could be eliminated with a phone call to the police.

The stranger staring back at him had glazed eyes, a slightly out-of-kilter nose that continued to stream blood, and a bruise eating up one side of his face. Brandon half expected a makeup artist to come dashing in to pat this and blot that and squirt a little extra red-tinted corn syrup on his face to offer a full blood effect for the camera.

Betty hurried from the bathroom, carrying several damp cloths. "Lie back, dear. Flat on your back. Good. Very good. I'll try not to hurt you. I would never, ever wish to hurt you. You know that, don't you? I would pluck out my own eyes rather than harm a hair on your head."

Brandon winced as she placed a cool, damp cloth over his nose. With another she gently began to cleanse the blood from his face.

"This is a very, very sad thing, and I'm sorry about it. It

all seems so tragic, considering that tonight was to be so special for you. Henry told me that you were going to propose to Miss James." She straightened and blotted her own face with the bloody cloth. "He was so thrilled about it. Positively glowing. Said he'd prayed, as had Bernie, for a woman like her to come along. Someone to make you happy at long last."

A sad smile turned up her mouth. "Of course, it's not for me to say whether Miss James will prove to be the woman of your dreams. I'm only an employee, aren't I? Not like I'm actually a member of this family. But I'll say this, and I hope you won't take it the wrong way, Mr. Brandon. Perhaps the problems of the last days are a sign that you should focus your energies and interests less on the female persuasion and more on helping Mr. Henry get through his difficult time losing Bernie, not to mention his own health."

Brandon stared at the ceiling and felt the blood drain down his throat. It tasted like copper wire in his mouth. As Betty continued to ramble—to preach—annoyance began to infiltrate his pain and fuel his anger. Christ, why wouldn't she shut up? A lunatic had just ransacked his home, and all she could talk about was his screwed-up priorities—as if he needed that reality rubbed in his face.

"—Simply feel that Henry and Bernie need your undivided attention. There will be plenty of time for other things once he and Bernie are gone. While Henry might tell you that he's thrilled about this scandalously rushed relationship with Miss James, truth be known, I suspect that he'd like—"

"Shut up, Betty," he said as he continued to stare at the ceiling.

"I beg your pardon?" She blinked at him.

"I said 'Shut up.' If I want your opinion, which I don't, I'll ask you for it."

Betty blinked again. Opened and closed her mouth. Wrung the washcloth in her hands so a thin rivulet of water streamed toward the floor. Her cheeks flushed.

Sitting up, Brandon closed his eyes at the sudden, intense pressure in his head. The room spun dizzily. He thought he might vomit. "What I do with my life and who I do it with is none of your business. I fully intend to marry her, so you may as well get used to the reality that there's going to be another woman living in this house very soon. If you have some kind of personal problem with Alyson, you'd better get over it."

"That sounds very much like an ultimatum, Mr. Brandon." Betty's voice quavered as she looked at him with grieved disbelief. Though he supposed he should feel guilty for his sharpness toward Betty, he didn't. The memory of Alyson turning her eyes up to his and saying "She doesn't like me" replaced the hurt hammering his head.

"I see." Betty drew back her shoulders. "My apologies for believing that my opinions actually matter to you." She walked to the door and looked back; the corners of her mouth turned down. "Forgive me for saying this, but my opinions did matter before she intruded into the family. She's changed you, Mr. Brandon. I only hope you open your eyes before it's too late."

After an exhaustive search and study of the premises, the Crime Scene Unit departed at just after one in the morning. Alyson fell into bed in Henry and Bernie's old room with her clothes on—dress, stockings that were riddled with snags and runs—she was too damn tired to take them off, had barely made it up the stairs, her feet like lead weights. She lay in the dark and counted the minutes until Brandon joined her, knowing even as she lay there in the shadows, her heart still beating double time with each slam of the wind against the house, that he wouldn't climb the stairs and join her.

For over an hour he'd driven the farm's perimeter in search of Rufous, whistling and calling the dog's name—no luck. The dog was gone. Now Brandon continued to sit in the dark kitchen among the food and rubble, smoking one cigarette after another, drinking one can of Pepsi after another, incapable of waking Henry, as Henry had requested, to tell him his dog had vanished.

Because they knew Rufous had not simply vanished.

Alyson had eventually given up her attempts to communicate with Brandon. He appeared totally unconcerned and unaffected by the injuries Jack Dillman had inflicted on his face, although it had taken an hour of ice packs to stop the bleeding from his nose. His remoteness frightened her. His lack of emotion terrified her. He had become an android. The deputies' questions about Anticipating and Mitsy Dillman had been responded to with a brevity that confounded her.

At four A.M., Alyson rolled out of bed and wearily descended the stairs. The stagnant stink of beer made her queasy. She flipped on the kitchen light to discover Brandon no longer there, frowned at the pile of cigarette butts he'd crushed out in an open container of sour cream. A noise from the den alerted her, and she cautiously hurried down the short hall to the room. Her heart stopped.

"What are you doing? What do you think you're doing?"

Calmly, he loaded Henry's Smith & Wesson .357 magnum.

Her gaze locked on the weapon, she moved across the room.

His head down, a cigarette between his teeth, Brandon said, "Go back to bed, Aly, and mind your own business."

"You *are* my business, Brandon. You made yourself my business when you asked me to marry you and I accepted. Who has more of a right to tell you that you're about to do something stupid than the future mother of your children? Please, put the gun away and come to bed. I'm too damn tired to get hysterical."

He snapped the chamber shut with a flip of his wrist. "A man has a right to protect his family. The law's going to do nothing to help us—she's basically one of their own, isn't she? Jack's sister. If they'd picked her up like they were supposed to, this wouldn't have happened."

"We don't know for sure that she did this. We don't know that she's Anticipating."

Removing the cigarette from his mouth, Brandon looked at her through curls of smoke as he tucked the gun into the waistband of his jeans. "You've certainly changed your tune. You sound like the goddamn deputies. 'Let's not rush to any conclusions. Let the Crime Scene Unit do their job.' Whose side are you on, anyway?"

"Yours. Henry's. If you get yourself killed or sent back to prison, what do you think that will do to him?"

"She's going to kill me, Aly. Or Henry. Or you. She's made that more than apparent tonight. If you think I'm simply going to stand around idly and let it happen, you've got another thing coming."

"Deputy Conroy said they'll put a watch on the house— twenty-four hours a day until she's in custody."

"So that means we sit around this farm for God knows how long, afraid to venture out because she could be squatting behind some tree with a rifle aimed at my head? I don't think so, Cupcake. I spent three damn years in prison already, thank you very much."

"Sugar, three years is going to be a drop in the old bucket compared to what you'll get if you shoot someone—if you even act like you're going to shoot someone. Your driving out through the front gate with that gun in your pants will be enough to revoke your parole. Please." Alyson struggled for an unsteady breath. "Put the gun away and come to bed. Once we get some sleep, we can look at this more objectively. Who knows? Perhaps by morning they'll have taken her into custody."

Brandon regarded her for a long, silent moment, resembling one of his macho, ego-driven movie characters, then he stepped around her and started for the door.

Alyson ran after him, grabbed his arm; he jerked it away. As they reached the kitchen, she attempted to dart past him and grab the car keys on the table. He shoved her hard enough so that she stumbled and went down hard on her butt. Concern briefly gave him pause; their gazes locked— his as dark and turbulent as the weather rattling the rafters— then he picked up the keys, turned on his heels, and went out the back door.

A rush of cold, wet wind barreled through the kitchen and

slammed Alyson where she sat on the floor, legs sprawled, dress hiked above the lace edge of her tattered stockings. God, oh God, what was she supposed to do now?

The sudden blast of the phone ringing made her jump. She stared at it dumbly as it rang again. Bernie's bedroom door opened and Henry stumbled out, squinting against the light as he grabbed the receiver and barked a hoarse hello. His eyes went to the open back door, then swung to Alyson as she pushed herself to her feet.

"Yes, yes, I understand. That's wonderful, Deputy. Terrific news. Yes, I'll tell him immediately. Thank you. Thank you, very much."

He hung up the phone. "They have Mitsy in custody—"

Alyson sprang for the door. The frigid wind drove the air from her lungs as she ran into the night and straight into the headlights of Brandon's car. He slammed on the brakes. The car skidded toward her as she threw up her hand to shield her eyes and stumbled back, bracing herself for the impact as she hit the wet ground.

The car stopped inches short of her. Brandon jumped out and ran to her, dropped to his knees and grabbed her. She locked her arms around him. "They have Mitsy in custody. Thank God, it's over."

Mildred lit her first cigarette of the morning. Her head hurt like hell. Having spent the entire weekend staring at the Pine Lodge walls, she felt like screaming. If that wasn't bad enough, the weather had turned miserable and she hadn't brought so much as a sweater. Rain mixed with sleet was predicted by nightfall. God, what she wouldn't give to be back in sunny California. Breathing Monday morning smog was heaven compared to rotting another day in this Petticoat Junction of a town. But, all in all, if her instincts proved correct, the mind-numbing boredom of the last few days would be worth it. Oh, yes, things were about to heat up in good old Ticky Creek, Texas. They were positively going to incinerate.

Smiling, she settled back against her bed pillows and checked her watch. Time to rock and roll. Eight A.M. Pacific time.

She situated the phone on her stomach, punched the numbers, and waited, humming to herself, and smoking.

"Good morning, *Galaxy Gazette*. How may I direct your call?"

"Alyson James, please."

Silence. "Who do you want?"

Mildred frowned. "A. J. Farrington, please."

The phone buzzed twice, clicked.

Mildred's heart skipped. If she was wrong about this—

"Editorial. This is Shana."

"Alyson James, please." She tapped her ashes into a empty Coke can.

"Who's calling, please?"

"Does Alyson James work there or not, honey? I haven't got all day."

"What's the nature of your call, ma'am?"

"I've got a lead for her."

"I could help you with that—"

Mildred laughed. "Tsk tsk, sweetheart. Not nice. I'm certain Miz James wouldn't be too thrilled to hear that her coworker attempted to steal her story."

Silence. "Will you hold, please?"

Mildred rolled her eyes. "Look, what's so freaking hard about answering a simple question? Does Alyson James work there or not?"

"Hold, please."

"Oh, for the love of—"

"This is Cheryl Flynn. How may I help you?"

"I . . . want . . . Alyson . . . James. A. J. Farrington. Whatever the hell she's calling herself now."

"And you are . . . ?"

"For the love of God Almighty, what difference does it make? I met the woman a few months back, okay? I've got a lead on a major story—"

"I can help you with that."

"No, you can't. Look, you tell me if Alyson James works there, or I'm taking my story to the *Enquirer*."

Silence. "Alyson James has taken an extended leave of absence. We're not certain when or if she's coming back. Therefore, I can help you."

Mildred closed her eyes and smiled. "Sweetheart, you've helped me tremendously already."

By Sunday night Henry's house had been restored to normal, or as normal as it was going to be until they could repaint the kitchen walls and the outside of the house that had been doused with red paint. After another long search for Rufous, turning up nothing, they had fallen into bed exhausted, and while Brandon had fallen asleep almost immediately, Alyson had stared at the ceiling and listened to every bump and groan of the wind.

The last days had played back through her head like a rewound video on Fast Forward. The Yamboree seemed like a surreal dream. The incident with Dillman might never have happened—if the evidence hadn't stared back at her every time she looked into Brandon's swollen, bruised face, which was often. With her head resting on the pillow next to his, she'd studied his sleeping features and imagined kissing him goodnight for the rest of their lives. Imagined giving him the children he craved. Imagined making up for all the sadness in his life.

But it was fear she'd experienced as she'd finally drifted off to sleep. Fear of losing him. That reality loomed greater with each passing hour. She could no longer avoid the inevitable. The time had come to tell him the truth, yet . . . she couldn't. Not yet. Not while he and Henry were still reeling over the destruction of their home and Anticipating's escalating threat.

Monday morning had brought news that though Mitsy was still in custody, keeping her there for much longer was going to prove difficult. There was nothing to tie her to the vandalism of Henry's house—yet. Her alibi for the period during which the vandalism had taken place was that she'd been fishing. A clerk from the Wonder Worm could prove she had purchased bait at seven-thirty sharp Saturday evening, but said clerk couldn't be located; he'd taken a trip to the Shreveport casinos and wasn't expected to return until tonight.

Also, there was nothing to link her to the Anticipating letters, although handwriting experts were going over them. Mitsy supposedly had an alibi for the night of Emerald's death—she was living in Santa Fe and could provide proof. The only thing they could hold her for was her assault on Alyson. However, considering she was Jack's sister, the likelihood of her making bail by noon Monday was very strong.

Brandon and Henry made a joint decision. Alyson was to check out of the Pine Lodge as soon as possible and move into Henry's house.

Brandon wasn't comfortable leaving Henry—since the vandalism Henry had suffered several spells. Alyson volunteered to take Henry's prescription to the drugstore to be refilled on her way to the motel. As she was leaving the farm, she was nearly sideswiped by Mildred, who had obviously gotten her car out of the shop at long last. Mildred was going to be in for some very unpleasant surprises. Her client was hardly going to be in the mood to tolerate her attempts at manipulation. The news that Alyson was moving in with Brandon would be enough to set Mildred off like a keg of gunpowder. God only knew how she'd react to the news that they were about to be married.

As she waited for Henry's prescription to be refilled, Alyson dropped off her film to be developed—all photos taken at the Yamboree. She'd been out of film during Dillman's assault on Brandon. Not that he'd ever know that. As long as there was the threat that she'd caught his abuse on film, and would use the shots against him if necessary, he'd be less likely to repeat such actions.

Alyson stepped out of the bitter cold into the Dime A Cup for coffee. A half-dozen patrons stared up at the television suspended from the ceiling, hypnotized by soap opera shenanigans.

She ordered coffee and settled back to think.

First on her list of things to do was phone the *Gazette* and resign. Cut the ties completely. That way, when she confessed all to Brandon, she wouldn't be lying about no longer being associated with the tabloid. She'd destroy the few tapes she already had on Carlyle—not that he'd given her much, but best to start clean.

Alyson checked her watch—noon—paid her tab, and returned to the drugstore. She picked up Henry's medicine and her photos, sat in the car while thick rain collected on the windshield, her body shivering thanks to the broken heater, and flipped through the two dozen black-and-white photos, smiling to herself. Brandon would be pleased with the shots of Henry and Bernie. She tossed them into the passenger seat, then headed for the motel.

Ice bit at Alyson's face as she ran to her room. Clutching the key in her hand, she reached for the door, stopped, and took a step back, thinking she'd run to the wrong place. Number ten. Not the wrong room. But—

The door was ajar and a Do Not Disturb sign hung on the knob. She had dropped by the Pine Lodge yesterday to pick up a change of clothes and her car, and though she couldn't be positive that she'd closed the door soundly as she left, she was positive she hadn't hung the Do Not Disturb sign on the door.

Perhaps the maid had put it there.

But why?

Alyson nudged the door open farther. The lights were out. She slid her hand up the wall and flipped the switch. A globe lamp over the kitchenette sink flashed on, dimly illuminating the room.

Cautious, she stepped into the room, did not close the door, tossed her purse aside, and moved on the balls of her feet toward the kitchenette—keys jutting from between her fingers in case she needed a weapon. Her eyes were fixed on the open bathroom door, the only place someone could hide, her heart accelerating with each step, her every breath sounding like a rush of wind in her ears.

The room heater kicked on with a sudden deep thud that vibrated the walls. Alyson jumped and dropped the keys. They made a loud *chink* as they hit the carpeted floor. Still, she didn't take her eyes off the tinted shower door even as she bent to retrieve the keys. Slowly, slowly she moved into the bathroom, reached for the stainless steel handle on the door, held her breath, and jerked it open.

Nothing.

Resting against the sink, Alyson pressed one hand to her heart, let out a breath, and gave a dry laugh. Only when her heart's pounding steadied did she return to the room, pull off her jacket, and toss it and the keys onto the chair with her purse. She closed the door against the cold wind and rush of freezing rain, and sank against it as she willed strength back into her knees.

Beads of ice scratched at the door, and it occurred to Alyson that if she didn't hurry and get her things packed and out of here, the roads might be too treacherous to travel. Tyler's Channel Four News had predicted accumulations of two to six inches by this time tomorrow. Just as well that they'd delayed their trip to Longview to get her birth certificate. Riding out the storm with Brandon in front of a roaring fire would give her time for confession, and the time to deal with the consequences of that confession.

She grabbed up her suitcase, already partially packed, tossed it on the bed.

The bed wasn't empty.

She hadn't noticed, thanks to the dim light and the dark bedspread—hadn't noticed the lump under the covers. Why should she, when the bed was so neatly made, not a solitary wrinkle in the paisley cover? But there was something there—something solid—something hard, about the size of a small child.

Alyson backed away, glanced at the door. Again at the bed. Tried to draw in a breath that stuttered like the frantic, frightened pounding of her heart. The rumble of the heater thumped like slow footsteps on a hollow wood floor. Each second that she stared down at the mound, the sound magnified until it seemed the walls were pulsing with the bump-bump-bump. Only then did she note the smell: musty heat and. . . .

Dragging the case off the bed, she flung it to one side, spilling her clothes around her feet, caught the corner of the bedspread, and yanked it hard. It billowed like a cape in the air before drifting to the floor.

She stared at the dog's corpse. Its gray muzzle was frozen in a snarl. The dim light made Rufous's teeth look like yellowed ivory.

Her hand flew to her mouth as the death stench washed over her. As she turned on her heels, her gaze swept the room, fixed on the mirror above the dresser. Something was there. She clawed for the light by the dresser, hands shaking so badly she could hardly grip the switch to turn it on. The sudden light blinded her as she tried to focus on the mirror. It read

YOU'RE NEXT BITCH

scrawled in her Crushed Cranberries lipstick.

Cold, horrifying realization slammed at her temples.

Mitsy Dillman was not Anticipating.

Mitsy Dillman had been in custody since three A.M. Sunday.

Alyson had dropped by the motel room at four yesterday afternoon. Anticipating had been here sometime after that.

Alyson grabbed her purse and keys—no way would she so much as glance toward the bed. Her ability to remain mentally and emotionally functional was dependent on focusing, on getting to Brandon as soon as possible.

She flung open the door.

Mildred stood there. Minuscule crystals of sleet shimmered like glitter in her dark hair. Her face was colorless except for the red slash of her lips, which were pulled up on both ends in something that vaguely resembled a smile. Only there was no friendliness in it. Her expression resembled someone who had just witnessed a portent of her own death.

Mildred knew, Alyson realized as her gaze shifted to the copy of the *Galaxy Gazette* in Mildred's hand. Suddenly the horrible thing in her bed ceased to matter. The expression on Mildred's face filled her with a dread that expanded to excruciating pain.

"What have you done?" The voice that leaked from her mouth rattled like dry bones. "Oh, my God, Mildred, what have you done?"

Seconds ticked by before Mildred responded. "Apparently . . . he cared more for you than I thought—"

"Foolish, self-centered, idiot! Do you realize what you've done to that family? Don't you care? Don't you think I've wanted to tell him?"

Mildred turned her face away. "Never thought I'd see the day he'd give a damn about a woman this much. Thought you were just another fling. Sure, I knew he'd be angry. Who could blame him? The *Galaxy Gazette* hasn't exactly been Carlyle-supportive over the years, has it?" Turning her gaze back to Alyson, she said, "Look, I don't give a damn about you. I think what you do to people and their reputations makes you as disgusting as snot. But I do care about Carlyle. He's . . . special. I was trying to protect him. He's been hurt enough, know what I'm saying?"

Alyson shoved Mildred aside and stepped into the freezing drizzle. A thin glaze of ice covered the parking lot. She skated to her car, was forced to swipe her hand over the windshield to rid it of accumulating sleet. The engine turned over reluctantly, and only as she pulled out onto the highway did she realize that she hadn't taken the time to slip on a jacket.

Her hands were numb with cold and the fierceness with which she gripped the steering wheel. The windshield wipers whined with the effort to smear the freezing rain from the glass.

The Carlyles' security gate stood open. Odd.

Car idling, Alyson parked outside the entrance and stared at the house in the distance. Henry's truck sat in the drive. Next to it, Betty's car. Brandon's Jag would, of course, be in the garage.

Easing off the brake, she moved up the drive.

The front door of the house opened.

Brandon stepped out, carrying a baseball bat in one hand. At first he looked no different than when he kissed her goodbye three hours ago. Still wearing the Hard Rock Café sweatshirt, jeans, and Roper boots, jaw unshaven. Oh, but there was a difference, she noted, her heart climbing up her throat. She hit the brakes and the car skidded. She shifted into Park.

"Please," she shouted as he moved toward her through the drizzle. "Brandon, listen to me! I wanted to tell you—"

He swung the bat as if he were trying for a grand slam out of the ballpark. She ducked as the bat connected with the driver's side window. Glass erupted over her head and shoulders, bit into her hands as she threw them up to shield her face. "Stop it!" she screamed, as he struck again, this time smashing the back passenger window. "Listen to me. Please listen to me. It's not what you think, Brandon—"

The windshield popped, and a thousand cracks webbed outward from the impact point. Brandon moved the car, shattering the headlights, moved to the passenger side and swung the bat against the glass, which flew over her head and shoulders like razor-sharp confetti.

Alyson began to cry, barely hearing the disintegrating glass as he continued to drive the bat into the windows, the taillights, and, when done with the glass, began to beat the car roof and doors, trunk, and hood.

Eyes closed, she rested her forehead against the steering wheel, hands clasped in her lap, cold biting at her wet cheeks.

Brandon jerked open the driver's door, scattering bits of glass over the ground. Twisting his fingers into her hair, he turned her head so she was forced to look into his eyes, which were like two deep bruises in his white face. She felt his hand trembling against her scalp.

"I loved you," he said softly, tightly, dryly. "I don't think I've ever loved another human being, aside from Bernie and Henry, like I loved you. More important, I trusted you, Miz Farrington."

"Please believe me. I came to Ticky Creek to get a story

that would help me make a break with the *Gazette*. I couldn't go through with it, not after getting to know you and Henry. Not after falling in love with you. I realized then that I could help you. Not simply with the autobiography, but with Anticipating. I love you, Brandon. That's not a lie. I swear it. I wanted to tell you Saturday night—I tried. You wouldn't listen. I was so damn afraid this would happen. That you wouldn't understand—"

"Get the hell away from me, Alyson."

As he backed away, she grabbed his arm. He tried to twist free. She held on, and he dragged her out of the car. Her feet slid out from under her, and she nearly pulled him down. "Dammit, you're going to listen to me," she wept. "If you want to hate me, fine. Maybe I deserve it, but please listen to me, Brandon. Something's happened. At my motel room—"

"Get off me, goddammit!" He planted one hand against her chest and shoved. She sprawled on her back hard enough to momentarily wind her. Above her the ice-heavy pine needles looked like glass daggers. Wet cold crept through her blouse and cut at her back.

Brandon towered over her, legs slightly spread, one hand a fist, the other holding the bat as if he intended to beat her with it. His face appeared whiter, if that was possible. The mean bruise over his right cheek looked like diluted watercolor. His eyes flashed with fierce anger under his lowered brows, and when he spoke again, the tone was low and ominous. "If you don't get the hell out of here now, I'm calling the law. If you come back on this property, or attempt to see me, or Henry, I'll have you arrested for trespassing." Turning on his heels, he headed for the house.

Alyson sat up and watched him walk away. "Mitsy is not Anticipating!" she called after him in a defeated voice so weak and full of tears, she suspected that even if he heard her, he didn't understand.

Entering the house, he slammed the door.

Alyson covered her face with her hands, and sobbed.

20

As Deputy Greene and the CSU combed Number Ten, Pine Lodge Motel, for evidence, Alyson moved her belongings to another room—one next to Mildred's. She briefly considered banging on her door, and when Mildred answered, punching her lights out. But that would be laying the blame at someone else's feet, and one thing she was very, very good at was accepting the consequences of her actions. She'd known all along that by refusing to be up-front with Brandon, she'd set herself up for a major disappointment. An understatement, of course. The crushing despair pressing in on her could not remotely be compared to disappointment.

Not bothering to turn on the heater, she removed her clothes and crawled into bed, under the covers, and listened to the shush of ice against the window—tried not to think of her short-lived romance with Mr. Hollywood or how much she hurt inside, even more than she had expected.

But it was better to dwell on the pain than the images of a dead dog and a psychotic stalker.

She didn't want to think that she was on some maniac's hit list; then again, since Brandon had virtually kicked her out of his life, that might have changed. Probably. Obviously she was no longer a threat to Anticipating. She only hoped Anticipating got the news before coming to call again. Alyson imagined painting a sign with what was left of her Crushed Cranberries lipstick and taping it to her motel door.

Dear Anticipating. News Flash! Lover Boy dumped me!

Perhaps she should call Alan, cry on his shoulder and whine in his ear. Then again, perhaps not. He'd only say, *A. J., I told you so* in that patient monotone; he'd try to convince her to return to San Francisco immediately; and she'd refuse, of course. She'd been a fighter all her life—stubborn, never say die, never give up; the harder she was beaten down, the more fiercely she fought back.

But that was neither here nor there. This situation wasn't about her. It was about Brandon. Someone wanted to hurt him. Someone was going to hurt him. Had already hurt him. She felt very certain now that Anticipating had been involved in Marcella's death. If he wasn't prepared to accept that reality, then she'd deal with the situation herself. Hell, at the *Gazette* she was notorious for tracking down the most inconsequential clues. She had an instinct for it.

By now, Alan had received copies of Anticipating's letters. If anyone could read between the lines, Alan could. He had an uncanny ability to shuck aside personas and get to the raw data. He gloried in revealing the Hannibal Lecter lurking in everyone's psyche. If there were clues to Anticipating's identity buried somewhere in those letters, Dr. Alan Rodgers would find them.

The phone rang at just after seven, jolting Alyson awake. For an instant, between phone rings, she lay in the dark, hearing Mildred's television babble through one wall, and through the other, the whoosh of a toilet flushing. Her heart raced with the hope that the caller would be Brandon. *Hey, baby, I miss you, let's kiss and make up. . . .*

She grabbed the receiver and sat up, fumbled for the lamp switch.

"Al? It's Henry."

She frowned and cleared her throat. "Henry? Oh, Henry. I've so wanted to talk to you. To explain—"

"Never mind all that, Al. I think I understand how you're feeling. I was shocked at first. Disappointed, I guess. But I can certainly appreciate your hesitancy to explain your situation. That's not why I'm calling."

"Did Deputy Greene contact you?"

Silence. When he spoke again, his voice trembled. "Yes. That's one of the reasons I'm calling. I'm extremely concerned, Al, about this escalating threat from Anticipating. I don't think it's a good idea for you to remain there alone. I must insist that you collect your things and come back to the farm."

She smiled and sank against the pillows. Henry's concern brought tears to her eyes—emotion that she had fought throughout the afternoon to deny. Now it surged like a tide inside her. She wanted to bury her face against his shoulder and cry like a baby. "I'd like nothing better, Henry, but I suspect your nephew isn't inclined to agree. I'm probably the last person, aside from Anticipating, that Brandon cares to see."

"That's another reason I'm calling, Al. I'm concerned about Brandon."

Alyson sat up; her hand tightened on the receiver. "What's wrong, Henry? What's happened?"

A long pause, then, "He said he needed to get away for a while. He had some thinking to do. I guess that's not so unusual. He often takes that damn speed machine out on the back roads when he needs to release a little steam. But not in this kind of weather. Al, he hasn't come back. And that's unusual. Normally he might be gone an hour or two—he left here just after two. That's five hours, Al. He hasn't called to check in, even though I paged him. The weather's getting pretty damn nasty. . . ."

Swinging her legs from the bed, Alyson said, "Try paging him again. I'll cruise around a little, see if I can find him, or at least someone who might have seen him. And, Henry, try not to worry. I'm sure everything is fine. Maybe he got caught up in the ice someplace. Maybe his pager isn't working."

"Maybe."

"You might give Deputy Greene a call . . . just to be on the alert."

"Yes, I've thought of that. I'll call him right now."

"Henry . . . just so you know beyond any shadow of a doubt. I love him desperately. And you, too."

"I know I can speak for Brandon when I say we love you as well, Al. We'll get over this. He's . . . hurt and confused right now. Once he's had time to reason all this through, he'll come around. As I pointed out to him after you left this afternoon, he's made his share of mistakes. Love means understanding and forgiving, right?"

"Right." She smiled. "I'll call you. Betty is with you, right?"

"Yes. She's here."

"And you found the prescription I left on the front porch?"

"Yes. I'm fine, Al, but I'll be much better when Brandon is home safe and sound."

Alyson replaced the receiver and grabbed for her clothes. She dressed in two minutes, was standing outside the motel room door in the freezing drizzle before recalling that there was no hope of driving what was left of her Rent A Heap. As she had left the Carlyle farm, the windshield had caved into her lap. She'd driven back to the motel with sleet coating her face and blurring her vision.

Her phone began to ring. She fumbled the key into the lock, finally managed to shove the door open in time to grab the receiver, praying Henry would announce that Brandon had safely found his way home.

First the sound of music blasted in her ear, then, "Alyson James? Is that Alyson James?"

"Yes." She plugged one ear, hoping to hear the caller better.

"Thank God. I took a guess you'd be stayin' at the Lodge.

This is Ruth Threadgill. At the River Road? You remember
I waited on you and Mr. Carlyle last week?"

"Yes." She nodded, feeling her stomach cramp. Somehow
she knew what Ruth would tell her—knew it as well as she
knew her own name.

"Look, I didn't know who else to call. Didn't think givin'
ol' Henry a ring was such a good idea, ya know what I'm
sayin'?"

"How bad is it?" she asked, closing her eyes.

"The man's shitfaced. He come in here around four lookin'
like roadkill and with a mad-on big as Dallas. Good thing
the place was empty, cuz this baby was lookin' for a fight.
He ordered his usual Chivas, only this time he didn't walk
away from it. Clyde locked him in the office. I reckon he
could stay here until he sleeps it off, but we're closin' this
place due to the weather."

"I'm on my way, Ruth."

She marched to Mildred's room, beat the door with her
fist. Mildred answered with a cigarette in one hand and a
beer in the other. She stared at Alyson with raccoon eyes.

"I need your car keys," Alyson said.

"For what?"

"Brandon's drunk."

Mildred rolled her eyes and shook her head. "Figures. I
told him last week it was only a matter of time—"

"You're just brimming with support for your client, aren't
you?" She shoved Mildred aside and stepped into the smoky
room. Mildred's purse lay on the bed. Alyson grabbed it and
dumped the contents out.

"You've got some nerve," Mildred declared. "Who the hell
do you think you are?"

Snatching up the keys, Alyson turned on Mildred. "Someone who obviously cares about him more than you. If you
had one splinter of common sense or conscience—not to
mention decency—you'd have come to me first with your
information. You'd have let me break it to him and Henry
as gently as possible. If you really suspected he was tottering
on the edge of drinking again, why did you push him? I'll

tell you why. Because when he's weak and vulnerable, you can manipulate him. Maybe you even thought you'd manage to seduce him back into your bed. Or maybe you're just a vile, mean bitch without the brains God gave a maggot."

Mildred barked a harsh laugh. "Look who's talking, Miss Stalkarazzi. Where were you on August 30, 1997? In Paris, no doubt, on the back of a freaking motorcycle chasing Diana to her death!"

Alyson moved toward the door, her face burning.

"He wouldn't be drunk if you hadn't broken his heart!" Mildred yelled after her. "So if you want to lay the blame at someone's feet, toots, lay it at your own. He stayed sober four freaking years until you came along."

Alyson scraped ice from the windshield with the keys. As she unlocked the door, Mildred stepped out into the sleet and slammed the motel door closed behind her. She ran to the passenger side of the car and jumped up and down, hugging herself to keep warm. The tip of the cigarette in her mouth glowed like a fat orange firefly.

"No way," Alyson declared. "You're not going with me."

Looking through the iced window, Mildred rattled the door handle. "Believe me, you want me to come. I've seen him smashed, remember? I know what that poison does to him." She said more firmly, "I'm serious, Alyson. He needs . . . handling. I'm used to the abuse. You, on the other hand, might get your feelings hurt."

Alyson turned the ignition and hit the lights. She watched falling spears of ice reflect the illumination like slivers of Christmas tinsel. With a sigh of resignation, she unlocked the passenger door.

Mildred tossed her cigarette away and climbed in, her teeth chattering.

So far so good. The highway remained clear of accumulation. Still, Alyson drove carefully, never allowing her speed to creep beyond forty-five.

Mildred settled back, gazed out the window into the dark. "Whatever you do, don't mention Cara. Never mention Cara when he's smashed. Don't even think her name. Just friendly advice. He'll want to argue. Just agree with everything he says. If he says its a sunny eighty-five degrees right now, nod your head and suggest a swim and a picnic.

"He might try to bully you. I recognize your willfulness, dear, but this is not the time to dig in your heels. It's a control thing with him. Must stem back to Cara's domination of him as a child or something. You try to force him into something he doesn't want to do, and you might as well walk a torch into a room full of dynamite. Directors were forced to take out extra insurance on themselves before working with him those last few years. Directing Hollywood's Hellion became both an obsession and a challenge.

"The damn sad thing is, he's so freaking brilliant when his head is on right. Name me another actor who could play a drugged-out rock star *and* Jesus Christ. He should have won another Oscar for his Jesus—would have, if there hadn't been so much controversy about his playing the role, considering his reputation was already on the skids. It didn't help that the *Gazette* ran that photo of him dressed as Jesus and throwing a punch at his costar."

Alyson frowned. "The photo certainly didn't hurt the movie. It was number one at the box office for God knows how long. Yes, Brandon was brilliant in the role. But he was too damn sexy. You can't have a sexy Jesus. When you look into Jesus' eyes, you should want to repent, not jump his bones."

Mildred smirked.

They drove in silence down the deserted highway, which was fast becoming icy the farther out of town they got. At long last, with a heavy sigh of relief and a flutter of nervousness in her stomach, Alyson turned the car in to the River Road parking lot. Brandon's Jag sat under a vapor light near the entrance.

Ruth greeted them at the door, her expression harried, and led them down a dark corridor. She glanced at Alyson. "Look, Sweetie, I don't know what happened between the two of you, ain't none of my business, but you better know up front that he ain't exactly gonna do handstands in excitement over seein' you. We can just be grateful this place has been dead because of the weather. He come in lookin' to fight an' get laid. If he came in here a month ago propositionin' me like he done today, I would of thought I died and went to heaven, but after seein' him look at you the way he done the other night, I figure I might be good for a lot of things, but I ain't good at rebounds, even if it is with Mr. Hollywood. Didn't help that he kept callin' me Alyson."

Reaching the office door, she slid the key into the lock, gave it a twist, and stepped back. "You're on your own, ladies. Good luck."

Mildred stepped forward. "Me first. I'm real good at ducking."

She eased the door open and cautiously stepped in. Alyson followed.

Brandon sat in Clyde's chair behind a massive oak desk. With his feet propped on the desk and crossed at the ankles, he smoked with one hand and held a glass of Chivas in the other. Alyson wasn't certain what she expected, but it wasn't this. He appeared perfectly normal, and she almost allowed herself to relax. It was the narrowing of his eyes when he saw her that stopped her in her tracks.

Mildred held up both hands. "We don't want any trouble, Brandon. We're simply here to help."

"Do I look like I need help?" His voice oozed a deep East Texas drawl and dripped with sarcasm.

Mildred looked at Alyson and rolled her eyes. "Now there's a loaded question for you." She cleared her throat. "The weather sucks big time. Ice and snow. You don't want to wreck that pretty car, so we came to give you a ride home."

"Liar." He laughed and smoked. "I keep telling myself I have to fire you, Mildred. Then you remind me that no one else will represent me. Then I tell myself I don't need an agent anyway, because I'd rather cut off both balls than go back to Hollywood. I'm sick to my stomach of getting ripped apart by producers and directors and agents—all a lot of parasites who can't survive without us, but always take great delight in beating us up. Oh, and let's not forget the tabloids. My, my, that was always fun, wasn't it? *B. C. Arrested on DUI Charges, B. C. Fired from Reiner Project, B. C. Drunk Again on Set, B. C. Murders Porn Queen During S&M Sexcapades.* That was my favorite, I think. No, on second thought, my favorite was *B. C. Sex-Fest with Mongolian Gay Midgets;* my head was superimposed on a three-foot-tall dwarf whose entire body was covered with penis tattoos. Let me think, the reporter on that one wouldn't have been Farrington, would it?"

"No it would not," Alyson piped up, even though Mildred turned a warning eye on her and shook her head.

Mildred smiled. "We're simply trying to help, Brandon. You obviously can't drive in your condition."

"I'd rather crawl in a box with two pissed-off rattlesnakes than leave here with either of you."

"The management wants to close this place. They want to go home while they can still get home. They can't close as long as you're here. You're a reasonable man, Brandon. You can understand their concern—"

"You're patronizing me, Mildred." He cut his eyes to Alyson. Suddenly the temperature in the room felt zero degrees. His words seemed to hang in the air like frozen vapor. "I really hate to be patronized. I rank that right up there with being used and lied to by people who are supposed to love me."

Alyson stepped forward, her gaze locked on Brandon's, which continued to smolder. "Henry's very concerned about you, Brandon."

"You stay away from my uncle, Miz Farrington. I don't give a damn about what you do to me, but when you bother my family—"

"Henry is confronting this sorry situation with a reasonable mind. I spoke with him. He's hurt, but he isn't angry. He's worried about you and wants you home safe. I told him I'd find you and take you home. So here I am."

"Go to hell."

Alyson turned to Mildred. "Leave. I'll handle this my own way."

Mildred scoffed. "Look, you don't have a clue—"

"I'm not afraid of him, Mildred." A lie, of course. She hardly relished a repeat of that afternoon's fit of temper, but aside from her wounded pride, she'd walked away physically unscathed . . . but then again, he hadn't been intoxicated. Judging by the nearly empty Chivas bottle on the desk, and the fact that he hadn't had a drink in over four years, he was probably beyond intoxicated. His being conscious astounded her.

"He's crazy when he's smashed," Mildred whispered. "Don't let this calm facade fool you. The least thing can set him off."

"He won't hurt me. Go." She caught Mildred's shoulders and turned her toward the door. "Go."

Mildred walked to the door, stopped, and looked back, her expression deeply concerned. "I'll be outside if you need me." She stepped outside and closed the door.

Alyson turned back to Brandon. A flush warmed her cheeks as he took a deep drink of Chivas, watching her over the lip of the glass. She could see the effects of the booze now. A sheen of perspiration covered his face despite the cold room. She moved toward him cautiously.

"I'm wondering how Henry is going to take your drinking again," she said.

"Don't get sanctimonious with me. You make a living off humiliating people. Destroying marriages, reputations, careers."

"I never ran a story that wasn't true—"

"My personal life is nobody's business!" he shouted so loudly she flinched.

"You're absolutely right." She shrugged. "I'm sorry. If I could take it back, I would. I'm not proud of what I did to you. Truth is, it's haunted me for years."

He barked a laugh, then took a deep drag of his cigarette and shook his head. "Like I'm supposed to believe that. You're training a goddamn Nikon on me from up in a goddamn tree, and I'm supposed to believe that."

"We occasionally do things out of desperation that we're not proud of." She pointed to the Chivas bottle. "Take that, for instance. I bet you're already regretting your decision to come here. If you could undo it, you would."

Looking away, Brandon pressed the glass against his forehead, as if the condensation would cool his hot brow.

"I don't think Henry is going to take the news of your drinking again nearly as well as he took the news that my coming to Ticky Creek was to land the story of a lifetime and not to help you write your autobiography. My objective has changed since I came to love you and Henry, but there's no changing the fact that you're an alcoholic, and you've just blown four years of sobriety. You have every right to want to hurt me, but you have no right or reason to destroy Henry."

Alyson sat on the edge of the desk. Brandon regarded her with a disturbing lack of emotion, which frightened her more than the possibility that he might take a swing at her. She removed the glass from his hand—he resisted for an instant, then released it—and set it aside. She took a deep breath. "I got my story the night you confessed you were, with Cara's consent, molested by Ralph Reilly. If a story's all I wanted, would I still be here?"

He stared, his eyes as cold and hard as sapphires.

"Have you even stopped to think what I've been through? The fear and guilt and confusion I've suffered over the last days when I imagined yours and Henry's reactions to the news I was a tabloid writer? Not just any tabloid writer, but the writer who broke the story of your alcoholism? I can sit here and apologize for the story, Brandon, but the bottom line is, if it hadn't been me, it would have been someone else. Would the story have been more legitimate and palatable coming from Barbara Walters or Dan Rather? Because, believe me, if Walter Cronkite had been standing in that police station the night they hauled your butt in for DUI, you better believe the story would have shown up on the six o'clock news."

Still, nothing.

"We have to leave this place. I'm going to take you back to the motel. I know you don't want Henry to see you like this. You can sleep it off in my room. Go home in the morning. At that point, if you never want to see me again, I'll leave Ticky Creek."

A flicker of some emotion passed over his face.

"Is that what you want?" she asked, doing her best to keep the pain from her voice. "Do you want me to get out of your life, Brandon?"

As if rousing from his trance, he blinked, and the coldness of his eyes became two blue flames. His jaw worked and his hands clenched. "I loved you," he said in a hoarse, vibrating whisper. "I don't think you know what that means. I've never let myself love anyone like that. I never trusted anyone like I trusted you. I told you things I've never shared with another human being. And all the while you were compiling my dirty little secrets, not for the autobiography you were supposedly here to help me write, but for some tabloid article—"

"Forget the *Gazette*, Brandon. It's history." She forced a smile. "I began questioning whether I could go through with it the morning I sat across from you at the Dime A Cup and saw the pain in your eyes when I presented you with *Hollywood Hellion*. I should have left Ticky Creek then. Maybe I'd already fallen in love with you a little. I simply couldn't walk away." She held her hand out to him. "Please."

He glanced at her hand, and his brows drew together. For the first time he appeared confused. Inebriation made his eyelids heavy, and when he spoke again, the angry words sounded slurred. "I don't think I can do that, Cupcake." His gaze slid back to hers. "When I was in prison, I made a vow that I'd never allow a woman to use me again. Or to hurt me. I was doing fine until you came here, screwing up my head with your beautiful eyes and incredible mouth."

He stood. As Alyson slid off the desk, he grabbed her arm and drew her close, saying through his teeth, "I've never hit a woman. Thought about it. Known a few who deserved it. Part of me wants to beat the hell out of you. The other part

wants to spread you over this desk and climb between your
legs one last time. Maybe being inside you again would obliterate this anger and remind me why I should forgive the lies.
But maybe I'm afraid of finding out that even that was a lie.
Maybe you won't feel so good in my arms. Or maybe you'll
taste as sweet or smell so damn alluring that I lose all common sense and fall in love with a stranger. What I'd do to
you wouldn't remotely resemble the love we once made, Miz
Farrington."

His hand fell away. His eyes closed. He swayed.

As Brandon slept like the dead in her bed, Alyson called
Henry. "He's fine," she assured him. "He's . . . resting."

"I'd like to talk to him, Al."

She glanced toward the bed. "He's sleeping. He's exhausted. I'll have him call you just as soon as he wakes up.
I promise."

Henry remained silent. She wanted to hang up the phone,
cut the connection before he outright asked her if Brandon
had been drinking. Then she realized that he already knew.

Finally he said, "I'm glad you're with him. He needs you.
You're good for him. He knows that. Brandon can be stubborn and temperamental, but he's not stupid. He knows a
good thing when he sees it. Tomorrow . . . when his head is
clear again, you'll work out your differences. You'll come
home, where you belong."

Tears rose to her eyes. "Home sounds good, Henry."

"Goodnight, Al. Give him a kiss for me. And tell him I
love him. Please."

Wiping her eyes, she nodded. "I'll tell him."

Sitting in a chair, the television on but muted, Alyson
watched Brandon sleep. A pain had centered behind her eyes
that made her temples ache. She shivered with cold, thought
of turning up the heat, then decided against it. From experience, she knew that heat only exacerbated the effects of a
hangover. Then she reminded herself that what Brandon

would feel upon waking up could hardly be compared with a simple hangover.

But worse, he'd now have one more cross to bear. First Henry and Bernie, then Anticipating. His disappointment over her *Gazette* association. Now the booze. She'd known enough alcoholics to realize that the consequences of this tumble from sobriety came with more than just the reawakening of his body's hunger for the drink. There would be depression and guilt. A sense of failure. A loss of hope. He'd search for the relief from those emotions in a bottle, and the cycle would begin again.

At just after two in the morning, Brandon opened his eyes. Alyson hurried to his side, stroked his brow, which felt damp with sweat. "Where the hell am I?" he slurred.

"My motel room."

"Thirsty as hell."

"I'll get you some water."

He shook his head and tried to get up. She forced him back down. "Would you prefer a cola? I'll get you one, but you must promise to stay in bed."

Groaning, he closed his eyes and pulled the pillow over his face.

She dug a dollar in change out of her purse, slid on her shoes and sweater, took one last glance at Brandon, who appeared to be sleeping again, and stepped out into the shock of bitter cold. Over the last hours the storm had settled its frozen hand solidly over the countryside. Beneath the parking lot lights the grounds and cars shimmered like ice mirrors.

The vending machines were in an alley behind the office, which was across the parking lot. Pulling her sweater more tightly around her, Alyson balanced her weight carefully on the ice and trudged forward.

Up ahead and to her right, sandwiched between a minivan and a Ram, a car idled. A cloud of vapor coiled from its exhaust pipe like a genie from Aladdin's lamp. As she walked past it, she glanced at the windshield, which stared back at her like an oblong black eye, reflecting the distant pole light like a glowing white iris. The car looked empty.

Her steps slowed.

She looked back at the motel room door, which remained slightly ajar. Again at the car, then allowed her gaze to sweep the parking lot, along the line of motel doors and windows, all of which, other than hers, were lightless.

The memory of the dead dog in her bed crept into her mind, along with the lipstick scrawl.

YOU'RE NEXT BITCH

Her teeth began to chatter. She stood in the middle of the parking lot, her body crawling with gooseflesh that had nothing to do with the cold.

This is ridiculous, she thought, vaguely aware that she gripped the coins so tightly their serrated edges bit into her flesh. Only she knew the fear wasn't ridiculous. Not at all. Someone sick enough to murder a dog and hide it in a person's bed was sick enough to hurt her.

She forced herself to breathe. Woodenly, she turned again toward the vending machines, which seemed to float in the distance like a mirage. With one last glance at the empty, idling car, she shuffled toward the machines.

The coins plinked into the machine's hollow belly. The cola thumped down the shaft and rolled into the catch. Alyson grabbed it and headed back to the room, retracing her footprints in the slush, slowed near the car, unable to look at it now for some odd reason—afraid that perhaps it would no longer be empty, that someone would be there behind the wheel staring out at her, someone who might have been hiding before, perhaps lying down in the seat. . . .

A sound behind her.

Her feet slid like skates on ice. She danced in place, dropped the cola, and watched helplessly as it rolled toward the growling car.

The figure moved up behind her, grabbed her arm. Her mouth flew open, but all sound caught in her throat and nothing came out—

"Careful," the voice said, followed by amused laughter as

the man steadied her on her feet. She looked around, into his
bearded face, or what she could see of it burrowed deep into
his raised coat collar. A knit cap covered his head, to just
above his bushy eyebrows. "Peggy Fleming you ain't," he
joked, then chased the cola can, sliding in the attempt. He
tossed it back to her, and without a backward glance, climbed
into the car and turned on the headlights. Alyson shuffled
aside as the car crept past her, tires crunching the ice.

She felt limp with relief and chagrin.

Back in the room, Alyson found Brandon asleep again.
Wearily, she dropped into the chair. Finally, she kicked off
her shoes, pulled off her sweater and climbed into the bed
next to him, laid her head on his shoulder, and closed her
eyes. She listened to his heartbeat until the sound lulled her
to sleep.

She stared bleary-eyed at the clock on the bedside table,
Nine-twenty. The bed beside her was empty. Her heart stam-
mered, then she heard the water running in the bathroom.

Alyson eased from the bed and walked to the partly open
bathroom door. Steam rolled over her, as did the smell of
toothpaste and soap. Hot water ran freely from the sink fau-
cet.

Brandon, a towel wrapped around his waist, pressed his
forehead against the fogged lavatory mirror, eyes closed, his
face pale. He made a sound in his throat.

"Are you okay?" she asked.

A moment passed before he responded. "Do I look okay
to you?"

"You look like hell."

He swallowed. "Please, shoot me and put me out of my
misery." Rotating his head, his temple still pressed against
the mirror, he looked at her with bloodshot eyes and pain
etching deep lines in his face. "Aly. . . ." He swallowed
again. "I fucked up."

"It's okay," she said softly, smiling. "We all fuck up occasionally, Brandon. I'm a perfect example. I'll forgive you if you forgive me."

Cautiously, she stepped into the hot room and against his body, damp with humidity and sweat. His arms wrapped around her tightly, almost too tightly, as if anger lingered. Sliding his hand into her hair, he twisted his fingers in it, pulled back her head and looked hard into her eyes.

"Forgive me," she whispered. *"Please."*

He pressed her back against the wall, body moving against hers as his hands slid down her body. His breath touched her temple. His lips brushed her mouth.

The phone rang.

The wall came down in Brandon's eyes, and with it the same condemnation that had cut her to the bone the day before. He backed away, and the moment vaporized like the steam swirling around them.

Her heart sinking, Alyson ran to the phone. "Hello?"

"Miss James? Miss James, is that you?"

Alyson frowned and looked around. Brandon, his face and hair dripping water, a towel in his hands, stood near the end of the bed, face ashen and eyes shadowed. He was shirtless. His jeans were only partially zipped.

"Who is this?" she asked. Brandon dropped into a chair and began wedging his feet into his boots.

"Betty Wilson."

"Betty?" Her gaze locked with Brandon's. His movements froze.

"I'm afraid something dreadful has happened," came Betty's trembling voice, loudly enough that Alyson was forced to hold the receiver slightly away from her ear. "We got a call around seven. From the Emergency Clinic."

Brandon grabbed the receiver from Alyson's hand.

"Someone said you and Mr. Brandon had been in an accident—that you were both critical and were being airlifted to Tyler General. Mr. Henry left for the clinic immediately. When I didn't hear from him, I called the clinic; they told me they knew nothing about it, there must be some mistake, and Mr. Henry had never arrived there. I'm terribly concerned that he's stranded in the ice, or worse."

"Have you called the police?" Brandon asked.

Betty began weeping. "Thank God, you're all right. We thought—"

"Did you call the police?" he shouted.

"No, not yet. But I will. Immediately."

Brandon slammed down the phone. Alyson jumped from the bed, grabbed for her socks and shoes.

"Don't bother," Brandon snapped as he reached for his shirt.

"Oh, no, you don't. No way are you leaving this room without me."

He turned on her, jaw tight, and jabbed one finger in her face. "Just because I was oblivious enough last night to climb back into your bed—"

"This isn't about us, Brandon. If you want to shut me out of your life, fine, but you can't shut me out of Henry's. That's Henry's choice to make, not yours. Besides"—she pointed at his hands—"you're shaking so badly, the last thing we need is for you to climb behind the wheel of a car— especially in these icy conditions."

He glared at her as he buttoned his shirt and she tugged on her socks. They shrugged on their jackets.

Low clouds turned daylight to dusk. Alyson gripped the steering wheel hard, her fear for Henry and her concern for Brandon adding to the stress of manipulating the car down the icy highway.

Here and there trucks had dumped sand and gravel to aid traction—always too little too late. Any town south of the Red River simply could not cope with such freakish weather.

She glanced at Brandon. He stared out over the frozen countryside, his lower lip caught between his teeth. She reached for his hand, curled her fingers around it. For a long moment he did nothing; no response, just sat still and cold. Then his fingers entwined with hers and squeezed so hard her bones felt crushed.

"What the hell happened to me?" he said. "What the hell was I thinking? I don't even remember reaching for it. Four fucking years blown. What was I thinking, Aly?"

"You weren't thinking, Brandon. You were reacting. You were sad and angry, and looking for a way to make those feelings less painful."

He shook his head, and when he looked at her, his eyes were dark pools of panic. "I'm unraveling. My whole fucking life is unraveling. I feel like I'm careening toward that goddamn guardrail again, and I can't stop it." Running his hand through his hair, he squeezed his eyes closed, gripped her numb hand more tightly. "We both know who made that phone call to Henry, don't we? What kind of lunatic pulls that kind of sick joke?"

In that instant Alyson realized that he hadn't heard about Rufous. Of course he wouldn't have. He'd been gone from the farm when Deputy Greene contacted Henry.

"Jesus," she heard him groan. He leaned forward, focusing on something in the distance that was little more than a dark blue blur in the cold haze. "Oh, Christ. Don't let that be Henry's truck. Please, God, don't let that be Henry."

Closer.

The old truck materialized through the mist, parked on the roadside, wipers scraping back and forth over a thin film of ice on the windshield.

"Stop the car," Brandon ordered. "Stop the goddamn car."

The Jag slid sideways as Brandon threw open the door and jumped out, slid to his knees, clawed his way back to his feet and ran, slipping and sliding, toward the truck. He couldn't breathe. The pressure in his head began to pulse like a heartbeat. He could see Henry now, sitting behind the wheel, only something wasn't right. His glasses looked askew on his face, and he was leaning—resting, yes, he was resting—against the door. He grabbed the door handle and yanked, sending slivers of thin ice to the ground and over his feet.

Henry slumped into his arms, the heavy, sudden weight propelling them to the ground.

The horn-rimmed glasses bounced on the frozen road.

"Henry?" Brandon took his uncle's cold face between his

hands and searched his dull blue eyes. "Ah, Henry. Oh, Jesus. Oh, no. Oh, God . . . no."

He looked up as Alyson dropped to her knees, fists pressed to her mouth to stop the sobs rising up her throat. Her eyes were big and tear-filled, reflecting the acknowledgment that he, in that terrible moment, refused—though it was there, filling him up inside, expanding with painful pressure, crawling up his throat and buzzing between his ears. His eyes suddenly felt too large for their sockets.

Suddenly her arms were around him, holding him as if she were fighting to keep him from falling off a precipice. She wept his name and cried, "I'm sorry. I'm so very sorry."

"The doctor's with him now," Alyson said softly into the phone. She pulled her jacket tighter around her as she sat on the front porch step, shivering and staring up at the ice-heavy tree branches. The temperature hovered at thirty degrees, but the precipitation had finally stopped. She did her best to swallow her emotion. Her eyes throbbed and her throat ached. "Alan, he just sits there, smoking, staring at nothing, unresponsive. I want desperately to comfort him—"

"He's in shock, A. J., not to mention denial. He's been forced over the years to keep his pain and anger bottled up inside him. No doubt he'll find a way to blame himself for this. Not good, considering everything else that's going on. When he rouses out of his stupor, he'll head for the bottle to punish himself. Or worse. Do you think he's suicidal?"

She shook her head, frowning, refusing to acknowledge that the possibility had coiled around her concerned and suspicious mind the last hours. "I don't know. I don't think so, but—"

"Don't leave him alone, whatever you do."

"You're joking, right? I can hardly get within three feet of him. Betty hasn't left his side for thirty seconds all day. I've seen dogs trained to kill guard with less ferociousness."

"How is she taking Henry's death?"

"Better than the rest of us, I'd say." Her voice trembled.

"I'm trying to handle this, Alan. I don't think I hurt this badly even with my grandmother's death. Don't get me wrong, I loved her devotedly. How could I not? She raised me, for God's sake. But when her time came, I was prepared. She'd been sick for so long—her passing was a relief. But this . . . I spoke to Henry just last night. He was fine."

She looked around, through the window where a single lamp burned. Brandon sat by it in a rocker, his head back and eyes closed. Standing, Alyson carefully moved down the icy steps, putting more distance between herself and the house. "Whoever made that phone call to Henry knew how it would affect him. Henry always carried a bottle of his medicine in his pocket, another in the glove compartment of the truck for a backup—Brandon insisted on it. Alan, the deputies went through that truck with a fine-tooth comb. His medicine wasn't there. Not on him. Not in the truck. Betty said when he got the call, he was so frantic to get to the hospital that he didn't take his medicine with him. She didn't realize until he'd left. Why would Anticipating strike out at Henry, Alan? What could she gain from his death?"

"Perhaps she saw him as an obstacle in her way. Or perhaps it was another punishment. Or a control issue. Could have been any of those reasons, or all of them." Alan sighed. "Look, it isn't the best time to discuss this, but this needs to be said, A. J. I think it's obvious that we're dealing with a very twisted individual. I've had time to read and reread these letters, and I've come to the conclusion that Anticipating is probably someone who, at one time, was very close to Carlyle. Personally. Not just some freak fan—unrequited love from afar sort of thing."

"A former lover?" she said, glancing again toward the window. Brandon stared out at her, his face blank of expression.

"I don't think so. More like a business associate. More likely an employee. Someone who came in direct contact with him enough to know his day-to-day activities, which is probably how she knew about Ticky Creek. It's quite common. An employee attempts to establish a personal relationship with a coworker, an employer, and is rejected or ignored. Eventually their adoration becomes frustrated, angry, worsening their already sorry self-esteem. These people are socially maladjusted and probably have never been involved in any sort of meaningful relationship.

"But aside from all that, there's more going on here than the unrealistic emotional investment that Anticipating is manifesting by her rants of love and extreme adoration for Carlyle. It's as if she's elevated him to a god and sees his human foibles as outrageous iniquities. Apparently, she believes her sole objective is to deliver him from evil, so to speak. Which would explain why she'd take out anyone she thinks is leading him down a path of damnation."

"But why Henry?"

Alan remained silent for a long moment, then, "Just a hunch, A. J. But wasn't Henry encouraging your relationship with Brandon?"

"Oh, God," she whispered into the phone. "Our last conversation, he insisted that I move into the farmhouse. More than that, Alan, he was highly supportive of our getting married as soon as possible."

"Then Anticipating has ingratiated herself into Carlyle's life more closely than we thought, if she was aware of your plans to marry. Listen to me, you've got to get into Carlyle's employee records. Get us names and addresses, phone numbers. The letters began around a year before his accident with Marcella. We'll focus on those who were working for him at that time. Are you hearing me, A. J.? There's something else. The last few notes included quotes from Keats's 'Ode to a Nightingale' *I have been half in love with easeful Death . . .* the individual has a death wish, A. J. I'm afraid she's tortured by more than her unrequited adoration for Carlyle. We've got to get to the bottom of this *now*."

Her gaze fixed on Betty, who stood framed in the window, staring down at her, limned by the lamplight behind her. Alyson couldn't see her face—the dusk was too thick—but she sensed the coldness of Betty's stare. As always, when she looked at Alyson, her eyes were like green marbles. "I'll see what I can do," she replied, then hit the Off button on the cell phone.

As Alyson entered the house, she heard Doc Simpson talking on the kitchen phone, voice a low monotone. From the corner of her right eye, she saw Betty moving toward her, so she turned to her left and entered the living room, where Brandon sat in the rocker, lighting another cigarette. Alyson dropped to one knee beside him and put her hand on his arm. "Talk to me, Brandon. Please. You can't continue this way."

"Leave him alone," came Betty's voice. "He's suffering. Can't you see that?"

Brandon looked at Alyson.

She tried to smile. "Don't hold it inside this way. Talk to me. We have to talk about what happened . . . and why."

"Why should he?" Betty demanded. "You're a liar and a fraud, Miss James. You broke his heart, and Henry's as well. I wouldn't be at all surprised if your behavior didn't provoke Henry's attack."

Alyson turned her head and stared into Betty's narrowed eyes. "I beg your pardon?"

"You heard me. I know how devastated he was. I spent the entire day comforting him. He adored you, and you repaid his kindness with deception."

Her hand closing more tightly on Brandon's arm, Alyson focused again on his eyes, which looked at her with an intensity that stabbed at her heart. She suddenly felt cold, as if the marrow in her bones had turned to ice. "I spoke with Henry about it, Brandon. He wasn't upset. Don't listen to her. We know what provoked that attack. The phone call—"

"Mr. Henry trusted you. He allowed you into his home, encouraged your relationship with Mr. Brandon, and all the while you were using them. Blood money, that's what you'll gain from your sleazy tabloid story, Miss James."

Jumping to her feet, Alyson turned on Betty, and slapped her. The sound snapped like a child's pop gun in the silence. Her eyes wide, Betty stumbled back; her hand flew to her cheek.

Brandon grabbed her, hauled her around so brutally she almost stumbled. His fingers closed like vises around her arms as he lifted her to her toes and shook her. His face looked feral. "Enough," he said through his teeth. "I want you out of my house, Alyson. Get the hell out of Ticky Creek, because if you don't—"

"Don't do this," she implored. "You have to listen to me, Brandon. I understand you're upset—"

He moved toward the door, dragging her with him. "Betty's going to take you back to the motel now. If you call me or come back here, I'll file charges against you."

"Surely you're not blaming me for—"

"Shut up."

"But—"

"I said 'Shut up.' " He shoved her out the door and down the icy porch steps.

She attempted to wrench away. He held her tighter until a hot numbness flashed down her arm. "I spoke with Alan," she announced, trying to keep her voice steady and rational. "He believes Anticipating is an acquaintance, very probably a former employee. She wanted to get rid of Henry because Henry encouraged our relationship, the way she got rid of Marcella because she saw Marcella as a threat. We need your employee records: names, addresses, phone numbers—"

"Do I look like a goddamn accountant to you?"

Opening the door of Betty's car, he pushed her down into the seat.

"Why won't you listen to me?" she cried, at last twisting her arm free.

Looking into her eyes, he said, "If you ever really gave a damn about me, Aly, just walk away. Walk away and don't look back. It's enough to deal with Henry's death. If something happened to you. . . ."

She touched his cheek, managed a watery smile. "You still care, don't you? You're doing this—pushing me away to protect me."

Some emotion flickered in his eyes, and suddenly he looked bone weary, and heartbreakingly sad. "I have to do this alone, Aly. Understand, please. It's . . . private, the pain. I can't explain it. I have to deal with it alone." Brandon shut the car door as Betty opened hers and threw Alyson's purse into her lap. The contents spilled around her feet. She hardly noticed, her focus still on Brandon as he backed away, his eyes full of turmoil and his face pale as chalk.

He stood in the cold long after Betty's car had disappeared beyond the security gate. The cold bit at his exposed skin. The lead weight in his chest had grown immeasurably heavier the moment the car, with Alyson in it, disappeared into the dark.

He didn't want to go back in the house. Not back to the emptiness. And the silence. And the memories. Then he'd be forced to acknowledge the hole of anger and grief that, minute by minute, expanded inside him, as if the seam of his reality were slowly dissolving stitch by stitch, swallowing him from the inside out.

Henry gone. It wasn't possible. Brandon expected him to appear in the distant barn door, wearing his cap and overalls. At any moment Henry would appear on the porch, eyes twinkling behind his glasses, and point out that Brandon would catch his death if he didn't get out of the cold. Henry would suggest hot chocolate, and when he thought Brandon wasn't looking, he'd sneak some brandy into his mug. They'd settle next to Bernie and stare at the television—grump over the idiotic questions on *Who Wants to Be a Millionaire*—and Henry would fall asleep with his glasses on.

Henry gone. It wasn't possible.

Sluggishly, he mounted the porch steps, glanced over his shoulder one last time, half expecting to see Betty returning with Alyson—no, not expecting it, exactly. Needing it. Wanting Aly back even before Betty's car lights had dimmed into the dark. Better this way. He simply couldn't deal with her getting hurt—not because of him.

He moved down the hallway to the kitchen. Doc Simpson sat at the table, looked up at Brandon with sad, weary eyes. Doc was slightly older than Henry, thinner, with a fluff of white hair that resembled cotton. "The phone hasn't stopped ringing. Folks passing on their condolences. I suspect they'll be trailing through here tomorrow like army ants."

"Why are you still here?" Brandon asked.

"Henry was a friend. A close friend. I know how he worried about you." He looked away, then back. "The funeral home called. Just like we thought. Heart attack. Massive. They'll have his body ready for viewing by noon tomorrow. They'll need clothes to bury him in, of course. Would you like me to do that for you? Drop off his clothes? It's on my way home."

Brandon stared down at the horn-rimmed glasses on the table. Their lenses were cracked, having hit the ground when Henry slumped out of the truck into Brandon's arms. He shrugged and pressed the heels of his hands into his eyes, as if the effort would block out the sight of those glasses.

Doc Simpson scraped back his chair and walked to Brandon, laid one hand on his shoulder. "I'm sorry, son. I know what he meant to you."

"No. You don't." Brandon shook his head. "You can't possibly know what he meant to me."

"If there's anything I can do—"

"There is." Brandon gave a quavering grin. "Bring him back."

Doc turned away, trudged up the stairs to Henry and Bernie's old room, where he'd poke through the closet and find Henry's only suit. Henry had bought it shortly after Brandon's return home, during one of Bernie's bad spells. "Best to be prepared," Henry had declared with an air of nonchalance that had not been reflected in his sorrowful eyes.

Brandon touched the glasses, but didn't pick them up.

He turned slowly toward Bernie's room.

She sat in her wheelchair facing the muted television, hands in her lap, blue eyes fixed on the television screen as if she were really watching it. He crossed the room and touched the Off button, moved to Bernie, stared down at her for a full minute before easing down onto his knees and reaching for her cold hand.

He searched her face, her eyes, the pressure and heat in

his throat becoming unbearable. Simply drawing in a breath felt impossibly difficult, as if his lungs had filled with water. "Bernie . . . he always held on to the hope that you were still with us. God, I'd like to believe that right now. I'd like to think there was something left. . . ."

A spasm flashed through him. His eyes burned. Emotion scraped up his throat like burning fragments of sharp glass. "He's gone, Bernie." The sound was ragged. "Henry's gone. I'm sorry. I'm so damn sorry."

The words—saying them at last—obliterated the numbing denial. Grief slammed him. It rose up from his chest in a terrible flame, erupted in a howl as he rocked back on his knees, eyes squeezed closed and fists shaking. On and on went the howl, as if every emotional wound of his past had been lanced and the old, festering memories and pain gushed forth in a fiery torrent. The tears spilled, then the sobs began, great gulps and shudders, crushing his chest, driving like a fist into his gut, bending him double. Clutching his belly, he rocked and groaned and sobbed, hating the sound of it, sickened by the feel of it, the awful helplessness, the wracking pain, the sinking, sinking despair of falling into a dark pit where no light would ever penetrate.

As if he had tumbled through a time warp, he became a boy again, face buried in his hands, ashamed that he couldn't stop the crying, more ashamed that he couldn't confess the reasons for his crying, sobbing at Bernie's feet while she wrapped her arms around him. *Hush, hush, my darling boy, my precious Brandon. There, there, dear, let me hold you, make it right. We love you, love you, love you, and always will—forever, Brandon, forever.*

Shaking, heaving, he laid his head on Bernie's lap, took her cold hand, and nestled it against his cheek.

21

"I'm outta here," Mildred declared as she threw a handful of panties into her suitcase. "The son of a bitch fired me. Coldcocked me just like that. 'You're fired, Mildred, now get the hell out of my life.' Just like that. Hung up in my ear. I called him back, and that freaking Doberman answered. Actually had the audacity to say I might, in some way, have caused Henry's heart attack. I was speechless. I mean—me, speechless? But I was. How the hell can·you respond to something like that?"

"How did he sound?" Alyson watched Mildred dig another armload of clothes out the dresser drawer.

Mildred straightened, stared thoughtfully at her reflection in the dresser mirror. "Tired, maybe. Sad, definitely. Drunk. . . ." She looked around at Alyson. "I couldn't tell. He was on and off so fast I simply couldn't tell. He holds his booze pretty damn well, as you know. He can be on the verge of passing out, and you wouldn't know until he was facedown on the floor. It's how he got away with his alcoholism so damn long. People just thought he was an ass on the set, a spoiled tyrant." She swallowed and shrugged. "He's a nice guy when he's sober. It's really hard not to like him, you know? Not that he's a total loser when he's boozed. You just don't want to corner him, you know what I'm saying? It's a little like poking a stick at a wounded animal. He just loses it."

Alyson paced, her hands on her hips. "I spoke with Deputy Greene. They have a couple of officers watching the place, one at the front gate, another at the back, at least for tonight."

"What about that Mitsy creature?"

"Deputy Greene put a car at Jack's place last night. She hasn't left the house since she was released from jail." Alyson stopped pacing and faced Mildred squarely. "If we're correct in our assumption that Anticipating made that bogus call to Henry, and that the disappearance of his medicine from the truck wasn't just coincidence, then Anticipating has to be someone close enough to Brandon to know his every move. More than that, she has to have access to the family." Alyson narrowed her eyes at Mildred and asked smoothly, "Did you know that Brandon and I were to be married this week?"

Mildred stared at her, clothes clutched to her chest. "No." She shook her head, disbelief widening her eyes. "Hey, you don't think that I. . . . Holy heck, you do, don't you? You think I'm Anticipating—"

"You're an employee, Mildred. You have a thing for Brandon. You slept with him—"

"Oh, my God!" The clothes spilled to her feet. "I might be a shark at business, Alyson, but I don't go around murdering dogs and old men. What happened between me and Brandon was just spur-of-the-moment lust brought on by too much champagne and too many Bloody Marys. I sleep with many of my clients, for God's sake. He was just better at it than most, drunk or not."

Pointing a finger at Alyson, Mildred added, "Hey, I wouldn't be in your shoes for anything. Women haven't nicknamed Brandon Mr. T for nothing. The man is walking testosterone. There isn't a woman alive who doesn't fantasize his jumping her. He's slept with every female costar he's worked with, and if you think marriage is going to stop him, you're in for a crash and burn, Sweetheart."

"You're wrong," Alyson said calmly. "He'd never cheat on me, Mildred. He's just a small town boy with small town dreams, thanks to Henry and Bernie. He desperately wants the sort of love and commitment his aunt and uncle shared. Why shouldn't he? They were the only positive role models in his life. They represented stability and emotional security."

"Yeah? Well, if he's so hot to trot with you, why did he tell you to get lost?"

"To protect me. If Anticipating would eliminate Henry, she'll come after me, and this time she won't stop with a dead dog in my bed and a warning scribbled on a mirror." Dragging both hands through her hair, Alyson closed her eyes. Had it been only twelve hours since the heart-stopping moment they'd discovered Henry's truck by the road? A flurry of fresh pain ripped through her. Not just pain. Fear. Cold and creeping, pebbling her flesh with goose bumps. "With Henry gone and me out of the way, there's nothing more to stand in Anticipating's way, is there?

"I have to get my hands on his payroll records—the employees working for him one year prior to Emerald Marcella's death. His only response to that was 'Do I look like a goddamn accountant?' " She turned to Mildred. "His accountant. Of course! What was I thinking? He told me—his accountant would obviously have those records. But who is his—"

"Middleton, Travis and Wolff. Fred Wolff. I use him as well."

"Will he give us Brandon's files?"

"If Brandon calls him—".

"He can't, Mildred. Think. If Anticipating were to discover that we're trying to nail her—"

"How the hell would she know that? She'd have to be living under Brandon's roof. . . ." Mildred stared back at her, the color draining from her face. Slowly, she sat on the bed,

her feet tangled in the panty hose and bras she had dropped.
"Betty."

Hearing her suspicion out in the open relieved a pressure
on Alyson, if only momentarily. Suddenly, her knees felt
wobbly, and the cold that had speared her minutes before
sank deeper into the very pit of her. Her throat closed. She
was forced to clear it twice before speaking.

"It all makes sense to a point. How Anticipating would
know his every move, day or night. How she could get in
and out of the farm to vandalize it. How she could manipulate Henry's medicine, removing it from the truck—"

Mildred shook her head. "Stop right there. Betty was with
Henry and Bernie when Henry got that call about an accident. Had to have been. He never would have driven away
from the farm and left Bernie unattended.

"Besides, they have no history together, not before she
went to work for Henry. Hey, I'm first in line to testify that
the woman defines the word 'creep,' okay? But you said
yourself, Anticipating has been around a long time—five
years. She's probably a former employee. At least an acquaintance. Betty's probably nothing more than some frumpy
old maid who's become too emotionally attached to her patient's family. It happens."

"I'll call the Texas Medical Board first thing in the morning. She'll have to have a license to nurse in this state. She
said she moved here from Kansas. I'll call the Kansas Medical Board as well. If there's a record of her working in
Kansas before moving to Ticky Creek, we'll have to eliminate her as a suspect."

Twisting her hands together, Mildred said more softly, "Jesus, Alyson, I wouldn't like to think he's over there alone
with her if you're right."

"If I'm right, Anticipating has him right where she wants
him. Isolated. Controlled. She worships him, Mildred. She
won't hurt him, not as long as her position in his life remains
stable and unthreatened. The smartest thing we can do now
is back off until we've got rock-solid proof that Betty is
Anticipating."

"But we should warn him—"

"I think he knows already. Or suspects. It's why he wanted me away from the farm, out of harm's way." She tried to swallow. "Please call Fred Wolff. Call him now, Mildred."

The shaking of his body roused him. Like the old days, the sorry poison slithered like snakes through his blood. His brain swam with voices and images that were as fleeting as ghost whispers. His eyes throbbed.

He floated while the blackness ebbed little by little. He wondered if he was awake or dreaming again. Or maybe he'd finally died and gone straight to hell, because that's what the terrible pain in his body felt like—torture. Fire and agony. Pins and needles. Perpetual nausea from being tossed endlessly on hundred-foot waves.

The booze did that to him, confused his reality. He had a vague memory of dancing, Ruth Threadgill laughing and blushing while he propositioned her. Her eyes had looked up into his with a yearning and pain that had speared him with guilt, because she knew she wasn't the one he needed to hold in that moment.

Stupid bastard. How could he have blown four years of sobriety?

Christ, he had to get home. To Henry and Bernie. Henry would know, of course. He always did. No matter how good he'd become at hiding the fact that he'd been drinking, Henry would take one look at his face, and that shadow of despondency and helplessness would settle in his uncle's eyes. Brandon could feel the punch of it in his gut.

Never again. I promise you, Henry, never again.

He opened his eyes, or thought he did. Couldn't really be certain, could he? Not until he'd sweated the alcohol out of his system, or pissed it away. The haze, of course, would remain, stuffing up his brain like thick cotton.

I promise you, Henry, never again.

There was a vague hint of light: streaks and shadows, swirls of mist like some cheap horror flick. Christ, it felt real, as real as the pounding in his head and the lead weight of his body. Something was there. Someone. Smiling down at him.

"There, there, Mr. Brandon. Sleep. I'm close at hand, here to take care of everything, now that Henry's gone."

Henry's gone.

Groaning, he closed his eyes. The memories crawled back, then the grief. He recognized it now. The pain squirming through his body wasn't from alcohol.

Cool hands stroked his brow.

"Aly?" he called. Had she come back? "Aly, is that you?" He tried to sit up, to remember. There was pain in his throat and chest—crying, yes, he'd been hysterical, and Doc Simpson had been there, bending over him, stabbing something into his arm. The world had instantaneously become melting colors and sounds, then the floor had opened up beneath him and he'd fallen into a hole of pitch darkness.

"Dreadful woman is gone," came the words. "You sent her away. Banished her and her sinful ways from your life."

Forcing open his eyes, he focused on Betty's smiling face. Only she wasn't smiling, exactly. Her mouth was pulled into a flat, thin semblance of a smile.

Alyson showered, hoping the hot, pounding water would re-lieve the tension in her shoulders. Impossible, of course. She felt as if someone had beat her with a tire iron. With water raining down over her head and steam almost suffocating her, she began to cry again. Squatting over the rusty drain, her face buried against her knees, she bawled so hard her ribs ached and her eyes throbbed.

The image replayed over and over in her mind's eye: Brandon sitting on the slushy road shoulder, cradling Henry in his arms, heartbreak and helplessness reflected in his eyes, rocking rocking rocking in the cold, pleading with God to give Henry back. It had taken two paramedics and Deputy Greene to pry Henry's body away from him. The worst had come when they brought out the body bag. Dear God, she prayed never to see such emotional anguish in another human's face as long as she lived—especially not Brandon's. How much suffering could one man endure before he broke?

That's what frightened her most. Was he despondent enough to harm himself?

No. Not as long as Bernie needed him. That, if nothing else, would give him the will to continue.

She dried and dressed and ordered room service, delivered by a gangly teenage boy with a severe case of acne. "Food's on the house," he declared as he bounced to ward off the cold. "Heard about Henry. Old dude was okay, not like most of the old farts around. He was cool, ya know? Helped him bale once. Paid me real good. Louise threw in a piece of coconut pie. She remembered Henry comin' in not long ago and ordering a piece. You tell Brandon we're real sorry. Henry's gonna be missed around here. Ya know?"

"I know," she replied, swallowing a fresh lump in her throat.

She choked down half the sandwich then tossed the leftovers into the trash. A half-dozen times she walked to the phone, wanting to call Brandon. But she'd never get past Betty, so why try? Best to leave well enough alone, for the time being. Still, she didn't like to think of him suffering through his loss alone. Like Mildred, she didn't like to think of him alone with Betty, if their suspicions about her were correct.

She'd call Alan. He, of course, would know exactly what to do. Perhaps he might even talk her out of believing that Betty Wilson was Anticipating. *Don't rush to any conclusions, A. J. And by the way, keep your nose out of this and let the police do their job.*

Grabbing up her purse, she dumped it out on the bed, spilling keys, gum wrappers, a partially smushed Twinkie, her change purse . . . and two phones.

Alyson frowned, picked up the spare phone, turned it over, examined it one way, then another. Then she remembered. Her purse had spilled in Betty's car. She'd been forced to scramble for her things in the dark. She must have grabbed Betty's phone . . . hidden under the car seat.

She tossed it on the bed as if it were a snake, wiped her hand on her T-shirt, shivered.

It's just a phone, she reminded herself. Creepy isn't contagious.

Sitting on the bed, she stared down at the phone, reluctantly reached for it. Just a phone. That's all. Samsung. Sprint. Worked just like every other cell phone. She flipped it open, punched the Power button, and waited for it to bleep at her with a green light in the small display window.

READY winked up at her.

She pressed the Recall button.

A number flashed-up. Henry's number. Called at seven-fifteen that morning.

I'm afraid something dreadful has happened. We got a call around seven. From the Emergency Clinic. Someone said you and Mr. Brandon had been in an accident—that you were both critical and were being airlifted to Tyler General. Mr. Henry left for the clinic immediately.

We got a call around seven. . . .

The motel phone rang.

"I finally got through to Fred," Mildred said. "He's in Cancun and won't be home until Friday. There won't be a problem accessing the files. He keeps everything on record for seven years. One big glitch. He won't cooperate unless he speaks to Brandon first. He'll give him a call tomorrow. Now before you panic, Alyson, I've told him everything, and he understands the seriousness of the situation. Fred is as slick as bat guano. He could ream Betty up the backside with a jackhammer and she'd think he was making sweet love to her. Try to get some rest, kiddo. I've got a hunch you're going to need it."

"I've got a hunch you're right," Alyson said, looking down at Betty's phone.

* * *

Alyson called the Texas Medical Board the next morning. Betty Wilson had applied for and received her Texas license seven months ago—shortly after Brandon returned to Ticky Creek, Mildred pointed out. Alyson followed up with a phone call to the Kansas Medical Board. Records indicated that Betty had worked at Kansas City Memorial Hospital for ten years, up until two months before she relocated to Texas.

"Well, that's that," Mildred declared as they drove to the funeral home to pay their respects to Henry. "Betty might be creepy, but she's obviously legit. It's like I said; she's become too involved in the Carlyles' lives. You've said yourself that they treat her like family; it's obviously gone to her head."

"But what about the phone call? Made to Henry's farm from her cell phone around the same time she said she got that bogus call from the clinic."

"Maybe she ran to the Sack-It-Quick or something—called Henry to make sure they had enough grape jelly for breakfast. She arrived back at the farm just as Anticipating called."

"That could be disproved by checking phone records, couldn't it? There'd be two calls on record; one from her, one from Anticipating."

"Law enforcment will have to get a warrant to check those records. And to do that, she'll have to be considered a suspect. They have to have a legitimate reason for prying into someone's personal business. This isn't exactly a police state, you know."

"Have you heard back from Fred Wolff? Was he able to reach Brandon?"

"Haven't heard. Fred's good and he's thorough, but he's not the best communicator in the world. Besides, the man is in Cancun."

Alyson shook her head. "Something just isn't right with Betty. I've felt it all along. I've got a uncanny ability to sniff out rotten character, and I'm telling you, something very mendacious is lurking under that woman's facade. My skin crawls when I'm within twenty feet of her."

Mildred pulled the car into the Roselawn Funeral Home

parking lot. The lot was full, and Mildred was forced to park on the street. Nervousness and despair rolled over in Alyson's chest as they walked up the sidewalk and through the front doors. Clusters of people crowded the corridor, conversations muted, expressions . . . expressionless. A man approached and, extending one cold hand, he said, "I assume you're here to see Henry Carlyle. The first sanctuary on your right. The funeral is at ten in the morning. A short service here, another at graveside." He turned and walked away.

"What do I say to Brandon?" Alyson blinked the rise of tears from her eyes. "I want to hold him—comfort him, not chitchat."

"Main thing is to see if he's keeping it together." Mildred caught her arm. "Let's get this show on the road. God, I hate funeral homes. When I die, I'm donating my whole freaking body to science. If there's anything left of me when they get done plucking my bones, I hope they grind me up and make fingernail polish or something."

"Harlot Red," Alyson said with an unsteady grin.

Mildred made a sound and headed down the corridor, Alyson trailing. She recognized most of the faces who turned to watch her. Janet from the Dime A Cup. The good old boys from Red Neck Feed. Several couples she recalled from the River Road but couldn't remember their names.

Giant, fragrant wreaths of roses, carnations, and lilies flanked the open coffin. Alyson fell back, a crush of emotion pressing on her chest. Mildred looked around, her face suddenly looking its fifty-odd years. She extended one hand toward Alyson. "We'll do this together," she said.

They clasped hands.

Alyson's heart raced, and her legs became lead.

They moved together to the coffin.

Henry rested within a cloud of blue satin, looking very distinguished in his navy blue suit.

Alyson thought she'd prepared herself. Then she realized, just as she had realized that blinding-bright summer morning when she first viewed her grandmother tucked into her Forever Rest container, that there could be no preparation for this.

A sob climbed her throat. She pressed her hand to her mouth and experienced a sweep of anguish and anger that made her head feel as if it would burst.

Someone slid an arm around her. She looked around, into Ruth Threadgill's bloodshot eyes.

Ruth tucked a Kleenex into Alyson's fist and smiled. "There just ain't no words to lighten the moment, is there? But I'll say this; Henry was a good, good man. He led a Christian life and he loved his family. Bernice and Brandon were his whole world. Him and Bernie had somethin' real special together. There weren't a one of us in Ticky Creek who didn't look at their union with a touch of envy. He just ain't been the same without her. He died a little more each day that he had to watch her fade away. If there's any justice in what's happened here, maybe it's in God's takin' him now as opposed to later. At least this way he don't have to watch her suffer no more. An' he won't have to suffer without her."

"I wish I'd known him longer," Alyson whispered. "I feel . . . robbed."

"His passin' is gonna leave a big empty space in our lives, that's for sure."

Alyson looked around. Her gaze slid over the milling visitors.

"He ain't here," Ruth said more quietly, and reached for another tissue. She blew her nose, gave a sniff, and shook her head. "Mr. Reed, the funeral director, says Brandon ain't been up yet. Ever'one's a bit shocked, considerin' how close they was an' all."

Mildred muttered a curse and walked away.

Alyson felt her face go cold, as if every ounce of blood had drained from her head and pooled in her legs.

Ruth noticed, and took Alyson's arm in her hand. "He's fine, Hon. I seen him this mornin'. Most of us here had a run by. You know, dropped off food and whatnot. I fried up a chicken and took it over. Janet dropped off a ham, I believe, and a pound cake."

"How did he look?" Alyson asked.

"Rough, of course, but that's to be expected. I'd say he was holdin' up pretty well. Kept to himself, mostly. Stayed close to Bernie. You know how it is. She's all he's got now. . . ." Her voice trailed off as she studied Alyson.

"What about Betty?" Alyson did her best to keep the concern from her voice, and the suspicion.

"Warm. Hospitable. Sad. Fluttered between Bernie and Brandon like a mother hen. Thank God Brandon's got her, right? Then again, maybe Brandon will see Bernie into a rest home now that Henry's gone. Never made much sense to any of us that Henry would want the responsibility of carin' for such an invalid. But that was Henry for you." Ruth smiled down at Henry and gave a quick soft sob. She patted Henry's folded hand like it was a child's. "Bless his heart, took his vows seriously, right to the end. Until death do us part." With a hiccup of emotion, Ruth turned on her heel and hurried away.

Dear God, if she didn't get out of here immediately, she was going to totally humiliate herself.

Alyson found Mildred in the hallway, smoking and pacing. By the time they got back to the car, dusk had fallen. "Drive to Brandon's," Alyson said. Mildred nodded, as if she were contemplating the trip already. They made the drive in silence.

Deputy Conroy sat in his patrol car outside the farm's security gate. As Mildred pulled into the drive and stopped, Conroy climbed out of his car and ambled to them, shoulders hunched from the cold, hat nudged back from his forehead. Bending, he smiled at them through the window.

"Ladies, y'all doin' all right tonight?"

"Right as rain." Mildred pointed to the house. "We've come to pay our respects to Mr. Carlyle."

Conroy smiled at Alyson. Only it wasn't a smile, exactly. More like a wince. "Sorry, but Mr. Carlyle ain't seein' nobody right now. He's gone into seclusion. You understand."

Mildred thumbed at Alyson. "This is his fiancée. I'm thinking he'll want to see her."

Conroy shook his head and averted his eyes. "That ain't the way I hear it, ma'am. I was told not to let anyone disturb Brandon this evening. Especially either of you."

"Brandon tell you that, or did Betty?" Mildred demanded, tapping her long red nails impatiently on the steering wheel.

"Well . . . Betty. But she said it was Brandon's request."

Alyson, leaning over Mildred, looked hard into Conroy's face. "Have you actually seen or spoken to Brandon yourself?"

"I didn't come on duty til three this afternoon, but I seen him walk down to the barn just before dusk."

"He hasn't been to the funeral home," Mildred declared, exasperated. "Don't you think that's a bit odd?"

He shrugged. "Not really, under the circumstances. If there's someone out there intent on doing him some harm, holed up in his house is probably the best."

"Unless he's holed up in the house with Anticipating," Mildred blurted.

Conroy raised his eyebrows. "You mean Betty? You're joking, right?" He rubbed his stomach. " 'Bout all Betty's guilty of is overindulging us. She brung me enough food for dinner to feed an army."

"Is that so?" Mildred laughed. "I'm glad to know the price of buying off law enforcement in Ticky Creek is cheap as a plate of fried chicken and pound cake."

Alyson grimaced.

Conroy frowned. "What's that supposed to mean?"

"Any of you yeehaws down at the sheriff's office run a background check on Betty Wilson? Like where was she the night this place was vandalized? Maybe checked out her apartment for a stolen Oscar—"

"She was at home Halloween night, and we don't go bull-dozing into people's homes around here without a good reason. This ain't *Law and Order*, ya know."

"I'd say burglarizing and vandalism is a damn good reason, Deputy. And how do you know she was home Halloween night? Because she said so?"

"Well . . . yes. Hell, Betty ain't got no motive to hurt the Carlyles. You got to have a motive—"

"Look, Barney, where I come from, everyone is guilty until proven innocent. She has access in and out of this place—"

"That back gate was open. If she wanted in, all she'd have had to do is drive right through."

"Well, duh." Mildred bumped her forehead with her fist. "It doesn't take an Einstein to figure she wouldn't be that stupid. Why don't we just take a little ride over to her place and check it out? Might be a little more productive than sitting here in the dark and burping up the onion you must have eaten with that fried chicken—"

"Mildred!" Alyson slapped Mildred's arm, making Mildred glare at her.

"Honey, we don't get what we want in my business by mollycoddling sluggards and idiots."

Deputy Conroy's eyes narrowed, and he cleared his throat. "Code of Criminal Procedure, Article 18.01, Sections B and C. No search warrant shall be issued for any purpose in this state unless sufficient facts are first presented to satisfy the issuing magistrate that probable cause does in fact exist for its issuance.

"Ma'am, in our opinion Betty Wilson has no more motive to harm Mr. Carlyle, his family, or home, than Miss James there."

"There's a big difference, Deputy," Mildred pointed out. "Miss James has an alibi for Saturday night. She was with Brandon and his family at the time. And as far as Henry is concerned—"

"Henry died of a heart attack."

"And the phone call?"

"A prank."

Alyson opened the car door. Mildred grabbed her arm. "What do you think you're doing?"

"I want to talk to Brandon," she said.

Conroy straightened, his hand going to the butt of his gun out of reflex.

Alyson, trailed by Deputy Conroy, walked to the security intercom and punched the call button. Nothing. She punched it again and tucked her hands into her armpits for warmth.

"This is Betty," came a voice so suddenly that both Alyson and Conroy jumped.

"This is Alyson. I'd like to see Brandon."

"That's impossible," came the terse response. "He doesn't wish to see you—"

"Put him on."

"He doesn't—"

"Betty, if you don't put him on, I'm going to climb this goddamn tree again and—"

Brandon's voice came on then—that smoky drawl that made her knees weak. For an instant she forgot the cold. Forgot the fear that had a painful hold on her heart.

"What do you want, Aly?"

Her eyes drifted closed as she floated on the sound of his voice. "I want to know that you're okay."

"I'm . . . fine. I'm resting, and I want to be left alone."

"I'd like to see you," she said more softly.

Silence.

"Please, Brandon. Just for five minutes. So I know you're okay."

"I'm tired, Aly. I'm going to bed."

Alyson shook her head. "It's seven o'clock—"

"I'm tired," he repeated, more forcefully. "I don't need any more hassles. It's enough that I got a call from my accountant today . . . I'm being audited. I've got to turn over my records for the last five years. . . ."

She looked back at Mildred, who smiled and gave her a thumbs-up. "Okay," she said. "I'll see you at the funeral tomorrow. And, Brandon, for what it's worth . . . I love you."

Nothing.

Finally, turning her eyes back to the house, she saw him in the window—silhouetted against the lamplight. Lifting her hand, she waved.

*   *   *

No doubt Henry's funeral would be recorded as the most attended service in the four-generation history of the Rose-lawn Funeral Home. Mourners spilled out of the building, across the frosty lawn, through the parking lot, and down the sidewalk.

Alyson and Mildred barely managed to wedge inside the chapel before the ushers were forced to tell those who followed that there was no room for them inside. Much to Alyson's frustration, she could see nothing more than the back of Brandon's head from her position, and though she did her best to listen to the half-dozen men who shared their thoughts and memories of their departed friend, she could only think about how Brandon must be hurting in that moment. That, even more than her sorrow for Henry, made her cry.

Afterward, the three-mile drive to the cemetery took an hour. Led by the white Cadillac hearse and family limo, the hundreds of cars crept at a snail's pace along the winding, blacktop road to Roselawn Hills, their headlights round white glows in the dull daylight.

The Carlyle plots were surrounded by wrought-iron fencing and situated on the highest hill under sprawling oak trees. No ordinary headstones there, but impressive blocks of towering marble and granite.

As Brandon and Betty were seated near the coffin covered with sprays of red roses, Deputies Greene and Conroy moved up beside them.

Mildred elbowed Alyson and pointed to Jack Dillman, who stood removed from the crowd. "He doesn't look like he's cried too many tears for Henry," Mildred commented.

As if he sensed their watching him, Dillman turned his gaze on them and stared. One corner of his mouth twitched, as if he were tempted to smirk.

"Wonder what kind of lock and key he's keeping that crazy sister of his under," Mildred whispered.

Alyson eased her way around the back of the crowd until she could peer over their shoulders well enough to glimpse Brandon.

Mildred, standing on her toes, could still see nothing. "What's he doing?" she asked.

"Nothing. Just . . . staring down at his hands, I think."

"What about Betty?"

"Emotionless as the Sphinx."

Unable to hear the service, they retreated to a distant bench and sat down.

"How do you think he'll react when you tell him we're leaving for California?" Mildred asked.

"He knows what we're doing, and why."

At long last the service ended. The mourners filed past the coffin one last time, briefly addressed Brandon, and wandered off to their cars. After what felt like an eternity, Brandon and Betty remained, alone except for Deputy Greene, who loitered close at hand.

With a resigned sigh, Alyson approached him. As he turned his dark blue eyes up to hers, the strength in her legs gave a little. The emotion she had kept inside rose up her throat in a burning rush, and she was forced to look away until she could trust herself to speak without sobbing.

Brandon stood and moved toward her.

She lifted her chin and forced a smile. Her gaze focused briefly on Betty, who watched them from her chair, expression stony.

"Hello," he said softly.

"You look exhausted," she said shakily, reaching to touch his cheek. "Are you sleeping at all?"

"Too much." He slid his hands into his trouser pockets. "I guess I'm just . . . tired . . . or something." He looked at Mildred, who remained in the distance. A lazy grin turned up his mouth. "I thought I fired her."

Alyson cleared her throat and spoke more loudly, surely loudly enough that Betty would hear her. "We're flying back to California this evening."

"I'll miss you."

"Will you?" She smiled, and felt heat suffuse her cheeks. "That's nice. Of course, I could always stay . . . just give me the word."

"I don't think that's such a good idea, Cupcake."

"Then I guess this is good-bye."

The word hung between them, the sound as disturbingly final as the open grave and coffin behind him.

His dark eyes never left hers as he offered one hand. A friendly shake—two acquaintances saying *good-bye, it's been fun, nice to know you, good luck.* She stared down at it for a moment, then took it, her heart catching as he wrapped his fingers around her hand, held it, warmth amid the crisp cold of the day. The words *I can't* tottered on the tip of her tongue.

Suddenly he pulled her into his arms, held her so fiercely she couldn't breathe, didn't want to. Dear God, he smelled good—felt good, fit her body so perfectly. The memories of their lovemaking rushed through her in a shimmering wave. She clung, closing her eyes as he turned his lips to her ear and whispered, "I miss you, Aly. I miss you so damn much."

"Are you okay?" she whispered back.

He nodded, and held her tighter.

"I won't be gone long, Brandon. I promise. I'll call you."

He kissed her cheek one last time and reluctantly pulled away. "Good-bye," he said again, and touched his fingertip to the tear on her cheek. "Good-bye." Then he turned and walked off.

Brandon sat in a chair next to Bernie's bed. Henry's chair. The cushions, molded to Henry's body after so many years, felt slightly uncomfortable, like wearing someone else's well-worn shoes. The muted television displayed a smirking Pat Sajak and bubbling Vanna White.

He looked at Bernie lying in her bed, head resting on her pillow, her hair like a gray cloud around her pale face. Her eyes stared at him.

Something was different. He couldn't quite shake the feeling that something in her faded blue stare had changed the last few days. A deep shadow of despair and age had settled amid the folds of loose skin around her eyes and mouth.

She's given up, he thought. Whatever energy Henry's faith and love had provided her was gone—the plug had been pulled on the life support.

He glanced at his watch. By now Alyson and Mildred would be on a plane headed back to California.

Brandon closed his eyes and sank deeper into the chair. He didn't want to think about Alyson right now. Didn't want to recall how pretty she'd looked at the cemetery, how red her eyes had been from crying, how good she'd felt in his arms, how much he missed her already. Such thoughts screwed up his reasoning. He had a hard enough time thinking clearly and rationally these days as it was. Depression and shock, Doc explained, not to mention grief. Eventually he'd pull out of it: a week from now, a month, a year. Until then, take life as it comes and know that Betty is there to see him through it.

Betty.

She appeared at the door, as she had an uncanny ability to do any time he thought about her. Funny, but he'd never really thought about her in the past—not as one would think of a friend or relative—never wondered about her existence away from the farm, never gave two thoughts about her past . . . aside from her nursing credentials, which had convinced Henry she would more than adequately replace the young woman who, before dying in an accident, had cared for Bernie.

But he'd been thinking about her more and more the last days. She continued to creep into his head anytime he roused from his depression and grief, and he found himself watching her with some instinctual rise of caution that had begun to gnaw at him while in her presence.

"Mr. Brandon, there's someone here to see you." She stepped to one side as Deputy Conroy moved to the door.

Conroy touched the brim of his hat, then hooked his thumbs over his gun belt. He appeared ill at ease, a bit edgy and uncertain. "Evening, Mr. Carlyle. Just thought I'd let you know we've been called back to the station. If you need anything, anything at all, don't hesitate to ring. We can be here in five minutes."

"We'll be just fine," Betty said behind him.

Conroy continued to watch Brandon, his eyes shadowed and intense under the brim of his Stetson. His mouth looked pressed, his expression thoughtful. "You sure you're okay, sir?"

"He's fine," Betty declared in a piqued tone. "He'll be much better when everyone stops badgering him. Good heavens, the man needs privacy right now, and the people of this town continue to parade through this house like it's Grand Central Station."

"Folks are just paying their respects," Conroy said. His eyes narrowed and his mouth pursed, and he slowly turned back to Betty. One hand reached into his coat pocket and withdrew a notebook which he flipped open and studied before raising his gaze back to hers. "Ma'am, would you mind tellin' me again just where you were on the night of October thirty-first between the hours of seven-thirty and eleven P.M.?"

Brandon left his chair and walked to the door. He slid his hands into his jeans pockets and leaned against the doorjamb. He watched deep color move into Betty's face.

Betty glared at Conroy, then at Brandon. "I told you. I was home. Alone, of course." Drawing herself up, she said, "I find your persistence in questioning me an outrageous insult."

"You wouldn't mind if we looked through your apartment, would you? You shouldn't, if you've got nothin' to hide." Then, as an afterthought, he added, "We can always get a search warrant. . . ."

Betty's mouth dropped open. She said nothing for a moment, then shook her head. "Of course I don't mind. Why should I?"

"Good." Conroy pocketed the notebook and smiled. "Why don't we take a run over there right now?"

"Now?" She blinked. "Oh, but I couldn't leave—"

"We'll be fine," Brandon said. "You'll want to get this cleared up, Betty. For both of our peace of mind."

She said nothing further, just flung aside the dish towel she was holding and headed for the stairs. "I'll get my coat and purse."

Standing shoulder to shoulder, Brandon and Deputy Conroy watched Betty ascend the staircase.

22

Apparently he was drinking again.

His head hurt like hell and his body felt like he'd been run through the baler. Memory, of course, was not an issue. He never remembered the drinking. Or the sorry behavior that went along with it. In years past, he'd simply wait for the phone to start ringing, sit for a confused half-hour and listen to tales of his previous night's escapades. Or, worse, pick up a newspaper or turn on the television to see his name or photograph before his bleary eyes. The dread and humiliation would sink like lead in his chest and stomach, and he'd promise himself to get help—again—even as he walked directly to the liquor cabinet and, with shaking hands, poured himself a glass of false courage and dignity.

But lying in bed that morning, he looked at his hands and found them steady. And when he thought of what he needed most at that moment to stop the ache inside him, it wasn't Chivas.

It was Alyson.

God, he missed her. The pain of it made him groan.

He showered. The hot water beating on his head and shoulders was of little help in alleviating the lethargy of his body or his head as he waited for the shaking, concentrated thirst for booze to assail him. Yet, it didn't, and an infinitesimal flicker of hope winked inside him. By the time he toweled off and dressed, he felt stronger.

Downstairs he found Betty in Bernie's room, sitting in Henry's chair. The curtains were still drawn against the day, the lamps unlit. Bernie remained in her bed. She hadn't been bathed yet, or fed. Or, by the smell of it, had her soiled garments changed.

Betty stared at the television where a televangelist, surrounded by a choir, gyrated across a stage.

Are you ready? I said, ARE YOU READY? He is coming. Yeeeees, praise Jeeeesus. The Resurrection is forthcoming. The Coming is now. Now. Noooow! Hallelujah! ARE YOU REEEEADY?

"Yes, yes, yes," Betty chanted softly, smiling and nodding.

Brandon flipped on the overhead light. Betty's head turned, and she gazed up at him dreamily.

"What the hell are you doing?" he demanded.

"They don't know." She giggled. "They haven't a clue. Can you imagine their reaction when they learn the truth?"

"What truth?"

She stood, still smiling. "The Lord said to Samuel, 'The Lord does not see as man sees; for man looks at the outward appearance, but the Lord looks at the heart.' Would you care for some breakfast?"

Something was *definitely* wrong with this picture.

Brandon walked to the television and slammed his fist against the Power button, cutting off the televangelist in midhowl. Then he moved to the window and flung open the curtains, spilling a wide band of sunlight over Bernie's bed.

From the kitchen came Betty's humming.

Closing his eyes, Brandon did his best to contain the streak of anger that made his head pound all the harder. A vague memory of last night began to tap at his brain: Betty and

Deputy Conroy returning from Betty's apartment. Deputy Conroy apologizing for putting Betty to so much inconvenience. Conroy continuing to stand in the kitchen door, studying Betty, then Brandon, before apologizing again and leaving. Brandon had trailed him to the door, watched as the deputy drove off in his patrol car, and Brandon had experienced . . . what? Not fear, exactly. Perhaps disappointment that Conroy's search of Betty's apartment hadn't turned up a clue that would justify the troubling doubts and suspicions that had nagged at him the last days.

The idea that Betty Wilson was Anticipating was absurd. And while her behavior since Henry's death had been odd, it could certainly be attributed to the same shock and grief that made him wander the house like a lost soul, listening for the sound of Henry's voice, imagining a presence that was no longer there but certainly real enough to make him turn, look, reach out for the strong, steady hand that had always been there to pick him up when he stumbled. Reality had been warped, time and space disjointed. He awoke every morning feeling more and more like a boat that had slipped its moorings and drifted out to sea with the tide. His thoughts were . . . aimless. If he thought at all. Even that was an effort. He slept. He drifted. He slept. And in between there were the vast black holes of nonexistent memory.

Brandon walked to the kitchen. "I don't want breakfast," he said to Betty's back. "I want you to take care of my aunt. That's what I'm paying you for. To take care of Bernie. I can get my own damn breakfast. I'm not helpless. She is."

Betty partially turned, an egg in one hand, a skillet in the other, looked at him with the same pleasant, albeit unconcerned, smile on her mouth. "Of course. Whatever you want, Mr. Brandon. You're in charge now." She put aside the egg and skillet and returned to Bernie's room.

He left the house through the back door. He needed fresh air and space—needed a few minutes to get control of his mounting frustration and irritation. The old house had become as confining as the prison cell in which he'd rotted for three years, a relic that was little more to him now than a faded souvenir of what once had been a child's utopia. He realized as he stood there, looking back at the clapboard house with its neat blue shutters, that it hadn't been the farm, the barn, the animals that offered him sanctuary from Cara's madness; it had been Henry and Bernie. They could have lived in a penthouse in Manhattan, and he would still have found respite from his nightmares.

After days of dismal weather, the bright daylight made his eyes ache. The temperature had warmed significantly, melting the ground frost and turning the dirt and grass along the path into a semi-spongy mire that made slurping sounds as he continued to the barn.

Hay scented the old building. Dust motes danced in the streaks of sunlight that found their way through the gaps between the weathered gray planks of the loft. A rabbit scurried from between two bales of pale green hay and bulleted into a copse outside the barn door. Brandon sat on the bale, elbows on his knees, and stared at his feet.

Suspicion followed by reason squirmed again in his thoughts.

There was absolutely nothing that could link Betty and Anticipating. And no matter how he might desire to place the blame for Henry's death on some anonymous stalker, he couldn't get around the fact that recently Henry had been extremely forgetful, not just with the handling of his medicine, but other things as well. Like believing he'd filled the boat motor with gas a few days before their last fishing trip.

And the vandalism? Why shouldn't he believe that Betty was home that night, as she always was, preferring her solitary existence to that of socializing at the Yamboree?

So where the hell was Anticipating?

He'd expected to hear from her by now. The last days he'd snatched mail from Betty's hand and shuffled through envelopes: big ones, small ones, first bills, then condolence cards—then the manila envelope with the return address Pine Lodge Motel. Black-and-white photos of Henry and Bernie at the Yamboree had spilled into his lap, and for an hour he'd sat staring at them with a sort of morbid fascination, as if Henry had suddenly materialized, allowing Brandon one last opportunity to burn his uncle's face into his memory before dissolving again into oblivion.

But no word from Anticipating.

He lay back on the hay, moved his face into a pool of sunlight, and drifted. He felt drained, like the character he'd once played in a movie—a young man who, night after night, was being relieved of his blood by a vampire girlfriend. The director had been an idiot, and the movie had never seen the light of day, thank God. No doubt it would turn up one day on Showtime or HBO, and everyone, thinking it his latest endeavor, would shake their heads and exchange banter like *So this is what Hollywood's Hellion has come to.*

Well, what do you expect from a man who cozies up to sheep?

Brother, did his career crash and burn!

He never had talent. Got by on his looks for too long.

Brandon? Brandon, son, wake up. I have to talk to you. Wake up, quick. I don't have long . . .

Raising his head, squinting from the sunlight in his eyes, Brandon focused on the figure standing in the barn door. A man's figure, limned by eerie light.

"Henry?" Surprise and gladness rushed through him. And relief. Yes, tremendous relief! Henry's dying had obviously been a dream. A nightmare.

What are you waiting for? Why haven't you gotten the hell out of here? Returned to L.A. with Al? What are you waiting on?

"Bernie—"

Is gone, Brandon. Gone. She's here with me. That's not Bernie. Not that bag of bones lying helpless in that bed. Get the hell out of here while you still can.

His eyes flew open, and Brandon stared toward the barn door—heart beating his chest wall like a prizefighter on a punching bag. The euphoria he'd experienced when looking into Henry's eyes vanished with crashing despair as he realized it had been nothing more than a dream. Fresh sadness filled him, and for a moment the raw, pulsating grief and hysteria that had consumed him the night of Henry's death whip-cracked through him, robbing him of breath and strength. He lay on the hay that he and Henry had sweated to bale in September, his hands pressed into his eyes, his throat convulsing as he tried desperately to fight back the sorrow.

Betty stood with her back to the door and the phone pressed to her ear. Her knuckles looked white and knobby as she gripped the receiver, listening. "Yes, I'll tell him," she said in a monotone, then slammed the receiver so hard a sampler on the wall pitched to one side.

"Who was that?" Brandon asked, closing the door behind him.

Her head whipped around, causing her red hair to fly about her shoulders. Green eyes glared at him. "A. J. Farrington, that's who. Can you believe it?"

"Alyson?" For the first time in days he felt a smile touch his mouth. Then he sobered. "Why didn't you call me?"

"And have her upset you again? It'll be a cold day in hell before I allow that woman to hurt you again with her deceit and harlot's seduction. Vile, vile creature! A serpent of evil. I knew it the moment I first saw her. She led you down the road to damnation, as so many others have. They used you. Fed on your soul like starving jackals. Satan is very, very crafty these days, sir."

She smiled and pointed to the plate of food flanked by a glass of orange juice.

He sat and stared down at the scrambled eggs, bacon, and toast. He drank his orange juice, forked the eggs, put down the fork, and sat back in the chair. Fresh irritation gnawed at him, and in his mind's eye he saw Alyson standing before him. *She doesn't like me. Betty doesn't like me.*

Betty scrubbed a butcher knife in a sink of frothy, steaming water, humming to herself.

"I intend to marry Alyson," he said to Betty's back.

She continued to scrub and hum.

"But you already knew that, didn't you, Betty? Henry told you—"

"Foolish man. Foolish, foolish man to encourage such a union. And to have invited her into this house . . . what was he thinking? How am I expected to fulfill my duty when I'm constantly confronted by these imbecilic actions? Oh, well, we all have our burdens to bear, don't we? They are there to test us. To make us stronger. To define our faith. His disciples were constantly forced to prove themselves, weren't they? I wonder how well they would have handled the sins and temptations of the twenty-first century."

Brandon shoved the chair back and stood. He dug a pack of cigarettes out of the kitchen drawer, along with a lighter, then moved down the hallway to the shadowed living room, sat in the rocker next to the lamp table and extension phone.

He knew in that very moment that the black holes of his memory the last days had not been caused by boozing any more than the aimlessness of his thoughts had been caused by depression. The soothing tongue of sedation slithered through his blood, licking at his consciousness. The last days he had attributed the lethargy to exhaustion—his body's need to rest and heal from its shock and grief. He'd simply closed his eyes and fallen . . . fallen . . . fallen. . . .

Shaking his head, Brandon blinked and tried to focus on the phone. He would fight it, the dark hole opening under him. His hands fumbled for the receiver, but the numbers blurred.

"What are you doing? What the *hell* are you doing?"

The phone slid to the floor with a loud ping of the ringer. Brandon stared down at it, feeling stupidly clumsy, then lifted his gaze back to Betty, who glared at him from the door. She held the soap-dripping butcher knife in one hand.

"What do you think you're doing?" she demanded again, only it wasn't her voice. Too deep and raspy. Like a boy tumbling headlong into adolescence, a clash of testosterone that made vocal cords temporarily retarded.

He glanced down at the phone as the shrill beep-beep-beep signaled that the receiver was off the hook. His cigarette lay beside it, smoldering as a dark smudge spread beneath the ash, sending a tendril of scorch-stink into the air.

"What have you given me?" he heard himself ask.

"Just something to relax you. To help you rest. You needn't worry. It won't harm you. Surely you don't think I'd harm you. My God, I've done everything in my power to protect you."

Unsteadily, he stood, swayed, not so sedated that he couldn't experience a rush of white-hot fury. "You killed him, didn't you? Henry. You removed his medicine—"

"He invited that harlot into this house to tempt you. My presence meant nothing any longer. I explained what a mistake he was making to encourage your relationship with that tramp—"

"Bitch."

Her eyes widened as he lunged toward her. She stumbled back, cried out as he clutched her throat in his hand and propelled her backward, slamming her against a wall so hard that the panes in the nearby windows clattered. Her mouth flew open in a shriek like a terrorized animal and she slashed out with the knife, driving it deep into his shoulder. Blood flew from the wound in a startling spray, spattering across her uniform and face, drawing an agonized wail of shock from her.

Pain exploded through him, and he rolled away. The searing heat of the wound momentarily drove the lethargy from his sluggish mind and body, and he staggered down the hallway toward the kitchen. *Think, think. The gun, he'd loaded the .357 on Halloween night with the intent of confronting Mitsy Dillman, had put it away in the gun cabinet without unloading it.*

Betty lumbered down the corridor behind him, her footsteps thundering like a bull's on the hardwood floor. In the kitchen she hit him, driving him over the harvest table, crashing the rooster to the floor and sending salt and pepper shakers flying toward the sink, where they splintered against the cupboard. He drove his elbow hard into her ribs—she grunted—he heaved backward and rolled, rammed his bloodied hand into her skull, twisting his fingers into her hair and—

Her hands closed around his neck and lifted him as if he were weightless, and in that surreal moment he knew he was dead—the certainty of it settled into his darkening consciousness with a calm acceptance that obliterated the pain in his shoulder and the fear that had rendered him momentarily mindless. He felt himself fly through the air and crash against the wall. He slid down the wall bonelessly as the dark drug of sedation and shock crushed down on him and through him. A bone-chilling cold replaced the fire in his shoulder. He stared down at his hands, the bloodied one gripping something that at first confused him—a scalp. Christ, he was holding her scalp; the orange-red of her hair clashed with the dark blood on his fingers. Slowly, he raised his gaze to her eyes, which were wide and bulging in rage—one green eye and one brown. The lost green contact gaped at him from her cheek.

23

"I don't like it." Alyson looked up as Alan walked into the room, glasses perched on the end of his nose as he read from a collection of dissertations on stalkers and their victims. "I've called Brandon three times. The first time Betty said he'd driven to the cemetery. I've called twice since then, and both times got a busy signal."

Alan dropped onto the sofa, tossed the notebook aside, and removed his glasses. He rubbed his eyes, and sighed wearily. "Have you heard anything from Ron?"

"Nothing yet." She stood and paced, her attention briefly roaming Ron Peterson's apartment. "Alan, are you sure this guy knows what he's doing?"

"He was the District Attorney's chief investigating officer, A. J. He knows what he's doing. He's in Carlyle's corner, okay? He felt from the word *go* that Brandon got a raw deal during the Emerald Marcella fiasco. If it had been left up to him, Carlyle would never have spent a day in prison, much less three years. He's got good instincts. If anyone can ferret out Anticipating, he can."

"He just seems . . . cocky."

"He's a rogue." Alan chuckled. "If he didn't give a damn about the truth, he'd still be with the D.A.'s office."

Alyson shook her head. "I've got this sick feeling that I shouldn't have left Ticky Creek when I did. If Betty is Anticipating—"

"If Betty is Anticipating, A. J., your presence and intrusion into the Carlyle household would only worsen the situation. Not only that, but you'd risk turning Anticipating's attention and wrath against you. Third parties who attempt to insulate a stalker's target often become victims themselves. Take Henry, for instance. We have no way of knowing for certain, of course, but I suspect that Anticipating decided he had, in some way, begun to hamper her ability to get up close and personal with Brandon. Either that, or she sacrificed him as an example of the control that she perceives she has over Carlyle. Perhaps it was a warning to you of what would happen if you continued your relationship with Brandon."

"There has to be something we can do. That the police can do."

"Anticipating has kept her distance, which in itself is very unusual. Stalkers who've gone as far as this one normally present themselves to the victim in a more obvious manner by now. They're very brazen, overconfident in their quest and ability to achieve their goal. Remember, in their twisted rationalization, they believe the object of their desire actually loves them, so remaining anonymous isn't going to get them the satisfaction they crave."

"Perhaps she's already presented herself," Alyson pointed out. "If Betty is Anticipating, she's right where she wants to be, isn't she? She's ingratiated herself into his life and family. He's become dependent on her. Fond of her. Certainly, she wouldn't risk it all by presenting herself as Anticipating."

"I think you need to take a giant step back off Betty. I'm

afraid you're allowing your focus to become skewed because she doesn't like you."

"She hates me, Alan."

He grinned and shrugged. "Okay, okay, she hates you." Replacing his glasses on his nose, he looked up at Alyson and winked. "I'm simply suggesting, sweetheart, that you step back a moment and look clearly at the big picture. Before Betty went to work for the Carlyles, she had no history, no ties with Brandon. We've come close to establishing that Anticipating had to be a close acquaintance or an employee."

"True." She nodded. "On the other hand. . . ." She flopped onto the sofa beside Alan. "I wasn't in Ticky Creek forty-eight hours before the town was buzzing about me and my reasons for being there."

"Whoa, wait a minute. I know where you're going with this, A. J. If some strange woman started hanging around and asking about Carlyle, the Ticky Creek residents would have been on to her. Need I remind you that you fell out of a flipping tree on top of Carlyle and got yourself arrested? You were as blatant as a bull in a china shop."

"We're talking about a secluded little town of less than five thousand people. And when it comes to Brandon . . . the people are obsessively protective of him. If someone moved in and showed excessive interest in Brandon, you better believe that town would rally. I shudder to imagine how they might have reacted if they'd learned I worked for the *Galaxy Gazette*." She took a deep breath and laid her head on Alan's shoulder. "God, I'm tired."

"Why don't you get some rest?" Alan slid his arm around her. "I'll wake you when Ron gets back."

"I can't. I'm ringing Brandon again. If he doesn't answer this time, I'm calling Deputy Greene."

The door opened and Ron walked in, his sport coat slung across one broad shoulder. Alyson sprang from the sofa, stopping him in his tracks. He looked like Don Johnson from his *Miami Vice* days.

"Give me good news, Peterson. If you don't, I'm liable to jump off this building and take you with me."

He flashed her a smile. "God, I love pushy women." He grinned. "Just spent the last two hours with Juanita Perez Darling, proprietor of Darling Domestics, which supplied Carlyle with housekeepers and cooks up to the time he sold his house and retired to Corcoran Prison. Aside from telling me numerous amusing anecdotes about your boyfriend, she established that the employees who worked for him can be accounted for. Most still work for her."

"And the ones who don't?"

"Are working for other agencies." He tossed his coat over the back of a chair, and grinned. "Quite a boy, our Brandon."

"What's that supposed to mean?"

"Poured booze instead of milk over his Bran Nubbins for breakfast."

"So he's a little eccentric." She laughed and glanced around at Alan, who shrugged and feigned a laugh back.

Ron removed his sunglasses and stepped around her, heading for the kitchen. "That was when he was in a good mood. Considering how highly you think of him, I won't annoy you with those times he wasn't in such a good mood. Let's just say that once he began spiraling down that bumpy road of self-destruction, the ride was rather hairy for anyone within shouting or striking distance."

"He was angry," she directed at Ron's back. "He has very good reasons for being angry." Turning on Alan so ferociously the grin froze on his face, she said, "You, of all people, should realize that behavior is a reflection of emotional health. Neither of you Neanderthals have a clue about what he was put through as a child."

Peterson popped open a beer can and leaned against the doorjamb.

Alyson took a deep breath, then wearily released it. "He was sexually molested for four years by the producer of *Those Foster Kids,* and Cara knew about it. In fact, she wrapped her son up in a big bright ribbon and delivered him to that creep's door—or should I say bed."

They stared at her, silent.

"Ralph Reilly, the producer of the show, gave a nine-year-old booze to relax him during his assaults. After four years of that, I'd say reaching for a bottle to kill emotional pain or fear would become second nature, wouldn't you?" She marched across the room and thrust her face into Ron's. "How dare you judge a man by what you read in the tabloid headlines? I'm sure Brandon would happily trade his money and fame if it meant turning back the clock and undoing the terror and humiliation he was forced to endure so Cara could have her fifteen minutes of glory."

"I'm sorry," Ron said softly, and averted his eyes. "Nothing personal, A. J. Actually, I like your boyfriend. During the Marcella investigation, I got the impression that he was extremely disturbed over the accident. In fact, he never came across like he felt he should get any kind of special consideration from the D.A.'s office because of who and what he was. I thought at the time that he rolled over too easily. Like he just . . . gave up the fight from the start."

Alyson turned away, paced to the phone. She did her best to will back the anger that brought hot tears to her eyes, and checked her watch. Six-thirty. Eight-thirty in Ticky Creek. Grabbing the phone, she dialed Brandon's number. Her heart squeezed in hope as the phone rang—no busy signal this time—and rang and rang—

She turned to Alan, the receiver still pressed to her ear. Panic closed off her throat. "Something's wrong," she wept. "I know it, Alan."

Alan left the sofa and walked to her. She buried her face in his shoulder as he held her, removing the receiver from her hand and placing it on the cradle. "Perhaps," he offered gently, "they've turned the phone off. If Betty is as protective of Brandon as you say, she'll want him to rest. Or she simply doesn't want you to talk to him. Come sit over here, and we'll go over this employee list again—"

"What's the point?" She shoved him away. "The domestics all check out—"

"There are gardeners, chauffeurs, pool services, secretaries—"

"This could take a month. We—don't—have—a—month, Alan. Betty is up to something."

"Betty Wilson has no ties to Brandon before—"

"Maybe someone connected to Betty does," Ron said and swigged his beer. "It's a long shot, of course, but certainly not out of the realm of possibility. Another thing, when you spoke to the Kansas Medical Board, did you think to have them cross-reference Betty for, say, a maiden name?"

"She told me she's never been married."

"Well." He smiled. "If she's as disreputable as you claim, why would you believe anything she says? First thing we do in the morning is call the Kansas Medical Board and do a cross-reference on her. See what we come up with. In the meantime, I'll spend the rest of the evening calling the names on the employee list—those who aren't associated with agencies and companies. There aren't many."

Alyson nodded and wiped the tears from her cheeks. "I'm calling Deputy Greene. I'll ask him to take a run out to the farm, just to be on the safe side."

Jack Dillman watched Dixie Bishop, dispatcher for the sheriff's office, waddle toward him with the speed of a lumbering turtle. Her girth took up most of the narrow corridor. She chewed a Baby Ruth in one hand. The other carried a slip of pink paper.

"Just the man I'm lookin' for," she declared, spitting a peanut through her lips. It stuck to the polka-dotted blouse pulled taut over her massive bosom.

Jack curled his lip and tried to remain calm. "This better not be important, Dixie. I got me a speech to write. I'm talkin' to the damn Elks Club tomorrow night—"

"Some woman called about Mr. Carlyle. Says she's tried to call the farm a few times and nobody's answered."

"And that's a reason to call out the National Guard?"

She shrugged and chewed. "Told her I'd send a car out, but all the boys are tied up right now. Maybe you want to run by the farm on your way home."

"That farm ain't on my way home. Jeezus." He shook his head and snatched the paper from her. "I'd like to know who the hell died and made Brandon Carlyle a goddamn national treasure. You'd think he was the goddamn president of these goddamn United States. Next thing you know, he and that goddamn movie star Injun senator will be runnin' for president and vice president—"

"Whitehorse," Dixie said, picking caramel from between her teeth with her fingernail. "John Whitehorse. I'd vote for that ticket, Jack. Sure as frogs go splat when they hop, you'd find a whole hell of a lot of women takin' a new interest in politics." She chuckled. "When you gonna get over this hump you got on for Brandon?"

"Son of a bitch knocked up my sister."

"You hated Brandon long before he knocked up your crazy sister. You hated him ever since he come out to the Homecomin' game your junior year and stole your touchdown thunder, not to mention Geena Beckett."

"Asshole done it on purpose."

Dixie rolled her eyes. "As if he knew to make his entrance just as you threw the game-winnin' touchdown." Popping the last plug of Baby Ruth into her mouth, she mumbled, "As if he needed the adulation of a lot of squealin', goo-goo-eyed Ticky Creek cheerleaders." She turned and ambled down the hall toward her office, tossing back over her shoulder, "Like it or not, he *is* a national treasure. You can bet your sweet butt that if somethin' happens to him on your watch, there won't be enough left of you or your career to use as catfish bait on Jim Benton's trotline."

"Jeezus!" He wadded up the pink slip and slammed it in the trash on his way out the door. The temperature had warmed drastically over the last twenty-four hours, so he didn't bother with a jacket, just climbed into the patrol car and peeled rubber over the macadam road surface.

He pulled through the Dairy Queen and ordered himself a Beltbuster with onion rings, and a steak finger basket for Mitsy, double on the cream gravy with an extra side of jalapeno ketchup. Food would be cold by the time she got it,

but so what? Thanks to the magistrate who declared she was
to be kept under lock and key at home and under Doc Simpson's care, she was about as coherent as a goddamn yam.
Wasn't enough that she was eating Xanax like it was Skittles,
but the old quack had supplied her with a lot of mood enhancers that sounded like aliens from outer space: Prozoids
and Zoloids or some such trash that would inevitably send
her careening through a post office somewhere, shooting people with his Taurus Raging Bull. Hell, it was gonna to be
tough enough getting voters to trust a man whose sister was
nutty as a Christmas fruitcake. How the hell was he gonna
explain that in order to keep her in line, he had to stuff her
full of mood pills? Jeezus. She was gonna be the death of
him and his career.

He pulled into the Carlyle drive. Security gate closed, of
course. The house sat in the distance, windows dark.

Jack munched an onion ring and listened to the radio
squawk. He didn't much like to acknowledge the tickling of
sadness that had occasionally afflicted him the last few days.
Though he hated Brandon with a sick passion, he'd never
had a problem with Henry or Bernice. They were good people and obeyed the law. Now Henry was gone, and seeing
the house sit there lightless drove home the reality that the
old man, who'd been an upstanding and respected Ticky
Creek citizen for over sixty years, was gone.

He climbed out of the car, chewing his onion ring, and
walked to the intercom. Punched the buzzer. Punched it
again. Licked ketchup and grease off his fingers, thinking the
jalapeño was a little on the biting side tonight. He walked
closer to the wrought-iron gate and stared through it at the
house. He stuffed the remainder of the onion ring into his
mouth, then caught a couple fence bars in his hands and gave
the gate an inquisitive shake.

Nothing wrong here. Hell, houses should be dark by nine
o'clock. And as far as the intercom . . . hell, Betty and Carlyle were probably in bed already. Doc mentioned that he'd
prescribed Brandon some powerful sedatives to get him over
the rough few days after the funeral. . . . And as far as the

unanswered phone calls . . . so what? There wasn't a rule
written someplace that people had to answer their stupid
phones all the time. That was what the ringer switch was for.
On if you want to take calls. Off if you don't. . . . Jeezus, so
what was he doing here, prancing around in the dark while
his Beltbuster and onion rings grew cold? He had a freaking
speech to write. How was he supposed to convince a lot of
old geezers to re-elect him if he wasted his time pandering
to Mr. National Treasure?

He walked to the car, hesitated, and looked back. No doubt
he was allowing Dixie's admonition to get under his skin.
*You can bet your sweet butt that if somethin' happens to him
on your watch, there won't be enough left of you or your
career to use as catfish bait on Jim Benton's trotline.*

"Ah, to hell with him." Jack dropped into the car and
reached for the radio mike. "Dixie dispatch, this is Jack.
Everythin' appears to be right as goddamn rain at the Carlyle
farm. Tell your freakin' caller to get a goddamn life and
leave mine alone. Over."

"That's an affirmative, Jack. See you in the mornin'."

"Right." He tossed the mike aside, stared through the dark
at the house, the smell of mustard and onions from his cooling Beltbuster making him a little queasy.

Ron propped his socked feet on the coffee table and crossed
them at the ankles. He nibbled on a cherry Pop-Tart, his gray
eyes fixed on Alyson, who watched him from the kitchen
door, a Twinkie in one hand, a diet Dr Pepper in the other.
Her eyes felt gritty from crying and lack of sleep. God, she
simply couldn't stop crying. She had never been a crier, or
one to panic, yet standing there waiting for Ron Peterson to
sweet-talk some Medical Board personnel out of information,
she felt as if she were unraveling.

"Andrea. What a great name. Anyone ever tell you you
have a terrific phone voice? Yeah? You having a good day
so far, Andrea?" He nodded and smiled and nibbled his Pop-
Tart. "Life is definitely too busy. Wouldn't it be nice if we

could just take, oh, say, twenty, thirty minutes each day to meditate in a soundproof room, away from deadlines and telephones and traffic? I mean, try dealing with L.A. traffic every day of your life. Do you know that the suicide rate is higher in California than anyplace else in this country?"

He grinned at Alyson and shrugged, as if to admit that he didn't have a clue about the country's suicide rate, nor did he really care.

"Well, Andrea, I have this problem. My mom in Texas is very, very ill, and it's imperative that I hire a home health care specialist as soon as possible. I've had a nice lady apply, but before I make my decision, I want to check out her credentials thoroughly. Betty Wilson, says she worked for KC General for ten years, I believe. Right. Good. What about before that, Andrea? What I mean is, has she always worked under the name of Wilson? Just in case I need to poke a little further into her work history and character references? I know that would take some digging, but we're talking about my mom here. Since I can't be in Texas with her, I have to feel extremely confident in the background of whomever I hire. Thanks, Andrea. God, you're a doll. Sure, I'll wait."

Alyson sat on the coffee table next to Ron's feet. He poked her with his toe and covered the receiver's mouthpiece with his hand. "Anyone ever tell you that eating a Twinkie in front of a man is asking for trouble?"

She forced a smile. "Seems I can recall a time or two recently when it had that effect on someone."

He laughed and pointed to the employee list beside her. She picked it up and looked it over. Apparently Peterson had narrowed the prospects down substantially. There were no more than a half-dozen names left to contact. Her heart sank.

"Yes, Andrea, I'm here." He grabbed a pencil, then the list from Alyson's hand, nodded, scribbled, nodded. "Okay, that's terrific. Hey, thanks, you've been a great help."

Ron hung up the phone just as Alan walked into the room. "Boyd," Ron said. "Her maiden name was Boyd. Betty Boyd."

Alyson briefly closed her eyes, and she did her best to

force back the rush of anticipation that made her dizzy. Ron ran his finger down the list. "I'll be damned."

Her heart stopped.

"Heavenly Hands Massage. William Boyd, Masseur to the Stars."

Alan put his hand on Alyson's shoulder. "Let's not get excited yet. It could be a coincidence."

"A coincidence?" Alyson laughed in disbelief. "I don't think so, Alan."

Ron called the number listed. It belonged to one Gerald Duncan—had belonged to him for a year. "So we take a drive to this address; check it out," Ron explained, tossing the remains of his Pop-Tart onto the coffee table. "If nothing else, maybe I'll have Boyd's heavenly hands work on me."

The address listed on the employee records was residential. At some time the shabby stucco one-story had been painted brick red. The color had faded in places, giving it a sickly, washed-out appearance. The house sat back from the street, surrounded by a chain-link fence. High weeds clustered at the base of the fence, along with a scattering of litter. A weathered sign hung on the gate, praying hands flanking HEAVENLY HANDS MASSAGE.

"Masseur to the Stars, huh?" Alan grinned. "If this is all this dude can manage, I suspect business hasn't been so good lately."

Alyson reached for the door handle.

"Hold your water." Ron shook his head. "One never approaches a potential suspect unless properly prepared."

"What's he going to do," she snapped, "pummel me with his heavenly hands?"

Ron smiled and looked at her through his sunglasses. "If you weren't so cute, I might get annoyed."

She sank back in her seat and chewed her lip.

He slid his hand under his coat, checked his gun as he surveyed the narrow street that was lined bumper to bumper with early model cars. "First thing we have to consider here:

this neighborhood. Seven out of ten times you find a business run out of a house in this kind of neighborhood, the business is a front for dopers. Or prostitutes. If that's the case, and strangers go marching up to the front door, chances are that fur is going to fly. Good old Boyd isn't going to be happy if he, in a panic, flushes his candy down the john."

Opening the car door, he said, "You two stay here. If anything looks promising, I'll give you a nod."

Alyson watched Peterson walk toward the house, his hands in his pockets in a nonthreatening fashion, his casual interest in the neighborhood far from reflecting the uncertainty he must have been feeling. A pack of German shepherds in the adjacent yard rushed the fence and began barking. The owner of the dogs, a bald, obese man wearing dingy yellow boxer shorts, stepped out on his porch and glared at Ron, then reentered his house without bothering to quiet the animals.

Alyson held her breath as Ron banged on the door.

Alan leaned forward, one arm slung over the back of Alyson's car seat, his face tense.

Ron knocked again, harder. The dogs yapped louder. The fat man came out of his house again, this time holding a beer can.

Sinking back into the seat, Alyson sighed. "I don't know how much more of this I can stand."

"Look on the bright side, at least we're making progress."

"Maybe. If Betty Boyd was employed at Kansas City General for ten years, up until two months before moving to Ticky Creek, she was obviously not traipsing around California stalking Brandon."

"Have you called Brandon this morning?"

She nodded. "Nothing. The dispatcher last night assured me that an officer checked the farm and everything was fine. But if I don't reach him by tonight, I'm calling Ruth Threadgill and having her take a run out to the farm."

Ron headed back to the car and disappointment settled in Alyson's chest.

Back in the car, Ron gave Alyson an apologetic smile. "Sorry. We'll come back later. In the meantime, I'll run Wil-

liam Boyd through the Drivers License Bureau and see if
he's still registered at this address."

According to the DLB, William Boyd still resided at that
address. An address cross-reference indicated that the residence was shared by one Thomasina Peacock. Further checks
revealed that neither had any history of arrests—not so much
as parking tickets.

They returned to the residence twice more through the
afternoon. No luck. Alyson continued to call the farm. No
answer. By seven that evening, Alyson could barely contain
her panic and mounting frustration. She was tempted to contact the Ticky Creek sheriff's office again and suggest that
Betty Boyd Wilson might have a connection to Anticipating.
Ron explained that without substantial proof to back up such
a claim, they wouldn't take her seriously. Alan added that if
Betty had ties to Anticipating, the last thing they wanted was
to rush in without enough proof to nail her. Obviously, Anticipating was capable of murder. The last thing they wanted
to do was corner her.

Dinner was another fast-food meal of burgers and fries. At
just after seven they headed one last time to Boyd's residence. A light burned in the window. As Ron climbed out
of the car, so did Alyson. Before he could protest, she said,
"If I have to sit waiting in this car another minute, I'm going
to explode. I'm a tabloid reporter, for God's sake. I'm accustomed to ducking when people see me coming."

Alan followed as they approached the house. Ron banged
on the door, which was opened so suddenly they jumped
back, Ron making an instinctive move toward his pistol. Alan
grabbed Alyson and shoved her behind him.

A petite woman in a skirt and blouse flipped on the porch
light.

"Thomasina Peacock?" Ron asked, sliding a shield from
his pocket and flashing it at her.

"Yes," she replied in a surprisingly deep and cautious
voice.

"Ron Peterson. Investigator for the D.A.'s office." Repocketing the shield, he smiled. "Sorry to disturb you, ma'am. We're looking for William Boyd. Is he available?"

"No," she replied with an exasperated roll of her dark eyes.

"Mind telling me when he'll be back?"

"Haven't a clue."

Ron smiled charmingly. "Does he still live here?"

"Your guess is as good as mine." She looked beyond Ron to Alyson and Alan, looked Alyson up and down, then refocused on Ron. "What's this about? Has he got himself in trouble?"

"Could we step inside and have a word with you? I promise we won't take up much of your time."

She shrugged and turned away. "Suit yourself."

The tiny house was cluttered and dimly lit. The air was rank with animal odor. As they followed Thomasina Peacock into the living room off the entrance hall, a half-dozen cats scattered, ducking behind the flowered sofa and a lopsided recliner. A macaw screeched from its cage near the window. Beside that was a forty-gallon aquarium.

Thomasina raked newspapers off the sofa and threw them onto a stack, then she flopped onto the recliner and crossed her legs. "So, what's this about?"

"William's association with Brandon Carlyle," Ron replied as they sat on the sofa.

"Brandon Carlyle is old news, isn't he? Heard he was off living in Tibet or something after he got out of prison."

"William worked for Carlyle?"

"Carlyle used his services. William is a damn good masseur. Or was. Haven't a clue what he's doing now. God knows."

"Then you're saying that William no longer lives here—"

"Rent's paid up until the end of the year. Again, what's this about?"

"Would you mind giving me a little background information on William? How long he worked for Carlyle—"

"Billy moved in with me eight years ago. We met at a

support group—hit it off. At the time, he was working as a nurse's aide at St. Mary's Hospital. He did the Heavenly Hands thing part-time—on his days off. We became fast friends, at least for a while. The dear just came with too much emotional baggage. After a while, things just got too heavy."

"Were you lovers?"

She tipped her head to one side and smiled. Her gaze wandered his face, then she laughed throatily. "Hardly, Mr. Peterson."

"Would you mind explaining what you mean by his coming 'with too much emotional baggage'?"

"Billy had issues." She shrugged. "I mean, we all have issues, right? But give me a break. There's more screwed up in Billy Boyd's head than just the obvious—which was why he was eventually asked to leave our support group."

"Please elaborate."

"Billy had family problems. Frankly, his father was a nut. I'm all for religion, okay? I occasionally attend the church of my choice. But from the sounds of it, this man was over the top, even drove his wife to suicide with his fire-and-brimstone damnations. The man formed his own denomination. Took his kids out of school, declaring the only book God deemed worthy of their studying was the Bible. They were allowed three hours of sleep a night. The remaining twenty-one hours were spent reading the Bible and praying. The old man was convinced that anyone could achieve perfection in mind, soul, and body if they were in total harmony with God. Just as convinced that if a human showed mental or physical flaws, or even illness, that was caused by spiritual weakness and work of Satan. Once he became aware of Billy's . . . physical defects, for lack of a better description, the old man became obsessed with saving him. Billy was beaten, starved, and prayed over virtually twenty-four hours a day."

She looked away. Her chin quivered, and she shrugged. "I did what I could to support the poor dear. But there comes a time when we must accept our limitations and gracefully bow out. The last year or two that Billy lived here, I rarely saw him. We spoke in passing. When he was home, he stayed closed up in his room. I could often hear him . . . praying."

"Is he still in touch with his father?" Alyson asked softly.

For the first time, Thomasina looked directly at Alyson. There was a shadow of envy in her expression. She fingered her jaw-length brown hair self-consciously and took a shaky breath. "He's dead. He was found a few years ago with a crucifix driven through his heart and the word *imposter* scrawled in his blood on the walls. You might recall the story. It was featured on *Unsolved Mysteries*."

Alyson sank deeper into the sofa, a wave of cold dread rushing through her. Alan wrapped warm fingers around her wrist and gently squeezed.

"When did you last speak to William?" Ron asked. There was an edge to his voice that hadn't been there before.

"He left here in January, I believe. Said he intended to travel. In March, he called to tell me there had been a death in the family, and that he wouldn't be coming back for a while. He sent me a check to cover the rent for the rest of the year."

"Do you know where he was calling from?"

"Yes. Kansas City."

Alyson sat forward. Alan drew her back.

Ron stood. "Would you mind if we take a look at William's room?"

Thomasina frowned. "It's locked—"

"Get the key."

"I don't have the key. He didn't leave it—"

Ron left the room. Alyson, followed by Alan, ran after him, Thomasina in pursuit.

"Just one moment," she cried. "You can't simply come into my house—"

"Which room is it, Miss Peacock?" Ron stopped at a closed door and rattled the knob.

"I demand to know what this is about."

Ron drove his shoulder into the door, once, twice; it exploded inward. Alyson shoved past him, swept her hands over the wall until locating the light switch.

"Oh, my God," Alyson whispered.

The walls were covered with crucifixes and papered with photographs of Brandon—only not just any photographs, Alyson noted with escalating horror. All depicted Brandon as Jesus Christ from *The Resurrection*, including a life-size theater display of Brandon nailed to the cross.

"Oh, boy," Alan said softly, adjusting the glasses on his nose. "We do got a problem here, folks."

Ron walked to the double closet and threw open the doors. The shelves were lined with wigs on foam forms. Women's clothes were on hangers, women's shoes were lined across the closet floor like soldiers in formation. There were photographs of a severe woman with a mass of red hair. Alyson took it from Ron and tilted it toward the light.

"Who's this?" Ron asked.

"That's Billy's sister, Betty," Thomasina explained as, with a flush of irritation coloring her face, she regarded the damage Ron had inflicted on her door. "You'll pay me for this damage, or I'll sue you. Do you hear me?"

Alyson shook her head. "This isn't *our* Betty."

"Of course it's Betty." Thomasina snatched the photograph from her. "Or *was* Betty. Betty was killed in a car accident. It was the reason Billy went to Kansas City. To bury her. He was his only surviving family member."

Alyson slowly raised her gaze to Alan, who stared hard at Thomasina before looking over at Ron.

"Whose clothes are these?" Ron thumbed toward the closet, his eyes narrowing as he focused harder on Thomasina's face.

She briefly averted her eyes, then gave him a thin smile. "Billy's, of course." Lifting her eyebrows, she said, "We're transsexuals, Mr. Peterson."

"I want you to sit on the sofa and keep your mouth closed, A. J. Not a peep out of you. Understand?"

Alyson looked across the room at Thomasina Peabody, then back at Alan.

"I sense there's more going on here than meets the eye," Alan told her. "If you want to help Brandon, we have to know exactly what we're dealing with."

"I'll tell you what we're dealing with," she said under her breath. "A lunatic. While you're exercising your shrink muscles, God only knows what could be happening to Brandon. We have to call Deputy Greene. Now, Alan."

Ron moved up behind Alyson, put his hands on her shoulders, and said softly, "Let the man do his job, A. J. From a cop's standpoint, the better we understand the criminal's mind, the better we're prepared to cope with any eventuality. Besides, we still have no hard evidence that this character is Anticipating. And even if he is, we don't know that he's capable of murder."

She glared into Alan's steady eyes while her frustration and fear mounted. Forcing herself to take a deep breath, she dropped onto the sofa, ignoring Ron as he sat down beside her and reached for her hand.

Thomasina sat nervously on the edge of her chair, her gaze locking on Alan as he dragged a chair over and sat down before her. Smiling, he reached for her hands, squeezed them reassuringly.

"Relax," he told her. "You haven't done anything wrong. Just tell us everything you know about William Boyd."

She nodded, glanced toward Alyson, and frowned. "What's he done?" she asked softly.

"We don't know that he's done anything. You say you met Betty eight years ago at a support group for transsexuals." She nodded. "Nice person?" he asked.

"Oh, yes. Very nice. One of the sweetest, kindest individuals I've ever had the pleasure of knowing."

"Was she working for Carlyle at that time?"

"Yes. As Billy, of course. That was before she decided to go through with the gender change. At that point we were still in the closet, so to speak." She smiled and blushed.

"Was she a tremendous fan of Carlyle's?"

She chewed her lip, then gave a hesitant nod. "She was quite enamored of him. I'm sorry to say it became an extreme source of frustration and discontent for her, as you can well imagine."

"She was in love with him, I take it."

"Very much."

"Obsessively?"

". . . Yes. After a while, it seemed her entire existence revolved around him. I tried to reason with her many times; after all, there was no hope for her, so why continue to put herself through it? But the obsession grew. Eventually, she quit her job at the hospital so she could focus on him."

"In what way?"

She averted her eyes, and her cheeks flushed with color.

"Did she write him letters?"

"Yes."

"Did she watch his house?"

"Yes. Once she even moved into his house when he was away. I told her she was going to get in trouble. Big trouble. That if she was found out, she'd go to jail. But he'd become like a drug to her. She couldn't get enough of him. She began making plans for her surgery, convinced that if she became a woman, she'd stand a chance with him."

"Did she ever give you any indication that she might harm him?"

Her eyes widened; she shook her head, looking at Alyson, then Ron, then back at Alan. "She would never have harmed him. Ever. At least. . . ." Sighing, she sank back in the chair, closed her eyes. "I don't know what happened. She began . . . changing. I didn't know her any longer. She became more and more reclusive. Depressed. She cried a lot. Around that time she became involved again in the church. Frankly, I was surprised. I'd gotten the impression over the last years that her experience with her father had so frightened her that she'd never step foot in a church again."

"About how long ago was this?"

She thought, frowning. "Four years, perhaps."

Alyson sat forward. "About the time that *Resurrection* was released?"

"Yes, I suppose so."

"How did she react to the Emerald Marcella incident?" Alan asked.

"Hard to say. As I mentioned, the behavior had become so odd. So unpredictable. I never knew what to expect. One day she'd be the sweet, considerate, timid individual that I adored. The next. . . ." She shrugged. "A disturbing stranger."

"In what way disturbing?"

She shuddered. "Very . . . intense. Focused. Domineering. Judgmental. Often cruel."

Alan smiled and regarded her thoughtfully. "He ridiculed you?"

"Yes, he. That was certainly no female, Dr. Rodgers. Everything about that dreadful individual was masculine—not like my Betty at all. The way he dressed. Walked. Talked. It was as if there were two personalities, and Billy was taking over. I saw less and less of Betty, my friend. She was so very sad. She broke my heart. I was afraid she'd take her own life. I often heard her talking to herself, carrying on complete conversations, back and forth. Arguing with herself. Once. . . ."

She looked away. Her hands clasped together in her lap, and her face drained of color. "She had bruises over her arms, her throat, her chest. When I asked her how she got them, she whispered, 'He did it.' I thought she'd become involved with someone—you know, in an abusive relationship. Then one night, I heard her crying, and there was that voice again. Not hers, his. I crept to her window and peeked in. She was pinching herself, hitting herself, saying horrible, hurtful things—"

"Such as?"

" 'Vile creature of perversion. Satan's seed.' It was as if her father was there, trying to drive demons from her, as if she'd become possessed by his spirit. After that, I often got the horrifying impression that I was looking straight into the Reverend Boyd's eyes."

*   *   *

"Beware of Billy Boy." Alyson watched traffic streak by them as they drove back to Ron's apartment as fast as the law would allow. She felt numb, although the first quivers of hysteria were beginning to rouse. "She was right again. Only she wasn't hearing it exactly right, was she? Not Billy Boy. Beware of Billy Boyd."

"Who?" Ron asked. "What the hell are you talking about?"

"Nora. She. . . ." Alyson laughed wearily and shook her head. "Never mind. You wouldn't believe me anyway."

"A. J., after today I'd believe anything."

"It's all so obvious now. Charlotte Minger—of course. Billy, not Betty, attacked her. She smelled infant formula, only it wasn't baby's milk. It was Ensure. That nutritional drink she feeds Bernie. And she made the call to Henry that morning. She might have walked to the barn—or to the bathroom, wherever. She removed his medicine from the truck, perhaps hid the other bottle so he couldn't find it. We'll never know for sure, of course. She took a chance he'd have an attack, and he did." Covering her face with her hands, she added, "Merciful God, what is she doing to Brandon?"

"We're dealing with a very complex situation here," Alan began. "A dissociative identity disorder, complicated by gender dysphoria. You have your host personality, which I must assume is the female. Then there's your Alter personality. Judging by what I've heard about the extreme abuse in this individual's childhood, the Alter probably manifested himself to protect the female. He's the macho personality who was better capable of dealing with Reverend Boyd's fire-and-brimstone mistreatment. Also, he'd be acceptable to the Reverend Boyd, whereas the female who now calls herself Betty would not.

"My greatest concern," Alan added, releasing a weary breath, "is that the Alter has gained the upper hand here, judging by the religious evidence decorating those bedroom walls and his abuse of the female. Little by little, he's eroded the more sensitive female's control. I suspect she'd never have murdered Emerald Marcella, or beat up Charlotte, or killed Henry's dog, or harmed Henry. While she might not have liked you—even hated your guts, A. J.—I doubt she'd have physically harmed you."

"Are these personalities aware of one another?" Ron asked.

"It's known as co-consciousness. These Alter personalities actually communicate and cooperate with one another. Or fight one another. Or bully one another. Just because they live in the same body and brain doesn't mean they have to like one another. It's like siblings. They might have the same parents and occupy the same house, but that doesn't mean they won't take a punch at one another if push comes to shove. The personalities can eventually merge, with the more powerful taking charge. I believe that's what could be happening here."

"What does all this mean for Brandon?" Alyson demanded.

"We hope that Betty still has enough influence that she won't allow Billy to hurt him."

Ron pulled the car into the parking lot outside his apartment building. Mildred's car was parked there. She sat in the dark, the tip of her cigarette glowing, briefly brightening her face as she took a deep drag.

A sense of foreboding stabbed Alyson. Before Ron managed to stop the car completely, she threw open the door and leaped out. Mildred's head slowly turned as Alyson approached her, her step slowing and her throat tightening as Mildred looked at her with mascara-smeared eyes, the streetlight reflecting off the tear streaks on her cheeks. "What's happened?" Alyson heard herself cry in a dry, weak voice.

"You haven't heard?" Mildred covered her mouth with her hand and sobbed, "He's dead. Brandon is dead."

24

"What the hell were you thinking?" Alan shouted into Mildred's tear-streaked face. Holding Alyson, rocking her as she sobbed so hard against his shoulder that her entire body convulsed, he added in a quieter voice, "If I wasn't a doctor, I'd punch your lights out. You don't blurt out that kind of information unless you know for a fact that it's true."

"Shut up! All of you!" Ron yelled. He turned up the television volume. A somber news correspondent stared into the camera while around her, people moved in swarms behind barricades. Police officers stood guard against any onlooker who attempted to breach their security.

"Brandon Carlyle was first reported missing this morning by Betty Wilson, a live-in health care provider employed by Mr. Carlyle to care for his invalid aunt. According to Miss Wilson, Carlyle mentioned to her yesterday that he was coming out to this creek you see behind me to fish—a creek that is notoriously dangerous to navigate."

"That's a lie!" Alyson shouted at the television. "Brandon would never have—"

"Quiet!" Ron repeated.

"When Carlyle didn't return last evening, and hadn't returned this morning, Miss Wilson contacted the local law enforcement, who found Carlyle's car at the docks where he kept his boat. A search crew was immediately dispatched. An hour later, the empty craft was found approximately two miles down the creek. Search crews from surrounding towns have been arriving since noon—"

Ron flipped to the next news channel.

"Sources have informed us that Carlyle's apparent depression stemmed from the very recent loss of his uncle."

Ron flipped again.

"Residents speculate that this might well be a suicide—"

"Sheriff's Department refuses to speculate on what may or may not have taken place here last evening. Until the body is located—"

"Miss Wilson admitted that recently Carlyle had started drinking again—"

"Carlyle spent three years in California's Corcoran State Prison on manslaughter charges—"

"Ticky Creek Sheriff's Department is attempting to locate a young woman who, until recently, was romantically involved with the missing actor. According to Betty Wilson, Carlyle began a relationship with Alyson James, who reports as A. J. Farrington for the *Galaxy Gazette*. According to Wilson, Miss James misrepresented herself to the family. Once Carlyle learned of it, the relationship was broken off. However, Wilson stated, Miss James continued to harass Carlyle by phone. Investigators are now looking into the possibility that Miss James could be tied to the stalker, Anticipating, who has beleaguered the actor for some time. . . ."

Ron hit the Off button.

"Son of a bitch." Alan shook his head in disbelief.

Alyson, clutching Alan's shirt, choked, "He's not dead. Alan, he's not dead. As long as there isn't a body—"

"There's always hope." He forced a smile and blotted the tears from her face with a paper napkin.

Mildred coughed a disbelieving laugh. "Right. Sure. He's just crawled off into those goddamn pine forests to contemplate life for a while."

"He would never have climbed into that boat alone," Alyson said, doing her best to remain rational. "He didn't like it even when he was with Henry. He knew that creek is dangerous. He'd never have gone fishing—"

"But if he was suicidal—" Mildred argued.

"He wasn't!" Alyson jumped from the sofa, her fists shaking. "If he wanted to kill himself, there are enough guns in that house to arm the next invasion on Kuwait. He'd simply have blown his brains out—"

"Quiet," Ron ordered in a thinly patient voice. "There's a greater issue here that we must deal with right now. And that's the fact that the sheriff is looking for A. J. as a possible suspect in Carlyle's disappearance."

"Stop it!" Dragging her hands through her hair, Alyson took a deep breath, then slowly released it. "There's no greater issue than Brandon's life. I refuse to accept that he's gone."

"A. J.," Alan said gently. "Hope is a good thing to hold on to, but in most cases—"

"I *don't* want to hear your theories any longer, Alan. I *don't* want to be rationalized to death. I *don't* want to be told ever, ever again that I should practice caution or risk agitating the psyche of a victimizer. If I'd gone to the sheriff when I first began to suspect Betty was Anticipating, Brandon would be alive. . . ." Her mouth snapped shut. The blood left her head, and she sank to the floor. Ron grabbed her, drew her against him, pressing her head against his chest. "Oh, my God," she cried dryly. "Oh, my God. He's dead, isn't he? He's someplace in that horrible water. She killed him—"

"Hold on," Ron urged softly. "Don't give up yet."

"If I hadn't left—"

"You were trying to help, A. J. We had to be certain you were right before we could act—"

"But we're too late. What does it matter, if we're too late?"

He picked her off the floor, carried her into the bedroom, and put her on the bed.

He held her there, his hands pressed against her shoulders. "You'll have to be strong through the next days, Alyson. It's going to be tough. You can't hold it together if you're exhausted."

"What are you going to do now?" she asked.

"Call the Ticky Creek authorities about Betty Wilson. We're going to get this issue of your possible involvement in Brandon's disappearance out of the way. Once she's in custody, at least temporarily for questioning, I think the situation will be . . . resolved fairly quickly."

Alyson awoke just after three. She staggered into Ron's living room, where the muted television flickered in the dark. Alan slept on the sofa. Mildred, curled up in a chair, mascara streaked over her cheeks like war paint, also slept. Her gaze locking on the television screen, Alyson sank onto the coffee table.

Video and photographs of Brandon rolled before her eyes, cataloging his life. Child actor, adolescent, adult; smiling, brooding, fighting. He stood on a stage in his dark tux, a twenty-year-old with a head of wild curls, holding an Oscar while the audience rewarded him with a standing ovation. He'd turned those bruise-blue eyes toward the camera and flashed that heart-stopping smile that had blown away the last vestiges of his childhood and securely entrenched him as the man women most fantasized over. The Sexiest Man in the World. Oscar winner.

She pressed the remote Off button and sat in the dark. Brandon as she had seen him that last time at Henry's funeral came back to her. Grief-stricken, bone-weary. His final goodbye had sent a chill through her that had left her with a

sinking despair and fear that she couldn't place until now—
as if he'd known he'd never see her again.

Returning to the bedroom, she crawled between the sheets.
With her cheek buried in the pillow, she allowed the hot tears
to flow.

"As expected, the world has converged on Ticky Creek,
Texas, a secluded village of less than five thousand people
buried in the heart of the deep East Texas pine woods. The
tragedy that brings us here now is one that, over the last few
years, has become far too familiar: a beloved public figure
cut down in his prime. And to make matters more shocking,
Betty Wilson, the nurse who reported Carlyle missing, is now
missing herself.

"Officers, following a lead, visited the Carlyle home this
morning, where Miss Wilson has been living. What they discovered there shocked them. Bernice Carlyle, Brandon Carlyle's aunt, was found dead, and apparently had been dead
for at least forty-eight hours. There were definite signs of a
struggle. Blood was found on the walls and floor. The Crime
Scene Unit spent the morning collecting evidence. Although
the sheriff declines to make comments at this time, we suspect that the investigation will now refocus on a possible
homicide as opposed to a boating accident or suicide."

"For the second day, search crews continue to drag Ticky
Creek in hopes of discovering the body of Brandon Carlyle.
Dogs have been brought in as well, and they're combing the
inhospitable terrain on both sides of this treacherous body of
water. Over the last five years, twenty-five people have
drowned in these waters, which are notorious for their un-
dertow. With each hour that passes, hope fades for finding
Carlyle alive. Weather forecasts are calling for storms tonight, which will certainly worsen the situation. In the meantime, the search continues for Betty Wilson. . . ."

*   *   *

"On this third day of Brandon Carlyle's disappearance,
Ticky Creek law officials have been forced to halt the search
due to inclement weather. Storms are predicted to continue
through the remainder of the week. In the meantime, fans of
the incredibly popular entertainer have been pouring in by
the thousands, as have friends and news media. Senator John
Whitehorse arrived this morning. Both, of course, were media darlings back before the senator became an outspoken
activist for the Native American population and ultimately
ran for the Senate. We asked the senator about his friendship
with Carlyle and what brought him to Ticky Creek."

"Brandon and I have remained friends for a great many
years. I'm here today because of that friendship—to show
my support, to pray, along with everyone else here, that he'll
be found alive. He's a tremendously gifted actor, and despite
the occasionally nasty rumors—most of which are untrue, I
might add—one of the nicest guys I've ever had the pleasure
of knowing."

"A distraught Cara Carlyle is in seclusion tonight at her
apartment in Manhattan. We could not reach her directly for
comment. However, a short time ago a spokesperson for Ms.
Carlyle read a statement: "I grieve for my son. Despite our
past differences, I continue to adore him and pray for his
safe return. Brandon, wherever you are, I love you, my darling."

"Liar!" Alyson shouted at the television screen, which was
filled with images of Cara Carlyle, eyes hidden behind sunglasses, as she ran from a limo into her apartment building.
Alyson hurled a pillow at the set, knocking a framed photograph of Ron's mother to the floor. Alan wrapped an arm
around her waist and hauled her toward the bedroom. "That

woman destroyed Brandon's life! How dare she lie to the public like that? I've got a good mind to—"

"To do absolutely nothing but get in bed and calm down. Christ, A. J., I don't know how much longer I can hold out before I have you committed." Alan dumped her on the bed and glared down at her through his lopsided glasses.

"Alan, I want to go to Ticky Creek."

"No way. Not going to happen. Not yet."

"That idiotic sheriff has all but buried Brandon. Jack Dillman has called off the search—"

"Suspended, Alyson, due to the weather."

"He could be out there somewhere, dying."

Alan raked one hand through his hair and sighed wearily.

"You believe he's dead already, don't you?" She glared up at him.

He looked away.

"Don't you?" she demanded in a steadier voice.

"Yes," he finally replied. "I do." Alan dropped onto the bed beside her. "I'm sorry. I wish I could continue to tell you otherwise, but at some point one has to start to face reality. We have no way of determining just how long Brandon's been gone. No one has seen him since the day of the funeral. Now Betty is gone—and Bernie is dead.

"Alyson, the blood they found was Brandon's. Something dreadful happened in that house—a confrontation, perhaps. Betty drove his body out to that creek, disposed of it, and returned to the house on foot, just like Brandon did the night you left him by the highway."

"But if she murdered him, why would she call attention to herself? It's almost as if she wanted people to know. Now she's missing . . . who's to say she isn't with Brandon? Perhaps it's a kidnapping situation."

Alan shook his head, removed his glasses, and rubbed his eyes, which were red from lack of sleep. "I've worked with the police on a great many very strange cases, and I have to admit this one is making me nuts. The normal rationale here is complicated by the apparent dissociative identity disorder. We're not simply dealing with one confused individual, we're dealing with two. Hell, for all we know, we could be dealing with a dozen. What we could actually be confronting here is one hand not knowing what the other is doing. If in fact there's no co-consciousness between the female who now calls herself Betty and the male, Billy, then Betty might not have a clue as to what Billy did with Brandon."

"There *has* to be a consciousness between the two," she argued.

"They share a mutual goal, which isn't unusual. That goal is Brandon Carlyle. Betty sees him as a romantic idol, an object of worship. Billy sees him as the twenty-first-century Jesus Christ—an object of worship. We mustn't forget that in times of stress and strife and weakness, Billy takes over. That's his job. Even if Betty *is* aware of Billy, and even if she *doesn't* applaud his behavior, she's still dependent on him for her survival."

He cupped Alyson's cheek with his hand and smiled wearily. "Your returning to Ticky Creek now would be a big, not to mention a dangerous, mistake. Those Ticky Creek residents are going to be out for blood. They know now about your association with the *Gazette*. They know you misrepresented yourself to Brandon. You're going to be a suspect in their eyes. Then, of course, there's Betty. If you return to Ticky Creek, you may put your life in jeopardy. Please take these sleeping pills and get some rest. We'll wake you if there's any news."

Reluctantly, Alyson slid the pills into her mouth . . . and tucked them under her tongue. She drank the water and handed Alan the glass. He left the room, closing the door behind him.

Alyson spat the pills into her hand. Reclining against her pillows, she listened to the drone of the television. She glanced at the bedside clock. Eight-thirty. Ron had mentioned his appointment would keep him out late. She hadn't heard from Mildred in two days.

Finally, she slid from the bed, grabbing the bottle of capsules as she did so and pouring another couple into her hand. Inching the door open, she looked out to see Alan sitting on the sofa with a selection of books open before him. Occasionally he glanced toward the television, then went back to scribbling notes on paper. An open soda can sat to one side.

She waited, her attention now and again shifting to the clock at her bedside. Plenty of time yet. Delta flight 1124 wouldn't leave LAX for Dallas until one-thirty.

After what felt like an eternity, Alan stood up and arched his back, tossed his pen onto his notes, and reached for the soda can, which apparently was empty. Alyson swore under her breath, then sighed in relief as he walked to the kitchen and retrieved another drink from the fridge, popped the lid, took a deep drink, then set it on the table by his books. He wandered into the bathroom and closed the door.

Alyson crossed the room, keeping one eye on the closed bathroom door as her fingers fumbled with the capsules, which had grown slightly gummy from her sweating hands that began to tremble before she dropped to one knee and emptied the white powder from each capsule into Alan's drink. She jumped as the toilet flushed; quickly, she blew away the powder residue she'd scattered over the can top and coffee table, then dashed back to the bedroom as the bathroom door opened. She dived for the bed, burying her face in the pillow. Her eyes squeezed closed as the bedroom door opened, allowing threads of television conversation to filter in.

"Hope of Brandon Carlyle's safe recovery fades tonight as. . . ."

The door closed softly.

Minutes dragged by. A half-hour. An hour. At ten o'clock she rolled from the bed and crept to the door.

Alan sprawled on the sofa, glasses shoved to the top of his head, pen still gripped between his fingers as he slept. Alyson tiptoed over to him, bent, and whispered, "Alan?" Nothing. She nudged him. "Alan, wake up." Nothing.

She retraced her steps to the bedroom, pulled her purse and packed bag from under the bed, returned to the living room, and grabbed the car keys from the end table. For a drawn-out moment, she stared down into Alan's sleeping

face, a well of sadness opening up inside her as she acknowledged that she might never see him again. Because he was
right. The monster that was Billy Boyd was still lurking
somewhere around Ticky Creek. And he wasn't going to be
pleased when she made her entrance back into Brandon's
life. Because regardless of what Alan and Ron believed, what
the investigators believed, Alyson was convinced that Brandon was still alive. Equally convinced that time was running
out.

Alyson pressed a kiss to Alan's cheek. "Please understand," she whispered, then slipped out the door and into the
night.

Midnight. The rains had finally eased, at least for the time
being. Jim Benton cautiously steered his boat up Ticky
Creek. With swollen waters came massive debris. Once he'd
nearly been capsized by the rusted-out chassis of a 1968
Volkswagon Beetle.

With his high-powered light focused on the swirling,
churning brown water ahead, he maneuvered his craft around
a bobbing tree trunk, drank his warm Coors, and tried not to
think about the last few days. The Carlyle thing was creeping
him out. The whole gosh-dang family gone just like that. It
was one thing for the old ones to go. Folks expected that.
Henry and Bernie were both ill, and had been for a while.
But Brandon. . . .

Jim belched and hunkered deeper into his jacket. No doubt
about it, folks were upset. The hordes of rubberneckers and
fans overrunning the town didn't help.

At last, he located the orange flags marking his trotline.
Each time he sidled the boat in place, the current drove him
back. A floating stump came bobbing up from nowhere and
rammed the hull of his boat so hard he almost flipped. By
the time he rectified the situation, he was sweating and on
the verge of puking from nerves. He was getting mighty tired
of fighting and fretting over this goddamn creek. If he didn't

make so much money selling catfish to the local restaurants, he'd pack it in and get a hobby.

Shivering, he frowned. Normally he wasn't a superstitious kind of guy, but considering everything that had happened lately . . . dragging the creek for Carlyle's body; Bernie found dead in her bed—and man, oh man, wasn't *that* weird, her being completely paralyzed, yet when they found her, her mouth was wide open, as if she'd been trying to scream; and all that blood in the house.

A rustle in the bushes brought his head around with a snap. He stared through the dark at the dense copse, feeling as if his eyeballs were about to pop out of his head. Grabbing a lamp, he directed the beam into the tangle of trees and briars. Again the racket, closer this time. He saw the vegetation shiver and sway.

"Gosh dang," he whispered through suddenly dry lips. "Gosh dang, gosh dang—"

The deer lifted its head and stared straight into Jim's light. In the blink of an eye, it whirled and sprang off into the dark. The air rushed from his lungs, and with a grunt of chagrin Jim put down his light and returned to the task of retrieving the trotline, which, judging by the weight of it, was going to make his trip out here more than a little profitable.

The first four hooks produced winners—three-pounders at least. Storms always churned up the big ones. Fifth hook had been cleaned of bait. The sixth had snagged on moss that made his fingers slimy as he removed it and rebaited. The line grew heavier near the middle of the creek. Gritting his teeth, he strained to lift it, cursing under his breath because it was pretty obvious that whatever was holding the line down was bigger than any catfish. There went his profits, for sure. Probably snared a tree limb.

"What the hell is that?" he said aloud, bending nearer the water, where the lamp beams formed disks of light on the moving surface. He heaved again, dragging the object closer. "What the heck. . . ."

His mouth fell open and he jerked back, nearly rising to

his feet, causing the boat to tip dangerously. Then he began screaming. . . .

Delta flight 1124 arrived at DFW Airport at six-thirty. By noon Alyson idled in a mire of traffic that stretched for miles along Highway 59 outside Ticky Creek. Cars were bumper-to-bumper along the shoulder of the road as people crowded the grassy verges of the Carlyle property. Mounds of flowers were piling up outside the security gate. Women sat on the wet grass with tears streaming from their eyes. News crews swarmed like vultures.

An hour and a half later, Alyson pulled her rental car into the River Road parking lot. Here, too, the congestion of cars flowed down the highway. She parked the Ford a quarter-mile down the shoulder and walked back to the restaurant, floppy hat pulled low over her brow, her eyes hidden behind dark glasses despite the escalating threat of rain.

God, she was tired. She tried to remember when she had last eaten. The smell of grease and barbecue wafting from the building made her light-headed.

Stepping inside the building, she was startled by the odd quietness. Although the place was packed with customers, the soft murmur of conversation felt disquieting, more like the people had gathered here for a wake instead of food. The idea made her stomach clench even tighter.

She saw Ruth, and waved.

Carrying a tray of drinks, Ruth looked at her strangely, obviously not recognizing her right away. The smile on her face dropped like a rock, and a sudden spear of fear jabbed at Alyson. She took a step back, only to stop short as Ruth nodded and mouthed, *In a minute.*

Turning her back to the room, Alyson stared out through the glass front doors. Rain had begun to fall again in a thick gray sheet. Her eyes drifted closed.

"Hon, ain't you a sight for sore eyes?"

Alyson looked over her shoulder and gave Ruth a weak smile. "Still talking to me?"

"I'm still thinkin' about it. In the meantime, follow me. You look like you need to sit before you fall down."

Alyson followed Ruth down the corridor past the rest rooms, to a stairway. Ruth's short, belled skirt swung from side to side as she ascended. "I ain't takin' you to Clyde's office today," she explained over her shoulder. "I suspect Clyde ain't gonna be too happy to see you. Not that anybody else in this town will be either. But I can't help but like you. Call it a character flaw. I always have a soft spot for the underdog."

They walked to the end of a hallway and Ruth shoved open a door. "I hide in here when I've had enough pinches on my ass to drive me to the point of punchin' someone in the nose. Ain't fancy, but it's clean and comfortable." Catching Alyson's shoulders from behind, Ruth ushered her to the cot. "Sit. Wanna beer or somethin'? Coke? Wine cooler?" Bending at the waist and peering into a small refrigerator, Ruth said, "I'm gonna need a beer for this, I think. I suggest the same for you."

"A beer would be great, thanks," Alyson managed as she removed her hat and glasses.

"You got it, Sugar." Ruth unscrewed the bottle top and flung it in the trash. She handed the beer to Alyson, her mouth turned down and her chin quivering. "I wondered if you'd come back. I'm glad you did."

Alyson drank deeply. The beer was cold enough to make her esophagus ache. She closed her eyes and waited for the pain to pass. "I won't let them give up, Ruth. I won't believe he's gone until I see him with my own eyes."

Ruth stared down at her. "Holy heck! You ain't heard, have ya?"

Alyson fixed her gaze on Ruth. A rush of heat followed by freezing cold swept through her. Hysteria coiled in her stomach, and though she took a shaky breath in an attempt to restrain it, she felt it crawl up her chest, destroying her control. Tears boiled up and spilled.

Ruth put her beer aside and reached for Alyson's hands.

"Oh, please," Alyson whimpered, "please, no."

"Jim Benton was collectin' his trotline last night. There was a . . . body. Caught up in them hooks and all—"

"Oh." She sank into Ruth's arm. "Oh, no."

Ruth held her tight, stroked her hair, rocked her. Her voice broke and trembled. "It was pretty bad. The decomposition and all—couldn't be identified, and was taken into Tyler—"

Alyson lifted her head, searched Ruth's face. "They don't know—you're saying they don't know if it's Brandon—"

"They're gonna check dental records. All they can definitely say is it was a male, slightly over six feet, dark brown hair. They're thinkin' it could be that White Sands football player who went missin' here a couple or more weeks ago. They never found him, ya know."

"It has to be," Alyson declared, sitting up straight, her hands gripping the beer bottle hard. "If the decomposition was that far along—"

"You can't never tell, Alyson. Not in these waters. What with the animals and fish and all—"

"It's not him!" she declared with such passion that Ruth backed away and nodded.

"Okay. Okay, it ain't him. We'll just keep our fingers crossed and keep prayin', okay? Meantime, why don't you lay yourself down on this cot and rest awhile?" She took the beer from Alyson's hands, caught her feet, and swung them up on the cot. "I'm gonna lock this door so nobody comes stumblin' in here by accident. The last thing we need right now is for Jack to come rollin' in here and haul your skinny carcass off to jail, which he would probably do just cuz he's pretty pissed right now in general, and would like nothin' better than to take a shot at somebody."

Ruth rambled on a few minutes, but Alyson wasn't listening. The hysteria that had threatened to overwhelm her moments before remained, little by little expanding in her chest, fast becoming fire that was oozing up her throat like lava through a vent. She was quite certain it would erupt from her mouth at any moment in a scream that would send

Clyde's customers thundering from the restaurant in a wild panic.

The door closed. Locked. She lay in the windowless room, listening to the steady thrum of rain on the roof. Closing her eyes would be impossible, of course. Even with them wide open, staring, the image rose up before her mind's eye: a faceless body tangled in fishhooks and storm debris.

"Please, God," she prayed aloud, "don't let it be Brandon."

But in that moment she imagined the heartbroken parents of a once vibrant young football player, heads bowed as they prayed, "Please, God, don't let it be our son."

25

"*Alyson? Sugar, wake up. You gotta wake up now.*"

Alyson forced open her burning eyes. Where was she?

"Wake up now." Ruth gently shook her.

Sudden awareness slammed her. Alyson bolted upright. She stared hard through the dim yellow lamplight into Ruth's face hovering above her. Ruth was smiling, and her eyes were brimming with tears.

"He's alive." Alyson grabbed Ruth's shoulders. "They found him and he's alive—"

"Good news, but not that good." Ruth shook her head. "The body was that kid from White Sands."

Closing her eyes, Alyson sank back on the cot. "What time is it?"

"Real late. We're closin' up. Just wanted you to know. You might as well stay here, cuz you ain't gonna find a motel with a vacancy from here to Shreveport. I think every reporter from every newspaper, tabloid rag, network and cable news show in both hemispheres is in town. You'll never guess who I fed tonight. Tom Brokaw, Charlie Gibson, Barbara Walters, and Senator Whitehorse. All at one table. I was so damn nervous I 'bout dumped the whole damn tray in the senator's lap."

Alyson sat up and tried to rub the sleep from her eyes. God, how long had she been out? She glanced at a clock on the wall. Two o'clock in the morning?

"Once Clyde is gone, you come on down to the kitchen. We'll fix you up with somethin' to eat and we'll talk about things. Give me twenty minutes to get Clyde on the road. Oh, and I brung you some readin' material. Thought you might want to catch up on the latest breakin' news. . . ." She gave Alyson a sympathetic smile before leaving the room.

Sitting on the edge of the cot, Alyson rubbed her eyes and massaged her temples. Only once in her life had she ever boozed so hard she'd lost consciousness. That had been ten years ago in New Orleans. Even then, the morning after had not left her head feeling so much like a gourd full of wet sand.

She stumbled to the refrigerator and fished out a cola. Her throat felt like sawdust, and burned as she drank. Her gaze fell on the newspapers Ruth had tossed on the table. Her own face stared back at her from the front page of the *Galaxy Gazette*.

HUNK'S MYSTERY LOVER IDENTIFIED
AS OUR OWN A.J. FARRINGTON!

She nudged aside the *Gazette*. The *Enquirer* pictured her with camera, superimposed into a photograph of Brandon shooting her the finger.

REPORTER GIVES NEW MEANING TO UNDERCOVER WORK

The *STAR*:

DID GIRLFRIEND'S BETRAYAL DRIVE
TINSEL TOWN TERROR TO SUICIDE?

The *GLOBE*:

FATAL ATTRACTION!
SHERIFF CONVINCED REPORTER IS STALKER ANTICIPATING

The irony of it all made her laugh so hard that she bent at the waist, a silent convulsion that squeezed her ribs and chest like steel bands and made her stomach contract in a knot. She couldn't breathe. Tears ran from her eyes and spotted the tips of her Ropers. She had invaded Carlyle's life in the hopes of claiming the story of a lifetime that would win her esteem—now esteem would be the last thing she'd glean from this affair. She was going to be the Monica Lewinsky of publishing—if there was anything left of her once the Ticky Creek residents, not to mention Brandon's rabid fans, got hold of her.

She waited another ten minutes before venturing downstairs. Ruth met her, ushered her to a table near the jukebox, then hurried back to the kitchen for drinks and food.

The empty building felt vast and cold. Sounds from the kitchen echoed off the exposed beams high overhead. Alyson stood and walked to the jukebox that glowed like something ethereal in the dark room. Fishing into her jeans pocket, she withdrew a quarter, slid it into the slot, and punched K5. The machine hummed and clicked. Alyson turned and focused on the dance floor, the memory of her swaying in Brandon's arms lifting like vapor in her mind even before Trisha Yearwood's voice floated down from the speakers.

Alyson ate brisket, bootlegger beans, and potato salad as if it were her last meal. By the time she pushed her plate back, she was forced to unsnap her jeans.

"Look," Ruth said, "if you're smart, you'll climb in your car and head back to Dallas as fast as you can. This town is on the verge of blowin' sky-high. Jack's ass is in a crack. Folks ain't happy cuz he didn't immediately bring in outside investigators and search crews. Fact is, it was Deputy Greene who rang up the Tyler and Longview law enforcement and asked for their help. Jack said he was tryin' to avoid a media circus unless it was absolutely necessary. Half the town residents are demandin' his resignation. He can kiss his sheriff job good-bye. He'd be lucky to get a job sellin' bait down at the Wonder Worm. And you can bet that if Brandon's dead, somebody somewhere is gonna crawl out of the woodwork and sue his butt for negligence."

As Alyson related the story of Billy aka Betty, Ruth smoked, her expression never once revealing her thoughts or emotions. Finally, she shook her head. "I always thought there were somethin' strange about that bird. She come in here occasionally, took a table out yonder on the deck, ate, and stared out at that damn water. Tipped good, though." She chuckled. "That must have been Billy, cuz women don't tip worth a damn."

For the first time in days, Alyson laughed—the good sort of laughter that bubbled up like clear, cool water from a spring. It soothed the ache in her chest. For a moment, however brief, her head cleared of its dull weight and pain, and she felt normal again.

Ruth gave a choked laugh that made her cough. Crushing out her cigarette, she waved at the cloud of smoke hanging around her head. "Between her and Mitsy Dillman, we could start our own funny farm. Hey, they'd probably become fast friends. If nothin' else, they could sit around and make Popsicle stick trivets and exchange fishin' stories."

"I wasn't aware that Betty fished," Alyson said as she reached for her beer.

"Well, I assume that's what she does when she goes up the creek at two in the mornin'. Mitsy, too. You see Betty go puttin' by, and then here comes Mitsy."

Alyson stared into Ruth's eyes. The smiles, little by little, slid from their faces.

"Two in the morning," Alyson repeated. "Why would she be out at that time of morning, especially when she was always at work by seven?"

"Guess that didn't give her too long to fish, did it?"

They drank their beers in silence.

The phone rang.

Jumping, they stared at the phone on the wall. "Who the heck on a stick would be callin' this place at three in the mornin'?" Ruth said, looking back at Alyson.

"Clyde—"

"Thinks I headed out right after him."

"Someone looking for her errant husband?"

"Everbody knows we close this place down at one-thirty."

The ringing stopped. The silence that filled the big room rang like echoing bells. Alyson relaxed into her chair. Ruth reached for her pack of Winstons.

The phone rang again.

Alyson gently placed her beer on the table. "Answer it," she said softly, the odd urgency in her voice bringing a rise of something cold up her back. "Quick, Ruth, answer it."

"Sure." Ruth ran to the phone, slowly raised the receiver to her ear. "River Road, this is Ruth. Hello? Hello? Is anyone—" She frowned and looked at Alyson. *Come here quick*, she mouthed, and waved her over. "Ma'am, you want to repeat that? You want Alyson James?"

Alyson stopped in her tracks.

Ruth fixed her gaze on Alyson's. "Nora who?"

Alyson sprang for the phone, tearing it out of Ruth's hand. "Nora?" she cried. "Nora, is that—"

"Listen to me, Alyson. They're screaming again. Just now, they're screaming—"

"Where is he, Nora? Is he alive?" She grabbed for a pencil on the bar.

"Alive. He's—you have to hurry. He's. . . ."

"Where is he?" Alyson screamed.

"I see . . . water. Flat, wide water and trees—they . . . it's not coming—"

"Please," she begged, clutching the receiver to her head.

Ruth pressed her ear as close to the receiver as she could, trying to overhear. Her arm encircled Alyson as if willing her strength.

"Please, Nora. Listen!"

"... A church. I see a ... crude building with—there's a road, only it's ... not a road, it's water."

Ruth said in a shaking voice, "Two miles north up the creek, down that old stagecoach road, or what used to be the old stagecoach road. It ain't nothin' more than a swamp now. There was an old coach house, turned into a chapel a while back by some religious nuts. . . ."

"Hurry," Nora stressed. "He's ... Billy isn't happy. He's raging. If you don't stop him now, it'll be too late."

The line went dead.

Ruth took the receiver from her and hung it up. "What the hell is that about?" she asked.

"I need a boat," Alyson said, looking into Ruth's panicked eyes.

"Who was that on the phone?"

"And a gun."

Ruth's mouth fell open.

"Now, Ruth. I need a boat and a gun now."

"Whoa, now. First of all, you're gonna tell me who that—"

"Her name is Nora—"

"And she says she knows where Brandon is." Ruth barked a sharp laugh. "What is she, a frickin' psychic?"

"Yes." Alyson nodded. "She is."

Ruth laughed again, then stopped as she saw the seriousness in Alyson's face. "You're jokin', right?"

"Please, we don't have time—"

"Sugar, you know how many of them fruitcakes have been bangin' on Jack Dillman's door the last few days?"

"I'll bet Clyde keeps a gun tucked away someplace. Where is it?"

"Look, hon, I know you're feelin' pretty desperate right now. We all are—"

"I'll tear this place apart if I have to, Ruth. Does he keep it near the cash register?" She shoved past Ruth and began pulling open drawers and doors.

"If she was so damn smart, how come she waited so long before contactin' you?" Ruth shouted. "For that matter, how come she didn't stop this thing before it ever started?"

"She's rusty."

"She's whaaat?"

Alyson started down the hall.

"Where you goin'?" Ruth shouted.

"To Clyde's office. Maybe he keeps a gun there."

"It's locked!"

"Then unlock it." Turning back to Ruth so suddenly that Ruth nearly stumbled, Alyson said, "Do you want Brandon's life on your conscience?"

"When the heck did I suddenly become the bad guy here?"

"Every minute you fight me, Ruth, is one less minute I have to reach Brandon in time."

"So we'll call Jack."

"Fine. You do that. You convince him why he should believe a psychic. And while you're at it, suggest that Alyson James would very much appreciate his cooperation."

"Even if I wanted to believe this Nora woman, I can't let you go sashayin' up this creek in a fishin' boat by yourself. What kind of friend would I be? Gawd Almighty, Alyson, you can't even swim. Have you forgot that?"

Alyson opened and closed her mouth. Yes. Apparently she had forgotten. Not just forgotten that she couldn't swim, but forgotten her fear of the water. "So I'll deal with it," she heard herself declare in a flat tone. She tried to take a deep breath. It wouldn't come. "Please, Ruth, listen to me. First, how did Nora know I was here? I've spoken with no one but you since I've been back. Nora has been right about every bit of information she's given me. She told me, 'Beware of Billy Boy,' only it wasn't Billy Boy, it was Billy Boyd. She knew Brandon called me Cupcake. No one else knew that, Ruth. It was his pet name for me because I . . . I love Twinkies.

"Please. If she's wrong, what's the harm of my going there? I'll simply turn around and come back."

"And if she's right?" Ruth gave a frightened laugh. "What happens if you get there and—"

"I need a gun."

Ruth chewed her lip, then, "Sweet Jesus, I gotta feelin'

I'm gonna regret this. Come on. Clyde keeps a Glock in his desk in case somebody decides they want to knock off the safe durin' work hours." She led Alyson down the hall.

Ruth unlocked the door and turned on the light. She proceeded to the desk, where she pulled out a drawer and reached far back, her face screwing into a frown of concentration. Finally, she pulled the gun out and put it on the desk. They both stared at it.

"You know anything about guns?" Ruth asked.

Alyson shrugged. "A little. I took a class once in self-defense. There were karate experts there, a cop. Someone brought in handguns." She reached for the automatic, kept it pointed toward the floor as she regarded it.

"He keeps it loaded," Ruth said in a whisper. "He showed me once. You flip the safety off here, then you just aim and fire. Says it's got a hard trigger on it. Means it ain't gonna go off on you too easy."

"What about a boat?" Alyson could feel the first real clutch of fear seizing hold of her throat.

"Clyde keeps his boat down at the docks. He was helpin' in the search, so I know it's already got whatever you need. Aly, I—"

"Don't," Alyson interrupted her. "We're wasting time."

With a resigned groan, Ruth led her out the door.

They took Ruth's car, driving south down 59, back toward town. The rain had stopped, thank God. The roads were wet, and reflected the light beams like oil slicks. With the gun in her lap, Alyson stared out into the dense, black trees crowding the road. When fear for her own safety began to take hold, she focused on Brandon and what might be happening to him in that very moment. *He's alive*, she mentally repeated to herself. *Dear Heavenly God, let Nora be right again.*

"I ain't gonna pull no punches," Ruth said as she drove. Her face glowed with a green tint from the dashboard lights. "These waters are treacherous now. They always are, but especially now, 'cause of these rains. Creek is up and fast—"

"Why didn't they search the compound?" Alyson interrupted. "Why didn't the searchers look there—"

"They've been lookin' for a drown victim, or a disposed body. The compound is nearly three miles north of the docks where the Carlyles kept their boat. Creek runs south. That's where the search and rescue teams focused. Look, don't nobody go there. We don't hunt there, we don't fish there. I went there once with my daddy. That was way back, maybe twenty years ago, and I don't mind tellin' you, it's a damn spooky place. Like somethin' prehistoric."

"Like Caddo Lake?"

"Honey, Caddo Lake is Disney World compared to this baygall. Never forget my daddy tellin' me about the Baygall Bogeyman."

Alyson gave her a dry smile. "Sounds like a story parents made up to keep their kids from exploring the baygall."

"Sugar, we don't need no bogeyman to keep kids out of that baygall. The place is a mire of mud and quicksand. Flood waters get trapped up in those flats, and it becomes a breedin' ground for snakes, frogs, and mosquitoes. I'll never forget the smell of that place. Like somethin' dead and rottin'."

They drove in silence then. Finally, Ruth turned down a gravel road. The car bumped in and out of water-filled trenches, inched along for a quarter-mile until the headlights splashed across the covered, compartmented docks sheltering a line of fishing boats that hung from cables over the water.

As Ruth stopped the car, she turned again to Alyson. "Please don't do this. You ain't got nothin' to go on but the word of some weirdo who thinks she's got a vision. Brandon wouldn't want you to do this. The man was deep in love with you. If he thought you was gonna risk your neck like this—"

"If you think I'd turn my back on someone who loves me that much, then it's pretty damn obvious you don't know me." Alyson smiled into Ruth's eyes. "I've waited my entire life to belong to somebody who loved me that deeply, Ruth. For twenty-nine years I ached with an emptiness so bottomless and dark, I didn't think I'd ever see the light. Then suddenly there were Brandon and Henry, and I felt like I'd come home at long last. That I belonged. I think Brandon felt that way, too. We just sort of . . . fit."

Ruth squeezed Alyson's hand. "And by the looks of you two together, I'd say you fit pretty damn good."

Alyson reached for her purse and took out pen and paper. "This is the name and number of my friend. If something happens, and I don't come back—"

"Don't even think about it—"

"If I don't come back, call him. His name is Dr. Alan Rodgers, and this is his number. He'll take care of everything." She laughed. "Knowing Alan, he's probably on his way here, he and Ron. Maybe here already." Taking a fortifying breath, she said, "Let's go."

Alyson turned the cable crank that lowered the aluminum fishing boat into the water. Ruth checked the gas in the motor, flipped a switch that turned on the lights on the bow, secured the paddle in the hooks, then gave her a brief lesson on steering.

"It's pretty simple. If you want to go right, you turn this thing left. Left, right. You got it? You want more power, rotate this doomaflicker. Got it?"

"I think so." Alyson nodded, keeping her eyes on Ruth's face and not on the water lapping against the hull of the boat.

"You want to kill the power, just hit this lever right here on the side of the motor. Once you get up into the baygall, you'll wanna kill it. You can never tell how deep the water is once you get up the road away. You don't want to ground the propellers. Not only that, but the vegetation gets pretty dense—water lilies—and they can act just like a lot of fishin' line around your propellers. They'll gum you up real quick and burn up the motor. Best you paddle your way in at the first sign of the lilies, understand?"

Ruth tossed her a life preserver that Alyson shrugged on like a coat. It felt tight around her chest, but Ruth nodded. "That's good. The last thing you want is to slide out of your vest." Then she tossed her a flashlight and toed open a metal box on the boat floor. "There's a couple knives in here in case you get caught up in vegetation and need to cut your way out. Your boat lights are fixed good so you don't have to worry much about seein' where you're goin'. Hell, Clyde has this baby rigged up so bright it looks like a frickin' Ferris wheel. Jim's always teasin' him that he blinds the damn fish with his lights then clubs 'em over the head."

Ruth nervously rubbed her hands up and down the butt of her jeans. "You go right up the middle of this water, you hear? Don't let yourself get pushed too close to the banks. Too much underbrush. This is a good motor, but in these currents you're gonna have a fight on your hands to keep her straight and steady. Three miles up you'll see the road on your right. 'Course it just looks like a wide gap in the trees. There's an old wagon wheel nailed to the tree on the left corner. At least most times you can see it. Maybe not now 'cuz of this rain, I don't know. Anyhow, you go up that road. Things will start to look real different real quick. You'll know what I mean. It's just . . . different. Pine trees will start givin way to cypress. The water gets dead still. Soon as you start to feel like you want to turn around and get the hell out real quick, you know you're in the right place."

"How far up is the compound?" Alyson asked. Her voice sounded thin. Her mouth felt dry.

"Mile, maybe. By then you'll be paddlin'. Flip your propeller up when you get there, so you don't drag. And remember, please remember, if you have to get out of the boat to push or pull it over a sandbar, the ground could give out from under you at any time. You can go from knee deep to real deep with no warnin'. You'll see the compound on high ground. It's surrounded by water, like an island. There's a fence. A high one, 'bout ten feet, maybe."

Alyson nodded and looked down at the boat. "Go call Jack. If he won't listen to you, call Tommy Greene, or the Tyler police. Call Barbara Walters or Senator Whitehorse. Get someone to listen."

"You bet I will," Ruth said, nodding. "They're gonna listen whether they want to or not."

Carefully, Alyson slid off the dock and into the boat,

which rocked dangerously as she stumbled to the back and dropped into the seat by the motor. Ruth showed her how to start the motor, which cranked the first time. The yellow and orange lights up front flashed on, illuminating the water for ten feet around her.

"Remember," Ruth yelled, "left is right and right is left, and use that thingamajig you got your hand on to regulate your speed. It's a little like drivin' a motorcycle!"

Alyson nodded, and with a slight rotation of the thingamajig, the boat slid smoothly away from the dock and through the black water.

Jack Dillman sat in his Barcalounger in the dark, staring at his image on the television screen, blundering his way through an inquisition by a Fox News correspondent he'd seriously considered punching. Only one thing had stopped him: he was in enough goddamn trouble as it was. Jeezus, how the hell had his career gone south so damn fast?

Carlyle again.

The son of a bitch had to go and get himself killed. Dixie'd been right. There wasn't a rock he could hide under that somebody wasn't gonna be there waitin' for him with a frickin' camera to satellite his humiliated face to ever' goddamn television in the civilized world. His town was lost under a sea of reporters, outside law enforcement, politicians, and fans with a hunger to tear him apart limb by limb—like on those old Tarzan movies he watched as a kid.

He was starting to get death threats. His car had been stoned twice, and windows of the courthouse had been busted by flying yams the size of cantaloupes. He had a meeting at ten in the morning with the Town Council, who would, no doubt, ask for his resignation.

All because of Carlyle. Frickin' Carlyle. Always Carlyle.

He turned up the television volume and winced as he watched himself gulp in nervousness and wipe sweat from his brow.

"Sheriff Dillman, can you explain why, when you were

first notified that something wasn't right at the Carlyle residence, you didn't follow through with the customary check? Didn't you, in fact, radio your dispatcher that everything checked out okay at the Carlyle residence when, in fact, you didn't actually check the residence at all? Sheriff Dillman, has it occurred to you that if you'd followed through with the check, you'd undoubtedly have discovered that some sort of confrontation had taken place at the residence, and that Carlyle was, indeed, missing at that very moment? Not only that, but when Carlyle's disappearance was first reported, you waited six hours before requesting help from outside search and rescue units.

"Sheriff, is it true that you've had a personal issue with Carlyle over the years? Did this cloud your judgment when it came to following through with your responsibilities as sheriff . . . ?"

"Sheriff, is it true that your own sister was arrested for. . . ."

"Can you tell us if you have any leads on the disappearance of Betty Wilson?"

"Do you feel she's more responsible for Carlyle's disappearance than you first believed?"

"There's talk of your resigning . . ."

"Sheriff, if Brandon Carlyle is dead, you'll certainly be held accountable. But on a more personal level, how are you feeling, knowing that a man so beloved by the world might have died due to your negligence?"

"No comment. No comment. No goddamn comment!"

Jeezus.

He hit the Power button, throwing the room into complete darkness except for the illuminated eyes of a black-and-white plastic Felix the Cat clock on the distant kitchen wall. Its tail moved from side to side, ticking in the silence.

The phone rang; he jumped. Jeez, if another frickin' reporter had somehow found his number—he had a goddamn mind not to answer it. Who the hell would be calling here this time of night except a frickin' reporter?

Cursing, he climbed out of the Barcalounger and stalked

to the phone. "Give me a goddamn break!" he yelled into it. "It's four in the mornin' and I—"

"Ruth. Ruth Threadgill. Jack, you ain't gonna believe this, but. . . ."

He stared down at his bare feet, listening, feeling his blood pressure rise even higher. "Wait a minute, wait a minute, you callin' me at four in the mornin' with some cockamamie story of a goddamn psychic? You been dippin' too damn heavy into Clyde's cheap whisky. Go to bed, Ruth—"

Rolling his eyes, he interrupted her again. "Look, when I get my hands on that Farrington woman. . . . She's a goddamn nut too, Ruth. She what? She's done whaaat? Jeezus. . . ." He kicked the wall, hurting his toe. Jumping up and down, he shouted, "I'm a goddamn laughin'stock as it is. If you think I'm haulin' my officers into that baygall on the word of some nutcase supposed psychic and a tabloid reporter, then you deserve to be slam-dunked in the Terrell loony bin along with the rest of 'em. Now go to bed and leave me the hell alone!" He slammed the phone down, causing it to ring like a bell.

Mitsy's door opened, and a spear of light stabbed through the dark and into his eyes. She stood in the doorway, a silhouette, hair standing out from her head in wild tufts, her thin shoulders slumped. A spear of pity replaced the wild and angry disbelief that had overwhelmed him momentarily. He suddenly felt weak with sadness, not just for himself but for Mitsy. The last days he'd watched her practically fade before his eyes.

"Sorry I woke you," he said, rubbing his throbbing toe with his other foot.

"Who was it?"

"Ruth Threadgill. Wasn't nothin' important. Go back to bed."

"What did she want?"

"Just spewin' on about some cockamamie story—" He waved it away and limped to his chair. "Forget it, Mitsy. I'm too damn tired to waste my breath. Jeez, people have gone plumb crazy over this goddamn Carlyle thing. I never figured Ruth for crazy."

Mitsy moved into the room, looking like a wraith in her long white gown, pale face, and blond hair. "Jack, I gotta talk to you about somethin'."

"Can't it wait, Mitsy? I gotta get some sleep. I gotta meetin' at ten with the Council." He dropped into the chair and heaved a weary sigh. "Shit, after this I'll be lucky to get a job as night security at Wal-Mart. We'll have to move. That's all there is to it."

Mitsy moved toward the sofa, wringing her hands. "I've been thinkin', Jack—"

"God help us. Don't think, Mitsy. If you start to feel like thinkin' again, go take some more Xanax and mood enhancers. I don't need no more thinkin' from anybody right now."

"About Brandon—"

"Jeezus."

"Fact is, I've been thinkin' real clear for a few days now. Clearer than I've ever thought, maybe, and I'm ashamed to say I've done some things that hurt a lot of people. But my thinkin' was scrambled, Jack. Like my brain was short-circuitin' on me."

"Well"—he drank his warm beer and winced—"I'm glad you're feelin' better. Now go back to bed. You'll feel even better after a decent night's sleep."

"I hated Brandon for a long time. And you know why, Jack?"

" 'Cause he knocked you up, Mitsy, and made it so you can't have no babies."

" 'Cause he made me feel special, Jack. 'Cause he made me feel like somethin' besides a piece of white trash good for nothin' but quickies in the backseat. I felt real special with Brandon cuz he took me out in public—took me to the picture show and nice restaurants, and even bought me some pretty presents. I asked him one time why he treated me so nice, and you know what he told me? He said, 'Because I know what it's like to be lonely.'

"I trapped him, Jack. I thought he'd take me away from

this place and these people, like if I could go away, I could get clean again. When I was with Brandon, I was somebody, and folks looked at me like I actually counted for somethin'. Then when he left, I was right back where I started. A nothin'. After feelin' what it was like to be a somethin', bein' a nothin' again hurt even worse."

"That don't excuse him knockin' you up, Mitsy."

"I told him I was on the pill."

He stared at her. "Just the same, he had a responsibility—"

"It wasn't his baby, Jack." She took a shuddering breath. "I was two months along when I coaxed him into the back-seat of my car. I don't know who the daddy was. I fully intended on passin' that baby off as his. Then Cara come along and give Mamma all that money to get rid of it. Mamma could of taken me to a decent doctor, but she didn't. She wanted that money to help pay for her divorce."

Jack closed his eyes and listened to the *tick tick tick* of Felix's tail. Mitsy moved up by the chair. She laid her hand on his arm. The light from the bedroom reflected off the tears in her eyes.

"It ain't him I've hated all this time, Jack. It's me. Now I'm so damn ashamed of myself, and scared. I'm real scared."

Sitting up, Jack covered Mitsy's hand with his. "Don't be cryin', Mitsy. Jeez, you know how I can't handle no woman cryin'."

"I know where he is. I've known all along, and I didn't say nothin' cause I was still so confused. . . ." She started to cry hard.

"What the hell are you sayin', Mitsy?"

"I followed her there a time or two. I seen what she was doin', Jack. She's buried him there . . . in the basement below the old chapel."

26

He awoke again to darkness. Impenetrable darkness and si-lence, and the fear that slid its cold hands around his throat each time he awakened in this suffocating abyss of nothing-ness. Not for the first time, he reached out in panic, certain that someone had mistakenly thought he was dead and had buried him deep, deep in the ground. Yet, his hand swept nothing but the moist, heavy air that smelled like rank creek sediment and the filmy vegetation that flourished just beneath the water's surface. And something else—something nau-seatingly sweet, like rotten meat.

Where the hell was he? How long had he been here?

He touched his face—a good indicator that he'd been here awhile. Then, there was the gnawing hollow in his belly.

His shoulder and arm were going from bad to worse. The skin of his arm was tight and hot. He could hardly open and close his hand. The deep pain pulsated with new fire when he tried to move.

Think.

Betty. In the blink of an eye the woman he'd known and trusted for months had become . . . something else. A monster.

God help him, his monster was back.

A noise.

With a scrape of metal and a groan of wood, a hole opened above, pouring light down a steep flight of stairs. It reminded him of sunlight pouring through a break in black storm clouds—a ray dancing with dust particles. Along with it came fresh, cool air that brushed over his hot brow like a breath.

He glanced around, noting that he was lying on a bare mattress on a wood bed frame in a room with damp wood walls and an earth floor that looked slick with mud. There were deep footprints partially filled with brown water leading toward him and back to the stairs.

A figure approached, holding a kerosene lamp out to light her way. Her heavy feet thumped on the wood steps as she descended. He recognized the muddy, thick-soled shoes as Betty's.

Brandon did his best to push himself into a sitting position. He gritted his teeth against the pain in his shoulder. His eyes throbbed from the assault of light on his pupils. His empty stomach rebelled and he gagged, heaving up nothing but bitter gas.

Betty stopped at the foot of the stairs. Her eyes were feverish, her mouth turned down. Her red wig, which still looked darker in places from his blood, sat slightly lopsided on her head. When she spoke, her voice sounded tremulous and frightened—not Betty's voice, exactly. There were hints of Billy's testosterone roughing up the edges.

"Oh, Mr. Brandon. Thank God, you're finally awake."

With effort and pain, he propped himself back against the wall. He wanted to kill her. Desperately.

"What the hell are you doing to me, Betty?"

"It's not me," she rushed to reply. "Please believe that. I wouldn't harm you. Not for the world." Lowering her voice to a whisper, she said, "It's him. I can't control him any longer. Perhaps I never could. I think. . . ." She covered her eyes briefly with her hand, which sported three broken nails. They made him think of the scratches on his neck, welts of fire and dry blood. "Now that I think about it, he took me over long ago. He's used me, used me to get what he wants."

"What does he want?"

She shuffled closer and extended the lamp toward him. The fleeting idea of jumping her danced in his head. Impossible. He could barely manage to sit up, much less tackle a body built like a linebacker.

The green contacts in her eyes were missing. Now the irises were black as pits, and the skin on her face looked chalky under the permanent patches of blush on her cheeks. He tried to see beyond the Betty facade, to the man who had once worked for him—Mr. Heavenly Hands himself, Masseur to the Stars. How had he missed it?

"You needn't bother," she said, as if reading his thoughts. "Even if I hadn't had the surgery, you wouldn't have recognized me. Oh, perhaps you would have thought me vaguely familiar. But the truth is, Mr. Brandon, while you paid me handsomely for my work, and occasionally chatted with me during our sessions, and even slipped me very generous Christmas bonuses, you never so much as looked at me.

"But that all changed, didn't it, the night we bumped into one another outside the Paramount Theater—just after the premier of that Mel Gibson movie you attended. It was the first time I allowed you to see me . . . dressed. I walked right up to you, wearing a red sequined gown—and that dreadful security guard grabbed me. You waved him away and smiled at me—the first time ever you looked into my eyes and acknowledged me as a person. My friend took our photograph together—I have it still, you with your arm around me—and you signed my book, *With Love, Brandon*. I knew at that moment that something special passed between us. That if I corrected this horrible mistake of my birth, perhaps, just perhaps, I might stand a chance . . . if you came to appreciate me enough. I realized I'd have to make myself invaluable to you. And I did. We were so close for a while, so very close, and then. . . ."

She sighed, and her face sagged. "I'm not sure when he came back. I thought he was long gone. And I was glad— very, very glad—when he left. He frightened me. But he was necessary. I understand that. Very necessary. I often looked at him with envy when we were younger. He was my hero . . . until I realized just what a manipulator he could be. And oh, so crafty. He made me do things I wasn't proud of, and when I refused, he did them and blamed them on me. But Father liked him. Oh, yes, he was the son Father always wanted. A disciple to follow in Father's footsteps." Lowering her voice to a whisper, she added, "Father got more than he bargained for, I'm afraid."

"You might tell me which of you is responsible for this," Brandon said through his teeth as he motioned around him with his good arm.

She shushed him with one finger pressed against her lips. "He doesn't like anger."

"He can kiss my ass. I'm dying here, Betty. My shoulder— it's infected, I think. And I'm starving. *One* of you is starving me to death. *Goddamnit*, this is a *fucking* nightmare, and you're a *fucking* lunatic—"

She stumbled back, nearly dropped the lantern. The flame flickered dangerously.

Grabbing his arm and hugging it close, Brandon rocked forward, doing his best to contain the overwhelming anger and frustration he'd allowed to get the better of him.

"You mustn't anger him," Betty wept, growing frantic. "I can't help you if you anger him. I may not be able to help you anyway. I've tried, Mr. Brandon. I've begged him. He won't listen. But you *must* listen. Your life depends on it." She swayed and covered her eyes with her hands. She cocked her head, and her eyes widened. "Oh, God. Oh, God, he's coming. Yes, he's there. . . ."

She stumbled toward the stairs, fell hard on them, and looked back at Brandon. Her face looked sad. Her eyes filled with tears that streamed like silver threads down her cheeks.

"Humor him," she said. "Don't let him see your weaknesses—"

"Don't leave," Brandon shouted as she crawled up the
stairs. "Betty, wait! Help me get out of here—"

"I can't. He's too strong. He'd destroy me." She looked
at him again; her face worked, and her eyes rolled. The light
and shadows cast upon her features by the lamp gave Brandon the horrifying sensation of watching the transformation
of Jekyll to Hyde.

"Please," Brandon begged, knowing even as he said it that
Betty was already beyond his reach. He watched as she
dragged herself up the steps, mumbling to herself. But he
knew there was much more to it than that—the voice was
changing back and forth, female to male.

Then the whole door slammed shut and darkness fell over
him . . . hard.

With his good hand, Brandon worked the bed leg back and
forth. Not easy. The slimy ooze under him made leverage
next to impossible. Every few minutes he was forced to stop
and lean against the wall while he caught his breath and
willed back the pain in his shoulder. Above him, the voices
raged: Betty's and Billy's. Betty's seemed to be fading. The
fight was almost gone from her. The weaker hers became,
the stronger Billy's grew.

On his knees in the mud, Brandon continued the task of
dismantling the bed. The wood was old and soft around the
nail heads. With each yank of the leg, the rusty nail squeaked
like a dry hinge; each time, he froze, certain the creature
upstairs would hear and come clamoring down. If he survived this, he was going to produce and direct a movie about
this nightmare.

With one last heave backward, the leg popped free. Landing on his back, his mouth flying open as pain tore through
him, Brandon fought to contain the agony that choked off
his breath and made every pore bead with sweat. Sprawled
in the mud, he was surprised to find the ooze actually soothed

the fire in his shoulder wound. His eyes drifted closed.

The shouting above stopped, and the more familiar silence washed over him. In some distant corner of his awareness, he wondered if he was dying. Images of his life winged at him from hazy gray corners of his mind: his father and Henry and Bernie—good memories, not the old haunting that for so long had crept out of his mind's closet at night and rattled like bones.

Then came Alyson. The images of her were vibrant with color and energy. And passion. Brandon could almost smell her, lying there in the dark. That memory, more than any other, made him shake. With her, he'd found happiness and contentment at long last, and now this. The loss of what might have been, filled him with an anger that turned the black void into a pulsating white heat.

Footsteps above—heavy and lumbering—forced him back to reality.

After several attempts, Brandon managed to sit up, to crawl onto his knees, then stumble to his feet. He slid the bed leg into the back of his loose jeans, then felt his way to the far side of the bed and eased down onto it, careful not to unbalance it toward the missing leg. Slumped against the wall, he used his right hand to lay his left across his lap.

The door opened, slowly.

The body descended, barefoot and silent. He wore a wrap of white linen that hung loose from his shoulders, molding to the breasts juxtaposed against Billy's masculinity. A bubble of nervous hilarity worked up Brandon's throat. He might have been watching a malevolent Mr. Clean descend a heavenly light beam. But he didn't laugh. No way. Because the momentary hilarity that rippled through him fast turned to cold terror as the doors of his boyhood memories began to creep open. Panic began to shoot through him, and the shaking started. Each tremble sent fresh pain through his shoulder and arm. He bit his lip hard to stem the groan working up his throat.

The lantern in one hand, the other holding a bundle of clothes, Billy paused at the foot of the stairs. The yellow light painted his skin red and gold, and transformed his eyes into pinpoints of fire. His smooth scalp glowed like an iridescent dome. The permanent makeup Betty had applied to her face gave Billy the look of a macabre clown when he smiled.

He said softly, "It's time."

Brandon frowned. "What the hell are you talking about?"

Billy's head tipped to one side as he regarded Brandon. "I've brought Your clothes. You'll want to change, of course. They will expect it."

He crossed the room. His bare feet sank in the mud, which erupted between his long, white toes. He placed the folded linen on the bed. He regarded Brandon again, then released a shaky breath. "What a shame that Father isn't alive to witness this."

"Witness what, Billy?"

His smile widened. "I had given up hope. We all had. That sly old Satan had little by little insinuated himself into our lives like a cancer, eating silently but deliberately at our souls. Sex, violence, cruelty, greed . . . the worshiping of false idols. The weak writhe together in their misery like snakes in a pit, serpents of poison, their words like venom, intent on destruction of their fellow man. It is time for You to walk among them. You will rise up and work miracles so that those who have given their souls to evil will recognize their idiocy and know, in the last moments of their miserable existences, what glory and blessings they will be denied in the ever after. The revelation foretold Your Coming, and now the sinners will perish by lightning bolts from Your hands."

Brandon stared into Billy's eyes, his mouth dry. "Jesus," he uttered, "you think I'm—"

"The world has converged, just as I'd hoped. The believers await You, pray for You. They weep for You, and suffer, lost as lambs without Your light to guide them. The world, my Lord, awaits your resurrection."

He sat perfectly still, feeling sweat rise on his skin, causing his wounds to burn. Oddly, in that moment a clarity crystallized in his mind. His senses expanded to an excruciating rawness. He could easily hear his own breathing, and the rapid pounding of his heart in his ears. Betty had warned him: *Whatever you do, don't let him see your weaknesses. Don't anger him.*

Billy dropped to his knees, put aside the lantern, and clasped his hands under his chin; he bowed his head.

"I have waged a war against the evils who would harm You, the demon spirits Satan cast into Your path to tempt You. I now throw myself on Your mercy, and ask that You bless me with the miracle of Your healing so that, at long last, I am cured of this distorted and repulsive abomination placed upon me by a woman whose body and spirit were possessed by wickedness."

Brandon glanced toward the stairs as sweat poured freely from his scalp, and ran down his cheeks and the back of his neck. What would happen if he made a run for it? His hand itched to reach for the bed leg in the back of his pants—not yet. Not yet. He would need better leverage, as weak as he was—

"Please," Billy cried, his voice strident and urgent. "So that I might walk at Your side as pure of body and spirit as You. You have healed the blind, the crippled, the sick—" His hand flew out and clamped on Brandon's leg as Brandon attempted to stand. The powerful fingers dug into Brandon's thigh muscle as fiercely as a cramp, wringing a short gasp of pain from him.

Billy slowly tipped back his head. His ember eyes fixed on Brandon's sweating face. His lips pulled back, exposing his teeth in something not even close to a smile. "Fix it," he demanded in a soft monotone that sent a fresh wave of dread crashing over Brandon.

Twisting his big hands into the linen garment he wore, Billy ripped it down the middle and flung it aside. Oily flesh reflecting the lamplight, he slowly stood, naked, trembling, and white-faced. Tears trickled down his cheeks as he spread his arms. His sagging breasts swayed like pendulums. His flaccid penis drooped between his legs.

A surge of sickness rose in Brandon's throat. He jumped

from the bed and scrambled toward the stairs—feet sliding
in the slick mire. Too late—those hands snared his bad arm,
and the immeasurable pain rocketed up his throat and filled
the room with an agonized howl. He hit the ground and
rolled, clutching his arm against him as blackness flirted with
his consciousness. Little by little the pain subsided as he lay
with his face partially buried in the fetid muck. It oozed
through his lips and into his left nostril.

Teeth clenching and grinding on grit, he rolled and did his
best to focus on Billy's face and not his body, which stood
over Brandon, legs slightly spread and hands fisted. An expression of confusion and anger twisted Billy's features as
he looked from Brandon's eyes to his shoulder and back to
his eyes. Brandon sensed his thoughts. Right about now Billy
must be realizing that something was pretty damn wrong with
this picture. If he were capable of working heavenly miracles,
he would hardly be suffering from a wound in his shoulder.
He glanced toward the mattress, where the bed leg had fallen
from his jeans when he bolted for the stairs. Billy apparently
hadn't noticed.

Brandon tried to sit up.

Billy reached down and hauled Brandon to his feet, pushed
him back to the bed. He dropped like a rock, falling against
the wall with a groan he couldn't swallow. Silent, Billy regarded him through narrowed eyes, bringing a cold, sick
sweat to Brandon's brow. His mind scrambled for thought,
then—

"Betty!" Brandon shouted, and spat mud from his mouth.
"Betty, I need you!"

Billy's eyes widened, and he frowned as his confusion
intensified. "Gone," Billy declared. "Betty is gone. What do
you want with—"

"Betty! I know you can hear me. Don't let him take control, Betty. Don't let him hurt me—"

"We don't need her any longer—"

"Betty, fight him!"

Billy stumbled back and grabbed his head. His eyes rolled
and his face contorted. His teeth bared as he growled, "I . . .

destroyed her. Gone. She's gone to hell. If your right eye causes you to sin, pluck it out and cast it from you; for it is more profitable for you that one of your members perish than for your whole body to be cast into hell. And if your right hand causes you to sin, then cut it off and cast it from you—"

"Betty, if you don't do something, he's going to kill me!"

His eyes bulging and his hands pressed against his ears, Billy roared, "Impostor! Spurious, unrighteous fiend, maggot of hell and wicked disciple of Satan—"

"Betty!" Brandon shouted again, so loudly that the sound ripped up his throat. His hand closing around the bed leg beside him, he surged to his feet, and as Billy lunged with clawed hands, Brandon swung the wood as hard as he could against Billy's head, knowing as he felt the impact that it would do little good. The worm-eaten wood gave a dull snap and disintegrated like pulp in his hand.

Billy recoiled momentarily, tottered back; a stream of blood poured down over his left ear.

Brandon stumbled for the stairs, reached them, and clawed his way up toward the dark hole, despair overtaking him as his weak legs burned and trembled in their attempts to climb.

"Impostor!" came the shriek from below.

Billy's hand seized Brandon's ankle. Brandon jerked and kicked and heaved himself up the stairs in an attempt to break his hold, but to no avail. He looked down into Billy's face and eyes, desperate for some hint that Betty could be rallied—

"Behold," Billy sneered, "let no one deceive by any means, for that day will not come unless the falling away comes first, and the man of sin is revealed, the son of perdition, who opposes and exalts himself above all that is called God or that is worshiped, so that he sits as God in the temple of God, showing himself that he is God. And the lawless one will be revealed, whom the Lord will consume with the breath of His mouth and destroy with the brightness of His coming!"

With a furious, guttural cry, Billy pulled Brandon down the stairs, propelled his sweating, naked body onto Brandon's, and closed his hands around his neck. Gasping for air and getting none, Brandon attempted with his last ounce of strength to drive his fist into Billy's jaw—no good, too weak. He clawed at the hands squeezing his life away, tried to fight back the encroaching fringe of darkness—no good. A weightlessness replaced the burning in his brain, and the fear that had momentarily consumed him vanished, replaced by an equanimity that filled him with a strange serenity even as he looked directly into Billy's eyes.

Billy's voice drifted to him through a tunnel: "And the temples of idols shall be razed and false gods crucified, in the name of our Father. Amen."

The lily pads formed a carpet over the water, which was black as ink. Having killed the motor as Ruth instructed, Alyson oared the boat through the vegetation at a snail's pace, her lungs and muscles burning with exertion and her panic mounting, her hope lost of reaching the compound before daylight. Then again, she felt thankful to have gotten this far.

Twice she had lost control of the boat in the currents, once caught up in an eddy that had spun her in a circle until she'd suffered something like pilot's disorientation in the dark. She'd lost her direction and, having fought her way out of the problem, had motored all the way back down the creek to the River Road before realizing she was headed in the wrong direction.

With a thump and shush, the boat slid onto a sandbar, bringing her to a sudden stop. Alyson focused the beam of her flashlight ahead. The lily pads reflected the beams like mullioned glass. Cypresses loomed out of the water, their branches forming a gnarled and twisted canopy overhead.

Silence rang in her ears. She told herself that the lack of insect and animal sounds was due to the season—the cold, of course, would drive them into their burrows—but she couldn't help thinking of the old baygall legend—and how once she had read a story about the dead zone, how animals would not reside in a place haunted by the living dead.

Alyson eased the oar down through the water, connecting with the ground no more than a foot beneath the surface. Leaving the boat was obviously a necessity in order to dislodge it, and sitting here shaking down to her Ropers wasn't getting it done.

Still, the thought of sliding into the dark water made her lungs quit. The air suddenly felt too thick to breathe. Her blouse beneath the life vest clung to her skin, soaked with sweat. She realized in that moment, as she closed her eyes and buried her face in her hands, just how infrequently she prayed—hadn't actually gotten on her knees and addressed God seriously since her grandmother's illness. Her faith had never been quite as strong after that, and had continued to be eroded by life through the years. Would He listen now? Would He think her a hypocrite?

"Please," she prayed into her hands, "please help me do this. I can't do it without You."

Slowly, she lifted her head.

Nothing had changed. No golden road lit by heavenly light had opened up before her. No giant, benevolent hand had reached down from the sky to pluck her out of this boat and drop her safely on terra firma. The water stretched before her as black as pitch. She then shone the light behind her, the way she had come, noting there wasn't a single sign that she had passed there. The lily pads she had disturbed had shifted back into place, covering her tracks.

Her throat tight, Alyson put down the flashlight and oar, thought on whether she should remove her boots, and decided she should. They were already heavy; filled with water, they would weigh a ton. She set them aside, by Clyde's gun. The hull's coldness crept through her socks and made her ankles ache.

She eased to her feet. The boat barely wobbled. It wouldn't, she reminded herself. It was beached, after all. Carefully, she stepped over the side with one foot.

The water felt shockingly cold, and she gasped. Her foot sank into deep mud, and panic seized her; she tried to draw it back, but the muck sucked at her, momentarily refusing to give her up. Sediment bloomed in a cloud around her shin as she struggled, falling back into the boat as she managed to release herself. Sprawled across the boat bottom, the stench of old fish scales flooding her nostrils, she stared at her foot propped on the side rim. Mud dripped off her sock, as did tendrils of vegetation.

Again. Alyson took a deep breath and slid her foot into the water. Not so cold this time. Her foot sank, sank, then stopped. Then with her right foot. She shuddered at the feel of the gelatinous mush oozing over her toes.

The boat, minus her weight, floated loose. She took a cautious, labored step forward, her hands nudging the light boat along the surface of the water while her shins caused the lily pads to wobble out of her way. Still, she was often forced to struggle to free her ankles from the plants that felt like prickly fingers clutching at her.

Traveling that way for possibly ten minutes, Alyson began to relax. This was far easier than rowing through the vegetation. She'd begun to make good time, and hope returned that she'd reach the compound before daylight. If Nora was right, the last thing she wanted was for Billy Boyd to see her coming.

The ground beneath her disappeared without warning.

She sank to her nostrils before the vest caught her weight. Gulping for air and getting a mouthful of scum-covered water, she thrashed and splashed, panic overwhelming her until the realization set in that she wouldn't sink, thanks to the vest. *Relax, relax,* her mind chanted as her teeth began to chatter from cold. From the corner of her eye she saw the boat drift away.

Oh, God. Oh, God. Alyson made an ineffectual lunge for it. It danced farther away, as if taunting her. Her arms tangled in the lily pads, and the harder she fought them, the farther the boat slipped into the dark.

She started to cry, hot angry tears, and slammed the water with her fists. Then she remembered Brandon's words: *The next time you find yourself in water over your head, try to relax. Whatever you do, don't fight the water, because the water will win every time.*

Closing her eyes, Alyson took several deep, slow breaths, forced her legs and arms to hang limply in the water while her heart pounded so fiercely, she wondered if she was having a heart attack. The cold seeped deeper into the muscles of her back and legs. Her teeth chattered harder.

Finally, as gently as possible, she paddled with her feet, barely rippling the water. She crept up to the boat, eased her hands up the side, and snared it. Her head fell in relief and exhaustion against the cold metal, and her eyes drifted closed. Now for the hard part: she had to heave herself into the boat and hope that she didn't capsize it.

On her third attempt, she managed it. Sodden and shivering, she lay on the boat bottom with her head resting on a cushion and her gaze fixed on the tree branches that dripped with moss and flower vines. The first flush of dawn crept in vaporish streams through the leaves. Fresh desperation swallowed her. She reached for the oar, struggled to sit up, shouldered away the gritty water running from her hair into her eyes, and began paddling again.

Little by little, the baygall emerged, brown water and gray lily pads; a thick layer of mist hovered just above the surface. Dead or dying trees rose out of the murk, their roots jutting from the water like gnarled, knobby knees. Egrets lifted into the air and soared silently above.

Alyson saw it then, the cross rising out of the mist. It floated in the hazy air like a sign from heaven. Paddling harder and faster, she drove the boat toward it, body warming, adrenaline flooding the once exhausted muscles that had threatened to quit on her.

The dilapidated pier appeared unexpectedly out of the haze. The boat rammed it hard. The sound echoed like a gunshot in the silence, and a cloud of white birds erupted from the trees. Alyson gently laid the paddle in the boat as her eyes searched the ground that stretched out before her. The compound had the eerie look of a vacated concentration camp. A towering chain-link fence topped by rolled barbed wire surrounded a barren, flat area upon which huts were scattered. In the center sat an ancient building with boarded windows. The cross rising from its roof leaned precariously to one side, as if the slightest wind would topple it.

Alyson removed her life vest, then tucked the gun into her jeans. She flipped open the metal tackle box and took the pocketknife, tied the boat to a rotting pier beam, grabbed her boots, stepped into the shallow water, and waded to shore. She wedged her wet feet into the boots, then hunkered down to consider her options.

If anyone had recently inhabited the place, it didn't show. It had the appearance of a ghost town, and she thought again of Ruth's Baygall Bogeyman, half expecting to see him materialize from the mist.

She located a gate not far from the pier. It had been secured closed with a length of rusty barbed wire. She pried open the pocketknife and wedged the blade between the strands, rotated the handle toward her until the uncoiled threads popped loose and fell to the ground. The gate swung open with a low, grating groan of metal on metal.

There was obviously no cover in which to hide between here and the chapel, so taking a deep breath to steady the fresh surge of nervousness settling in her stomach, Alyson struck out as fast as her boots and water-weighted clothes would allow, keeping her gaze locked on the closed chapel door, certain that at any moment it would fly open and Billy Boyd would come flying out, prepared to wage war in the name of all Christianity.

He didn't, and upon reaching the building, Alyson flattened her back against it and slid to the ground, fighting for breath and allowing the frantic racing of her heart to ease. Her eyes drifted closed. Her mind remained blank, oddly removed from the reality of what she was doing, or about to do.

How long she sat there, she couldn't guess. Rousing, her shoulders heavy with dread, Alyson removed the gun from her jeans and, with surprisingly steady fingers, eased off the safety. Her mind turned over the memory of the self-defense class she'd taken. The instructor had shown them the basics of preparing to shoot a firearm, the firing of it, and what to expect. Except that the peashooter Alyson had handled that day could hardly compare to the cannon in her hand now. No doubt about it, this monster could stop a bull elephant in its tracks. That thought gave her the courage to push herself to her feet and move toward the door.

With the gun pointed up in her right hand, Alyson nudged open the old door, inch by inch to avoid sound, eased her body through the narrow opening and into the cold, shadowed room where dawn intruded only in gray light spears that seeped through the boards over the windows and the holes in the roof. Odd how they all converged near the front of the chapel, as if spotlights were trained purposefully on the dais.

Her gaze swept the rotting pews, the walls, her senses expanding to painful pinpoints. She moved down the aisle, looking right, then left, watching for any motion in the shadows. There were closed doors leading into other rooms. Her gaze swung back to the dais where the streaks of gray light grew brighter. As her eyes focused, a form began to take shape.

Alyson froze.

She felt, in that infinitesimal space of time, that she had actually left her body, that she hovered on a surreal plane of disbelief, like one stumbling through a nightmare, aware they're dreaming but incapable of tearing themselves from the horrible, albeit fascinating, image. Surely what lay before her was the result of her fear and the exhaustion of the last long days—

"Oh, my God," she heard herself say aloud. Her legs moved, cold bones creaking. Forgotten, the gun dropped to her side as her stride lengthened and her eyes focused more clearly on Brandon's body stretched out on the cross—

She tripped and nearly fell, stumbled into a run until she fell against his naked torso. She backed away, too horrified to scream, too terrified to touch him. A groan worked up her throat.

His eyes slowly opened.

She stared into them for seconds before reality slugged her. Dear Merciful God in heaven, he was still alive!

"Hurry," he said in a voice dry as dust, "before he comes back."

Her gaze still locked on his, Alyson put the gun aside and dug the knife from her pocket. For the first time since pulling away from the boat docks, she shook so badly that she feared she was incapable of functioning. Her brain felt scrambled. She dropped the knife, fumbled for it before picking it up and managing to spring open the blade.

There were large rusty nails and a hammer on the floor near the crucifix. With fresh fear, Alyson realized that if she hadn't arrived when she did, Billy would have driven them through Brandon's hands and feet, completing the crucifixion.

She sawed through the ropes at his ankles, then those looped over his shoulders and passing across his chest. He groaned and twisted in pain as she touched his shoulder and arm, which looked infected and swollen. The dulling knife gnawed pitifully at the bindings at his wrists.

As she cut through the final rope, the breath rushed from him; he reached for her, dragged her into his good arm and held her as fiercely as he could, his face buried in her hair. His body shook.

"I'd given up hope of ever seeing you again," he whispered.

"You're not going to get rid of me that easily, Carlyle." Smiling into his weak eyes, Alyson did her best to steady her voice. He looked like death warmed over: gaunt and pale and filthy. The injury on his shoulder looked bad. Very bad. And smelled even worse. "You promised me the story of a lifetime, and by gosh, I'm going to get it if it kills me."

"Where are the others?" His eyes narrowed. "Aly, where the hell are the others?"

"There are no others."

"You came alone—?"

"Ruth called Jack. I couldn't wait, Brandon. I couldn't risk their wasting precious time—"

"How did you know I was here?"

"Nora."

He stared at her in disbelief, then his cracked lips curled in a grin. "Remind me to thank her."

"I suspect you'll want to do more than thank her," she said. "Now let's get out of here—"

She knew, even before she turned her head that Billy was back. She saw the horror in Brandon's eyes as he looked over her shoulder.

Brandon drove his hand into Alyson's chest, propelling her away from him. He rolled off the cross just as Billy plunged the spike deep into the wood where Brandon's heart would have been. He landed on his feet, spun in time to duck the hammer Billy swung at his head. Dizzied by the movement, Brandon stumbled like a drunk, tried to regain his footing as Billy lunged—

Alyson threw herself on Billy's back, sank her fingernails into his cheeks. With a wail of pain, he flung her aside as effortlessly as a rag doll. She crashed into a broken pew, and before she could recover, he lifted her with one hand and drove his fist into her cheek. As if in slow motion, Brandon watched her head snap back.

Blood spread across her face like the thick red haze of absolute fury that rose up in Brandon's brain as he launched himself into Billy with a force that lifted Billy off his feet. They hit the floor in a cloud of dust and scattering lumber. Billy grunted from the impact. Jagged, lightning pain ripped through Brandon's shoulder; consciousness flickered, and his mind desperately fought to hold on. If he succumbed to the blackness, Billy would win. He'd kill them both—*not Alyson*, he thought, drifting as he rolled onto his back. *Please, not Alyson*—

"Jeezus!"

Jack Dillman came barreling down the aisle like a bull-dozer, teeth bared and gun drawn. In one fluid move, Billy jumped to his feet, swinging a two-by-four as hard as he could. It slammed into Dillman with the force of a battering ram, knocking him partially to his knees. Billy was on him before he could shake free of his shock. They wrestled for the gun, feet scuffling for a foothold on the dusty, lumber-littered floor.

The gun erupted with an ear-shattering explosion. Jack stumbled back, his face white as paste. Blood pumped from a black hole in his side. He stared down at it dumbly, his blue lips moving soundlessly. Turning his gaze on Brandon, he croaked, "Oh, shit," and toppled onto his face.

Lying on his back amid debris, dust dancing in the shafts of yellow light streaming through the holes in the roof, Brandon opened his eyes and stared up into the barrel of Jack's gun.

Billy smiled. His teeth were bloody. "There is a better punishment for you than just killing you. Far better. Atonement is attained only through sufficient suffering. Oh, sweet impostor, you shall suffer. Until your dying breath your hell will be walking this earth, knowing that because of you, she is lost." Bending nearer, the blood from his mouth dripping on Brandon's cheek, he whispered, "Rest assured that by the time I finish driving the demons from her, she'll welcome death. Say a prayer for her, lover boy. She's going to need it."

Then Billy slung Alyson over his shoulder and was gone.

Brandon struggled to sit up. The room swam. He shook his head, fighting back unconsciousness. Rocking onto his knees, he focused on Dillman. Blood pooled under his belly—no help there. Grabbing the end of a pew, Brandon heaved himself to his feet, tottered. He searched for the gun Alyson had brought with her—no luck, he determined with rising panic. Billy must have taken it. He fixed his gaze on the door and forced himself to move. He stumbled, caught himself, dragged in a deep breath, and ran out of the chapel, into the sunlight.

In the distance Billy climbed into a boat and lowered Alyson into it.

Brandon ran.

Billy cranked the motor. Nothing. He cranked again.

Brandon's legs moved faster, eating up the ground. The pain subsided, replaced by the numbing elixir of adrenaline. For an exhilarating time he felt weightless. The world was soundless except for the rush of air in and out of his lungs and the distant deep thump of his heart in his ears. The sunlight pulsated brilliantly, white light flooding with gentle heat on his head and bare shoulders.

Billy cranked a third time. A roar responded. Water rushed up in froth and foam.

Alyson lifted her head, groggy and confused.

Brandon burst through the gate and hit the pier, which trembled like a dying animal beneath his footfalls. Alyson turned her frightened eyes toward him. He yelled, "Jump, Alyson! Jump! Jump now!"

Alyson glanced horrified, at the water, then at Billy, who grabbed for her leg as she scrambled to sit up. She drove the toe of her boot into his arm so that he howled in pain. Then she belly flopped into the water.

Brandon leaped from the pier.

Billy looked up, his eyes flying wide. He made a fumbling grab for the gun in his pants—managed to clear it just as Brandon hit the boat, which heaved dangerously to one side with the impact. Billy swung the gun barrel toward him. Brandon grabbed it, threw his weight into Billy so the impetus took them over the side and into the water.

The water closed over his head with a cold shock. He desperately hung on to the gun, shoving the barrel away as he planted his feet on the muddy bottom and stood up.

They erupted from the water with a great gasp for air, struggling for the weapon. Billy's strength was wearing Brandon down—he wasn't going to make it, couldn't keep up the fight. Billy knew it, the sneer on his mouth turned into a smiling grimace.

Looking into Billy's eyes, Brandon called, "Betty! Please, Betty, help me! Help me!"

The change was as brief but as bright as the flash of a

comet in the night sky. Billy's face changed, his eyes softened. His grip on the gun weakened, allowing Brandon to
swing the barrel away from himself and toward Billy—

"Do it," rushed Betty's voice. "Quickly, quickly, Mr.
Brandon. Do it now!"

It was the sound of Betty's voice that made him freeze,
the heartbreaking shadow of desperation in the eyes as she
fought valiantly to contain the monster. Then, as if acknowl-
edging Brandon's quandary, she wrenched the gun from his
hand and turned it on herself.

The gunshot was little more than a muffled bump under
the water. A look of surprise rushed over Billy's features;
his eyes flew wide and his mouth fell open.

Brandon stumbled back, his gaze still locked on the face
that appeared to shift and change like the glass pieces in a
kaleidoscope. With a groan, the body slowly, silently, slid
like a sinking ship below the surface and disappeared.

Brandon closed his eyes, covered his face with his dripping hands while the frantic fear and adrenaline left him so
suddenly that it felt as if every bone in his body had vaporized. Then realization slammed him—

"Alyson." He searched the water, fresh panic surging
through him. God, oh God, this would be too cruel. Then he
saw her, clinging to the pier. She flung herself into the water,
splashed and stumbled her way to him, laughing and crying,
her hands reaching desperately for him as he pulled her
against his body and steadied her. They clung, pressed,
rocked with the gentle motion of the cold water.

"I love you," he said.

"I love you," she said.

Wearily, supporting one another, they waded out of the
water, trudged through the mud to solid ground, both beginning to shiver as the brisk morning air bit at their wet skin.

"Down!" came the distant shout, sounding almost like the
cry of a bird. "Down, get down—behind you!"

Brandon looked up.

Dillman staggered toward them, one hand holding his

bloody side, the other waving a gun. "Behind you!" he shouted again.

Brandon turned.

As Billy rose out of the water, sunlight sparkled on his head like gold glitter. He raised the gun, pointed it—

Brandon shoved Alyson aside.

The gun blast resounded like a lightning strike, reverberated through the trees, sending flocks of startled egrets rising into the air.

Brandon stared down the barrel of Billy's gun, waiting for the pain to start; slowly, he shifted his gaze to Billy's oddly blank face, and the bullet hole in his forehead. The gun slid from Billy's hand, then he drifted backward, settled gently into the water and momentarily floated like flotsam before sinking from sight.

Alyson's arms came around him. They sank to the ground.

Dillman staggered up, plopped down beside them, bloody hand gripping his side. He narrowed his eyes as he looked at Brandon. "You're a goddamn pain in the ass, Carlyle."

"You're right." Brandon gave him an exhausted grin. "A big pain in the ass. And by the way . . . thanks, Jack."

Giving a grunt, Dillman looked at Alyson, then away. "Let's get somethin' straight—for the record. I did this for only one reason. Figured by savin' your Hollywood hind end, I'd keep my job and win me a few votes come election time. It ain't as if I like you or nothin'."

"Just the same." Brandon offered his hand.

A flush crept up Dillman's pale cheeks as he stared at it. Then, raising his eyes to Brandon's, he muttered, "Jeezus," and took it.

EPILOGUE

Alyson stood at Brandon's bedside, her hand holding his, watching as he slept. A needle in his arm dripped fluid into his vein—electrolytes to hydrate him. It would be a while before he could stomach solid food.

After twelve hours in the hospital, he was beginning to rouse. His color was better. All vital signs stable. She looked toward the muted television near the ceiling. The morning's rescue played out over the silent screen: helicopters and boats converging on the compound, law enforcement officers carrying weapons piling out of choppers like soldiers invading some Middle Eastern country. She watched Brandon and Jack being placed on gurneys and carried onto the Air Ambulances that would transport them to Tyler General. She watched herself climb in after them.

His hand squeezed hers. With a skip of her heart, she smiled down into his sleepy eyes.

"Do I look as bad as I feel?" he asked.

"Never. I assure you." She pressed a kiss to his warm

forehead. "Looking better by the minute, Carlyle. Soon you'll be as good as new, and the women will be swooning at your feet again."

He groaned. "I've had enough of fanatic fans, thank you very much." Lifting his hand, he gently touched her swollen face. "God, I'm sorry, Cupcake. Sorry you got involved in this nightmare. If you'd died because of me—"

"Get this straight," she said firmly and stared hard into his bloodshot eyes. "None of this is your fault, Brandon. What happened to Henry and Bernie and Emerald Marcella—it was the work of a very disturbed individual." More softly, she added, "Alan said this kind of reaction is to be expected. He warned me; once the shock of all this wears off and reality hits hard again, you'll go through some tough periods. Fear. Grief. Guilt. Paranoia—"

"Great." He grinned weakly. "Gives me something to look forward to."

"I'll be there with you." Then she added softly, "If you still want me to be."

"As if I'd ever go anywhere again for the rest of my life without you." He pulled her close. "Aly, all I could think about in that damn black hole was you. Sometimes, when I thought I might never see you again, I wanted to give up hope."

She kissed him, lightly. "Are you up to a few visitors? They're out in the hall, have been for hours." He nodded, and Alyson walked to the door.

Mildred stalked into the room, steel-tipped high heels clicking, dark hair swept atop her head, earrings dangling. She flashed Alyson a resolute look before marching over to Brandon's bed. He narrowed his eyes at her, and she lifted her chin and pointed one long, red-lacquered nail at him.

"Look, you, I've put up with your arrogant bullshit for too long—got paid squat diddly for it, too. If you think you're going to fire me before I've gotten some freaking commissions out of your hide, you've got another thing coming. Furthermore—"

"Fine."

"What?"

"I said fine. If I rehire you, will you go away and leave me alone?"

"Let's get something straight, Bubba. I'm a damn good agent—"

"That remains to be seen."

"I could still get you seven million for that Scorsese movie."

"Thirty."

"Fifteen, tops."

"Thirty-five."

Pursing her lips, Mildred narrowed her eyes, then said through her teeth, "Carlyle, I'm going to get you thirty-five million for that movie if it's the last thing I ever do, then I'm going to shove it so far up your—"

"Excuse me . . . ?"

They looked toward the door.

Charlotte Minger beamed at them, exposing a mouth full of thread-thin wires. She shambled in, limping, her eyes twinkling. The injuries on her face were healing but still red.

Reaching for Brandon's hand, she bent and pressed a kiss to his cheek. "Man, am I ever glad to see you. Hey, you look almost as bad as me."

He grinned and cupped her cheek in his hand. "Sorry about what happened to you, Charlotte."

"My fault. Shouldn'ta done what I did. What matters is we both pulled through okay. Right?" Her eyes widening, she managed an unsteady bounce of excitement. "God, you'll never believe it. Do you know who I met in the hallway? Johnny Whitehorse. Oh—my—God. That man is sooo gorgeous! My mom is gonna bring up his poster—that one of him walking half-naked down Fifth Avenue? And he's gonna autograph it for me. Like, I almost fainted right there at his feet."

As Brandon raised one eyebrow and gave her a lopsided smirk, she covered her mouth and giggled. "Sorry. Course you know there ain't nobody like you, Brandon, even if you are gettin' sorta old."

The door bumped open. Jack Dillman rolled into the room in a wheelchair. Mitsy trailed him, heels dragging, chewing the fingernail of her right thumb. There were no signs of Marilyn tonight. She had curled her own hair and anchored it back from her face with a child's red plastic barrettes. Her jeans were baggy, and the sweater she wore drooped nearly to her knees. She kept her eyes averted as she stopped just inside the door.

Jack looked back at her. "Git up here, Mitsy. I ain't got all frickin' night. Jeez, I ain't even supposed to be out of bed. If I bleed the hell to death, who's gonna take care of your skinny behind?"

Cautious, she moved to the foot of the bed. Her big eyes finally raised to Brandon's. Her chin trembled. "Sorry," she mumbled.

"Louder," Jack ordered.

"Sorry." She took a deep breath. "I was crazy for a while, I guess. I'm still a little crazy. Probably always will be. But I'm gettin' better ever day." She glanced at Alyson and as quickly looked away. More softly, she added, "I lied to you 'bout that baby. It wasn't yours. I guess that'll relieve you some, knowin' it wasn't your kid that I. . . ." Tears rose in her eyes. "All I ever wanted to be was a movie star. Is that so much to ask? Well?" she said, looking around at the different faces. "Is it? You told me you'd help me get an agent, and then you went off, left me waitin' and hopin', stuck in Ticky Creek, Texas, like a stupid wart on a log."

"I'm sorry." Brandon extended his hand to her.

She sprang around the bed and grabbed it, clutched it to her cheek while tears spilled down her face. "I just wanted to be somethin', Brandon. I wanted to count for somethin'. You were the first person ever made me feel special, like I had a chance."

"I'm sorry," he repeated in a thick voice and closed his hand more tightly around hers.

"If that baby had been yours, I never, ever would of got rid of it. I loved you so much my heart still hurts to think about it. I'm sorry I hurt you. I'm sorry my stupid brother hurt you. He's just a big dumb dog turd with a turnip for brains, and if he thinks he's gonna keep treatin' me like I'm worthless, he's got another think comin'." Lifting her chin and squaring her shoulders, Mitsy glared at Jack. His brow lowered, and he sank back in his chair.

Laughing, Brandon drew her close, closer, tugged her down so he could whisper in her ear. She gasped. Nodded. Her body began to vibrate like a plucked fiddle string. When she backed away from the bed, her normally colorless face glowed like red neon.

Brandon looked at Mildred, a smirk curling his lips. He crooked his finger at her. Her eyes widened—looked from Brandon to Mitsy, widened even farther as Mitsy jigged in place.

Eyes narrowing, cheeks burning with hot color, Mildred flashed Brandon a look that said *You wouldn't dare*.

He nodded, his smirk turning to smugness. *Oh, yes, I would*, his eyes responded.

The door opened again and Alan walked in, followed by Ron Peterson, followed by Senator Whitehorse. While Mitsy cornered Mildred and Charlotte attached herself to Whitehorse, Alyson introduced Brandon to Alan and Ron, then stepped back and watched the interplay between the people crowded around Brandon's bed.

Funny how such a short time ago their faces had been shadows of despair and desperation, and how with the simple words "I'm sorry," their lives had been changed in the blink of an eye. Even Dillman sat with a grin on his face, an expression bordering on pride as he watched Mitsy. New hope electrified the air, and as Alyson focused on Brandon's face, she watched his sadness fade away. He looked . . . at peace. His eyes shone with a serenity that transformed the haggardness of his features. It was as if he were healing before her eyes.

The phone rang. She picked it up. Listened.

Brandon looked at her.

She smiled at him. "I'll be right down," she said into the phone, then gently replaced the receiver. "I have to step down the hall a minute," she told him, and dropped a kiss onto his mouth.

Stepping into the quiet corridor, Alyson briefly closed her eyes, took a deep breath, squared her shoulders. She marched down the hallway, eyes focused straight ahead, only vaguely aware of the nurses who watched her go.

A group of suited men loitered outside a waiting room. They turned to watch her approach. One stepped forward. "Alyson James?"

"Get out of my way," she snapped, shoved him aside, then hit the closed door.

Cara Carlyle looked up from the magazine she was reading and into Alyson's face.

Alyson's first thought was that the camera didn't come close to doing her justice, incapable of capturing the absolute perfection of her bone structure and skin, or the coldness of her presence. Her eyes were two ice blue stones, and with new awareness Alyson realized what it must have been like for Brandon, as a child, to have looked into those emotionless spheres, craving love, tolerating hell in hopes of earning it. Impossible, of course. The woman unfolding from the chair was incapable of loving anything or anyone other than herself.

"Miss James, I assume," Cara said with a lift of one eyebrow.

"What the hell are you doing here?" Alyson demanded in a trembling voice.

Cara's red lips curved. "I should think that's obvious. I'm here to see my son."

"Over my dead body. If you think I'm allowing you to hurt him any more than he's already been hurt, then you're as stupid as you are vile and vicious."

Her eyes narrowing, Cara purred, "Who do you think you are?"

"I'm the woman who loves him. Who intends to marry him. Who intends to have his children. Who intends to spend the rest of my life making up for the misery you've caused him. How you can even show your face here amazes me.

You don't deserve to occupy the same town as Brandon, much less the same building."

"I don't care who you are. You're not going to stand between me and what's mine."

"Think again." Alyson moved toward her.

Cara's eyes widened and hot color suffused her face. She backed away, dropping the magazine to the floor. "Touch me, and I'll have you arrested. I'll sue you—"

"You'd love that, wouldn't you? Nothing like scandal to manipulate the press and gain people's sympathies. Is that why you came here, Cara? Looking for free publicity? Play the concerned Mommy Dearest and get your face blasted across the tabloids—wind up on Jay Leno or Oprah?

"You used Brandon all his life to bolster your career. If it hadn't been for him, you'd be back in Ticky Creek flipping burgers at the Dime A Cup. Enough is enough, Cara. Because of some mother-son bond, he might have rolled over and tolerated your abuse—but now you're going to have me to deal with, and I won't put up with it. I'll spill my guts—everything I know about you and your sordid secrets. Oh, yes, Cara, he told me, and I'll never, ever forget the look in his eyes when he did. I don't think I've ever seen so much pain, humiliation, and heartbreak. And the sad, befuddling reality is, if I let you walk into that room right now, and you asked for his forgiveness, he'd forgive you."

Cara glared at her, expressionless, then drew back her shoulders. "You could spill your guts, of course. But it would be your word against mine. If, as you say, there is that bond between us, he'll keep his mouth shut, just as he has for the last twenty-five years. Now, if you'll excuse me, I intend to see my son."

Sweeping her purse off the chair, Cara tucked it under her arm, stepped around Alyson, and walked to the door.

"Don't do it," Alyson said to her back, stopping Cara in her tracks. "Please. If there's one molecule of decency in your body, if there's the tiniest spark in your heart of a mother's love for her son, leave him alone. He's suffered enough. Let him bask in the love I can give him—the love he's craved all his life. Just leave him in peace, and let him heal."

A heartbeat passed. Cara reached for the door, and left the room. The door swung closed behind her.

Alyson felt the last spark of energy drain from her. Her body suddenly felt every bone-jarring bruise Billy Boyd had inflicted on her. The last days of fear and anxiety crushed down on her shoulders, and the need to cry rose bitter as bile in her throat.

Forcing her legs to move, she ran for the door, threw it open, and rushed into the corridor, searched the long hallway to Brandon's room, expecting to see Cara and her entourage. They weren't there.

She turned.

Cara stood at the elevators, flanked by her suited companions. Her head slowly turned, and her blue gaze met Alyson's. The elevator opened; she stepped inside. The door slid shut behind her.

Alyson closed her eyes in relief. When she opened them again, she focused on a figure standing at the STAIR EXIT door. Pleasure swept through her, replacing the distress of Cara's presence.

"Nora."

Nora smiled.

Alyson walked to her. "I hoped you'd come."

"How is he?"

"Very tired. Very weak. But he's going to be fine, in time. Thanks to you, of course. He'd like to see you. He wants to repay you—"

"Not necessary." Nora clutched her purse to her chest.

"Surely there's some way we can thank you."

"You can thank me by not telling anyone about my part in this."

"How are they?" Alyson grinned and pointed her finger upward.

"Quiet, thank goodness."

"That's good."

"Yes." Nora smiled and nodded. "That's very good." She

backed toward the door. "I have to go now. Please give him my best."

"Will we see you again?"

She shrugged. "You never know."

A clatter of noise near the nurses' desk made Alyson look away briefly. When she turned again to Nora, her friend was gone. Alyson felt a trembling of sadness in her chest, and something else, a quivering of wonder and a fresh flame of faith. Nice to know there were still a few people out there willing to help lost souls—wanting nothing in return but knowing that they had mattered.

As Alyson moved down the corridor to Brandon's room, the nurses paused, their eyes bright with curiosity.

Brandon's guests piled out the door. Alan walked to greet her, opened his arms, took her against his chest, and held her. "You okay?" he asked.

She nodded.

"He's holding it together better than I expected. I suspect that will change when—"

"I know," she muttered into his shoulder. Tilting her head, she looked into his eyes and said, "Will you shut up being a shrink for a minute and just be my friend?"

"Of course." He grinned. "I wish you happily ever after, A. J."

She pinched his cheek and smiled. "Sugar, when he's ready to have his brain washed and tumble-dried, we'll give you a call." Kissing his mouth, she said, "Thanks. I wouldn't have made it through this nightmare without you."

"I only did the head work. You marched into harm's way to save the day. Got yourself one hell of a story while you were at it."

"Yeah." Her smiled widened. "I did, didn't I?"

She walked to the door, glanced around the watchful faces, then back to Alan, who, with his hands in his pockets, looked at her fondly. "I love you," she said.

He gave her a wink.

The door opened and a nurse stepped out. "I've given him something to help him rest," she said.

Except for the dim white night-light above Brandon's bed, the room was dark. His eyes were closed.

Alyson tiptoed around the bed, to the windows overlooking the parking lot. She waited.

Nora left the building. She paused in the glow of a streetlight, turned her head up toward Alyson. Alyson waved, then watched as Nora walked away and dissolved in the darkness.

Brandon opened his eyes. He studied her face, reached for her hand. "Everything okay, Cupcake?"

"Do you believe in angels?" she asked.

"Of course. I'm looking at one now."

"Sweet talker." Pulling back the sheet, she climbed into the bed, carefully nestled her body against his, and laid her head on his shoulder. "I have a feeling that our lives are only going to get better and better now that we have one another."

His arm closed around her. She felt a shudder of emotion ripple through him. His breathing became uneven. "No more nightmares?" His voice sounded groggy.

"No more nightmares."

"Kiss me."

She gently cupped his cheek in her hand, and turned his face to hers. His eyelids were heavy. He struggled to keep them open. Pressing her lips to his, she kissed them tenderly, awash with an emotion that filled her with a peace so vibrant she couldn't breathe. She had come home, at long last.

"Aly," he whispered, his voice fading as she pressed one finger lightly on his lips, and smiled into his eyes.

"I love you, too," she said.